the Cheetah Girls

the Cheetah Girls

Growl Power Forever

Volumes 9–12

Deborah Gregory

JUMP AT THE SUN

HYPERION PAPERBACKS FOR CHILDREN
NEW YORK

Printed in the United States of America
First Compiled edition, 2004
1 3 5 7 9 10 8 6 4 2
This book is set in 12-point Palatino.
ISBN: 0-7868-5163-5
Library of Congress Catalog Card Number on file.

Visit www.cheetahrama.com

Acknowledgments

I have to give it up to the Jump at the Sun peeps here—Andrea Pinkney, Lisa Holton, and Ken Geist—for letting the Cheetah Girls run wild. Also, Anath Garber, the one person who helped me find my Cheetah Girl powers. And, Lita Richardson, the one person who now has my back in the jiggy jungle. Primo thanks to the cover girl Cheetahs: Arike, Brandi, Imani, Jeni, and Mia. And to all the Cheetah Girls around the globe: Get diggity with the growl power, baby!

Contents

The Cheetah Girls Credo

To earn my spots and rightful place in the world, I solemnly swear to honor and uphold the Cheetah Girls oath:

- Cheetah Girls don't litter, they glitter. I will help my family, friends, and other Cheetah Girls whenever they need my love, support, or a *really* big hug.

- All Cheetah Girls are created equal, but we are not alike. We come in different sizes, shapes, and colors, and hail from different cultures. I will not judge others by the color of their spots, but by their character.

- A true Cheetah Girl doesn't spend more time doing her hair than her homework. Hair extensions may be career extensions, but talent and skills will pay my bills.
- True Cheetah Girls *can* achieve without a weave—or a wiggle, jiggle, or a giggle. I promise to rely (mostly) on my brains, heart, and courage to reach my cheetah-licious potential!
- A brave Cheetah Girl isn't afraid to admit when she's scared. I promise to get on my knees and summon the growl power of the Cheetah Girls who came before me—including my mom, grandmoms, and the Supremes—and ask them to help me be strong.
- All Cheetah Girls make mistakes. I promise to admit when I'm wrong and will work to make it right. I'll also say I'm sorry, even when I don't want to.
- Grown-ups are not always right, but they are bigger, older, and louder. I will treat my teachers, parents, and people of authority with respect—and expect them to do the same!

- True Cheetah Girls don't run with wolves or hang with hyenas. True Cheetahs pick much better friends. I will not try to get other people's approval by acting like a copycat.

- To become the Cheetah Girl that only *I* can be, I promise not to follow anyone else's dreams but my own. No matter how much I quiver, shake, shiver, and quake!

- Cheetah Girls were born for adventure. I promise to learn a language other than my own and travel around the world to meet my fellow Cheetah Girls.

the Cheetah Girls

Showdown at the Okie-Dokie

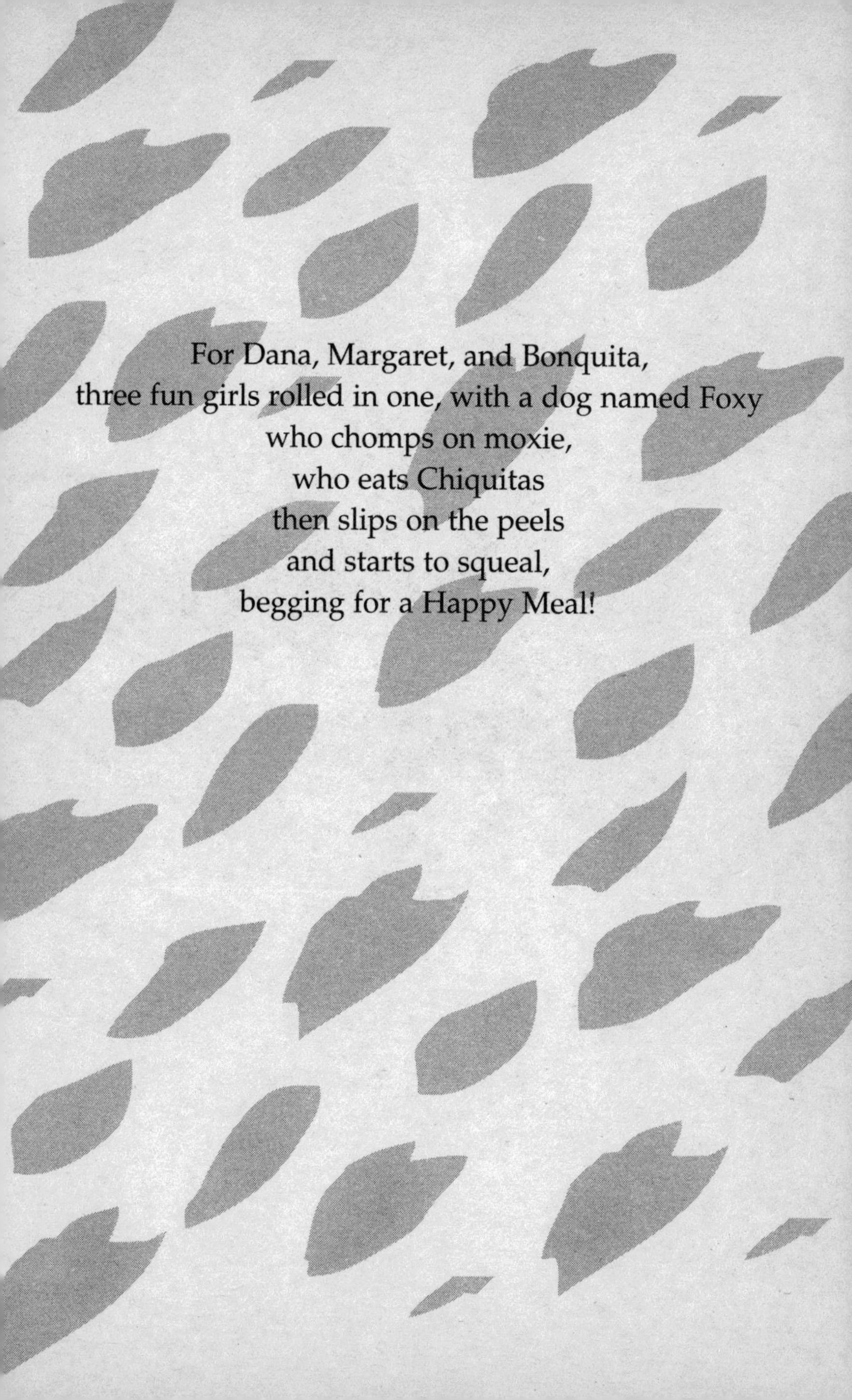

For Dana, Margaret, and Bonquita,
three fun girls rolled in one, with a dog named Foxy
who chomps on moxie,
who eats Chiquitas
then slips on the peels
and starts to squeal,
begging for a Happy Meal!

Chapter 1

I still cannot believe that the Cheetah Girls are boostin' in Houston! That's right, Kats and Kittys, we, your favorite girl group, are backstage, chillin' in the talent holding area, after performing on the very stage that Karma's Children, one of the biggest girl groups in the world, will grace in about fifteen minutes!

Okay, so we only got to growl one song, as one of Karma's Children's opening acts—but that brings us one crispy drumstick closer to making our dreams 'cuzome true in the jiggy jungle, right?

Cooling my heels on the dingy green couch, I imagine how toodly it will be when we have our own dressing room, just like Karma's

Children. Not that we have managed to get a peek inside *theirs* yet—it's right down the hall from ours—but we're not blowing this Popsicle stand until we do. I mean, how could we come all the way to Houston from the Big Apple and not meet our favorite girl group, or snag a photo op with them, if you catch my drift, swift?

We, of course, are me—Galleria "Bubbles" Garibaldi; Chanel "Chuchie" Simmons; Dorinda "Do' Re Mi" Rogers; and the twins, Anginette and Aquanette Walker (whom we have finally stopped calling the "Huggy Bear" twins).

In addition to us, four other groups were also chosen to perform as opening acts for this shindigable benefit concert — "Houston Helps Its Own"—which is raising much-needed duckets for the city's biggest homeless shelter. In order to get chosen, you had to hail from hot-diggity Houston, but the twins pulled a few strings to get us here.

The other wannabes on the bill are: the kiddie rap duo, Miggy and Mo; the alternative rappers, Diamonds in the Ruff; the rock 'n' roll group Moody Gardens; and the blues combo

Fish 'N' Chips—which has just gotten a new member: none other than the twins' uncle Skeeter, who plays a mean harmonica!

Of course, Karma's Children are the "mane" attraction (they really do have oodles of hair!). They're the only reason why peeps shelled out fifty duckets apiece for tonight's benefit. Everyone wants to see Houston's very own girl group "wiggle, squiggle, shake, and bake" right here in their own backyard. The place is the Turtle Dome Arena, in back of the Kemah Boardwalk in boot-i-ful Galveston Bay—surrounded by oodles of beautiful water. Trust me, we have nothing like this back in the Big Apple.

Now, let me explain how we pulled off this extra-coolio holiday hookup: first, Aquanette and Anginette came down to Houston to visit their family for Thanksgiving, but ended up getting an audition for this benefit. Once they landed a spot in the lineup, they got the "Houston Helps Its Own" benefit committee to fly us down, too. Then, once the Cheetah Girls were "in there like swimwear," the twins hooked up these homeless guys—Fish 'N' Chips—by putting in a good word for them. If those weren't enough good deeds for the day, they also brought Uncle Skeeter along to the concert—and he hooked up with Fish 'N' Chips as a special guest star on their bill! I guess you could say the twins have been "doubly busy."

I gaze over at Uncle Skeeter, who is humming a melody while wiping his harmonica like it's Aladdin's lamp.

"Lemme hear your flow again," I coax Do' Re Mi, who has become very fascinated with Mr. Fred Fish's banjo. All night, she's been trying to perfect this blues/rap riff she has created:

I'm sitting on the porch
just minding my bizness
trying to light a torch
but my bugaboo cat
is eating like a horse!

Of course, Fish 'N' Chips, who are old-school blues musicians, are fascinated with how Dorinda mixes rap riffs with blues beats. "That's right, keep plucking," Fred instructs her.

"Psst! They're done—here they come," Chanel says, motioning to us.

Miggy and Mo have just finished performing, and their eyes are twinkling like shiny Christmas balls as they run backstage to join us. We made friends with them at the audition for this event—they're only ten or so, and they're sooo cute! They've got freckles that make you heckle!

"Act like you know, Miggy and Mo!" I shout to them as they run over to the punch bowl.

"Are your freckles real, *mamacitas*?" Chuchie asks the pint-size rappers.

"Sí, sí!" Miggy giggles, getting a whiff of Chanel's Spanglish accent.

Personally, I think it's way past Miggy and Mo's bedtime: right about now, they deserve some Krispy Kremes and a dream. I glance over at their mom, Mrs. Majors, but she is engrossed in her knitting. She's making gifts for Christmas, which is right around the corner.

"She moves those things faster than chopsticks," I mouth to Chanel. I wonder if Mrs. Majors likes managing her kids, the way my mom likes managing us.

I feel bad about Mom being in New York by herself, but I'm not looking forward to talking to her on the phone later. See, I have to beg her to let me stay here for a few more days, so we can check out this event Miggy and Mo told us about. It's an urban rodeo at the Okie-Dokie Corral, and they're going to be performing there. We figured that the Cheetah Girls should at least wander over yonder and check it out, you know what I'm saying? Maybe they need some more warm-up acts!

"Even if we don't get into the show, I wanna try to ride a bull at least once, 'cuz I've never been to a rodeo before," I exclaim in my fake Southern drawl.

Miggy and Mo let out tiny squeals of laughter. Now, the alternative rap group Diamonds in the Ruff are glaring in our direction. We've left them alone, because they've been radiating attitude, but all of a sudden they seem supa-dupa interested in our flow.

I pretend I don't notice them staring at us, but I can't help checking out their fashion tragedy out of the corner of my eye. The two girls are wearing these wanna-be cowboy outfits: each one has on a white, ten-gallon cowboy hat covered in rhinestones, a red bandanna around her neck, rhinestone platform heels, and blue jeans so tight she probably had to slide into them from a parachute.

"Are y'all going to try out for the show at the Okie-Dokie Corral, too?" I turn and ask them because they're still staring at us on the sneaky tip.

"We're already booked for that," the taller one with the longer weave says matter-of-factly, rolling her eyes like pool balls. "They're not looking for any more groups. So I don't know what those kids told you."

Miggy and Mo don't say a word, but their mother has finally looked up from her knitting needles. "Are y'all 'bout done, Miggy?"

"Yes, Mom, we're finished," Miggy says, grabbing her sister's arm and walking over to their mother. Mo smiles at me as she passes, and whispers into my ear, "You should go over to the Okie-Dokie and try to get in anyway."

"Oh, we will, Mo, so act like you know," I whisper back. I look over at their mom again. She is finally packing up her knitting needles and balls of yarn. I'm glad my mom is our manager, 'cuz she would've never let those rhinestone-studded wannabes talk to us like that. Actually, it's probably better Mom isn't here—for *their* sakes.

"They're just a bunch of kids," the taller member of Diamonds in the Ruff says. "They don't know nothing—I'm tellin' you, you'll just be wasting your time going over there."

"What's your name?" Dorinda asks, trying to squash the situation.

"Diamond," the "weava" girl says in the same nasty tone. "How old are y'all?"

Dorinda doesn't say a word.

"Fourteen," I say calmly. I wonder why Diamond is trying to stop us from checking out the Okie-Dokie Corral situation. Maybe there's a pot of gold hidden there in one of the barns or something, I chuckle to myself, looking again at the ten-gallon rhinestone-covered "bowls" on their heads. I'll bet the only thing Diamonds in the Ruff know about a rodeo is how to clap when the clown comes out. Pleez, don't try it!

Chuchie takes a sip of punch, then hands me a cupful. "Hmm, Aqua, even the punch tastes better down here!" Chuchie coos.

"Lemme taste it," Aqua says, taking a whiff before she sips the punch, like she's doing an autopsy report or something. The twins' Granddaddy Walker runs a funeral parlor down here, and they've always been fascinated by everything to do with the dead—like horror movies and that kind of stuff.

"What's in it?" Angie asks her sister.

"I don't know, but Chanel is right, it's good!" Aqua says, chuckling.

"Let's have a toast," I say, trying to ignore Diamonds in the Ruff, who are still glued to our groove.

Aquanette pours punch for each of us, then we lift our paper cups and make a toast: "Whatever makes us clever—forever!"

"Come on, Sparkle, we'd better get ready," Diamond says to her partner, waving her hand like she can't be bothered with us anymore. It's their turn to go on after Moody Gardens. Once they leave the holding area, I take a deep breath.

"If you ask me, Miss Rhinestone is a little rough around the edges!" quips Aqua after guzzling her punch.

We giggle so loud that Mrs. Walker, the twins' mother, comes over to the couch.

"Aren't you going into the audience to see those girls perform?" she asks, her eyes twinkling.

"No thank you, ma'am," Aqua huffs.

"Okay—but I hope you're not going to let jealousy keep you from seeing Karma's Children later?" Mrs. Walker says gently. "You'll be sitting back here all by yourselves."

I nudge Aqua gently. The twins are a little green with Gucci envy over Karma's Children's success—I guess because they're both from the same hometown or something. I'll never forget the first time we met the twins in New York, at the Pizza Pit. Aqua told us the reason why they moved to New York was because "There ain't enough room in Houston for Karma's Children and us!"

We thought that was mad funny, even though we didn't really like the twins at first—that's probably because *we* were jealous about how dopalicious they could sing.

"Miz Aquanette, I just want you to know that we're not missing Karma's Children perform—not for all the turkey in Turkey!" I say, trying to coerce the twins to come out into the audience with us.

I look at my watch. It's only a matter of minutes before that quasi-rap/quasi-wack attack group, Diamonds in the Ruff, gets off the stage and makes room for the real stars of the show. "Let's go now, so we can get good standing room!"

"I don't even want to miss Karma's Children's entrance," Chuchie whines. "Anyway, we should be taking notes, and not gloat!"

"Word," Dorinda seconds. "It's not like we've got our stage thing down yet."

"All right," Aqua says, giving in. "Let's go see what those heffas have got that we don't."

"Thank gooseness," I say, relieved. "After all, we wouldn't be hanging in boostin' Houston if it wasn't for you two!"

"Oh, you know we weren't performing here without y'all!" Angie pipes in.

"I know, but I just wanna give y'all props for your manager skills, looking out for us—even though next time you'd better let my mom do the negotiating. If my dad hadn't gone to Italy and left her in New York by herself, she would've come down here and hit you over the head with a drumstick!"

"I know that's right," Aqua says, looking a little scared.

"Don't feel bad—I'm kinda scared to call her later myself," I admit. "I know she wants me to come back right after Thanksgiving, but I just wanna see if we can get on the bill at that urban rodeo."

"Well, you'd better call, 'cuz your mother doesn't play, Galleria," Aqua says, giving me a look.

I stuff my Miss Wiggy camera into my backpack, just in case I get a photo op with Karma's Children.

"What are you doing with the camera?" Aqua asks, noticing. "They told us we can't take any pictures."

"I know, but we're gonna bum-rush our way into Karma's Children's dressing room after the performance—so we can get a picture with them."

"I don't know," Aqua says hesitantly. "I'm not going to jail or anything just for a picture. . . ."

I give Aqua a look, like, "Cut the flimflam and get with the program!"

"Okay, I should have known you would have a plan, Miss Galleria," Aqua says, chuckling. "Maybe I'd better ask Mom if we can borrow *her* camera, too."

"I'm going with y'all!" Mrs. Walker says from behind me. "Don't worry, I've already got the camera!"

Chapter 2

I can't believe how many people are packed like shimmy-shaking sardines into the tiny Turtle Dome Arena, just to see Karma's Children! I mean, they're *everywhere*—squeezed into the bleachers, spilling out into the aisles, running back and forth to the concession stands—and mostly, it seems, they're bumping into *us* as we try to make our way down to the front, so we can see Karma's Children "shake and bake."

People are beaming at us as we pass, probably because we still have our fierce cheetah costumes on. "Go, Cheetahs! Y'all were great!" this girl yells as we pass.

We try to keep squeezing by, but given the gridlock, I should've known it would be a matter of moments before there was commotion in the ocean.

"OW!!" Dorinda moans, as this girl nails her in the toe with the pointy metal spike on one of her skyscraper heels. The girl, who's towering over tiny Dorinda like King Kong, wobbles, trying to regain her balance, then plops a big spill from her soda right on Aquanette's shoulder!

"Oh, honey, I'm so sorry," King Kong lady says, trying to wipe Aquanette's costume clean with a soggy napkin.

"Oh, that's okay," Aquanette yells over the deafening din of the crowd. We keep moving forward, and leave King Kong lady in the dust.

"I can't blame peeps for trying to get their money's worth," Dorinda says, hobbling along on her one good foot. I guess she's right: fifty duckets in the bucket, even for a good cause like this, is a lot to shell out for concert tickets.

"When Chutney Dallas came to town, you couldn't get a ticket for less than seventy-five dollars," Mrs. Walker informs us, as we find a tiny centimeter of space where we can stand huddled together and wait for Karma's Children.

"That's all?" I mutter. I'm surprised you could even get to see Chutney Dallas, the biggest singer in the universe, for a measly seventy-five duckets. But that's probably just the way it is down here. In the Big Apple, I'll bet even the cheapest tickets in the nosebleed section cost more than that.

"What did you say?" Mrs. Walker asks me, trying to make out my words over the noise.

"Nothing," I mouth back, because I don't want her to take it the wrong way—like the Big Apple has betta chedda or something.

The lights get dim, and the crowd roars. "Karma! Karma! Karma!" When the lights go up, a blond girl is standing onstage. She's wearing a rhinestone tiara and a blue sequined gown, with a banner across it that says MISS HOUSTON. She walks toward the microphone but almost trips over her dress.

"Ouch," I say, wincing at Dorinda, who is nestled to my left. "That reminds me of when you did a lickety-split in your costume onstage." My mom made our cheetah costumes, and Dorinda's was a little too tight in the cushion department, if you catch my drift, swift—but she was too afraid to say anything until disaster struck onstage!

"Oh, don't remind me. I'll never forget everybody looking at my bloomers," she moans.

I tug on the tail of her cheetah costume, and Dorinda makes a comical grimace.

Finally, pulling the hem of her gown from under her heels, "Miss Houston" giggles nervously into the microphone. "I hope there are no judges in the house tonight!" she says. "Thank goodness I didn't do that at the Miss Houston contest, or the only title I'd have won would have been 'Miss Clumsy'!"

We all smile at her corny joke. "I wonder how she did win," I mutter.

"Hi, everyone. I'm Miss Houston, Amanda Darby—"

The crowd claps and screams, "Howdy, Houston!!"

"Thank you—and I promise to get my dress shortened!" Miss Houston says, exploding into another round of giggles. "Seriously, though—tonight is a very special night for me, because I get to speak at a wonderful event—'Houston Helps Its Own' . . ."

The crowd interrupts her with another round of applause. "At this rate, we'd better move sleeping cots into the back!" Chanel mutters.

"You're right about that, Glitterbug," I shoot back to Chuchie. With all the glitter pomade she has put in her hair, she looks like one of those fireflies you see in July.

"We do take care of our own in Houston—and that's why a percentage of all the ticket proceeds will be used to rebuild Montgomery Homeless Shelter. I know fifty dollars is a lot of money to pay, but just remember—your dollars are working for our city!"

The crowd claps again.

"We want Backstabba!!" I yell, but of course, you can't hear me screaming over the noise. Backstabba is the lead singer of Karma's Children. A lot of people tell me I look like her, but I don't think so. She's taller and thinner, and her hair doesn't get wack frizzy attacks like mine. As a matter of facto, I'll bet nobody's does!

"We want to thank all the wonderful groups who were up here on the stage tonight, performing gratis on behalf of our benefit—and these are all groups from Houston, I might add!"

Now we're all clapping, and Chanel screams, "Yeah for the Cheetah Girls!"

"Aren't Miggy and Mo just the cutest things?" Miss Houston says, beaming.

I feel a pang in my chest. How come she didn't mention us? Chanel and Dorinda look at me, but I just roll my eyes and wave my hands in the air, like I don't care. "Yo! The Cheetah Girls are in the house!" I yell, my words swallowed up in the general chaos.

"Well, *all* the groups were great," Miss Houston gushes, just in case she's stepped on anyone else's toes—and believe me, she has!

"It's time now to introduce you to a group of girls who make us *soooh* proud. They've won two Grammy Awards, the Teen Peoples' Choice Award, um—" Miss Houston pauses to look at her cue cards. "I'm sorry—one *Soul Train* Award. And the best part is, they were born and raised right here in Houston! Please, let's give a warm welcome to our very own girl group—Karma's Children!"

I squeeze Chuchie. This is so live! I can't wait till someone announces *us* like that, and we get to hear people clap so loud, calling our names, panting for "more, more, more" till the big score!

Suddenly, we see spec-taculous lights beaming across the stage in all directions. Smoke comes pouring out onto the stage. Chuchie screams. The crowd chants, "Karma, Karma, Karma!"

"Omigod, the stage is on fire!" Aquanette yells. We chuckle. She and Angie can be so naïve sometimes!

Out of the smoke, Karma's Children emerge, wearing white satin jumpsuits covered by big white capes. "Omigod, they're wearing white in November!" Chanel shouts.

"Yeah, but they're dope costumes," Dorinda points out. And she should know—she majors in Costume Design at Fashion Industries East, where Chuchie and I also go to school. We major in fashion marketing, though. (And in case you didn't know, Aqua and Angie go to Performing Arts League. The rest of us are thinking of transferring there next year. If things keep flowing the right way for the Cheetah Girls, it's a definite!)

"For true," I scream back at Do' Re Mi. "But

we're not going to wear white after Labor Day or before Memorial Day—that's a Cheetah Girls rule!"

"Word!" Dorinda seconds, and we all do a Cheetah Girls handshake. I can feel the electricity in Chanel's and Dorinda's palms. This is the kind of moment I want to remember forever.

"Omigod, look how big Backstabba got!" Angie shrieks, pulling my arm.

She *is* a lot taller than I remember, but then again, I've never seen her this "up close and personal." Okay, we're stuck in left field, and I can't see her face that well—but we're in the house! Close enough to see that she's one tall girlina!

Backstabba is the leader of the group. She stands poised in the middle of the stage, hiding behind her cape. She is so dopalicious! I think she's about seventeen years old, but she looks older now, because they've gotten themselves more supa-dupa glammed up.

The four of them have been performing together since they were about nine. That's younger than we were when we started—and look how famous they are now! The other three members of the group—Greedi, Peace, and Luvbug—stand in a half circle behind Backstabba, with their hands above their heads.

I notice Dorinda's eyes popping. She's probably taking choreography notes. The beat to the song comes on, and she looks at me, puzzled.

"This must be one of the songs off their *new* album," I tell her.

We know every song they've ever done. Their biggest hit so far is, "Yes, Yes, Yes," which went double platinum—and that's supa-dupa better than the Midas touch! I can't wait till they drop this new album.

As if reading my mind, Backstabba pouts and breathes into the mike, "We love you Houston—that's why we're giving you a preview of the songs from our new album, which drops with Santa."

Chuchie looks at me, puzzled. "What happened?"

"She means, releases at Christmas."

I notice that Backstabba's hair is way longer than I remember it. She's definitely working extensions. "Hair extensions are career extensions. . . ." I hum to myself. Oh, that is so coolio!

I fight off the urge to pull my Kitty Kat notebook out of my cheetah backpack and scribble my idea down quickly, like I always do when I think of a song lyric. But I realize now is not the time. Instead, I repeat the words to myself a few more times, so I won't forget them, and make a mental note to write them down later.

Right now, it's all about the beat. I start clapping, then Dorinda, Chanel, and the twins pick it up with me.

Backstabba steps from behind the cape, in a cutout jumpsuit with rhinestones. *Wow!* Everybody is digging the "glitter-glam, thank you, ma'am" trip. The cape drops to the floor, and she starts singing the group's new song:

"Mr. Dream, why don't you come clean
and take the clouds you left behind
because you're so mean
Mr. Dream, why don't you float away
no one will complain
just come back another day
and stop playing your games."

All of sudden, a guy wearing a ten-gallon cowboy hat stands up in front of Dorinda, and she can't see a thing! Everybody looks at me, like I'm supposed to be the spokesperson for our crew—which I usually am. But there is no way I'm lassoing that cowboy!

Thank gooseness Mrs. Walker comes to our defense. She taps the guy on his elbow, 'cuz even *she* can't reach his shoulder! I don't hear what she says, but the guy crouches down a bit.

Dorinda still can't see, so I trade places with her. If you ask me, I say they should make tall people stand in the back, so we shorties don't get a complex.

Grooving to the music, I get caught up in my fantasies—all the wishes I hope come true for the Cheetah Girls. I can just see us, wooing the crowd like Karma's Children does. They seem to have the flavor that everybody savors—especially in Houston—but one day, I know *we* will be the flavor of the century (or at least the year!).

After a one-hour set, Backstabba steps up to the mike to say good night to the city she so obviously loves. The crowd is not having it: "More, more, more!!" they chant.

"Good night, Houston. We love you—and we will always come back home!" Backstabba chuckles breathlessly into the mike. She beams a supa-karat smile—almost brighter than the necklace dangling around her neck.

"I heard Jiggie Jim gave her that necklace," Chuchie says knowingly, like she is Miss Clucky, the gossip columnist.

"I'll bet you'd like to get a munch on those karats," I tease Chuchie.

"That's right, *mamacita,* I would," Chuchie shoots back.

I look over at Dorinda, and I can see her eyes glistening with tears. I give her a hug, and she hugs me back, hard. "We're gonna do it, Do' Re Mi—don't you worry," I say.

Chanel hugs Dorinda from the other side. The twins and their mother are looking on, beaming. Meanwhile, we're all trying not to get pushed around by the millions of people who are stampeding the joint like wild cattle.

"I guess we'd better get moving before we get stomped!" I say.

Chanel gives me a look, like, "What's the plan, Spam?"

I motion for everyone to follow me, as we try to plow our way down to Karma's Children's dressing room.

"Maybe we should use a smoke machine for *our* show," Chanel coos right behind me.

"Yeah—if it's good enough for the goose, it's good enough for the gander—and the Cheetahs!" I second. Sure, it's stealing some of their flavor, but I figure special effects, like smoke machines, are fair game. It's not like we're stealing their *songs* or anything!

"I felt like I was floating to paradise, listening to them," Dorinda chimes in.

"Yeah—we're doing fine on cloud nine!" I start humming, as we form a choo-choo train to make our move.

"You really think we should try to get in?" Dorinda asks in her squeaky voice.

"Why not? The most they can do is send us into the kitchen to wash the dishes, right?" I reply, getting up my courage. "We're not leaving until we get an intro, so act like you know, *girlitas*!"

The twins give me that look, like they know I'm not going to give up until we accomplish our mission.

The Mighty Man security guard has other intentions, however, 'cuz he stops us right in our cheetah tracks. "You can't go that way, ladies. Exit stage right."

Well, I'm not going to let this not-so-jolly giant stand in the way of my dig-able idea! Thinking fast, I moan, "We are the Cheetah Girls, and we left our wallets in the holding area."

"You can go to the holding area, but you have to go *that* way," he says, pointing to a path that short-circuits the one I want.

My face drops like a broken platter.

"Keep going," Mighty Man insists, pointing his hand in the *un*desired direction. I hear some noise on his walkie-talkie, and I give ground. I don't want to cause any static with the man, know what I'm sayin'?

"Let's go," Mrs. Walker says softly. I can feel the back of my neck burning with anger and embarrassment.

"I wish my mom was here," I mutter to Chanel as we head to the back exit. "She'd put Mr. Mighty Man in his place—with a can of Mace!" I feel like we just got nipped at the heels by a stupid hyena with pointy fangs.

We're all quiet as we hit the fresh air and head for the parking lot, on our way to Mrs. Walker's car. "Let me take a picture of you girls together," Mrs. Walker says chirpily. I guess she's trying to make us feel better, but I don't feel like being a nice Cheetah Girl right now—I mean, I'm mad as a hatter!

Chanel pulls me by the arm, and we stop in front of Mrs. Walker's car and strike a pose for a photo.

"Smile!" Mrs. Walker instructs us as she snaps the picture. Even though I don't feel like smiling, I do. "One more," Mrs. Walker pleads as I start to walk away.

She takes one more shot of us, then holds out the instant picture. I don't reach for it, but Dorinda does. "I'll take it," she says.

All of a sudden, this guy with hair so red it looks like it's on fire walks toward our car. "Aquanette, how you doin'?" he mumbles so low that at first, Aquanette doesn't hear him. Besides, she is too busy goggling at the picture. You'd think she'd never seen herself in her cheetah costume before. Well, I guess we should take pictures more often.

I poke her in the side to turn around. "Omigod, it's Beethead!" she coos.

Beethead just blushes, and looks down at his shoes, stifling a laugh.

"How are you doin'?" Aqua asks him, all

coo-ey goo-ey. Then, remembering her manners, she introduces Beethead to us. "This is Major Knowles—he's the reason I have seven stitches in my left knee!" she says, guffawing. Aqua is in fine form tonight—and I can tell by the way she looks at "Beethead" that she likes him.

Major is getting supa distressed. "I didn't mean for you to get hurt or anything."

"I know," Aqua says, patting his back. Then she tells us the story. They were playing on swings, it seems, and he threw a rock to see if he could reach her head. She fell off the swing, and hit her knee on a sharp rock. "That's what I get for showing off—" she starts to say.

All of a sudden, we hear a bunch of girls screaming, "Angie! Aqua!"

Aqua turns and says to her mom, "Who's that? Omigod!" In a matter of seconds, a whole group of kids is swarming around the twins, as if Aqua and Angie are Karma's Children or something. They start hugging the twins, jumping up and down.

"Clarissa, girl, you look so good! I'm so glad you got rid of those bangs," Aqua exclaims. Then she turns to us excitedly. "These girls belong to Kats and Kittys, too!"

"Oh, that's *la dopa*!" Chanel coos back.

Aqua tells them all about our group, and how we're members of Kats and Kittys Klub's New York chapter, but I'm not really listening. I feel like I have sort of floated out of my body.

All this attention the twins are getting is making me homesick for New York, for the first time since I've been down here. I wish we were back home, where we know people from school who would come backstage to congratulate us, like at the Kats and Kittys Halloween Bash last month. Looking into that crowd when we performed, and seeing some of the kids I went to junior high school with—that was a feeling I'll never forget. So I know how the twins feel right about now—and I'm a little jealous, I guess.

"I can't believe you went to New York and got in a group," the girl called Clarissa exclaims.

"Jasmine, when did you cut your hair?" Angie asks another girl, touching her short 'do.

"I guess after y'all left. Look at *your* hair—and those costumes!" Jasmine says loudly.

Clarissa senses that I'm not feeling it, so she smiles at me and says, "Y'all were great."

"Thank you," I say, taking a deep sigh, like

our vocal coach, Drinka Champagne, taught us to do whenever we get ready to sing—or whenever we're upset. I can hear her voice in my head, saying: "Clear those vocal cords."

We were great tonight, all right—but not great enough to get into Karma's Children's dressing room and hang. That's the real deal-io.

After we say good night to the bunch of "groupies" who are ogling the twins, we finally pile into Mrs. Walker's car. The twins are beaming as bright as the moonlight.

Beethead says he has to head off, too. "Say hi to your guinea pigs for me!" he chuckles.

"We will!" Aqua says, giggling as she gets into the car. Angie and Aqua brought those guinea pigs—Porgy and Bess—all the way from New York, just so they wouldn't be left alone with Mr. Walker and his crazy girlfriend, High Priestess Abala Shaballa. I guess they were afraid the High Priestess would use Porgy and Bess for one of her magic potions—cook them up in her steaming pot of who-knows-what. Anyhow, those two guinea pigs have been tearing up Grandma Selby's garden patch all week long!

"Omigod, can you believe how short

Jasmine cut her hair?" Aqua asks Angie. "If I had hair like hers, I would never cut it." The two of them sort of ignore us for a while, and gab on about their friends from Houston.

Finally, Dorinda pipes up, "Wow, Backstabba really looked dope. Is her hair longer than it was before?"

"I beweave it is," I say, chuckling. Then, suddenly, I remember the hook I came up with before. "Hair extensions are career extensions. . . !"

"Oh, that's so dope!" Dorinda gasps.

Taking my Kitty Kat notebook out of my backpack, I scribble madly. Then I start thinking. "I'm gonna add this to that Cheetah Girls Credo I'm working on for us."

"That's right, *mamacita*," Chanel coos. "Keep writing down stuff for us, 'cuz talent and skills will pay our bills!"

The twins chuckle. "That's right, Miss Chanel. You know that's right."

"That's it!" I exclaim loudly. "We just flipped some new flam!" I scribble some more. "Hair extensions may be career extensions, but talent and skills will pay my bills!"

"I like that!" Dorinda says approvingly.

I heave a deep sigh. Weaving words anyhoo I pleez always makes me feel better. Things may not be going our way, and nobody may be growlin' for more of the Cheetah Girls *yet*. But you just wait—one day, people will be trying to get into *our* dressing room, and know our every thought—and even what we had for breakfast.

Meanwhile, they can't take away our dreams!

Chapter 3

What started as a coolio adventure is turning into a real "turkey fest." The first bad vibe was last night, when Diamonds in the Ruff dissed us. Then that grumpy Mighty Man security guard prevented us from stepping into paradise (Karma's Children's dressing room, that is)—and now, my mom is acting wicky-wacky on the phone! I feel like I'm being beaten over the head with a drumstick. I don't have to be back to school until Monday, but Mom is determined that I come home before then.

"Galleria, you're full of stuffing! I'm not sitting home by myself on Thanksgiving! Not one more day!" Mom screams into the phone.

Mrs. Walker hovers by the dining-room table. My crew is sitting around, too—listening to me duke it out with Mom over the phone.

"But Mom, we wanna see if we can at least get into the Urban Rodeo show. It'll be good exposure for us!"

"If you want exposure, you can open the window and stick your head out! I don't care about any rodeo. Now, don't make me come down there and lasso you myself!"

I feel my ears burning. What is *wrong* with her? Nobody is more upset about Nona being in the hospital with a broken hip than I am. I mean, Nona's *my* grandmother, not hers! I was supa crushed that she couldn't come to New York and spend Thanksgiving with us, and that Daddy had to go to Italy to see her.

All of a sudden, I blurt out, "Mom, how come it's always Daddy's relatives we see? I mean . . . why don't *you* have any family?"

Mom starts crying into the phone. "How could you ask me something like that right now?" She is crying so hard, I can't even understand the rest of what she is saying.

I can't believe I asked her that—but I guess

. . . Well, to tell you the truth, I've always kind of felt that my mom was hiding something from me. I don't know why I feel that way—but somehow, I know it's true. It's little things, like tonight on the phone, that make me so sure.

Why can't she be open with me? I'm her daughter, for goodness' sake! I want her to tell me the *truth*. Whatever it is, it can't be that bad, can it?

Dorinda motions for me to give her the receiver. "Please let me talk to her," she whispers.

"Good luck, duck. You talk to her, *pleez*," I say, gladly giving Dorinda the cordless phone.

"Ms. Dorothea?" Dorinda whispers into the receiver. Cradling it to her ear, she walks into the other room.

Chanel looks at me, like, "Wazzup with that?"

But I don't care what's up. Right now, I'm just happy to get a break from Mom's wicky-wacky behavior.

"Is everything okay, Galleria?" Mrs. Walker asks me.

"No. My mom says she doesn't want me wearing out my welcome or anything. She wants me to come home. She doesn't care about any rodeo."

"I'll talk to her, and let her know you're welcome to stay here," Mrs. Walker says confidently.

All of a sudden, I wish I was in Chanel's shoes. Her mom, Juanita, is off in Paris with her boyfriend, Mr. Tycoon. Chuchie is happy to be away from her mom. Why is *my* mom always breathing down my throat? Why can't she just leave me alone for a change, like Juanita does with Chanel? I mean, sometimes Mom just suffocates me. I'm even starting to wonder if it's a good idea, her being the Cheetah Girls' manager. . . .

Aquanette puts down the breakfast plates. I shoot her a smile. "I can't believe Mom doesn't even care about us trying to get into the Urban Rodeo. Usually, she's the one pushing us to do more, more, more!"

"Yeah, well, it is Thanksgiving, Galleria," Aquanette says, taking Mom's side. "All she can probably think about is being with her family."

Dorinda walks back into the room and hands the phone to Mrs. Walker. "She wants to talk to you."

"What were you two talking about?" I ask Do' Re Mi.

"Oh, it was just girl talk," Dorinda says.

"Girl talk? My mom is forty-two years old and you're fourteen." I chuckle sarcastically, even though I feel a twinge of jealousy. I love Dorinda, just like she's my sister—I'm not jealous of her being close to my mom, but something is bothering me. . . . It's like they've been keeping a secret from me or something.

I think back to the day of Dorinda's surprise adoption party. We all helped her foster mother, Mrs. Bosco, plan the party, and everything went great—even though later we found out Dorinda didn't get adopted after all.

Anyway, a weird thing happened at that party. My mom was in the bathroom, boo-hooing about something as usual (I'm sorry, but my mom cries even more than me). Dorinda went in there to talk to her, and they've been acting real chummy ever since. I don't know what they talked about, but it sure must have been important, because neither one of them will tell me what it was—and now, here we go with more secrets!

Dorinda squirms in her chair. "She just feels bad about being alone—so I tried to talk to her. Okay, Galleria?" Dorinda yells at me.

"Okay, Do' Re Mi—just be chill-io," I say, backing off. "Why is everybody being so sensitive?" What I really want to know is, if Dorinda was able to talk some sense into my mom when I wasn't. "Did she say I could stay?"

"Only if we get the gig at the Okie-Dokie," Dorinda says matter-of-factly.

"Yes!" I jump up and down with dee-light. "Ya-hoo!"

"Bubbles, we didn't exactly get the gig yet, *está bien?*" Chanel squeaks at me.

"I know, Chuchie, but we're in the flow, so you never know!" I say. "We should burn some of those candles of yours for good luck."

"Oh, I left my Santeria candles at home," Chuchie says sarcastically.

"Yeah, but they must sell them at Piggly Wiggly's," I persist. "Come on, Chuchie, wax is wax and that's a facto."

"Piggly Wiggly?" Aqua asks in surprise. "We don't have that supermarket down here."

"Really?"

"Uh-uh. Our big chain is the Garden of Eden Supermarkets," Angie explains.

"That's too bad—I'll betcha if your father's girlfriend, Abala Shaballa Cuckoo, came down here, she'd be very disappointed," I howl. "You know how much she loves those cuckoo ingredients they sell at Piggly Wiggly's for the witch's brew she makes!"

Aqua and Angie give me a look, like *I'm* the one concocting witch's brew. *Omigod*—I forgot about Mrs. Walker! She's been right here in the room the whole time—and she probably didn't know about their father's new girlfriend! Not until I just opened my big mouth, that is!

I put my head in my hands. I'm just stepping on everybody's toes—like the girl with skyscraper heels who stepped on Dorinda's toes last night at the concert.

Luckily, Mrs. Walker is across the room, talking on the phone. We all look at her, trying to see if she caught a whiff of my riff. Feeling our gaze, she automatically turns and smiles, while muttering, "Huh, huh," to my mom. I take a deep, relieved breath.

Aqua mouths to me, "Not one more word about *her*!"

I mouth back, "What did you say?"

"You *know* what she said," Angie hisses. I can tell they *are not playin'*.

"Okay, sassy-frassy," I say, embarrassed. I've never heard Angie speak up before, but I guess the twins really don't want their mother to find out about the "wicked witch of the north," who is posing as their father's girlfriend.

Aqua scurries to the kitchen to put the breakfast grub-a-dub on the table, and we begin eating.

Mrs. Walker finally gets off the phone. She sure can talk. "Galleria, your mom is real nice. Don't worry—we're not changing the return date on y'all's plane tickets—not just yet."

"Thank you, Mrs. Walker," I say politely. Suddenly, I wish I had the twins' mother for a mom instead of mine. She's so nice and calm—not a drama queen like my mom.

Mrs. Walker pauses as if she's contemplating something. "Girls, I would prefer if you called me Junifred instead of Mrs. Walker," she says. "I'm sure Aquanette and Anginette have told you that I'm divorced from their father."

"Oh—I'm sorry . . . Junifred," I say warmly.

"Yes, ma'am, they do know," Aqua says awkwardly, then throws me a look, like I'd better not say one more peep about their Daddykin's girlfriend, Abala Shaballa, or the twins are gonna lasso me with a rope around my neck!

Mrs. Walker doesn't catch the glare, because she is too busy looking at her pretty gold watch. "I can't believe what time it is. You know I have to go over to Eden and shop for Big Momma."

Aqua jumps to explain. "Our grandmother walks with a cane, so she doesn't get around like she used to. But wait till you eat her food—her fried chicken and peach cobbler—you're gonna wanna slap your momma!"

"Well, I wanna do that already!" I blurt out. We all giggle nervously.

"What time is Skeeter coming?" Mrs. Walker asks, smiling softly at our silliness.

"He should be here by now," Aqua moans. Then they look at each other like, "Uh-oh, not 'Tales from the Tomb' again!"

See, last time the twins' Uncle Skeeter went missing, we found him in his daddy's mausoleum—you know, one of those big tombs you see in cemeteries. He was hiding out there, feeling so low he couldn't get any lower. Then we found him, and hooked him up with Fish 'N' Chips as the third member of their band. He's been ridin' high ever since—until now, that is. He's supposed to be taking us over to the Okie-Dokie Corral, where we will try to weasel an audition for the Urban Rodeo celebrations. I can tell we're all a little worried that he's not here.

Mrs. Walker makes a "shoo" motion with her hands, like, "bad thoughts be long gone." "Skeeter never did get anywhere on time. Don't expect that to change," she tells us.

Aqua and Angie laugh. They seem so much more comfortable around their mother than they are with their father.

"If he doesn't show, *I'll* take y'all to the rodeo, all right?" Mrs. Walker offers.

"Yes, ma'am," we all say.

Just then, we hear a car horn honking. "That's him!" Angie says, jumping up and running outside like it's Christmas. Aqua runs after her, and the rest of us grab our cheetah backpacks and head out to join them.

Skeeter drives a red Cadillac convertible

with the top down. If that isn't enough, he is wearing a red fedora and a red fake-fur jacket. He is grinning from ear to ear as he waves us inside.

"Can you believe Uncle Skeeter's outfit?" Aqua says, seeing the look on my face.

"I got it at Born Again Threads, baby," Skeeter explains. "I was gonna wear it to the benefit the other night, but I figured with all the trouble I'd already caused your momma, I'd better put on that flower shirt she got me for my birthday!" He slaps his metallic purple bell-bottoms, laughing.

"Ooh, this is *la dopa*!" Chuchie exclaims as she hops in. Chuchie would do anything to glide in a ride. Me? I'm a typical New York *girlina*—Mr. Taxi, pleez! Let someone else do the driving, okay?

"We iz so glad you're here," Aqua tells him. "Ma has to go buy groceries for Big Momma—and we thought she was gonna tiptoe through the turnips if you didn't get here in time!"

"Not to worry—life is a flurry, so you girls just sit back and enjoy. It's time to saddle 'em up and ride 'em, cowgirls!"

Chapter 4

I have never been to a rodeo before, let alone an "urban rodeo," so I'm kind of excited about finding out the real deal-io. As if reading my mind, Aqua is on the case like Mace, trying to find out more details. Apparently, a lot has gone down in boostin' Houston since the twins moved to the Big Apple in search of their rainbow. "I don't remember them having an urban rodeo here before, do you, Uncle Skeeter?" she asks, nestling up to her favorite uncle.

I start feeling sad again, thinking about my Italian aunt—Zia Donatella—who was supposed to come over to the States with Nona for the Thanksgiving holidays—but who never got airborne because of Nona's *tragedia*. Daddy hopped on a plane to Turin right away to be with Nona, and I'll bet he's lonely without me and Mom. He'd better be, I think, fuming inside. He's not the one who has to put up with how grumpy Mom is acting—*I* do.

"That's 'cuz they ain't never had no 'urban rodeo' in Houston before," Skeeter says. "I can tell you that for sho'. I heard some promoters from Philly are doing it—just throwing in a little soul flavor for entertainment in between some bulldogging. I heard they got big acts coming down here, too."

"Is that right?" Aqua mumbles.

"Yessirree, trying to bring some flavor down to the Lone Star State, I reckon," Skeeter chuckles.

"What's bulldogging?" Dorinda asks. She's definitely the most athletic one of our crew—what with her skateboarding moves, she probably can't wait to saddle up.

"Steer wrestling—that's what regular folks call it," Skeeter explains. "See, when you're competing in the bulldogging contest, you gotta get one o' them hazers to help you."

"A hazer?" Dorinda asks hesitantly.

"Yeah—that's the guy that keeps the steer—

you do know what a steer is, don't you?" Skeeter interrupts himself, chuckling.

Do' Re Mi looks at Chuchie, who shrugs her shoulders. The twins burst out laughing.

"I know it's something you ride, that's what I'm talking about," Do' Re Mi says, smirking and folding her arms across her tiny chest.

"That's right—it's something you ride, all right—and they be winning some serious cash doing it, too," Skeeter says, slapping his knee. "Boy, you get that hazer running that baby in a straight line, all you got to do is slide off your horse and grab its horn, then wrestle it to the ground."

He nods his head, satisfied with his explanation, while Do' Re Mi, Chuchie, and I look at each other like, "Where's the mall? Yikes!"

"Now, I know you two aren't any bulldogging queens, you know what I mean?" I hiss at Aqua and Angie.

"No, ma'am, we izn't," Aqua admits with a smile, "but that doesn't mean we don't enjoy watching it."

"Where's the Okie-Dokie Corral at?" Dorinda asks.

"On Rat Tail Road," Skeeter says, pointing

to a huge billboard on the highway as we approach it.

"Ay, *Dios mío!* Krusher is performing!" Chuchie squeals.

"And MC Rabbitt!" gasps Dorinda. "Bring on the Forty Karats, that's what I'm talking about!"

"Omigod—and Sista Fudge too!" the twins exclaim.

Of course, my eyes bug out when I see that Karma's Children are also on the bill. I guess everybody is still sore that we didn't snag at least one measly autograph from Houston's finest, but there's always one last chance, last dance, if you get my drift.

Then, suddenly, I get a bad case of the squigglies. How are we gonna pull off this hoedown? Even if it's an *urban* rodeo, they probably aren't gonna let us perform with headliners like these.

Do' Re Mi sees the look on my face. "Miggy and Mo said *they* were booked at the Okie-Dokie, right?"

"Yeah," I say, still feeling queasy and uneasy.

"I wonder where the, um, unknown acts

perform at?" Angie asks apprehensively.

"Probably in the barnyard, with the baby bulls who stubbed their little bitty toes during a hayride!" I say sarcastically.

"Well, I'd rather have a hayday than no payday!" smirks Do' Re Mi.

"That's a song!" Chuchie squeals.

"I got a hayday. That's my best payday," I hum nervously, as the rest of the Cheetah Girls join in.

"Hay, ho! Hay, ho! Hay, ho!" we chant for the chorus, causing Skeeter to chuckle.

We drive for twenty more minutes before we see the big red barnyard. "Hey, ho, here we are!" Skeeter says in sing song style as he drives up to the entrance of the Okie-Dokie Corral. "Come on, girls, let's go rope 'em in!"

"It sure looks like a big barnyard," Dorinda observes.

"Wow, they must have built this just for the show!" Aqua exclaims as we walk toward the wide entrance. Once inside, we see millions of men running around—carpenters banging their hammers, men in construction caps wielding electric drills. Sparks are flying everywhere. There is also lots of sawdust on the floor, and piles of wood.

Skeeter makes eye contact with this guy in a red baseball cap, with greasy-looking, stringy hair hanging out of it. The guy motions for us to step aside, and talks with Skeeter. I can't hear what they're saying because of all the noise. He motions for us to walk back outside and into another building—the office.

"They're building all the booths for the event," Skeeter explains. "We've got to find a guy named Mr. Steer—he's handling the talent."

"Well, talent is what we are," Aqua mumbles.

"The corral where they're gonna have the stock events is in the back," Skeeter goes on to explain.

"What's that?" Dorinda asks.

"The main events of the rodeo," Aqua says proudly.

"The rough stock events are where the cowboys—or the cowgirls, 'cuz you know we got a lot of 'em down here—" Skeeter chuckles, then coughs. "Anyway, they get on these wild bucking horses, you know, or sometimes they use bulls—whichever—and they try to ride those babies for however long they can."

"See, they win by how the judges award the points—you know, for their form, and how well they spur the animals," Aqua adds.

"How much do they win?" I ask, 'cuz now I'm curious.

"For first prize?"

"Yeah," I say. "Like, what other prize is there?"

Aqua chuckles. "They could get up to five thousand dollars."

"For those kinda duckets we should forget singing, and just become cowgirls!!" I heckle.

"You know they got all-girl rodeos now, too," Skeeter says.

"Yeah—they do bull riding, too," Angie says, laughing.

"Bull riding?"

Seeing my face, Skeeter smiles and says, "They don't have to spur the bull, they just gotta stay on him for eight seconds, by holding on to an unknotted rope around his belly with one hand!"

"Ooh, *mira*, look at the cows!" Chuchie exclaims, pointing to some cattle being led down the plank of a big truck.

"Chuchie—look at the horns. Those are *cattle*," I correct her.

"What happened? That's what I meant," Chuchie retorts, fascinated with the cattle being rounded up to go in the corral.

"Those are longhorns," Skeeter says, stopping to stare at the procession.

"Yeah—they've definitely got long horns," Do' Re Mi says.

"You ever seen one before?" Aqua asks, putting her arms around Do' Re Mi's tiny shoulders.

"They got them at the zoo in the Bronx?" Do' Re Mi asks mischievously.

"Probably not."

"Well—then I've never seen one!"

"What's the letter *B* doing on their behinds?" I ask.

"You gotta brand those babies, so nobody will steal 'em. Rodeo livestock is costing a pretty penny these days," Skeeter says.

"How much?" Chuchie asks, like she's in the market for a longhorn.

"One of these is gonna cost you about ten thousand dollars—but you gonna spend about twenty-five thousand for a champion bronco, that's for sure."

All this talk about duckets makes me wonder if the Okie-Dokie entertainers are gonna get any in their buckets. "Do you think they'll be paying talent?"

"Probably in grits, if you're lucky," Skeeter says, looking at me. "But that's the first thing I'm gonna ask Mr. Steer when we find him."

Once inside the one-story building, we see two more men—one in a powder-blue suit, and another in a red one. They are in a heated dispute. "See, he thinks he's slick," the one in red is yelling, "shipping the lights at the last minute. You ain't gonna see a church mouse singing up on that stage, let alone Sista Fudge, dog."

We stand by nervously as the two continue to duke it out.

"He's my cuzzin, dog—doing us a favor. What am I supposed to do?" the man in the blue suit counters.

"Yeah—well, the lights are out on cuzz, 'cuz you're paying him out of your share, dog!"

All of a sudden, the barking duo notice our presence. "Wazzup?" the man in red asks.

"We're looking for Mr. Steer," Skeeter says.

"You talent?"

"Yessirree." Skeeter puffs out his chest.

"He'll be right back," the man in red says, then remembers his manners. "We're the Rashad brothers—the promoters."

"Is that right?" Skeeter says, perking up. "I heard you guys are from Philly."

"You heard about us, huh? Yeah—that's right, we're from Philly, and we're definitely learning a thing or two down here, boy," he says, shaking his head. "This has been a trip. Our cuzzin Reggie lives down here, and he's been after us for years to put on an event down here—"

Before the dukin' duo can get in any more details about their urban rodeo drama, a tall man wearing a ten-gallon cowboy hat walks in. "Can I help you folks?" he asks.

Suddenly, I feel jitters again. I brush down my cheetah skirt automatically. I'll bet he's the man we're looking for, and after Skeeter introduces us, I can tell I'm right.

"I'm sorry, but we don't have any more slots available for the Sassy-sparilla Saloon Competition—but let's see what you got, since you came all this way." Mr. Steer takes off his hat and rests it on the long wooden table behind him.

I guess the Sassy-sparilla Saloon must be the contest for wanna-be stars, like us and Miggy and Mo. Funny they didn't mention anything about a contest. I wonder what the prize is? We should have asked them for more details.

I feel myself sinking. I shoulda known we weren't getting in to this shindig. Chuchie is bugging her eyes at me, like, "What are we supposed to do?"

I guess "see what you got" is our cue to perform. Suddenly taking charge, I hear myself say, "We're gonna perform our latest song for you—'It's Raining Benjamins.'"

"All right. Sounds good to me."

We stand together and begin:

"For the first time in her-story
there's a weather forecast
that looks like the mighty cash . . ."

While we're singing, I can't help but look at Mr. Steer to see how he's reacting. I mean, it's kinda weird, performing for someone who's wearing a ten-gallon hat that covers his eyes, if you catch my drift. Maybe he doesn't like our kind of music. Out of the corner of my eye, I see Skeeter. He is just beaming at us, and clapping along until we finish.

"Okay, girls, I'll tell you what. I'm gonna give you a slot in the contest—the opening slot. That's the best I can do for ya," Mr. Steer says apologetically. "I know it's not much, and we ain't paying, so it's up to you."

I want to jump up and down and throw a lasso around Mr. Steer's neck, I'm so amped. Whoopee!!

"What's the Sassy-sparilla Saloon?" Do' Re Mi asks Mr. Steer.

"That's one of the saloons where customers will be served beverages and food," Mr. Steer explains. "We've got about, let's see—counting the Bronco Burger, five places set up where customers can eat and drink. The Sassy-sparilla is for young people, so we thought about putting on a contest—you know, like a warm-up show before the All-Girls Rodeo event."

"Oh," I say. "What's the, um, prize for winning the contest?"

"Oh, nothing much—just a bronze cowgirl statue . . . and two tickets to AstroWorld for the Holiday in the Park Celebration."

"Oh," I say nonchalantly, trying not to seem too interested. I can tell that Skeeter doesn't get it: the Cheetah Girls always keep their eyes on the prize—and no prize is ever too small. "How many performers will there be?"

"You mean on the main stage?" Mr. Steer asks.

I feel a twinge of jealousy. I wish *we* could perform on the main stage. "No, I mean performing, um, with us."

"Oh—I'm sorry. We have six groups—all local, like yourselves," Mr. Steer says. "Miggy and Mo, CMG, Diamonds in the Ruff, HF—Houston's Finest—and the Cowgirls. I believe that's it."

Chuchie and I look at each other like we can't believe our ears. He did say all the groups were from Houston—and the CMG we know said they were from Oakland.

"Did you say CMG?" I ask Mr. Steer, not letting the fat cat out of the bag.

"Yes, I did. The Cash Money Girls."

"We performed with them, um, in Hollywood," I say, 'cuz I want Mr. Steer to know that we aren't just some group of wanna-be kids. I mean, we have had a few gigs, okay?

"Is that right?" Mr. Steer asks, smiling. "I know they moved out to California, but they are originally from right here."

Chuchie and I look at each other again, our eyes shouting. "Yeah, they said they'd moved to Oakland." I still can't believe it's the same Cash Money Girls we performed with at the Tinkerbell Lounge in Hollywood!

"I'm gonna have to run right now—we're doing a sound check for the main stage—but lemme show you girls the Sassy-sparilla Saloon." Mr. Steer ambles along in front of us, and we follow him to the saloon, which is getting its sign hammered on as we walk in.

"Construction sure took a long time around here," Mr. Steer says, motioning for us to walk under the ladder and through the doorway.

"That's bad luck," whispers Chuchie.

"Too bad," I whisper back, going in.

"This is nice," Aqua says, looking around at the wooden bar with heaps of sawdust on the floor. I glance over and see the small—and I do mean small—stage area.

The Rashad brothers have stopped fighting, and they wave good-bye to us as we walk back outside. Suddenly, I feel sorry for them. "It must be hard putting together an event like this," I say.

"Well, we won't have to worry about lights—'cuz we're performing in a barn," Aqua says sarcastically—which makes me wonder if she's disappointed in our hookup.

Once we are alone, I repeat the name of the group like a mantra: "CMG. CMG . . ."

"I can't believe they were frontin' like that—like they were so hardcore—from Oakland," Do' Re Mi says, shaking her head.

"Yeah, throwing money onstage, talking about the Benjamins alrighty, alrooty, tooty, frutti!" I heckle, making fun of them. "At least we got that dope idea of throwing money onstage from them." Like I said—special effects are fair game for copying.

"I told you it was a good idea," Aqua says, shaking her head. "Remember what Drinka Champagne says: 'You always got to have a theme' . . ."

"—and a dream!" Angie and I finish in unison.

"Aqua—you never heard of them before?" I ask, still puzzled about the origins of CMG.

"No, ma'am—but we don't know *everybody*

in Houston, Miz Galleria," Aqua says, bugging her eyes. "This ain't a one-horse town, you know."

"Three million people live here," Angie says, coming to her sister's defense.

"Well, I can't believe it's the same girls, coming off so hard like lard," I mutter.

"Lard ain't hard," Aqua says, confused.

"You know what I'm saying," I hiss, trying to make my point.

"Yeah, we understand," Angie says, shaking her head.

"Well, at least we got in there," Do' Re Mi says, shrugging her tiny shoulders.

"Yeah, in there like swimwear," I mutter back, feeling better already.

"Do you think all five of us are gonna fit on that stage?" Aqua asks, concerned.

"Not if you keep eating three pieces of cornbread for breakfast," I snicker back.

"Well, then I guess we'd better start dieting now," Chanel pipes up.

"Not a chance," Aqua says, shaking her head. "We have to go over to Big Momma's, and then to Granddaddy Walker's for Thanksgiving!"

"And eat two Thanksgiving dinners!" Angie pipes in.

"We'll be as fat as cows headed off for slaughter!" Chuchie moans.

"Well, then I got a new song we can sing," I say, smirking.

"Word?" Do' Re Mi says, her eyes widening.

"Yeah—'Can I Get a Moo!'"

Chapter 5

Chuchie is jumping around like a hot tamale, just because we're finally going to my namesake—the infamous Galleria Mall in downtown Houston. Of course, we're all down with hanging out at the mall, but we also have to buy some more fake Benjamins for our gig at the Okie-Dokie Corral. No matter how many times I say that word, it sounds like music to my ears: "We got a gig at the thingamajig," I hum aloud.

Aqua and Angie are telling their mother (for the tenth time) the story of how my mom named me after this mall, because she bought her first pair of Gucci shoes here, when she was two months pregnant with me.

"Is that story really true?" Mrs. Walker asks me, amused.

"Hard to believe, but true," I respond. "If you knew my mother—you would believe it."

After we park the car in the mall garage, Mrs. Walker tells us the game plan: "Y'all pick me up from Tender Tendrils in an hour—I'm just getting a quick touch-up."

Aqua gives her a mother a look. "It doesn't look like a quick one to me," she says. "You let your roots go too long, Ma—they may send you down the street to the magic shop instead!"

"I said one hour, or Reesy will keep me there all day, running her mouth about her ulcers, boyfriend problems, and late mortgage payments!"

"All right," Aqua concedes.

"Check this mall," Do' Re Mi says, looking around at all the beautiful stores like she's Alice in Wonderland. Out in the middle of the walkway, this guy has a table set up with CDs, and a sign that says $5.

"How come the CDs only cost five dollars?" Do' Re Mi asks me.

"'Cuz they're *bootleg* CDs," I retort, but I gaze at the table anyway. I could use the new Chutney Dallas CD. "Are these just like the real ones?" I ask the guy selling them.

"Word is bond," he responds, "and I'll give you two for nine, 'cuz you're fine."

"Omigod, Sista Fudge has got a new album!" Aqua says, reaching into her cheetah backpack for her wallet.

"Hold up, Aqua," I say, pulling her aside. "Listen, you know when you buy bootleg CDs, the artist doesn't get any money for it."

"Yeah, you're right," Aqua says, nodding her head.

"One day, they could be selling our CDs on that table, and you know we'd be mad as hatters if we didn't collect our duckets in a bucket. Am I right?" I look over my shoulder at Mr. Bootlegger, to make sure he doesn't peep our conversation.

"You sure are right," Angie agrees.

"How come they don't get caught doing it?" Do' Re Mi asks.

"'Cuz peeps is just happy to buy the CDs for less—they don't care about the artists, but *we do*, you get my flow?"

We walk away from the table, and the guy keeps harassing us from a distance. "Don't sleep on this, cutie!" he yells after me.

"I wish he'd kill the noise," I moan, walking arm in arm with Do' Re Mi. Suddenly, I stop dead in my tracks, and gaze at the window of a store called Who Shot the Sheriff?

"Ooh, those are nice," Aqua and Angie coo simultaneously, because they've spotted the same gagulous items that I have: cheetah-spotted cowgirl hats!

"Chuchie! Come on, Calamity Jane!" I yell, and motion for her to come check out our latest cheetah-licious find. "*Girlitas,* I think it's time we rock this town by getting us a hot-diggity getup," I say boldly, like I'm the trail boss leading my cowgirls into Dodge.

"What happened?" Chuchie says, catching up to us out of breath. Then she spots the prize: "Ooh, those are *la dopa*!"

Inside the store, Do' Re Mi peeps these funny-looking leather pants. "Check this, yo—I wonder . . ."

"Those are leather chaps," says the sales clerk, who has an upturned white mustache and a red face.

"Oh, um, word," Dorinda says nervously, putting them down.

"Lemme show you how a real cowgirl would wear them," the sales clerk says, strapping the pants around her waist. The leather chaps are so long on tiny Dorinda that they're dragging on the floor, but the jolly man pays it no mind.

"See, now, if you were wrestling steer, these would protect your legs from cattle horns, rope burns, scratches, and other hazards of the profession," he explains.

"Good thing I just go to high school!" Do' Re Mi says, chuckling.

"Where you gals from?" the clerk asks us, amused.

"The Big Apple," I explain.

"Is that right over by the Pear Tree Inn?" he asks, puzzled.

We burst out laughing. Sometimes I forget there are peeps who don't quite get our flow. "No, sir, that's what we call Manhattan," I explain.

"Oh," the clerk says, 'cuz now he gets it. "Sometimes I can't understand you young people. So what can I do fer you today?"

"We were wondering how much those hats are?" I say, keeping my fingers crossed that our latest cheetah find doesn't cost more than the duckets we have in the bucket, if you get my drift. Otherwise, we'll just have to buy one hat, and cut it up into five pieces!

"The Stetsons?" he says.

"Stetsons," Do' Re Mi repeats after him.

"Why, those happen to be on sale. I can give them to you for fifteen apiece," the sales clerk responds.

"Awright!" I say, relieved.

Chanel makes her long señorita face again. "I don't have *any* money left. *Nada* for Prada," she moans, cracking a joke.

"Here, Chuchie," I say, whipping some duckets out of my fat cheetah wallet. I know that Chuchie has been paying back her mom every penny she owes her for charging up her credit card. Her bucket is always empty these days—like a broken piñata. "Just stop jumping up and down—or I'm not giving it to you. You're making me dizzy, Chuchie, I swear!"

"Está bien, mamacita!" Chuchie says, giving me a hug.

"We'll take five of them," I tell the beaming salesclerk.

Aquanette tries on one of the spotted Stetsons, but it sits on top of her head like a muffin. "This one is too small. Here, Dorinda," Aqua says, handing it to Do' Re Mi, who has the tiniest head in our crew.

"Don't worry, I'll bring out some bigger sizes," the clerk says, stepping into the back.

"Ooh, put this on, Dorinda," Chuchie says, trying to hang a canteen around Do' Re Mi's shoulder. "*Mira,* now you look like a real cheetah cowgirl!"

"Chuchie, we're not in a desert!" I chuckle, fingering the circular metal canteen on a strap. "This would make a dope purse, though."

"All right, young ladies, why don't you try these on?" the salesclerk says, returning with an armful of spotted Stetsons.

"Are they really gonna stay on?" I ask, twiddling the adjustable string.

"Yeah, just make sure to adjust it tight enough under your chin, but not so tight you strangle yourself," the salesclerk chuckles.

Once we're outside, I catch a glimpse of the five of us in the store window, and I like what I see. "The hats look really dope with our outfits," I say, feeling the soft pile on my cheetah blazer, then touching the brim of the hat. "It's show time at the world-famous Galleria! I could get used to boostin' Houston."

"Everybody is so nice down here," Do' Re Mi says, hugging Aqua and Angie. Since we left New York, Do' Re Mi hasn't said one word about her foster mother, Mrs. Bosco, or her ten foster brothers and sisters. I get the feeling she is happy to be with us, and away from all that foster-care madness. No matter how much my mom gets on my last nerve, I'll never understand what Do' Re Mi goes through on a 24/7 basis. Never.

"Yes, ma'am, they are nice," Aqua says proudly. "I mean, we've got a few crabs in the barrel, but mostly everybody is real good people."

We decide to prowl around the mall in our new cheetah Stetsons, causing a stir in a Minute Rice second. A group of boys hanging around the mall starts shouting out to us.

"Isn't that the guy who was at the benefit?" I ask, pointing to the redhead in the bunch.

"Yeah—that's Beethead," Aqua says, beaming.

"You like him!" I taunt her. "Wait till I go back to New York and tell your father!"

"You do that, Miss Galleria, and I'm gonna tell High Priestess Abala Shaballa that you just love her 'health shakes,' okay?" But I can tell that Aqua is too busy goospitating at Beethead to care what her father thinks about boys. (He won't let them date until they're "older," and he won't say how *much* older!)

The other boys hanging with Beethead are just standing there, gaping at us like they're monkeys in a tree looking down at a bunch of bananas. If they keep it up, I'm gonna make sure one of them slips on a peel.

"Hey, Beethead," Aqua says, then nervously adjusts the strings on her hat.

"Where y'all going?" he asks, obviously amused by our Cheetah gear.

"Nowhere—we've just gotta buy something for our show, then meet up with my mother," Aqua explains. I can tell she is nervous.

"What show?" Beethead asks.

"Oh, we're gonna perform at the Okie-Dokie," Aqua says, flossing a little. I'm not used to seeing Miss Humble passing up her pie like this, so I just chill and take in the sight.

"We heard that's gonna be wack," Beethead announces, then looks at his boys.

"What, are y'all gonna ride in the rodeo or something?" a boy with buck teeth blurts out.

"No, we're singers," I hiss back.

"Our group is called the Cheetah Girls," Aqua says. "I told you that before."

"Oh, yeah," Beethead says, like he's embarrassed for his friend, who's like a dog with a bone, 'cuz he just won't leave it alone.

"I like your jacket," Buck Teeth says to me. "Can I touch it?" he asks, feeling my lapel. "Wow, what kind of fabric is this?"

"It's pony," I shoot back at him. "Give me a dollar, I'll let you ride it!"

Now Beethead is laughing at *his* crew, not ours. "Oh, snaps, that's ill!"

"Come on, we've got a show to get ready for," I say, pulling Do' Re Mi and Chuchie by the arms. Aqua and Angie can stand there holding court with the monkey boys if they'd like to. "We'd better get some Benjies for our show before the fake bank closes!"

The three of us skip past all the beautiful stores in the Galleria, like we're following the yellow brick road. We break into a cowboy song, adding a few laced lyrics of our own:

"Oh, give me a home where the buffalo roam
Where the deer and the antelope play,
Where seldom is heard a discouraging word,
And the skies are not cloudy all day—
'cuz it's a payday!!"

Chapter 6

Why, oh, why, did Mrs. Walker have to tell Chuchie about the Thanksgiving Day Dinosaur Dash? If she'd only known what a Road Runner accident-waiting-to-happen Chuchie is, she'd have squashed that suggestion.

Just think—we could be at Big Momma's right now—licking our lips on juicy drumsticks, instead of standing out here on Houston Hill, waiting for the wacky races to begin. The Dinosaur Dash consists of two races—one for kids, one for teens—and it's an annual event in Houston. Actually, the twins' cousins—Egyptian and India—were the real instigators behind this Dino Dash madness. When we returned from the mall yesterday, they called us and gave us a blow-by-blow of their handmade green costumes for the race. Actually, their costumes are cuter than Chuchie's: they made little green skirts with fringed hems and matching vests of felt. Chuchie's paper costume looks more like a "thesaurus" than a "tyrannosaurus," if you get my drift.

Aside from Chuchie, the only one of us who's digging all this dinosaur stuff is Do' Re Mi: she's checking out all the contestants' costumes. "That one is dope," she says excitedly. "It's a velociraptor—they have ferocious fangs."

"He looks like a cross between a praying mantis and Tricky Martian, if you ask me," I snarl, looking at the fake green antennae he's wearing on top of his green, paper-covered helmet.

"Yeah, well, he could do some serious damage with that eight-foot tail, if you ask me," Aqua moans, trying to stay out of his way as he runs by, wagging it in our direction.

"What do you get if you win this race? A dozen dinosaur eggs?" I ask the twins.

"No, I think they make a donation to the Museum of Natural Science in your name, that's all—it's just for a good cause," Aqua replies, waving at Egyptian and India like she's a Homecoming Queen on a Houston float. "Ooh, look how cute Egyptian and India look!" she beams as her two cousins scurry up the hill, their green-fringed paper skirts flapping in the wind.

When the teen division Dinosaur Dash begins, I find myself rooting for Chuchie anyway. "Go, Chuchie! Go, Chuchie!" I've got to give it to my *señorita,* she will run a race for any reason—even if the prize is a box of Gobblers.

Chuchie is a really good runner, because she has really long legs and all that energy. "Go, Chuchie!" I scream again—until this boy with red hair gains on her, and makes a mad dash for the finish line.

"Dag on!" Aqua groans. "Chanel almost won!"

"Ain't that Beethead?" Angie asks.

"I can't tell with that green bandana on his forehead—wait a minute, that *is* Beethead!" Aqua exclaims.

After the race, we all head over to the "Dino Bash" at the museum, and wait for Chuchie, Egyptian, and India. "If you ask me, this music is a little 'prehistoric,'" I moan, listening to the corny grooves blasting from the speakers.

"It's early rock 'n' roll—Chubby Checker," Mrs. Walker explains as she starts twisting her hips.

"Oh," I say, embarrassed. Mom has us schooled on the '70s music scene, but anything before that, we're clueless. We all start twisting our hips like Mrs. Walker, and mashing our feet.

"It's called 'The Twist,'" Mrs. Walker explains.

"That makes sense," Do' Re Mi chuckles, twisting her little matchstick butt for all it's worth.

"Ooh, that made me sweat," Aqua exclaims, as we pile over to the table to get some Tastee T-Rex Punch and congratulate Chuchie, Egyptian, and India, who are getting special goody bags for participating in the Dash.

"I almost won!" India says, jumping up and down.

"Yes, you did," I tell her, even though she was so far back in the race I almost didn't see her.

"This tastes like Tropical Punch to me," says Chuchie.

"Yo, wazzup, Aquanette?" says Beethead, coming from behind the crowd.

"Hi, Beethead," Aqua says, acting nervous again. She *definitely* likes him. "How come when we saw you at the mall, you didn't tell us you were running in the Dinosaur Dash?"

"Oh, you know, I was with my crew—they think it's kinda corny, but I've been doing it every year since I was nine," he chuckles. "I just can't get into the costume thing."

"Well, at least you wore a green bandanna," Aqua points out, as Beethead shoves it into his pocket.

Then Aqua says something that causes me to choke on my Tastee T. "You wanna dance, Beethead?" I didn't know she could be so forward!

"I'm not dancing to that wack music," Beethead says, sucking his teeth.

"Come on—I'm gonna show you how to do 'the twist'!" Aqua insists, pulling his hand.

Beethead, however, won't budge, and Aqua seems disappointed. He just wants to talk. "I'm gonna check y'all out at the Okie-Dokie tomorrow night," he tells us.

"I thought you said it was corny," Aqua responds.

"Yeah—well, I can eat a few corn fritters

and see a stupid all-girl rodeo just to catch your show, you know," Beethead says, joking.

"Did you see us at the Turtle Dome?" Do' Re Mi asks him. I guess she doesn't remember meeting him afterward in the parking lot.

"Yeah—y'all were awright. How'd you come up with that song—and throwing the money at the audience?" Beethead asks offhandedly, like he's trying not to seem too interested in our girl group.

"I don't know, that's just how we flow," I respond, flossing. No use telling him where we got the idea for the money-throwing . . .

Chuchie gives me a Popeye look, then blurts out, "Galleria and I thought the words up together. *Está bien?"*

"Well, anyway, my mom said she heard that song—or something like it—before you was singing it," Beethead says, sipping his punch, like, "What you know about that, huh?"

I don't believe him, and I'm starting not to like him, so I challenge the Beet. "Yeah?"

"She said there was a song called 'It's Raining Men,' or 'Cats,' or something like that," Beethead says, getting confused.

"I never heard it," I counter.

"That's 'cuz you're young—I'm talking about when she was younger," Beethead says, giving me attitude.

I still don't believe him, but I'll ask my mom after Thanksgiving—'cuz I can't bear the thought of talking to her before I get back home. One thing is for sure, I've had enough of Mr. Beethead for a while. Basta pasta, okay?

Luckily, Mrs. Walker wanders over. "Ooh, I've done twisted enough for Chubby Checker *and* Fats Domino," she says, grabbing a nakpin from the refreshment table and patting the sweat from her forehead.

"I wonder why all the singers from the '50s had names of fat people," I say to Aqua, ignoring Beethead.

"That's it!" he exclaims, pointing his finger at me. "Two Tons of Fun—that's the name of the group."

"What group?" I ask, annoyed.

"The group from a long time ago that made that song I told you about—'It's Raining Men.' I think they were called Two Tons of Fun or The Weather Girls or something—that's what my mom said."

"Oh," Aqua says, like she could care less.

"Well, our song is *original.*"

"And *la dopa*!" Chuchie blurts out.

"I'm ready to bounce from this Popsicle stand," I whisper to Do' Re Mi, who is standing with her arms across her chest and tapping her feet.

"Me, too," she agrees, chuckling. "Let's not keep Big Momma waiting—or the candied yams and rice and beans!"

Chapter 7

Cruising to Big Momma's house in Mrs. Walker's coolio Katmobile, I can't get the Chubby Checker song out of my mind. "'Let's twist again, like we did last summer—ooh, ooh!'"

Mrs. Walker joins in, and we bop along. I can tell she had a good time at the race. She was dancing with some guy with a bald head the whole time.

"Ma, I saw you dancing with that good-looking man," Aqua says, teasing her mother.

"What good-looking man? Reecy Weathers from the pharmacy? You've got to be kidding me," Mrs. Walker says, waving her hand at Aqua.

"Well, I don't think Mr. Chips Carter would like it one bit," Aqua says, teasing her mother. We all know there's a little flirting going on between Mr. Chips, of Fish 'N' Chips, and Mrs. Walker. And he *is* a good-looking gobble fester.

"Well, Mr. Chips Carter ain't paying no mortgage around here, so I guess I can do as I please," Mrs. Walker says, adjusting her Gucci shades. Then she gets real quiet.

Aqua gets quiet too. See, Mr. Chips Carter and Mr. Fred Fish both live in the Montgomery Homeless Shelter, so paying a mortgage would be, well, out of the question.

"Mrs. Walker, have you ever heard of a song called 'It's Raining Men?'" I ask.

"I think I do remember that one. Why?"

"Nothing," I tell her. "It's just that that guy, Beetjuice, was kinda insinuating that we were biting someone else's flavor from back in the day."

"I'm not exactly sure I follow you," she says.

"Have you ever heard our song before? 'It's Raining Benjamins'?"

"I think so," she says, not sure. "But so many songs sound alike these days."

"I wish I could drive this car," Chuchie says to Mrs. Walker, oblivious to what's going on.

"Ooh, you're not going to get me arrested!" Mrs. Walker chuckles. "Come back when you're sixteen, though, and we'll spin a few wheels."

I like the idea of us coming back when we're sixteen. I hope Mrs. Walker really means it. Suddenly, I get a pang of guilt as I think of my mom sitting at home with my little dog Toto. She's probably eating a whole tin of Godiva chocolates all by herself. She can't even pretend that she's cooking a ten-course meal: Mom only pulls that charade when we have company coming over.

"Is Skeeter gonna be there?" Aqua asks as we pull into their grandmother's driveway. "He should be here by now. He spent all morning volunteering at the Montgomery Shelter, serving food."

"Oh, that's good—that's real good," Angie says approvingly. Now that Skeeter has hooked up with Fish 'N' Chips, he's been spending a lot of time at the homeless shelter where they live. Today, the homeless population gets a big fat serving of Thanksgiving dinner—so he went over at the crack of dawn to help.

"Hold this," Mrs. Walker says to Aqua, handing her a casserole dish. "That's all Skeeter needs, is to feel like he belongs—just like all of us," she says, smoothing down her skirt. "I know I'm risking my life bringing over this macaroni and cheese, but I can't just sit back and watch Big Momma do *everything* all by herself."

Once we step inside Big Momma's house, we hurry into the living room before she makes a crack. The twins' grandmother, who is just like her name, doesn't like people standing on ceremony, if you get my drift. I think it makes her uncomfortable.

Do' Re Mi doesn't get it, though, and she just stands there waiting for an engraved invitation. Sure enough, we hear Big Momma's booming voice all the way in the living room, "Don't just stand there, child. Take off your coat, 'cuz the pawnshop's closed!"

"Is Skeeter here?" Aqua asks in a concerned voice.

"No," Egyptian says hesitantly.

"He and Big Momma are fighting again," India pipes up. "She doesn't like him spending time with his girlfriend."

Big Momma waddles into the living room, so we all disperse and head for the dining-room table. "I hope y'all ain't expecting none of my strawberry rhubarb pie," she tells the twins, "'cuz those guinea pig critters of yours put an end to that—they ate *all* my strawberries!"

"We'll take them home today, Big Momma," Aqua assures her.

"That's good, 'cuz Bessie and Messy done worn out their welcome in this house!"

"Big Momma, their names are Porgy and Bess!" Aqua protests.

"Well, their names are mud in this house until they replant my strawberry patch!" Big Momma says, and I don't get the feeling she's joking, either. I sure wouldn't want her mad at *me,* that's all I'm saying.

"We'll fix it!" India pipes up, then runs to the bookshelf and comes back with a book on gardening.

"Bless your little heart—but there ain't

nothing in there on the kind of planting I do," Big Momma explains. "You follow these instructions and you wouldn't even grow enough weeds for the mice to eat, child!"

"When we eating?" Egyptian asks, bored.

"Right now, baby," Big Momma coos back.

"Big Momma made the peach cobbler I like!" India says, smiling.

"Is there a peach cobbler you don't like?" Big Momma chuckles.

"Daddy's home!" India yells suddenly, dropping the gardening book like it's a hot biscuit and running to the door.

A look of relief washes over Aqua's face, while Big Momma gets up slowly, saying "Lemme get food on the table."

I can tell there is definitely some static between her and Skeeter. It must be kinda hard, living at your mother's house when you're old enough to drive your own car, you know what I mean, jelly bean? Suddenly, I get a case of the squigglies in my stomach. What if the Cheetah Girls don't make any money for a long time? Dear God, pleez don't let me live at my mom's house forever!

"Well, looky, cooky, we sure got a full house

today!" Skeeter says, filing into the dining room with his daughters practically walking in his footsteps.

"Aqua, why don't you bless the food," Big Momma says as we sit down to eat. She hasn't looked at her son once, I've noticed, but that doesn't stop him from talking up a storm after Aqua says the blessing. Mostly, he can't seem to brag enough about his nieces—and us, too.

"You should have seen them singing for Mr. Steer at the Okie-Dokie Corral, Big Momma," Skeeter starts in, his eyes beaming.

"Do y'all get to ride the horses, too?" asks India. Obviously, that's all she cares about.

"No, but we can go to the rodeo after we perform, if you want to," Aqua coos.

"Everything is coming up green, you know what I mean!" Skeeter sings in a really loud voice. Then he lets out a deep guffaw from the bottom of his chest. "I love that song—'It's Raining Benjamins,' baby!"

Big Momma gives Skeeter a look, like he'd better shut up and pass the peas.

"India, could you pass me the hot sauce, please," Aqua asks nervously. Then she pours almost the whole bottle on her collard greens!

She knows better than that, I huff to myself. "Better watch those precious vocal cords," I tell her, trying to keep the situation "Lite FM," if you get my whiff.

Aqua doesn't even look up from her plate. She must really be nervous.

All of a sudden, the earthquake we've been waiting for finally erupts. "Skeeter—that woman called here today," Big Momma announces, "but I told her I don't have any son that's single enough to be dating. The only son I got ain't even legally divorced from his wife yet!"

"Hmm, Hmm," Skeeter says, like he's not even listening. Then he hums the chorus from our song again: "It's Raining Benjamins for a change and some pork chops! It's Raining Benjamins . . ." If I didn't know any better, I'd swear Skeeter has been sippin' when he was out tippin', if you catch my drift.

India and Egyptian let out tiny snickers. Then the table gets quiet, just like it does right before a cyclone. But Big Momma surprises us all by turning to Aqua and Angie and asking, "How y'all come up with the songs?"

"Chanel, um, I mean, Galleria and Chanel wrote the song, Big Momma," Aqua says proudly.

"We just made it up," Chuchie adds. "I had a dream where there was money falling from the sky, and we were trying to grab all of it."

"That sounds like good inspiration to me," Big Momma says with a chuckle.

I take a deep breath and relax. I guess Big Momma just needed to have her say, even if Skeeter doesn't seem to be paying her any attention. It kinda reminds me of how Chanel and her mother fight. Nothing Chuchie does is okay with Auntie Juanita, so Chuchie does as she pleases until she gets into real trouble. Then she starts crying, and running to me and my mom (who is her godmother).

"Big Momma, do you know what fenugreek is?" Aqua asks hesitantly.

"Nothing but herbs," Big Momma says, coughing into her napkin.

"Oh," Aqua says, seeming relieved. I wonder why she wanted to know that?

"Herbs that shouldn't be messed with," Big Momma continues.

Now a look of concern comes over Aqua's

face, and she turns to look at Angie. Those two always communicate secretly. . . .

Ding! Suddenly I know what Aqua is getting at—they're talking about all that hukalakahookie stuff that High Priestess Abala Shaballa gives to their father "for his health." They're worried she might be messing with his mind somehow, because he seems to believe everything Abala tells him—kinda like a robot. If it was my Daddy, I'd be worried too!

"Why you wanna know?" Big Momma asks. "Y'all ain't doing any more of those autopsy reports, like you used to do when you wuz little?"

"No, Big Momma. We were just playing around. It's nothing—just something I saw on Daddy's nightstand—maybe some kind of supplement," Aqua says, but I can tell she's not telling the whole truth.

"Back in the slavery days, desperate women used to mix fenugreek with Sargasso sticks to chain a man's heart to them for life, in case they got separated or sold off to a different master on another plantation," Big Momma explains.

"You mean, like stuff they do in witchcraft?" Chuchie gasps, perking up.

"No, I mean stuff that stubborn, foolish women used to do when they wanted to keep a man," Big Momma says. "Sounds like John Walker done gone up to New York and got himself mixed up with—"

"Ma!" Mrs. Walker says sharply. Now Aqua and Angie look like they've swallowed twin canaries, instead of Big Momma's candied yams.

"After I lost Selby, it didn't make no nevermind to me if I never picked up after a man again," Big Momma says, sighing. She starts sucking on a neck bone, remembering her dead husband.

I watch in amazement: Big Momma can suck a neck bone cleaner than my pooch, Toto! "I'm sure you feel the same way, Junifred, now that you ain't got no man."

"We'd better be getting over to Granddaddy Walker's," Mrs. Walker huffs, getting up from the table.

"How's he doing?" Big Momma asks, like she was just talking about the weather.

"His blood pressure is up," Mrs. Walker says, brushing crumbs off the table. Then she mutters under her breath, "and so is mine."

I can hardly stand up, I'm so full. I've never had a five-course dinner before, and I'm grateful that Big Momma is letting us get up from her table! I think she is sad that we're leaving and going to Granddaddy Walker's house, but she just snorts at her daughter, "Junifred, tell Selma I said thank you. She outdid herself with that last bouquet."

Selma is the twins' step-grandmother—she married their Granddaddy Walker after their Grandma Winnie died of cancer. Granddaddy Walker owns the biggest funeral parlor in Houston. He buried the twins' maternal grandfather, Selby Jasper (Big Momma's husband). Selma always puts big bouquets outside Mr. Jasper's mausoleum—apparently, free of charge.

"Yes, ma'am, I will," Mrs. Walker says, motioning for us to wait outside by the car.

"Bye, Egyptian and India," Aqua says, kissing her cousins together.

"Y'all gonna go and sleep with dead people now?" India asks, her eyes looking sleepy after eating two slices of peach cobbler and one slice of sweet potato pie.

"We'll see if Granddaddy Walker lets us

commune with the dead. Then we might even have a séance," Aqua chuckles.

"Ooh, can we come too?" India asks, perking up.

"No, y'all stay here with Big Momma and your Daddy," Skeeter tells the girls.

"I'll be right out; y'all wait by the car," Mrs. Walker says, standing with her arms folded.

Once we're outside, Aqua whispers, "Ma is gonna give Big Momma an earful."

"What happened?" Chuchie asks, like a nosy posy.

"Wake up, Chuchie. You don't have to be a divette detective with a pig snout to figure this one out," I hiss at her.

"I'm telling y'all," Aqua says, getting upset, "as soon as we get back to New York, we're putting an end to this High Priestess drama. I'm not gonna let Abala Shaballa chain Daddy to her for life!" Then she sees Mrs. Walker coming outside, so she shuts up quick.

"Now, let's head on over to Granddaddy Walker for Round Two," Mrs. Walker says, chuckling.

I wonder what she means, but I'm sure we'll be finding out soon enough.

"At least it'll be quieter over there," Mrs. Walker says, sticking the key in the ignition. "Right now, the only people I'm in the mood for are dead ones!"

The twins' paternal grandfather and step-grandmother live on the third floor of the building that houses their beautiful funeral parlor, Rest In Peace. Selma Walker is a lot younger than her husband, and if her eyes didn't move, I'd swear she was a stuffed parakeet. I mean, she doesn't move a limb the whole time we're sitting at the dining room table.

The only person who seems to be eating besides Granddaddy Walker is Do' Re Mi. How can she eat after all that food at Big Momma's? I have only been able to move my food from one side of my plate to the other.

Granddaddy Walker is really nice, too. "What's that y'all got around your necks?" he asks, admiring our Cheetah Girls chokers, which we're wearing for Thanksgiving.

"They're our Cheetah Girls chokers—we made them," Aqua explains proudly.

"Well, I'll be, I think those would look mighty nice on some of the corpses, don't you,

Selma?" Granddaddy Walker says, his eyes twinkling. I can't tell if he's joking or not, but I decide to stay out of it.

"Yes indeed-y, they would look nice—especially on Wilma Burrows," Selma says, dabbing her lips daintily with her napkin.

"Who's Wilma Burrows?" Aqua asks.

"Oh, that's the corpse downstairs in the mahogany coffin, waiting to be stuffed in the morning," Granddaddy Walker says, then saws away at the turkey breast on his plate.

Suddenly, I feel like I'm having dinner with the Addams family, if you get my whiff. "Yeah, Miss Wilma used to be a dancing fool," Selma adds. "Gonna bury her in her favorite red dress and red tap-dancing shoes. That's what she wanted."

Suddenly, I gain interest in my "handpicked and homemade" cranberry sauce. "I never had cranberry sauce that didn't come out of a can," I tell Selma, smiling.

"What kind of singing do you do?" she asks me, almost causing me to jump. I look over at her—and her lips are closed. How does she do that—talking through closed lips? I wonder if she is a ventriloquist or something.

"Um, we call our music global groove," I explain, turning to look at Granddaddy Walker as well.

"If I didn't have to get Wilma trussed up tomorrow, I'd go see y'all at the rodeo," he says. "Wouldn't that be something, seeing my granddaughters singing!"

"Well, y'all will see us performing one day, Granddaddy," Aqua says, giving him a big hug.

All of sudden, Selma is interested in our show, so we explain the whole thing again. "At the end of the song, we throw fake Benjamins in the air, so the audience can catch them!" I say excitedly.

"Benjamins?" Granddaddy Walker asks, amused.

"You know, duckets—one-hundred-dollar bills."

"Oh," he says, getting a good chuckle.

"It was our idea to come up with that stunt—you know, throwing money in the air," Aqua says proudly.

Oops! Actually, it wasn't our idea originally—but I decide not to say anything. What's the harm in Aqua letting her granddaddy think the idea was ours? "I don't know," I say. "This one may be our best song so far."

"Yes, ma'am," Aqua tells Selma, "we love them all—but I think people really love 'It's Raining Benjamins.'"

"Do they have a lot of other people performing there?" Granddaddy Walker asks.

"Oh yeah—it's a contest," I explain. "We know a few of the groups—One of them, CMG, we met in Hollywood when we performed at the Tinkerbell Lounge."

"It'll be dope seeing them again," Do' Re Mi says.

"Yeah, but this other group, Diamonds in the Ruff, they gave us drama—we performed with them at the 'Houston Helps Its Own' benefit at Kemah," Aqua adds.

"Yeah—but Miggy and Mo are nice, so we'll have a good time," Chuchie says cheerfully.

"I just hope we win first prize for a change and some coins," I blurt out.

"Yeah, that would be nice," Angie agrees, crossing her arms. "That would be real nice."

"Well, I guess we'd better head on back," Mrs. Walker says suddenly.

"No, Junifred, y'all stay right here with us,

and go back in the morning," Granddaddy Walker says. "I don't get to see my girls, now that they've done gone and moved to New Yawk—let 'em stay the night at least."

"Of course," Mrs. Walker says, smiling.

Do' Re Mi and Chuchie look at me, and I know what they're thinking: We're gonna spend the night in a funeral parlor. Yikes!

There are four bedrooms on the third floor of Granddaddy Walker's palatial digs. Mrs. Walker kisses us good night and goes to sleep in her own bedroom, next door to Granddaddy Walker and Selma.

Before she retires, Selma gives us all pajamas from the closet. "These have all been worn by good folks, but they're clean, so don't you worry."

"Angie and I are gonna sleep in the smaller bedroom—the three of y'all can have the bigger one," Aqua tells us.

"Playing favorites?" I ask her.

"No, you're welcome to share the twin bed with me and Angie, but I think the three of you would be more comfortable in a king-size bed," Aqua says, bugging her eyes.

"Don't you have a queen-size one?" Do' Re Mi quips.

"Okay, we're going," I mutter. "Too bad we can't sleep in the coffins downstairs."

"Well, we wouldn't want to disturb Wilma," Aqua says, then hits me with her pillow and scurries into her bedroom.

"I hope we do win first prize—even if it's just some hokie statue," I mumble to Chuchie and Do' Re Mi as we drift off to sleep.

"*Sí, mamacita*, I could put it with my doll collection," Chuchie says, giggling.

"Who says *you'd* get to keep it?" I tease her.

Timidly, Do' Re Mi mutters, "Who *would* get to keep it?"

"I don't know—let's just win it first, then we'll worry about the flurry," I chuckle, then doze off to sleep like a log.

Tap, tap, tap, rap a tap. Tap, tap, tap, rap a tap.

"You hear that?" I whisper, shaking Chuchie's shoulder.

"What happened?" she mumbles back, but then bolts up in the bed.

"I hear it," Do' Re Mi says, her voice quivering. "It sounds like someone is—tap-dancing!"

The three of us lie there for what seems like hours. The noise doesn't stop.

"Let's go see Aqua and Angie," I whisper, and the three of us tiptoe out of the bedroom and into theirs.

Aqua and Angie are sitting straight up in the bed. "I think Wilma is having one last dance!" Aqua says.

"Let's go tell her to shut up!" I whine at the twins.

We all tiptoe down the creaky staircase into the Rest In Peace Funeral Parlor on the first floor. "I don't think anybody is resting in peace tonight!" I whisper.

When we turn on the light, everything seems still and peaceful. The five of us look at the beautiful wooden coffin in the corner of the room. "Who's gonna open it?" I ask, suddenly losing my gumption.

"I will," Aqua volunteers. "We're not scared of dead people!"

"Do you need help?" Do' Re Mi asks as Aqua struggles with the lid.

"Dag on, I forgot how heavy these things are."

"Forgot?"

Aqua turns and chuckles at me. "We used to come look at the dead people all the time!"

I should have known the twins were a little kooky when we met them. Why else would they walk around with bottles of hot sauce in their purses?

When Aqua and Angie open the lid of the coffin, I gasp. "There's nobody in there!"

"She really *did* go dancing!" Chuchie exclaims, grabbing onto me.

"Let go of me, Chuchie," I whisper harshly. Everything's making me jumpy now. I can feel a bad case of the spookies coming on strong.

"Last dance, last chance?" Do' Re Mi says in a squeaky voice.

We look all over the funeral parlor for Wilma Burrows's corpse, and come up with *nada*. "I can't believe it. *No lo creo!*" Chuchie says, getting scared. We hightail it back to our bedrooms, and pull the covers over our heads.

Tap, tap, tap, rap a tap!

"She can dance all night for all I care. I'm not getting out of bed!" I moan to Chuchie, who has dug her heels into the mattress and won't budge from my side.

Since Wilma has kept us up for half the night, I feel it's only fitting that I pay my respects to her, so I yell, "Good night, disco queen! Party on, girl!"

Chapter 8

I don't think I have ever woken up more tired in my whole life. But now is not the time to think about that, because we have to get sassy-fied and be at the Okie-Dokie Corral by noon, for the contest at the Sassy-sparilla Saloon!

Driving back to the twins' house, Mrs. Walker makes the mistake of asking us, "So, did you girls sleep okay?"

"Peachy keen," I say, telling a big fat fib-eroni. Because nobody has gotten up the nerve to talk about Miss Wilma's ghost dancing in the moonlight, I decide to ask Mrs. Walker if she heard anything strange last night.

"No, I didn't—why?" she responds.

"'Cuz it sounded like somebody was tap-dancing all night!" Aqua moans.

"Really?" Mrs. Walker responds, surprised.

"Do you think it's possible for a corpse to get out of a coffin and start dancing?" Angie asks her mom.

"Have y'all been drinking Granddaddy Walker's 'embombing' fluid?" Mrs. Walker asks, amused.

"I wish we did—'cuz maybe we woulda gotten more sleep!" groans Aqua.

"Ma—'member once when we slept at Granddaddy Walker's, and we heard someone hammering all night?" Aqua asks.

"No, not really . . . Oh, wait a minute, was that the time y'all wanted to sleep in my bed 'cuz you were scared?"

'Yes!" Aqua says. "That was the time Granddaddy Walker was burying a carpenter . . ."

"Oh, I get your point," Mrs. Walker says, looking into the car mirror before switching lanes. "Lemme tell you one thing I know—when souls aren't happy, they keep doing what made them happy in real life before they died."

"Really?" Aqua responds, then turns to look

at me, like, "finally, we got an answer to last night's situation."

"No—not really!" Mrs. Walker says, flipping the script. "You probably just heard the wind blowing at the window, or a tree or something."

"Well, then that tree sure has perfect rhythm!" Aqua says, folding her arms across her chest.

"Now I know why my mom is so grumpy sometimes in the morning," I sigh. "It's because she's tired. I mean, what I could really use right now is a double-whammy-jammy Frappuccino."

"I wonder how a corpse could disappear out of a coffin?" Do' Re Mi ponders, fidgeting with the snaps on her jacket.

"I don't wanna know," Chuchie moans, then puts her hands together as though she's praying.

"Chuchie, what are you doing?" I ask.

"Praying that we win the contest today."

"We prayed last night," Aqua reminds her.

"I have a feeling that we *are* going to win," I say. Then I think about that nasty group, Diamonds in the Ruff. In a few hours, we'll be seeing them again. "Could you believe those rhinestone wannabes trying to stop us from getting in the contest?" I say, shaking my head at the memory.

"They sure did try to stop us," Angie says, nodding her head. "That's 'cuz they know we're the real deal—and we're gonna steal their Happy Meal!"

The guy at the entrance of the Okie-Dokie Corral tries to charge us the ten-dollar admission price.

"We're performing in the contest at the Sassy-sparilla," I protest.

"Talent enters over there," he points, then keeps on talking to the other customers. "Right this way, folks."

The peeps piling into the Okie-Dokie Corral are just like I imagined they would be. "Look at how they're decked out," I exclaim to my crew as we head toward the Sassy-sparilla Saloon. People are roaming around with bandannas tied around their necks, cowboy hats, and cowboy boots with spurs and all! Vendors selling cotton candy, bags of peanuts, and cowboy paraphernalia are everywhere. There are also peeps standing around shouting and giving out flyers.

A cowboy clown on stilts with a red curly wig shoves a flyer in our faces: "Showdown at the Sassy-sparilla Saloon at high noon!" he shouts. The flyer is advertising the contest we're in, and the All-Girl Rodeo afterward.

"Ooh, look—that's the thing we're doing!" Chuchie explains to the guy.

"Good luck, Cheetahs!" he shouts down at us.

"Hey, how'd you know we we're the Cheetah Girls?" I ask him, suddenly feeling puffed up. Wow, peeps must be talking about us already!

"Well, look at yer outfits—y'all look like cheetahs if I've ever seen one." He cackles like a hyena. "I like your hats!"

"Thank you," Do' Re Mi says, peering up at him from under the wide brim of her cheetah-fied Stetson. "I like your hair!"

"Thank you, Cheetah," he says goofily. "I just took it out of the washing machine this mornin'!"

Chuchie heckles, then whispers, "I knew it was a wig!"

"Ray Charles could see it's a wig, Chuchie,"

I say, dragging her in the direction we're headed, past the cotton-candy vendor.

"Let's get some afterward," Chuchie says, eyeing the pink confection.

"I can't wait to see the rodeo later," Do' Re Mi says, hitching up her pants like she just got off a horse.

Waiters and waitresses in red-checked shirts are still setting up inside the dark Sassy-sparilla Saloon, spreading red-checkered table-cloths on the wooden tables in the center of the room. A boy is putting carnations in little glass vases on the tables of the two rows of booths that line the walls.

I get a squiggly feeling in my stomach: What if nobody comes? Who wants to see a bunch of kids performing, anyway?

"Can I help you, young ladies?" says an older lady, wearing a straw bonnet covered with pretty flowers.

"We're the Cheetah Girls," I say proudly, but when that doesn't get a response, I quickly add, "We're here to perform in the Miss Sassy contest."

"Oh, yes, of course—pardon me," says the cheerful lady. "I shoulda known by your outfits you were performing—you're the first girls to arrive. The dressing room where you can change—even though y'all look fine just like you are—is right in the back."

"Thank you," I say politely.

"Now if you'll excuse me, I've got to make sure the rest of our deliveries don't get ruined. They've already broken a whole crate of eggs!"

"Do you mind if I go, and come back right before the show starts?" Mrs. Walker asks the lady.

"No, ma'am, suit yourself. Just come back and grab yourself a table," the lady says cheerfully. "Just ask for me—Mrs. Owens—if you need anything."

"Good luck—and I'll be sitting right in the front, clapping up a storm when y'all come out," Mrs. Walker says to Aqua and Angie, then kisses us all good-bye.

When I open the door of our so-called dressing room, I'm in shock. "We're *all* supposed to fit in *here*?" I moan in disbelief.

"It's a good thing *Madrina* isn't here to see this," Chuchie says, referring to my mom, who as our manager would never stand for something like this. Chuchie barges into the tiny room ahead of me.

"She would have a sassy fit!" I moan, grateful that Mom is in New York, cooling her heels for a while.

"I wonder if the Rashad brothers are gonna be here," I mutter. Then realize that they probably have more important things to do—like handle the show on the main stage tonight.

"Mr. Steer didn't say anything about us getting into the concert tonight for free," Do' Re Mi says.

"Maybe if we win, they'll let us go," Chuchie says.

"Maybe, oh, baby," I sigh, then reach into my cheetah backpack for the cassette with our tracks on it. After dumping almost everything out, I still can't find it—and I start to panic. "Omigod, I can't find our tape!"

"Here, I got it!" Chuchie says, taking it out of her knapsack. "Remember, Bubbles, you told me to hold it?"

"I musta really been scared last night if I did that!" I groan, and Chuchie makes a face. "I'm sorry, Chuchie, but you're always losing things!"

There is a knock on the door. "Come in!" I

say cheerfully. The lady in the bonnet peeks her head in, and I say, "Oh, we forgot to give you the tape for our music."

"Right," she says, taking it. "I'll give it to Mr. Steer. Um, I just wanted to make sure you were decent, because one of the other groups is here."

"Bring 'em in!" Aqua says.

I take a deep breath, bracing myself for the rhinestone-studded ones, but much to my surprise, in walks CMG—the Cash Money Girls. For a second, I panic, because I've completely forgotten their names.

"Wazzup?" I exclaim nervously to the girl with platinum-blond hair piled high on her head. I'm so embarrassed, because my mind is still blinkety-blank. I can't remember her name!

Ding! I know they were named after dead presidents. Okay, so which ones?

"Ooh, look at y'all," says the CMG rapper with Miss Piggy eyelashes. Then she registers surprise in her face, those foot-long lashes fluttering. "Oh, hold up, I remember y'all—from New York, right?"

"Well, actually, my sister and I are from right here in Houston," Aqua says, as if she's baiting "flutter-lids." "Where were *y'all* from again?"

"Well, actually, see . . . we moved to Oakland a few years ago, but we did grow up here," says the one with the upswept braids and big hoop earrings.

"Oh," Aqua says, like she's not letting them off the hook so easy.

I try to get her attention, to motion for her to chill, but she doesn't look in my direction. It's gonna be hard enough as it is, putting up with the attitude of the rhinestone-studded wannabes when they arrive—we sure don't need more static in the attic, if you get my whiff.

"Y'all never been to Oakland, right?" asks Miss Piggy–lashes.

"No, we haven't," I say, trying to be nice.

"See, they're into this whole hard-core thing—so you gotta go out there and represent if you want to get a rep, you know what I'm saying?"

"Yeah."

"They think Houston is corny, okay?" the platinum blonde says, then puts out her hand for a high five from Aqua. "So, until we make it, we gonna cover all our bases!"

Do' Re Mi and I exchange glances, like, "Yeah, we get your trip, alrighty, alrooty, 'cuz you're frontin'!"

"What are your names again?" Miss Piggy–lashes asks me.

I introduce us. Then there is a long pause.

"Y'all don't remember our names? How could you forget them?" Miss Piggy–lashes says, whipping out her chain-link minidress, featuring dollar bills. I try to pretend it isn't true by just smiling.

"I'm Georgia Washington," Blondie says, extending her hand.

"Right!" Chuchie says excitedly. "You have the names of the dead presidents!"

The CMG girls laugh, then Abrahamma Lincoln and Benjamina Franklin (not a president, but . . .) introduce themselves to us again.

There is another knock on the door, but before we can respond, it's flung open, and we're faced with those rhinestone-studded wannabes, Diamonds in the Ruff. I can't wait to see how they'll react when they see that their playa-hating moves didn't work on the

Cheetah Girls—'cuz we got more pounce to the ounce, baby!

Diamond, who is the taller and skinnier one, prances into the room, trying to pretend that she doesn't see us—which is next to impossible, since we're holed in a closet, okay? After she makes a big deal of dropping her duffel bag on the floor, she looks up—and our eyes lock for a split second. Then she looks away, like I was just a fly flitting around or something.

Sparkle, whose stringy weave peeks out from under her white ten-gallon, rhinestone-covered cowboy hat, doesn't even look at us at all. She just props herself against the wall and pulls out a nail file.

What I'm wondering is, how do they sit down in those suction-cup-tight jeans?

Mr. Steer, the talent coordinator, knocks on the door, and asks if everything is all right. What I wanna say is, "Can we unpack the can of sardines, pleez? How are we all supposed to fit into this tin can of a room?"

Sensing the tension in the room, Mr. Steer finally pipes up, "I know it's a little crowded in here, but if it's any consolation, the house is filling up with folks!"

I sure could use a soda, but since no one has offered us anything to drink, I decide to squash my thirst.

"You know, some of the acts are sitting at the tables, too," Mr. Steer informs us. "You don't have to stay in here if you don't want to."

Now Miggy and Mo squeeze into the crowded dressing room, but I'm so happy to see them, I don't even care that I'm being squashed and suffocated.

"Wazzup, Miggy!" I shout excitedly.

"Wow, you got in!" Miggy exclaims. Their mother smiles at us, too. "I didn't get a chance to introduce myself at the last event, but I'm Mrs. Majors," she says.

Mo whispers something in her mother's ear, then beams at me with mischievous eyes.

"Mr. Steer, can the girls get anything to drink?" Mrs. Majors asks.

"You go, Mo!" I wanna shout, but I feel a little sheepish. How come *we* didn't get up the nerve to ask for ourselves? I guess we are feeling kinda spooked from last night's ghost-fest, and now this Diamonds in the Ruff drama.

"Oh, sure! Didn't Mrs. Owens tell you? You can just go out to the bar and get anything you want. Everything is on the house!" Mr. Steer seems like he's embarrassed for slipping in the southern hospitality department. Still, peeps sure are a lot nicer down here than they are in the Big Apple!

"Now, I just wanted to let you girls know that we're gonna be starting in fifteen minutes. Mrs. Owens will announce each of you, so just come on out when you hear your names called," Mr. Steer tips the brim of his hat as he leaves.

"You'd better keep the door open, then," Mrs. Majors says to Miggy. "I'm gonna go sit at a table in the front."

"Say hi to our mother for us!" Aqua says nervously to Mrs. Majors. "Remember, she was with us at the homeless benefit—the lady with the leopard scarf around her neck?"

"Yes, of course, I remember her. I'll go see if she's out there," Mrs. Majors says. As she leaves, I see her knitting needles sticking straight up out of her purse. I hope she doesn't poke anybody with those lethal weapons!

"Good luck," Abrahamma yells to us as they head out the door to sit in the audience. "It's too hot in here! We'll be representing for you from the front!"

"Right!" I yell back. I mean, it is a contest, so whoever gets the most applause will be the winner. So why would they be clapping for us?

I try to ignore Diamonds in the Ruff as we pack up our makeup, getting "ready for Freddy and down for anything," but the glare of rhinestones is hard to ignore, if you catch my drift.

We do our Cheetah Girls prayer, then our breathing exercises. Now we're starting to get excited, just like we do before every show. When we release each other's hands, Aqua yells, "It's showtime at the Okie-Dokie!"

Chapter 9

I'm so lost in my thoughts, scribbling notes in my Kitty Kat notebook, that I don't even hear Mrs. Owens begin her introductions. Luckily, Aqua does. "She's on the stage!" she hisses.

Now I can hear corny country music playing in the background, and it sounds like Mrs. Owens is trying to sing "Home on the Range" on top of it.

"She sounds more like a hyena out on the prairie!" I groan to my crew. "What have we gotten ourselves into?"

"Let's just keep our eye on the prize!" Do' Re Mi chuckles, then shrugs her shoulders.

"Yippee-yay!" Mrs. Owens finishes her

wack rendition. "Now before any of y'all get the wrong idea, I am not one of the Miss Sassy contestants tonight!" The audience claps really loud and does a few catcalls, no doubt relieved by Mrs. Owens's announcement. "But we've got some real sassy talent, waiting to come out here and give you a wild ride on the old frontier!"

"How wack-a-doodle-do can you get?" I grumble to my crew. By now, the five of us are huddled in the hallway, waiting for her to announce us, since we're the first "victims."

"These hats are really hot," I complain to Aqua, lifting up the brim in front so I can pat my forehead with my raggedy tissue. "They're making us sweat like a bunch of coyotes!"

Finally, Mrs. Owens says the magic words: "Let's give a hand for our first Sassy contestants—the Cheetah Girls—who I can assure you, sing a whole lot better than I do!"

They should just call this the Miss Corny Festival, I say to myself as I climb the three tiny steps to the stage. The stairs are so creaky, I almost fall backward, but Aqua catches me and pushes me forward again.

Mrs. Owens is standing there on the tiny

stage, with the cordless mike posed in her outstretched hand. Where are the mike stands from rehearsal? I wonder, panicking inside till it feels like my heart is pumping pure Kool-Aid.

Chuchie and Do' Re Mi shoot me puzzled looks as we crowd the stage, but I just shrug my shoulders. By now, I realize that the Sassy-sparilla is definitely a one-horse saloon, if you get my whiff. Thank gooseness we have at least one mike—and if the fairy cowgirls are smiling down on us, maybe it'll work somehow.

As the tape track starts in, I motion for Do' Re Mi, Chuchie, Aqua, and Angie to flank me from both sides. Aqua puts up the cheetah umbrella, and we all stand under it until the right beat. Then, I proceed to sing into the mike.

Screech! Screech! Honk! The wack microphone does everything but start oinking! The people seated at the front tables cover their ears—including the Cash Money Girls, who give us a look, like, "Better you than us!"

I pause a minute, to give the audio peeps some time to adjust the sound levels for human noises. Then, clutching the microphone with my clammy hands, I start in again. Meanwhile, the rest of my crew starts clapping, and the audience joins in:

"For the first time in her-*story*
there's a weather forecast
that looks like the mighty cash. . . ."

I happen to look up and catch the facial expressions of CMG—which have gone from amused to horrified in a matter of seconds. I feel my throat starting to constrict, so I try to breathe through my diaphragm, and take shallower breaths, the way Drinka Champagne taught us.

When we start to sing the chorus, I move the microphone closer to the twins, because they have the strongest voices in the group:

"It's Raining Benjamins
for a change and some coins
It's raining Benjamins
I heard that, so let's make some noise
It's raining Benjamins . . . again!"

The audience is clapping, but I guess it's

'cuz they feel sorry for us. I mean, what a master disaster! The five of us throw money into the audience. I try real hard not to look at the faces of CMG, or I'll faint—'cuz I can't take any more drama and kaflamma from this wack-a-doodle situation! But no matter how I try, I feel their eyes glaring at us, like mean panthers! What did we ever do to anybody? Why is everybody always trying to block our rainbow, you know?

I can't run offstage and into the dressing room fast enough. Miggy sees the expression on my face, so she blurts out, "Go get 'em, Cheetahs!"

"No, *you* go get 'em," I tell her, gasping to catch my breath, "and watch out for that mike, 'cuz it bites!"

I look up and see Diamond and Sparkle, from Diamonds in the Ruff, still standing in the same spot where we left them—and still throwing us attitude!

"We'll see you in a minute," Mo says cheerfully, as they exit the dressing room to go do their song. As they do, the three members of CMG come in and slam the door. Uh-oh—here's the real reason for my frightquake. What were those ferocious expressions about? I don't have a clue—but I can tell I'm about to find out!

The five of us start backing up against the wall, while Georgia Washington starts walking toward *me*—pointing the acrylic tip on her left index finger like it's a lethal weapon—which it is!

"I cannot believe that you nickel-and-dime wannabe jungle-snatchers had the nerve to bite our flavor like a couple of hyenas!" she screams, in a booming voice that could wake all the dead presidents lying in cemeteries all across America.

"Georgia, let me handle this," Abrahamma Lincoln says, stepping in front of her. Pointing her finger in Aqua's face, she goes on: "Not only did you have the nerve to copy our song, but you have the absolute gall to sing it in our faces! Well, let us break it down for you—we may have grown up here, but we ain't no corny, country pigeons like you!"

"That's right," Georgia adds. "We're up in Oakland now—and we don't play that. You got your thing, we got ours—so why you frontin'?"

"Miss Abrahamma, we didn't mean anything—" Aqua starts to say, but Benjamina Franklin cuts her off.

"Save that drama for your momma! Now, how are we supposed to walk out there and do our song—*which you stole from us*?"

"And how are we supposed to finish our finale by throwing Benjamins at the audience when you stole *that* from us, too!" Abrahamma says, spraying spit in our faces.

"You know the only reason we don't pounce on you like pork chops and leave the bones for the stray dogs?" Georgia Washington asks me menacingly. I keep quiet, knowing she isn't waiting for an answer. "'Cuz you high school wannabe cubs ain't gonna win first prize with your tacky hoedown version of our song and our flavor, my neighbor! So you better go home and start dipping your Lorna Doones and sipping your milk now. You dig?"

"We're gonna finish this later," Benjamina growls. "If you have any brains left under those tacky cowboy hats, you'd be smart enough to know—you corny cheetahs had better bounce before we come back and pounce!"

As the Cash Money Girls storm out of the dressing room, Chuchie breaks down crying. Diamond and Sparkle stand there like nothing has happened. I catch Diamond sneaking a peek at us, with a satisfied smirk on her face.

"Stop crying, Chuchie!" I yell in frustration.

"I wish *Madrina* was here!" Chuchie says through her tears.

For the first time since I've been in Houston, I'm wishing the same thing. If Mom was here, she would send those fake ATM machines packin' back to Oakland, and they wouldn't come back, either!

Miggy and Mo burst into the dressing room again. "What happened?" Miggy asks, looking at Chuchie with her big blue eyes.

"CMG—th-the Cash Money Girls—think we stole their flavor," I stammer.

"And we did!" Aqua blurts out.

"It was *your* idea to throw money at the end, just like they did!" I hiss back at her.

"Yes, it was my idea—but I didn't know it was wrong, or I would never have done it!" Aqua says, sounding like a Bible school teacher.

"I hope they win, so they'll leave us alone," Angie says wincing.

"Did we really bite their lyrics, too?" Do' Re Mi asks quietly.

"They're gonna go on now," Miggy says, trying to be nice. "I'm gonna go out and see them."

We all crouch by the door so we can hear CMG rapping:

"Yeah, we roll with Lincoln,
What are you thinkin'?
But it's all about the Benjamins,
Baby, not maybe, just mighty, awrighty!"

"I don't know . . ." I say tentatively. "It doesn't *sound* like our song. . . ."

I can feel that my face is flushed like a strawberry patch, because I'm so embarrassed. Deep down, I know they are right—we *did* bite their flavor! I mean, when Chuchie came to me with the first line of the song, the rest of it just came to me so easy! I guess I was just remembering what I'd heard CMG do in L.A. But I swear, it never occurred to me that that's where I got the inspiration—this has all come as a total shock to me!

"Groups bite each other's flavor all the time—that's what we savor," Do' Re Mi flexes, trying to make us feel better. "I think our song has different enough words that it's original. I mean, it's kinda the same, but not really. I just don't think they shoulda come at us like that. That's all I'm saying."

"Well, I don't wanna be here when they come back," I say, getting a serious case of the spookies.

"We *can't* leave till the contest is over!" Aqua protests.

"We don't have to worry, 'cuz we ain't gonna win anyway," I say, my voice cracking because I'm so upset. "I sounded like Donald Duck singing into that wack microphone."

"Excuse us," says Diamond, as she and Sparkle try to move past us so they can go out and sing.

For the next little while, we are so spaced out from our Okie-Dokie drama that we don't even care what the other groups are singing. Finally, Miggy comes back into the dressing room, bringing us back down to reality. "The last act—the Cowgirls—are going on now," she tells us.

"Good looking out, Miggy," I say softly. If it wasn't for her and Mo, we would have definitely blown this one-horse Popsicle stand by now.

I go to the open dressing room door and listen to the Cowgirls strut their stuff:

"Yippee-yay yo
That's how we flow
Yippee-yay yo
Where's the place to go?"

Aqua and Angie have gone into the house to hear the Cowgirls sing, but Chuchie and I stand huddled together by the dressing room door, like we're frozen, or dozin' on our feet.

It seems like the end of time before Mrs. Owens gets back on stage and asks all the groups to come out. I trudge onstage with the rest of my crew, like lambs being led to slaughter. The bright lights catch us right in the face as Mrs. Owens asks the audience to clap. "Go, Cheetahs! Go, Cheetahs!" the audience chants.

For one magical second, I feel my heart racing just like it usually does when we perform—like I'm on top of the world, and I've just found out it's one big, edible cupcake filled with cream.

I force myself not to look around. I know

CMG is in the audience. I can feel them glaring at us like a pack of predators eyeing their next kill.

We step off the stage, so that Miggy and Mo can go up. We even clap along with the audience in their favor. When Mrs. Owens calls the Cash Money Girls up to the stage, my heart sinks into my shoes.

They start cheering for themselves, and I can feel Abrahamma staring down at us, just egging us on to look at them. I think about her foot-long acrylic tips, and almost wet my Cheetah bloomers!

"Okay, ladies and gentlemen," Mrs. Owens says excitedly. "I know most of you want to head on over to our All-Girl Rodeo and watch them rope in those ferocious bulls! So I won't keep you waiting any longer. The lucky winner of our Miss Sassy contest is—the Cheetah Girls!"

I feel my legs turn to linguini, and suddenly, I'm fighting back tears. For months, we've wanted so badly to win something—and when we finally do, it turns into a Nightmare at the Okie-Dokie! It's so unfair!

We climb onto the stage to accept the

trophy, and Mrs. Owens shakes my hand like it's a slot machine or something. "Congratulations. And girls, besides your beautiful trophy, the Sassy-sparilla Saloon is also giving you six tickets to visit AstroWorld, for their Holiday in the Park Celebration!"

I try my best to smile at Mrs. Owens, but I can't manage it. The audience is clapping so loud, but all I wanna do is burst into tears!

"Boo! Boo!" yells Abrahamma. "They're a bunch of wannabes!"

On automatic, I make my way off the stage, and the rest of my crew follows along behind me. Out of the corner of my eye, I see Mrs. Walker. "Meet us outside!" I call to her. Then I keep pushing forward through the crowd, desperately trying to outrun CMG!

Miggy and Mo come running up behind us. "Hey, Cheetah Girls, don't you want to come to the All-Girl Rodeo?"

"No, Miggy, we'll catch up to you later," I tell her. My heart is pounding with fear that any second the Cash Money Girls are gonna come barging into the parking lot, looking for payback.

"Here comes Ma!" Aqua says, relieved.

"Thank God," I moan. "If High Priestess Abala Shaballa came right now on a broomstick to whisk us away, I'd get on—just get us outta here!!"

Chapter 10

Mrs. Walker is trying to help us, but—I can't even believe I'm saying this—the only person who can pull this rabbit out of the tragedy hat is my mom.

"I don't think those girls had a right to talk to you like that," Mrs. Walker says, trying to be helpful. But she just doesn't get it. See, the music biz is small, and beef jerky travels fast across the land.

"That's all the Cheetah Girls need, is to get a rep as song biters—even before we get a record deal," I try to explain. But Mrs. Walker just looks at me like I'm overreacting.

"I'm so glad Uncle Skeeter didn't show up and see that mess," Aqua says tearfully. She rests her arms on the table, then covers her face in her hands.

"I've gotta call my mom," I say very quietly to Mrs. Walker.

"Go ahead," she says, placing the telephone right in front of me on the dining room table.

As soon as I hear my mom's voice, I burst into tears like a real crocodile. I don't know if it's because I'm so kaflooeyed, or if hearing the sound of Toto's barking in the background makes me miss them both. Mom listens patiently, but she can hardly understand me. After a few minutes, I stop blubbering, and she gets the whiff of our terrible situation.

"You know, I hate to tell you this, but they're right—you're lucky the song wasn't recorded, or they would be able to sue you for copyright infringement," Mom sighs.

I hate when she's right. "But it's *not* recorded—*yet*," I say, trying to plead my case.

"Exactly—so the only thing they can do is tar and feather you, and go around telling people that the Cheetah Girls are the biggest thieves in the jiggy jungle, darling," Mom says sternly. "And let me tell you something—when customers get a whiff that your product is a mirage, you might as well go searching for water in the desert, because the charade is over. You understand?"

"Yes, Mom," I say, finally giving in. "What should I do?" I ask, hoping she'll magically make everything better, just like when I was little.

"Do the right thing," Mom pronounces. "That's all I'm gonna say, Galleria. Now I've gotta go finish the spring collection—or we'll be homeless next season. I leave this situation in your capable hands. You'll know what to do."

After a few more tears, a Cheetah Girls Council meeting, and a healthy dose of Mrs. Walker's chicken and waffles, we decide on the right thing to do. Well, actually, we get a little unlikely help from our fellow wannabe stars—Diamonds in the Ruff, that is.

"Are you sure that's Diamonds in the Ruff on the phone?" I ask Mrs. Walker in disbelief.

"Yes, ma'am, that's what she said."

"Hello?" I say nervously into the receiver, thinking it must be a trick. I imagine one of the Cash Money Girls reaching her hand through the receiver and yanking my hair out.

"Hi, this is Diamond—'member I performed with y'all yesterday?" Diamond's voice carries just a tinge of the attitude that we have come to know and hate. "Listen, I hope you don't mind, but Miggy and Mo gave us your phone number," she continues, probably sensing my coolness.

"Yes?" I say, still hesitant about the situation, but at least trying to be chill.

"We just wanted to know if we could help you squash the drama with CMG," Diamond says, kinda nervously. "After you left, we were talking with them, and I think I know a way you can deal with the situation."

"What? Why would you wanna help us?" I blurt out, because the suspense is killing me softly.

"'Cuz we feel bad for dissing y'all, that's all—I mean, we're all in this music biz thing together," Diamond says, kinda being humble. "You know what I'm sayin'?"

"Okay," I say, finally softening. Chuchie, Aqua, Do' Re Mi, and Angie are hanging onto my every word. "So, what's the master plan?"

"We'll all meet up at AstroWorld—inside,

by the Texas Cyclone ride," Diamond says.

"Okay," I agree, though I'm still not sold on this chess move. "What time should we be there?"

"It's live at five," Diamond says, chuckling for the first time since I've met her.

When I hang up, Aqua and Angie are just as skeptical as I am. "Why are Diamonds in the Ruff volunteering to help us now?" Aqua asks. "They didn't do anything when we almost got lasso-ed by those wannabe fake-money heffas!"

"Why is your backpack so heavy?" Chuchie moans, handing it to me in the car.

"Don't worry, I just packed for the occasion," I explain.

"What happened? What occasion?" Chuchie asks, puzzled.

"You'll see," I tell her. "Trust me."

"Y'all should at least go on a few rides while you're there," Mrs. Walker says, like our excursion to AstroWorld is a family picnic instead of a showdown, continued from the Okie-Dokie Corral.

"I shoulda packed a water pistol!" I mutter, squirming uncomfortably in the back-seat.

Even Chuchie is kinda quiet and serious for a change and some coins. That is, until we get to AstroWorld, and she sees the humongous fake mountain of snow inside! "Ooh, where did they get all this snow?" she exclaims, as we try to find our way to the Texas Cyclone Ride.

"They import it every year for the Holiday in the Park Celebration," Aqua says proudly.

Dorinda stops to look at all the kids snow-balling and sledding down the mountain. All of a sudden, I feel a pang of sadness for her. She has probably never seen anything like this before. It's all my fault that I got my crew mixed up in this madness, I realize. Why did I ever agree to write that song with Chuchie?

"Do they ever have any real snow here?" Dorinda asks Mrs. Walker.

"Not since I was born. And that was a long time ago!"

"Not since 1929," Angie pipes up.

"Nineteen twenty-nine what?" I ask.

"That was the last time they had a White

Christmas in Houston, that's what," Angie repeats. "They told us that in school, I think."

"Okay, this is where I leave you girls," Mrs. Walker says softly. "See—the Texas Cyclone is right over there. I'll be waiting right by the Viper ride. Good luck!"

"Thanks, Ma," Aqua says, then takes a deep breath.

I'm so glad Mrs. Walker didn't insist on meeting the Cash Money Girls and Diamonds in the Ruff with us. We got ourselves into this drama and kaflamma, so we should get ourselves out of it.

"I really would feel better if I had that water pistol," I moan to Chuchie, then put my arm in hers.

"I've got a bad case of the spookies," Chuchie moans.

"We all do," Aqua pipes up.

"It's showdown—um, show *time*," Do' Re Mi says under her breath.

I catch sight of Diamond's sparkly cowboy hat. "I wonder why they wear costumes off-stage too," I mumble to Chuchie. "That's kind of tick-tacky."

All of sudden, I stop myself. I *can't* be nasty to these girls—I just wanna squash this beef, and I think I know exactly how.

"Wazzup?" I say to Diamond, who gives us a big smile when we walk over. Wow, she looks prettier when she smiles, I think. I look around, but see no sight of our "cash-flow problem."

"They're here. They just went to get some popcorn," Diamond says, reading my glance.

Popcorn, at a time like this? Maybe this is a trick! I shriek inside.

Do' Re Mi turns first, and catches the grand entrance of the Cash Money Girls, who are wearing white vinyl jackets and boots. Surrounded by all this fake snow, they seem, well, right in their element. *Shhh!* I tell myself again, then repeat the mantra I've been saying all morning, "Squash the beef! Squash the beef!"

Georgia, who is clearly the leader of this "counterfeit ring," puts her hands on her hips and gets right to the point. "So what are y'all gonna do to squash this situation?"

"Um . . ." I say, speaking up. "We're just a bunch of kids, like you said, and we don't know things about the music business like you do." *Ouch, that hurt!* I'm screaming inside.

"Well, you'd better learn, straight up!" Abrahamma says, starting in.

"Let's just chill. We're here for a reason," Diamond says, intervening. I can't believe how nice she's being!

"Um, we are real sorry about what happened," Aqua pipes up, but I touch her arm as a way of saying, "let me continue what I started."

"I think the only fair thing is to promise you that we'll kill the song."

"You'd better," Georgia says, like we still haven't eaten enough humble pie.

"And we want you to have this," I say, pulling out the Miss Sassy trophy from my backpack. "You deserve it—after all, it was your idea for the song, and that's probably what the audience liked."

"Well, it's obvious that the competition was rigged—just like the one y'all did at the Apollo, girl!" Georgia says, unexpectedly flipping the script. Now she's thrown me off guard. I can't believe she remembered what we told her about the Apollo Amateur Hour. About those rappers Stak Chedda winning.

"Come on, give it up!" she continues. "You know that group, Stak Chedda, didn't deserve one piece of burnt toast for that madness they were bringing!"

We all start laughing together—except for Abrahamma, who still isn't giving it up. "You know, y'all can keep that cheesy trophy," she says.

I feel my cheeks burning, and I start to stutter, "No, um—"

"Abrahamma—would you stop?" Georgia says, flicking her wrist at her peeps. "Like they said, they're just a bunch of kids."

Ouch. That hurts, too. I wish peeps would stop calling us "a bunch of kids." It's bad enough *I* had to say it!

I swallow my pride and bite my lip, repeating my mantra of the day over and over again. The five of us wait quietly, while Georgia looks down at her white boots like she's thinking about something.

"You keep the trophy, okay?" she finally says. "But we don't ever wanna hear that you been bitin' our flavor."

"Yes, ma'am," Aqua says nervously—which causes all three members of CMG to chuckle.

Even Diamonds in the Ruff get into the mix. "Now that's what I'm talking about!" says Sparkle, who has been quiet the whole time.

"So, we're straight?" I ask nervously, still not believing we've gotten off so easily. "Have we squashed this beef?"

I look right at Abrahamma, even though I don't want to. Like Mom says, "Always look people in the eye, or they'll treat you like a cockroach and try to crush you."

"I'm beef-less," Abrahamma relents. "What about you, Georgia? Benjamina?"

"Hmm. Hmm," they mumble. And just like that, it's over. We're off the hook—and it's like a ten-ton weight is off our backs. Good old Diamonds in the Ruff! Who'd have ever thought they'd be the ones to ride to our rescue?!

When we get back into the car, Mrs. Walker seems to sense how calm and relaxed we are. "Did y'all work it out?"

"Yes, ma'am," I say, imitating the twins. Then I just rest my head on the car door, and let the wind blow through my hair.

"Good," says Mrs. Walker. "I'm gonna take y'all to the Spindletop Restaurant—my treat!"

"Yum, yum," I coo.

"I can't believe you were gonna give them our trophy!" Chuchie says, giggling.

"Whatever makes them clever—that's all I was trying to do, Chuchie," I say softly. "I'm just glad it's over."

"You know, I wish we had gone to see the All-Girls Rodeo," Do' Re Mi says wistfully.

"Next time we come, we'll make sure we do that," I say, without turning around to look at Do' Re Mi. I know we'll back in boostin' Houston. I can just feel it.

"We should go see Sista Fudge in concert at the Okie-Dokie tonight, Angie says.

"We got Sista Fudge money?" I ask, then chuckle, 'cuz it sounds like something my mom would say. I can't wait to go back to New York and give her and Toto the biggest hug in the world! "You think they'll let us in for free?"

"We can sure try—after today, I feel like we can do anything!" Do' Re Mi says, egging us on.

"You know what?" Aqua says, her eyes bugging wide like they do when she gets a bright idea. "Let's bring the cassette for 'It's Raining Benjamins' over to Granddaddy Walker's funeral parlor."

"Why?" I ask, puzzled, "You gonna give it a proper burial, or something kooky like that?"

"No," Aqua says matter-of-factly. "So Wilma Burrows will have some Cheetah Girls music to dance to when she gets up in the middle of the night!"

"But, Aqua," Do' Re Mi says, "her corpse wasn't in the coffin. What if she never comes back there?"

Suddenly, I feel like I'm in the Twilight Zone again. I'm not sure who's more cuckoo—High Priestess Abala Shaballa, or my crew!

"Don't worry," Aqua says shaking her head like Buddha. "Trust me, she'll be back."

"Yeah, well, guess what, Houston?" I say, yelling at the top of my lungs in the speeding car. "The Cheetah Girls will be back, too!!!"

Showdown at the Okie-Dokie

Yes, we thought it was all about the Benjies—
those crispy, tasty, certified papers—
disappearing like vapors,
'cuz of our Cheetah Girl capers.
That's right, y'all,
We got our coats pulled
at the Okie-Dokie Corral
and fleeced to the street by an Oakland crew
like a bunch of cubs who ain't for true.

We was looking for a payday
but all we got was a hayday
Down in boostin' Houston
where the word on the street is,
Gotcha—hee haw, hee haw!

Now the Benjies definitely ain't droppin'
but there's no stoppin'
our record-toppin' ways
'Cuz divettes stick together
in any kind of weather
and we'll be back for another intro
till then we're saying good-bye to the rodeo.
Hey, ho, hey ho, hey, ho
We bite the Big Apple
and we still got the flow!!

Think a naughty thought
And you'll get caught.
Write a song and try to sing along
with someone else's lyrics
and there's madness you'll experience.

We was looking for a payday
but all we got was a hayday
Down in boostin' Houston
where the word on the street is,
Gotcha—hee haw, hee haw!

The Benjies definitely ain't droppin'
but there's no stoppin'
our record-toppin' ways
Let's get that payday
and later for the hayday.
Hee haw. Hee haw!!
(Do you think they was really gonna hit us, Bubbles?)
(No, they were gonna kiss us, Chuchie!!
The next time you get the bright idea
to crib someone's lyrics,
I'm gonna wack you back to the Okie-Dokie . . . !)

The Cheetah Girls Glossary

A bad case of the squigglies: Nervous. A pit in your stomach.

Basta pasta: Enough. Chill. As in: "Basta pasta, okay?"

Beef: Drama. Kaflamma. As in: "I got beef with her." Or: "We're beef-less now."

Boostin': Representing.

Deal-io: Deal.

Drama and kaflamma: Drama times two.

Drama queen: Someone who tends to get dramatic and cause static.

Duckets: Money. Loot. Benjamins. Dollars.

Frightquake: An attack of scaredy-cat-itis so severe, it may actually require immediate medical attention!

Get my whiff?: Do you get my drift?

Gobblefester: Cute man.

Goospitating: Staring at someone like they're lunch.

Gridlock: Traffic jam.

Growled: Sang with flava.

Hukalaka-hookie: Nonsense. As in, "What a bunch of hukalaka-hookie!"

Keep It Lite FM: When you don't want to cause any static about something.

Laced: Phat, dope, coolio, large.

Live: Dope. Funny, as in: "I thought that was too live!"

Mamacita: Spanglish term of endearment that you can use to address your crew, or peeps you like, as in: "Hey, *mamacita,* did you do the math homework today?"

On the case like Mace: Checking out a situation.

Photo op: A chance to get a picture taken that will be worth a thousand memories (and may bring duckets in the bucket too!).

Pleez: Please.

Sassy-frassy: Smart aleck.

Spec-taculous: Spectacular. Dope.

Thank gooseness: Thank goodness.

Toodly: The "bestest." The most coolio.

Wicky-wacky: Wack. Not cool.

Cuchifrita, Ballerina

For Amanda Barber,
my old school friend,
who's got the slander—
'cuz what's good for the goose
is good for the gander.
Quack, quack!

Chapter 1

Bubbles is plopped in the seat next to mine on the plane—and she is sleeping with her cheetah jacket covering her head, which makes her look like one of those blob creatures from the Wack Lagoon. I think she's doing it because she doesn't want to talk to me. Although she hasn't said it (yet), I know Bubbles thinks the whole drama that went down in Houston is my fault. *La culpa mía*. Well, I'm not going to feel guilty! I stick one of my purple glitter star stickers on my bubble gum pink pants. Ooo, that looks *tan coolio*!

Feeling defiant doesn't get me out of the Dumpster, though. It's a sad Sunday, because the Cheetah Girls—that's Galleria "Bubbles"

Garibaldi, Dorinda "Do' Re Mi" Rogers, the twins (Aquanette and Anginette Walker), and, of course, me—Chanel "Chuchie" Simmons—are flying back to the Big Apple and going back to school. Our little gobblefest in Houston is definitely over. *Terminado*. I should be grateful that the Cheetah Girls got to spend Thanksgiving in the twins' hometown—even if it turned into *una tragedia*.

Actually, it was more like an episode on the Spanish soap opera *Oh, No, Loco!* See, the Cheetah Girls performed in the Miss Sassy-sparilla Contest at the Okie-Dokie Corral. Best of all, we won first place, because we sang this coolio song—"It's Raining Benjamins"—that I, Chanel Coco Cristalle Duarte Rodríguez Domingo Simmons, helped write. (I've decided if we ever publish a Cheetah Girls song together, I'm going use my whole name on the credit. Hee, hee—Dominican stylin'.)

Anyway, it was obvious the Cheetah Girls deserved to win the contest, because we had our lyrics and choreography down. Everyone could tell, because at the end of the song, when we threw the fake Benjamins at the audience, they clapped loud enough to chase away a herd of buffalo.

After we collected our Miss Sassy trophy, though, our luck went south. One of the losing groups, CMG—the Cash Money Girls—got bitten by the green-eyed monster, and decided to run us out of town. They went around telling anybody who would listen that the Cheetah Girls stole the lyrics from *their* song "Benjamin Fever"—and even stole their routine bite for bite!

Well, all right, I did use a *couple* of words from "Benjamin Fever" for our song "It's Raining Benjamins." But how was I supposed to know you're not supposed to do that? When we called *Madrina* (my godmother and Bubbles's mom) in New York, she told us that we had perpetrated "copyright infringement." And okay, we did throw fake Benjies at the audience, just like CMG does. But I don't care what anybody says—our song was better than theirs, *está bien?*

Sticking more stickers on my pants, I let out a deep sigh. I guess the Cash Money Girls had reason to be jealous. See, we had performed on a bill with them once before—at the Tinkerbell Lounge in West Hollywood, for a New Talent Showcase sponsored by Def Duck Records.

(Yes, the same label that has Kahlua Alexander.) We got a lot of attention after the showcase, so maybe CMG thought the record company liked us better than them. Little do they know we're still sitting around waiting for a record deal, and to get into the studio with Def Duck producer Mouse Almighty.

I sink back into my seat, and try to cover my face with the little airline pillow, but it falls into my lap. Maybe I should try to write another song? No, I don't think Bubbles would like that. Without even realizing it, I start humming the chorus to the song that caused all the drama:

"It's raining Benjamins for a change
and some coins.
It's raining Benjamins . . . again!"

I just can't get that song out of my head, but I guess I'd better not let it fly out of my *boca grande,* because the Cheetah Girls promised CMG we would never sing "It's Raining Benjamins" again in public. I stick some more glitter star stickers on my pants legs, and before I know it, they look like the Hollywood Walk of Fame on Hollywood Boulevard. Well, we sure aren't strolling on the Walk of Fame right now!

I can't believe Bubbles let the Cash Money Girls bully us around like that. She even offered to give them our Miss Sassy trophy! *We* won it, not them! Luckily, CMG said, "No, thanks."

The truth is, I wish *I* could take home the Miss Sassy trophy. I'd like to show it to Mom, so she can see that the Cheetah Girls are the best singing group in the jiggy jungle. But Bubbles decided that the twins should keep it. After all, they're the reason we got to spend Thanksgiving in Happenin' Houston in the first place.

"Miss, could you please put your bags under your seat?" the flight attendant says to Aqua, snapping me out of my Houston memories.

"We don't put our purses on the floor, ma'am, 'cuz it's bad luck," Aqua explains earnestly. "You won't have any money left if you do that." She gives the flight attendant a look like she should understand. "You know, it's a Southern thing."

I don't think the lady understands, because she just says, "Miss, you're gonna have to put your bags underneath the seat or in the overhead compartments."

"We'll do that, then," Angie says quietly. She waits until the lady walks away, then hides her purse under her blanket.

Even though I don't believe in their superstitions (only mine!), I can't blame the twins. It seems like they have a lot of rules in airplanes. For example, you can't polish your nails. You can't keep your belongings in your lap. You can't let animals sit in an airline seat, even though the twins paid seventy-five duckets for a seat for their guinea pigs, Porgy and Bess, so they could take them along. Seventy-five duckets! I'd buy twenty pairs of cheetah anklets from Oophelia's catalog before I parted with those kind of duckets for two furry creatures that chomp on carrots.

Don't get me wrong, I love pets. I even bought my little brother, Pucci, a cute little African pygmy hedgehog for his birthday—Mr. Cuckoo. "I hope Pucci has been taking good care of Mr. Cuckoo while I've been away in Houston," I say to the twins. Pucci's been staying with our *abuela*—our grandma—over Thanksgiving.

"I'm sure he's okay," Aqua chuckles back.

"You never know," I counter. Thinking about

Mom, I start nervously smoothing out my hair again. She's back now, from her trip to Paris with her boyfriend, Mr. Tycoon.

I feel flutters in my stomach, and a pang—*un poco dolor*—in my chest. I wish I had a nice family, like the twins. All my mother and I do is fight, and my brother Pucci only speaks to me when he feels like it. Of course, now he's being nice to me because I bought him Mr. Cuckoo.

I wonder if Daddy and his girlfriend, Princess Pamela, are back from Transylvania, Romania. That's where they went for Thanksgiving, so she could be with her family. I'll bet if I lived with them, Mom would miss me. Then she'd be sorry she gave me such a hard time. . . .

"I wonder if Pucci will let me take Mr. Cuckoo to the annual Blessing of the Insects and Their Four-Legged Friends at St. John's tonight," I say to Angie. "Probably not, but I'm going to take him anyway. Do you want to bring Porgy and Bess?"

"No, we have to go straight to our church with Daddy," Angie explains.

Maybe Bubbles will bring her dog, Toto, I think. I decide I'll ask her later, when she wakes up. Then I look around, and see that the lady sitting across the aisle is smiling at me.

"Howdy do," the lady says in a Southern twang, which I'm used to now after spending a week in Houston.

"Hi," I say back, smiling.

"Y'all ain't from *Youston*, are you?"

"No, we're from New York," I say beaming, then add, "we're singers."

"Is that right?" the lady says excitedly. "Do you sing rip-rap?"

I look at Dorinda for help, but she is lost in her book, so I shrug my shoulders and ask politely, "Do you mean hip-hop?"

"Why, yes—isn't that the same thing?" the lady asks, amused at her own cuckooness, I guess.

"Um, yeah," I say, trying to be nice, "but not exactly. We mix all kinds of music and vibes together."

"Oh," the lady says. "Well, variety is the spice of life."

"We must be very spicy, then, because we mix a lot of music!"

The nice lady sees me eyeing the crumpled newspaper resting on her lap. "Would you like to see the paper?" she asks me. I nod yes, and she hands it to me.

"Ooo, Krusher's new album is out!" I coo to no one in particular, as I gape at the full-page advertisement for my favorite singer in the whole world. His eyes look so dreamy . . . like he's smiling right at me!

Dorinda takes her nose out of her book and peers over my shoulder.

"I think you have *un coco* on Krusher!" I tease Dorinda.

"I think he's cute, but I'm not mackin' him like you are," Dorinda says, throwing me a sly look.

"What happened? I'm gonna write him a letter," I say, like I have made a very big decision in my life, *mi vida loca*. Suddenly, I feel a sting in my chest, remembering the 1-900-KRUSHER contest that I entered. How could I have lost that? The deejay lady who won the stupid contest couldn't possibly feel the same way I feel about him.

"How old is he?" Dorinda asks, yawning.

"Nineteen," I say dreamily, touching his picture.

Dorinda gives me a funny look. "You really are goo-goo ga-ga for him!"

I get so embarrassed that I flip the page quickly. "You'll see," I say firmly. "What if we get to perform with him—I mean after we become famous, *está bien*?"

"We don't even have a record deal yet," Dorinda reminds me, sighing heavily and spoiling my *gran fantasía*.

"Maybe Def Duck records forgot about us," I say sadly.

"I hear that," Dorinda says matter-of-factly, but I can tell she feels sad, too.

My heart flutters even more when I turn the next page of the newspaper. It's a full-page ad for the American Ballet Theatre. A beautiful girl who looks a little older than me is pictured in a ballerina tutu, standing on her tippy-toes in pointe shoes with her arms outstretched over head. REACH FOR THE STARS! is sprawled across the picture in big letters. Underneath it says, "Auditions for the Junior Corps Division begin soon. Deadline for applications, November 24."

That's three days ago. This paper must be a week old!

I shoot a quick glance at Dorinda, to see if she notices how excited I am. Luckily, she's too busy staring at the picture in the ad to notice.

My heart is pounding like a jackhammer—I didn't realize the auditions were coming up so soon! See, about a month ago, I secretly sent in my application—and I've been waiting to hear from them ever since, practicing hard in case I got an audition. Now I realize that the first thing I have to do after school tomorrow is find out if I got an audition for the Junior Corps!

"Can you do that?" Dorinda asks chuckling.

"What happened?" I ask absentmindedly. Then I realize Dorinda is asking about the exquisite ballet pose in the picture. *"Sí, mamacita,"* I say defensively.

Dorinda giggles, because I fell in the twins' bedroom in Houston while trying to do a *battement tendu jeté* to the side, then leap across the room. I sprained my ankle, and it still hurts.

"The area rug in the twins' bedroom was slippery—that's all!" I complain.

"Is your ankle okay?" Dorinda asks gingerly.

"There's nothing wrong with my ankle," I shoot back. "It was just a little sprain. It's okay, *está bien?"* I stare adoringly at the ballerina in the picture, who is obviously playing the part of Princess Aurora in "Sleeping Beauty"—my favorite classical ballet. Mom took me to see it when I was little. In my fantasies, I sometimes pretend that I am Princess Aurora.

"How long did you and Bubbles take ballet classes?" Dorinda asks, nudging me out of my daydream.

"Lemme see—we started when we were six or seven, then stopped in the sixth grade—no, it was the year Bubbles won the intermediate spelling contest . . . um, the second semester in seventh grade. I think that spelling contest went to her head."

"Well, you know how Bubbles likes the lyrical flow," Dorinda chuckles, like I should stop complaining. "Why didn't you keep doing it though—even after Bubbles stopped?"

I look at Dorinda like she is cuckoo. She knows that Bubbles and I are like sisters. Whatever Bubbles does, I do. That's just the way it is, ever since I can remember.

But now I'm beginning to wonder. I miss ballet, and this may be my last chance to prove I can do it—even if Mom thinks I can't. I can hear her now: "Chanel, your butt sticks out too much to be a ballet dancer!"

"I don't know, Dorinda—Bubbles didn't want to do it anymore, and I didn't want to do it by myself," I respond.

"I wish *I* could do it," Dorinda says wistfully.

Suddenly, I feel bad for whining. Dorinda never even had the chance to take ballet lessons, because she lives in a foster home, and they don't have any money. She probably could've danced circles around all the snobby girls that were in our class.

Now I know why Dorinda tried out for Mo' Money Monique's tour without telling us: *she wanted to see if she could do it.* Maybe I could do *this* without telling anybody, too. . . .

"Did you really want to go on tour with Mo' Money Monique?" I tease Dorinda. I know how badly she feels for trying out without telling us a little bo-peep about it.

"I guess not. I just wanted to make my teacher happy—she wanted me to do it," Dorinda says, trying to justify her actions.

Suddenly I hear the words come out of my mouth. "I'm going to try to get into the Junior Ballet Corps."

"Word?" Dorinda asks, surprised.

"*Sí, mamacita*—this may be my 'last chance,

last dance,' and I'm going to do it," I say, convincing myself. "You'll see."

The nice lady is looking over at us. "You seem to be really enjoying that newspaper. Why don't you keep it?"

"Really?" I ask.

"Of course," she says, waving her hand.

I look one last time at the picture of the ballerina, then fold it up carefully. I put it into my cheetah backpack, like it's a wish I have to put in Aladdin's lamp. In some ways, it is—I *have* to convince Mom to let me spread my wings again!

Chapter 2

As soon as I put my key in the front door, I start feeling nervous again. *Ay, Dios*, please don't let Mom pick a fight with me!

I've made up my mind that I'm going to tell Mom that I'm trying to get into the American Ballet Theatre's Junior Corps division. I know Mom is not feeling me these days, *está bien*, and part of it is my fault. *Tengo la culpa*. See, I got the *baboso* idea to charge up her credit card after she let me use it to buy me a new outfit. You can bet Mom is never gonna let me forget about that *catástrofe*. She will probably be telling my grandchildren the story when she's old and in a rocking chair! *Qué horrible!*

Maybe Mom will be happy for a change, now

that she got to spend a whole week in Paris with Mr. Tycoon. He is her new boyfriend, and she seems to be pretty cuckoo about him—even though he never looks me straight in the eye, or asks me anything about myself. I don't think the tycoon approves of my being in a singing group. Well, neither does Mom—so I guess they are perfect for each other!

Suddenly, I hear this screeching noise—*Whhrrrr, whrrrr, whrrrr*—coming in my direction from down the hallway. Just as I'm looking up, not only do I almost get my head sawed off by a fast-moving blur, but I trip and fall on my butt, letting out an involuntary scream. "Aaayeee!"

"So how was your trip, *loco* Coco?" Pucci giggles, making his way back toward me on this—scooter? Pucci likes to call me by my middle name—Coco—so he can prefix it with *loco*—crazy. He thinks he's funny. I'll show him.

"*Baboso*," I wince, eyeing the shiny silver scooter with the big purple Flammerstein and Schwimmer logo on its deck. That store is really expensive—that scooter had to cost at least $100! "Where did you get this?" I ask Pucci, grabbing his wrist.

"None of your business!" he smirks back, then wiggles his way out of my grip and makes a mad dash back down the hallway.

"Pucci!" I hear Mom's muffled voice yelling from the den. "I told you not to ride that thing in the house, *está bíen?*"

Pucci scoots by like a *loco* Road Runner, then comes back down the hallway again.

"You heard *Mamí—párate*!" I hiss at Pucci until he finally stops.

"Why'd you have to come home?" he asks, scowling at me.

I ignore my pain-in-the-poot-butt brother. "Who got you that thing?" I demand.

Seeing me eye his new prized possession, Pucci huffs, "*Mamí* got it for me in Paris."

"*Por qué*?" I ask astounded. "It's not your birthday!"

"'Cuz I *wanted* one!" Pucci shoots back, grinning like the Cheshire cat—large and in charge.

That is so unfair! I say to myself. Mom would never buy me anything "just cause I wanted it."

"Is Daddy back?" I ask Pucci, feeling the need to complain to somebody about Mom.

"Yup—he called me."

"Where?"

"At Abuela's house," Pucci snaps, like I'm stupid. "Daddy met Dracula—and he brought back his teeth." Snorting like Mr. Piggy, Pucci scurries away.

"He did not. And get off that thing!" I yell. Pucci is always telling fib-eronis. But who knows, maybe Daddy did meet some of Dracula's relatives in Transylvania! See, his girlfriend, Princess Pamela, is almost like royalty in her native land. She comes from a long line of Gypsy pyschics—and they are treated with respect in Romania—not like here.

I grab the newspaper out of my suitcase, and walk into the den. If I'm going to have a fight with Mom, it might as well be over something really important.

Anyway, I need to get this handled right away, because the auditions are coming up really soon. On the way into the den, I'm thinking, Mom can't say no. If she doesn't like me singing with the Cheetah Girls, why can't I join a ballet group? She wanted me to be a ballerina—and I stopped because Bubbles got tired of it. She should be happy that I want to do it again.

Ay, Dios mío! I gasp when I see Mom. What has she got on her *face*? I know that she does her beauty mask every Sunday afternoon, but this isn't like her yucky yellow mask—it's a lot scarier! It's a white plastic thing that kinda looks like a hockey mask, but creepier—and it's vibrating! I try not to stare, but her whole face is covered—except for the two holes for her eyes, the two dots for her nose, and the round hole for her mouth. Usually, when she does her mask ritual, she looks like the Mummy—but now she more resembles Hannibal the Cannibal in that scary movie we saw, *Silence of the Lambchops*, or whatever it's called.

Mom is sitting on the couch, flipping the pages of *Hola!* magazine. She looks up at me, her brown eyes like two beads peering out of the holes. Suddenly I feel too nervous to ask—because I can't even look at her!

"Don't stand there staring at me," Mom moans in a muffled voice. "This is a new skin-tightening mask. I got it in *Parrris*, at Maison Bouche—the most prestigious skin care *institoot in Parrrris*," Mom says, stretching out the rrr's. Wow, I think—her phony French accent has gotten better.

Wait a minute—how do I know this is my mother? Maybe this hockey face is really a clone, because Mr. Tycoon got rid of Mom!

"What's that noise coming from it?" I ask gingerly, backing up against the wall in case she tries to attack me or something.

"It vibrates to get the circulation going in the skin," Mom moans, like she wants me to stop bothering her. Now I'm sure the spooky hockey lady is Mom, and not a clone, because she is annoyed with me as usual. Defeated, I rest the weight of my body against the bookcase.

"Thank you for letting me go to Houston. We had a really good time," I say, telling *una poca mentira*—a little fib-eroni—so she'll be in a better mood. I'm not going to let her know what really happened.

"That's nice," she says, no longer looking at me, but engrossed in the pages of the magazine again. Mom is writing a book—*It's Raining Tycoons*—about women who date oil tycoons from Arabia. She is constantly doing research now, trying to find candidates—even though the book company told her she has to get a ghost writer or they won't publish it, because her writing isn't that good.

"We ate fried alligator sandwiches in Houston," I say, giggling.

"Eeuw—that sounds disgusting!" Pucci blurts out, sticking his big head into the den. He's so nosy, he gets on my nerves! I throw him a quick scowl and squint my eyes at him. "Too bad the alligator didn't bite you!" he snaps at me.

"Shut up, Pucci," I snap back, because I can't resist.

"*Mamí,* can I go to the park now?" Pucci asks. I should have known he was angling for something from Mom—he sure didn't come in here to see me!

"Did you clean your room?" Mom asks him.

"Yeah," Pucci says, rubbing his head.

"I don't want you going to the park by yourself."

"Moham is coming with me," Pucci protests.

"I don't want you two going any farther than the park on Thompson Street, *tú entiendes?"* Mom says, but I know she's really telling him, "You two had better not go uptown on those scooters."

"Okay," Pucci says, like he's kinda disappointed.

The doorbell rings and nobody moves. "Excuse me," Mom says, looking at us like we're *loco*. "It's the butler's night off—go answer the door!"

Pucci runs to the door, and I hear him talking to Moham. Then the two of them come into the den.

"You told Moham he could pick you up without checking with me first?" Mom asks, in that muffled, facial mask voice. It sounds like she's wearing a muzzle!

"He's just coming over. I didn't tell him I was going," Pucci protests.

Moham stands very politely in the doorway, waiting. He is so nice, I don't understand how Pucci and he can be friends.

Mom is not very happy about Moham being in the den. She is staring at his muddy sneakers.

"Hello, Mrs. Simmons," he says, staring warily at her fright mask.

"Hello, Moham."

"I'll . . . see you later," Moham says, scurrying out of the room followed by Pucci.

"I'm taking Mr. Cuckoo Cougar to the Blessing of the Insects and Their Four-Legged Friends," I call after Pucci.

"I don't want you taking him anywhere!" Pucci yells, turning around and glaring at me.

"You two stop it!" Mom shouts, as loud as she can with her hockey mask over her face.

"I want Mr. Cuckoo to be *blessed*!" I hiss.

"Pucci, let her take him to church!" Mom commands.

"Awright, but nothing better happen to him," Pucci says, shooting me a dirty look.

Moham smiles serenely, then asks curiously, "Where is it?"

"Saint John the Divine," I reply.

"Maybe I should bring my turtle," he chuckles.

"Don't laugh—there are people there with fishbowls, too!" I exclaim.

"We're not going there," Pucci mutters to Moham.

"Don't worry," Moham tells him. "We're Muslim—my mother wouldn't approve anyway." Moham drags his scooter out the front door, and Pucci is right behind him.

I go back into the den, to push my ballet scheme with Mom. I start by chatting away about Houston, to get her in a better mood.

"You should have seen the restaurant Mrs. Walker took us to," I say cheerfully. Mom loves five-star bistros, and I guess the Spindletop Café counts.

"That was very nice of her," Mom says, like, "I know I didn't pay for that."

I feel guilty, because I'm not telling Mom the real reason why Mrs. Walker took the Cheetah Girls to the Spindletop. It was because she felt sorry for the whole *tragedia* that happened between us and the Cash Money Girls.

Sighing, I realize that the real reason I don't want to tell Mom what happened is because she'll just be, like, "I told you so." She doesn't really want me to be in the Cheetah Girls, because she says it's only gonna bring me heartache.

I don't want to admit it, but in a way she's right. We sure have had a lot of heartaches, belly-aches, and toothaches, if you ask me. But it's all worth it when things go right. And anyway, it's *my* life, not hers. Truth is, I'm afraid she's gonna take the same attitude about me and ballet.

"What's the name of the restaurant?" Mom asks me.

"Um, it's called the Spindletop. It has a revolving rooftop, so when you're sitting inside, looking out at all the skyscrapers, it seems like they're moving—but it's because you're rotating!"

"I'm dizzy just listening to you," Mom says, dismissing me.

Suddenly, I'm getting annoyed with her. So what if it wasn't the Gay Paree Café or something? Maybe if she would've taken me to Paris with her, I would *know* what a five-star bistro is!

I wince at the thought. I don't want to go anywhere with Mom. I would rather spend fifty years in a Chinese torture dungeon!

"Kashmir took me to the most fabulous restaurant in Paris," Mom says, wistfully, calling the tycoon by his first name. "La Butte Chaillot."

It sounds like she said, "Da butt Shall Move," so I don't try to pronounce the name of the restaurant, but I want to seem interested in her *historia*. I must have ballet on my brain, because it seems like I can't concentrate on anything. "What kind of food did they have at, um, the restaurant?" I ask, knowing how Mom loves to talk about food, even though she doesn't eat much.

"Oh," Mom says, perking up, like she's surprised I'm interested. "The chef is *renowned*—Guy Petit Le Fleur. The food is what you call country bistro cuisine—sophisticated, of course. . . ."

Of course, I think to myself, wondering if

Mom is gonna have any skin left once she takes that contraption off her face.

"The snails were so delicious—oh, and the oysters with cream *mousse*. I could have stayed in Paris and never come home," Mom says, like she really means it.

Now I'm angry. She likes that tycoon of hers better than she does me! And did she say she ate *moose*? Well, I wish it ate her and she didn't come back!

Suddenly, I feel guilty for thinking something so awful. After all, Mom let me go to Houston and spend Thanksgiving with my friends. I should be grateful!

Suddenly, just as I'm about to broach the subject of ballet, I feel a wave of light-headedness come over me. Maybe it's because I haven't eaten since last night's dinner. The twins' family kept feeding us so much that I must have gained at least five pounds! So I made up my mind then and there to stop eating until I lost the weight again.

Not eating on the airplane was easy—their food is totally wack—but I guess Miss Cuchifrita's gotta eat her three square meals every day, 'cuz now I'm feeling dizzy. I clutch at the newspaper as it falls from my hand and drops to the floor.

"What's that?" Mom asks, not noticing my little fit of dizziness. Recovering before she sees me stumble, I grab the newspaper off the floor and show it to her.

"Um, look at this," I say, fumbling to find the page with the ad for American Ballet Theatre. I try to remember to breathe while Mom looks at the ad, so I don't pass out altogether.

"So, what do you want to show me?"

"Um," I say, feeling my throat constricting, "I want to try out for the Junior Ballet Corps Division."

"Chanel, you haven't taken ballet classes with Mrs. Bermudez in two years. What makes you think you can get into the Junior Corps?"

"I practice all the time—really hard," I say, flustered.

"You call doing a few *tendu* exercises every once in a while practicing?" Mom retorts in a nasty voice.

I try not to let Mom's remark get to me, but my voice cracks. "I do practice! I do my warm-up exercises five times a week, then *adagios* at the barre in the exercise studio, then floor exercises, and then—"

Mom cuts me off before I finish—which is good, 'cuz I was about to blurt out that I can't work at the barre in the exercise studio because *she* is always in there, practicing her stupid belly dancing just to impress her boyfriend!

"If you want to try out, fine—but don't expect me to pay for any more classes," she says, without putting up any more of a fight.

I can't believe it! She didn't even try to talk me out of it! I feel guilty and sad now, for thinking all those bad things about Mom. All she ever really wants is for me to do what she says. I'll bet if I went along with her more often, we wouldn't be fighting all the time.

"But I don't think you should try out for the Junior Corps—" she blurts out, deciding after all to argue with me. I should have known it was too good to be true!

"But that's the only way I'm gonna get in without paying!" I whine.

"The Junior Ballet Corps Division?" Mom repeats, surprised. "You want to get into the *professional* company?" She gives me a look like she thinks I'm cuckoo, then says, "And what about your singing group?"

I stand there, with tears forming in my eyes. "I—I'll just have to do both," I stammer. "I'm fourteen years old. This is my last chance to see if I can be a ballerina, *Mamí*. I want to try."

Mom softens. "I don't think you're ready for it, Chanel, but I'm not going to stop you. If you get in, then we'll talk about it." Then she adds, "Maybe your father will pay for everything."

She looks away and pretends to read her magazine, but I think she's embarrassed that she snapped again about Daddy. She always tries to pretend it doesn't bother her that he loves Princess Pamela and not her.

Right now, I don't want to think about Mom and Daddy fighting, or how sad I feel because I don't see Daddy as much as I'd like. Obviously, he doesn't love *me* any more, either.

"Thank you, *Mamí*, you'll see—I'm gonna get into the Junior Ballet Corps Division—then I'll decide if I want to be a ballerina or not." I bend over to touch her ponytail.

"What are you thanking me for?" Mom asks.

"Um . . ." I stutter, because I am still scheming, "because . . . you're going to give me money to buy new pointe shoes?"

"Ohhh . . ." Mom says, pausing. "Oh, all right. Go get my purse."

"Yes! I love you, *Mamí*!" I prance all the way to her bedroom to get her purse, and when I open the door, I gasp. I can't believe all the shopping bags flung around the room! She must have brought back everything but the Eiffel Tower!

I feel my temples getting hot again. How could she buy Pucci a scooter? *I wonder if she brought me back anything?*

I resist the urge to peek in the shopping bags. That's all I need is for her to catch me — I'd be grounded for life. Maybe she's gonna surprise me later, I think, trying to calm down. What counts now is that I'm gonna show her—and everybody else—that I can be a ballerina.

I hear the doorbell ring again, and Mom yells, "What is this, Halloween?"

I run to the door and answer it. "It's the delivery guy with flowers, *Mamí*," I say, feeling my face get flushed, because I know the flowers are not for me. I mean, Krusher doesn't know where I live, *está bien?* And who else would ever send me flowers?

"Thank you," I say to the guy, and take the big box tied with bright red ribbon to Mom. I love boxes with big ribbons!

"Ooo!" Mom says, her face lighting up, because we both know who the flowers are from—Mr. Tycoon. Mr. Sheik. Mr. Moneybags.

I don't know if I'm gonna make it as a Cheetah Girl, or as a ballerina, or even something else I don't know about yet. But one day, I'm going to get more flowers than anybody has ever seen—even if I have to send them to myself!

Chapter 3

After I clean up my room, dust off the twenty-seven dolls in my collection, and put them back on the shelves, I kneel down and say a silent prayer: *Please let me get into the American Ballet Theatre Junior Corps.*

Then I tiptoe over to my red Princess phone to call Daddy. I want to see him and Princess Pamela, and hear all about Transylvania, and about Dracula's relatives. If Daddy is back, then he is probably at one of his restaurants—The Return of the Killer Tacos—because Daddy works even on Sundays.

"Chanel!" yells Mom from her bedroom. I feel so guilty about calling Daddy that I automatically hang up the receiver, even though someone has already picked up the phone. Mom would be upset if she knew I was calling Daddy—and even more upset if I talked to Princess Pamela.

"Coming, *Mamí*!" I yell back, so she doesn't get suspicious. Suddenly, I get excited—maybe Mom's calling for me because she brought me a present from Paris! The last time she went there, she brought me these coolio French berets—which I love, even though when it's really hot they make me break out around my forehead.

Right now I can't afford to break out, because I want to look perfect for my audition at the American Ballet Theatre—if I even get one, of course. The judges at dance auditions sit very prim and proper, while you dance and sweat your heart out—and they're judging every *adagio* step, every *petit allegro*, every *port de bras* arm movement—which should be as graceful as a swan floating on a pond.

I prance down the hallway to Mom's bedroom, fantasizing that I'm Princess Aurora in *Sleeping Beauty*, waiting to get kissed so I can wake up after sleeping for a thousand years. *"Sí, Mamí?"* I say cheerfully, peeking into her bedroom. Now that she has given me fifty dollars to buy a new pair of pointe shoes, I don't feel so mad at her for bringing Pucci that stupid scooter.

"I got you something," Mom says, handing me a shiny pink box. It can't be another French beret, because the box is too big.

I feel my heart fluttering as I open the flesh-colored satin ribbon—which reminds me of the beautiful ribbons I sew so carefully onto my pointe shoes. "Ooo," I sigh as I tear into the creamy layers of tissue paper and see the pink netting underneath. "Aaaaah, *Mamí*!" I exclaim as I hold up a powder pink tutu. *La más bonita!*

"Nobody makes a tutu like the French. *Nadie*. It has sixteen rows of tulle net." Mom is trying to act nonchalant. Then she abruptly barks, "I've gotta get this thing off my face. I'll be right back!"

I think Mom ran into the bathroom because she doesn't want me to hug her.

I try not to let the disappointment show in my face when she comes back out of her private bathroom. Now she sits in front of her vanity table, and opens one of the fifty jars she has lined up in neat rows.

That's when I get a good look at her. *Cuatro* yuks! Her face looks lighter than the rest of her body! I think that hockey mask sucked all the oxygen out of her, like a vampire or something. She's lucky she still has skin on her face after wearing that suction trap!

"You know, Chanel, I always wanted you to be a ballerina," Mom says, heaving a deep sigh and slathering cream all over her face. I think it would be better for you than being in that singing group." Then she frowns. "Just because Bubbles doesn't have the discipline for ballet, doesn't mean *you* shouldn't do it."

"I know, *Mamí,*" I say, getting teary-eyed, because I think she is finally trying to tell me that I'm good at something. "Thank you for the tutu."

"De nada, amor," Mom says, beaming at my reflection in her mirror. "You know, the French invented ballet, too."

"Really?" I say, surprised.

"Of course, Chanel—why do you think all the movements are in French—*plié, pirouette*?" Mom sounds a little annoyed with me. *"Por qué?"*

I stand dumbfounded, clutching my new tutu, because I can't think of an answer. I should have known the reason why Mom liked ballet. She likes *anything* French—even five-day-old *croissants*!

"I knew that, *Mamí*, I just forgot," I say, telling a *poco* fib-eroni. I know God will forgive me. I try to seem interested in Mom's trip to Paris, so she will get off my case.

"Did you go to anyplace interesting, like the Eiffel Tower?" I ask.

"No, Chanel," Mom snipes. "I did not go to the Eiffel Tower—that's for tourists."

Now I feel like a complete *babosa*, because of course only tourists would go see the Eiffel Tower, and Mom does *not* consider herself a tourist in Paris. The silence is very uncomfortable. Then, *gracias gooseness*, Mom says, "We did go to the Musée d'Orsay—you know, most of the exhibits there come from the Louvre."

"Sí, Mamí," I say, nodding. I wonder what the Louvre is, but I don't ask. Knowing Mom and Mr. Tycoon, it must be someplace where snobby people go.

"Oh, the sculpture!" she sighs wistfully. I never heard her speak that way about art, but I guess now that Mr. Tycoon is her boyfriend, she's learning a lot of new things. "When you walk in the center aisle, there is this wonderful series of busts—thirty-six of them."

Did Mom say busts? Does she mean they had ladies' breasts in the museum? I don't say anything, because I don't know what she's talking about, and I don't want her to think I'm stupid or something.

"Then I saw this bronze statue that took my breath away—'Young Dancer of Fourteen,' by Edgar Degas. The statue looked just like you, Chanel, with her feet poised in second position, and long braids down her back. That's why I went and bought you the tutu."

I feel the tears welling up in my eyes, so I look down at my shoes, but the change in Mom's voice snaps me out of my sadness.

"I still don't think you should try out for the Junior Ballet Corps Division yet," she pronounces in a tone of warning. "But if you've got your mind made up, you'd better start practicing every day."

"I will," I say defensively. "Can I use the exercise studio now?"

"Okay, but I wanna get in there soon and do my belly dancing," Mom says, rubbing her calf. "I didn't exercise the whole time I was in Paris, and I ate like a *puerco*. I know I'm gonna pay for it on the scale."

"You don't look like *un puerco*," I say jokingly. Mom is very skinny, but she is always imagining that she puts on weight.

Suddenly I think, again, *maybe I put on weight, too!* I tried not to eat too much food in Houston, but you know Southern hospitality—and besides, it was Thanksgiving. . . . I hold the tutu up against my stomach and look at myself from the side in the mirror. My butt is sticking out even more than usual!

"Tuck your butt in," Mom warns me, like she's reading my mind.

Now I remember why else I gave up ballet—it wasn't *just* because of Bubbles. I thought my butt stuck out too much for me to be a ballerina! I hold the tutu tighter against my chest, and try not to think about it.

"I'm going to exercise now," I tell Mom. Trying to fight back tears, I blurt out, "I've never forgotten that you took me to see *Sleeping Beauty* when I was little."

"Did I?" Mom says, like she doesn't remember.

"I'm already fourteen, *Mamí*, and I want to

be Sleeping Beauty—Princess Aurora, I mean—before it's too late."

"That's true—you are getting older, and the decisions you make now will affect the rest of your life—that's all I've been trying to tell you, *mija*."

"I know, *Mamí*," I sigh, then run out of her bedroom, because I want to cry. Suddenly I don't trust her. Why didn't she give me a hard time about auditioning for American Ballet Theatre? Maybe she wants me to get back into ballet because she thinks I'm a terrible singer. *Maybe that's why she doesn't want me to be in the Cheetah Girls.*

Mom is waiting for me to finish exercising, but right this minute I'm too upset to concentrate. I run into my bedroom instead, and pick up the receiver on my red Princess telephone. While the phone rings, I hold my breath, because I know that Bubbles probably doesn't want to talk to me. She hardly said a word to me the whole way home from the airport.

"Hi, *mamacita*," I squeal into the receiver, trying to sound cheerful. "I, um, was wondering if you would bring Toto and come with me to the Blessing of the Insects and their Four-Legged

Friends Ceremony," I say. When Bubbles doesn't say anything, I add, "I'm gonna bring Mr. Cuckoo—'cuz stupid Pucci won't do it."

"Sure," Bubbles says, surprisingly cheerful. "That'll give Toto something to do. He's been walking around the house sulking because I left him alone all week. And by the way . . ."

I know that tone of voice. It means Bubbles has good news. No wonder she didn't yell at me about Houston! "Mom's got this tight idea," she says proudly. "I'll tell you when I see you."

"Okay!" I can't wait to hear about *Madrina*'s great idea. She always has *la dopa* ideas—that's why she's our manager, and my godmother for life.

"I'll meet you in front of the cathedral at five o'clock," Bubbles says. Then she yells to Toto, who is barking in the background, "Hold your hot dogs, Toto, I'm coming!"

When I become a famous ballerina, and get my own apartment, the first thing I'm going to do is get a dog just like Toto! For a second, I get mad again at Mom, then realize that I shouldn't be. It's not her fault she's allergic to dog and cat fur. And besides, she did buy me a tutu in Paris! How many girls at American

Ballet Theatre can say that, huh? *Nadie, está bien?* Nobody but me.

Oops—I guess I'm not in American Ballet Theatre *yet*. But you just wait until I leap across the stage—I'll be the most beautiful Dominican Princess Aurora the world has ever seen! I pick up my new tutu and stare at it. It's the most beautiful one I've ever seen. I guess Mom really does love me, even though sometimes I think she is disappointed in me.

Staring at my tutu, I remember again the time Mom took me to see *Sleeping Beauty* at Lincoln Center. I was five years old, and wearing a pretty pink dress with ribbons in my hair. Mom kept showing me off to all the ladies in the balcony where we were sitting. It was one of the few times I remember going anywhere alone with Mom—Pucci was too little to go, and Daddy was working at his restaurant. He was always working back then.

I loved *Sleeping Beauty,* even though I got very scared when the wicked fairy Carabosse appeared—uninvited—and put the curse on the baby princess, telling her parents that she would die on her sixteenth birthday.

What will happen to *me* on my sixteenth

birthday? I don't want to think about that right now. Instead, I carefully put down my new tutu, and slip into my black footless cotton unitard and my old pink ballet shoes. Uh-oh—they're a little tight. I reach under my bed, feeling for the shoe box that contains the can of shoe spray I use to stretch my shoes. I can't afford to get any blisters right before my audition!

Dragging the box from under the bed, I take out my very first pair of pointe shoes—all moth-eaten and old, and so tiny! Mom bought them for me when I was seven years old. . . .

I start crying like a baby, and plop to the floor. Mom was so disappointed when I stopped going to Ballet Hispanico. I remember that Bubbles didn't like our teacher, Mrs. Bermudez. She thought she was too mean. I can still remember Bubbles poking her mouth out at Mrs. Bermudez. In ballet school, the teacher conducts the class and students are expected to follow whatever she says. Bubbles hated that. She doesn't like teachers telling her what to do.

I can see Mrs. Bermudez now—her black hair slicked back into a tight bun on top of her head, and her skinny lips accented by red lipstick. "Don't let your backside stick out, Chanel!" she would say sternly when I did my *grands pliés*, which are very deep, and require the upper body to remain perfectly straight.

Wiping away my tears, I put my old pointe shoes back, and take out the can of shoe stretch spray I was looking for all along.

After spraying inside my ballet shoes, I walk on *demi-pointe* to the exercise studio until my shoes dry and mold to my feet. I look at my profile in the exercise studio mirror. Suddenly it hits me—not only my butt, but my stomach is sticking out! I suck it in and stand up straight. I'm not going to eat dinner tonight—even if Mom makes my favorite Dominican-style *arroz con pollo*! No dinner for Miss Cuchifrita!

Now it's time to stop fussing around, or I'll be late meeting Bubbles at the cathedral, and I don't want her yelling at me. I'm always late for everything, it seems. I put my hand on the barre and start my *pliés*, then do my *tendu* exercises to warm up my feet, then *dégagés* and *ronds des jambes*, on the floor and off—making sure to keep my heel forward. That is so hard, I hate it!

My favorite part of the workout is the cooldown. That's when I do my *grand battements* in each direction—these are big, controlled kicks, and they're fun to do. I can hear Mrs. Bermudez in my head: "Chanel, don't lean forward—stay straight." When you're doing *grand battements*, you're only supposed to move the hip sockets and below—the upper body should be perfectly still. "Think of the beautiful swan swimming across the pond," Mrs. Bermudez used to tell us.

I am a beautiful swan, I tell myself. Then, suddenly, a voice inside me shrieks, *What if I'm really the ugly duckling?*

I put my arms high over head, making my movements as graceful as ever, moving my arms from fifth position to first and open to second position, then gloat in the mirror at my reflection. I am *not* an ugly ducking—because no ugly duckling in the world does *ports de bras* as graceful as mine!

I sure hope I got the audition appointment—because if I get to try out, there's no doubt this *girlita* is gonna make it into the Junior Corps!

Chapter 4

The Blessing of the Insects and Their Four-Legged Friends Ceremony at the Cathedral of St. John the Divine, at 112th Street and Amsterdam Avenue, is very popular—*muy popularo.* It coincides with the Feast of St. Cucaracha of Washington Heights, a saint who loved animals and nature. Of course, St. Cucaracha is one of *my* favorite saints, too. I know Mom would croak if she heard me say that, but it's true! She hates animals because they shed a lot of hair, which makes her sneeze and gets all over the furniture. I'm sorry, but I think Mom sheds more hair than any animal I've ever met.

Standing at the bottom of the steps in front of the beautiful cathedral, I lift my heels so that I can balance myself on my tippy-toes and look over the crowd. Sure enough, I see Bubbles coming toward me, wearing a red knit hat with a big red pom-pom on top. It bops to her beat, like a cherry on an ice cream sundae. I guess there's no way I would be able to miss her in that outfit!

"Where's Mr. Cuckoo?" Bubbles asks, before she even gives one of her usual flippy salutations.

"I didn't want to bring his cage," I explain in a whiny voice. I don't mean to sound like that, but I'm still nervous about Bubbles being mad at me, even though I'm trying to pretend I'm not. *Qué broma*, what a joke. I mean, the tension between us is thicker than nutty Nutella spread, *está bien?* I open my backpack, so Bubbles can see Mr. Cuckoo nestled in a towel inside.

"Ohhh, he looks smaller," Bubbles says, concerned, like he's not being taken care of properly or something.

"He's *bigger* than he was when we bought him," I insist.

"Oh. Well, maybe it's the way he looks wrapped up in that towel—you know, the background contrast is so close to his color,"

Bubbles says, like she's doing an assignment in one of our art composition classes at school.

Toto stands up and rests his paws on my leg. "Hi, Toto!" I exclaim, bending down to fix his cheetah jacket, which is riding up toward his neck. "Oh, you need a haircut, boo-boo!"

"Why don't *you* give it to him?" Bubbles asks, *muy sarcástico.*

"If you want me to, I can do it later," I reply.

"Mom is gonna take him to the Doggies Can Be Down Spa next week, so he'll get a cut there and a pawd-icure," Bubbles explains. I wish I went to as many different beauty parlors as Toto goes to, *está bien?*

"Are you going up?" asks this lady behind me, like she's annoyed because Bubbles and I are just hanging out on the cathedral steps.

I turn around to look at her, and catch the Wicked Witch expression on her face. *La gente* in *Nueva York* can be so rude! But I can't be mad at her for long, because the parrot atop her shoulder squawks at me, "Hello, pretty!"

"He's so beautiful!" I exclaim, admiring the parrot's red plumage, which is brighter than my favorite shade of S.N.A.P.S. lipstick—Raven Red. "What kind of parrot is he?"

"It's a girl," the Wicked Witch lady snaps back.

"Oh, I'm sorry."

"That's okay," the lady says, softening. "She's an Eclectus Parrot—the males and females have completely different colors. The males are bright green."

"Oh," I say, fascinated. "Has he—I mean, *she*—ever been to St. John's for a blessing before?"

"No, it's her first time—and from the looks of this crowd, it may be her last," the Wicked Witch lady snipes at me, looking around in disgust.

It is getting pretty crowded. I mean, St. John's Cathedral looks like it's going to the dogs . . . and cats and fish and—"Ooo, look, Bubbles, somebody brought an elephant!"

"That's nutso," Bubbles squawks. Toto starts barking, because the crowd is getting too close to him, so Bubbles picks him up, even though he weighs a ton. "Come here, Fatso," she says, rubbing his underbelly as he lies floppy-style in her arms.

The dumbo jumbo elephant is flanked by police officers on horses, and luckily, is ushered through a side entrance of the cathedral—or else we would have had a stampede!

"I wonder whose pet that is?" I ask in disbelief. I mean, there are so many rich people in New York, maybe some little boy who lives in a castle is the proud owner of Mr. Dumbo Jumbo. As much as I love pets, the one thing I wouldn't want is an elephant—because they stink too much, and I don't like smelly things around me all the time.

"I heard they're expecting four thousand people," the Wicked Witch says, turning slowly back to the front so that her prized parrot doesn't get jolted from her shoulder. "But it looks more like forty thousand if you ask me."

It's a good thing nobody is asking her. I look around at the crowd again—and see kids with fishbowls filled with lizards, frogs, and fish.

"There's a Chihuahua, Chuchie," Bubbles say, turning to her right.

"*Ay, Dios*—there are three of them!" I say, counting the three ladies with kerchiefs holding my favorite little dogs in their arms. As much as I love Toto, what I really want is a Chihuahua, imported straight from Mexico and into my arms!

"We're finally moving," moans the lady, giving me and Bubbles our cue to move up the cathedral steps.

Even though I'm eager to hear about *Madrina*'s great idea, I'm more anxious to tell Bubbles about my decision to try out for the American Ballet Theatre. I just want to get it over with, *está bien?*

"*Mamí* brought me a tutu from Paris," I say, turning to Bubbles with a smile. I can feel the squigglies starting in my stomach again.

"Really?" Bubbles asks, bouncing Toto up and down in her arms.

"In that big city of soufflé and dreams, why would she get you a tutu?" Bubbles asks, crinkling her nose.

"Y-you know, *Mamí* wants me to be a . . . ballerina," I stammer.

"Yeah, well, wants and wishes are best bestowed by fairy godmothers with magic wands," Bubbles snorts.

"*I* want to be a ballerina, too," I blurt out. Immediately, I feel my stomach get more squiggly.

"Chuchie—your days of sashay on the pirouette tip are long over. Don't you think, pink?" Bubbles asks, raising her eyebrow at me.

"No, I don't," I reply, holding my ground. "I'm going to try and get into the American Ballet Theatre." Wincing, I quickly add, "the

Junior Ballet Corps Division." I don't want Bubbles to think I've completely gone cuckoo.

"Are you serious?" Bubbles asks, surprised.

"Sí, mamacita."

"Well, I hope this crusade is a lot better planned than your songwriting fiasco," Bubbles says, poking her mouth out.

There. She finally said it. It is all *my* fault that *we* wrote a song *together* called "It's Raining Benjamins," and copied some of the words from the Cash Money Girls. If Bubbles was supposed to know so much about songwriting, then how come *she* didn't know about copyright infringement?

"Bubbles, I-I didn't write the song by myself," I say, stuttering. "You said yourself that I only wrote two lines of it."

Bubbles shoots me a look, and I realize that I've made a big boo-boo. See, Dorinda told me what Bubbles said behind my back, and I guess I shouldn't have repeated it to Bubbles's face.

"Dorinda didn't tell me—I, um, just knew you felt that way," I say, feeling my face turn deep red.

"If Dorinda didn't tell you, then how did you know I said that?" Bubbles asks. "I guess you are just the queen of the crystal ball?"

"Um . . . I guess because . . . she didn't tell me anything! *Nada*," I say, trying to tell a *poco* fib-eroni about my fib-eroni. If I don't stop, I'm gonna start confusing myself!

"But see, that's not the point, Chuchie," Bubbles says, getting so angry at me that she doesn't care if everyone around us on the cathedral stairs hears. "The point to this joint, is that you wanted to write this song *together*, when *I* could have been thinking up an *original* song."

"Yeah, but you came up with some of the words, too!" I hiss at Bubbles.

"Yeah, but I'm not the one who had a so-called dream about Benjamins falling from the sky, and you and I grabbing them like a couple of Mary Poppins wannabes!" Bubbles is glaring at me now, and pointing. "The idea for the song came from *you*."

"I *did* have the dream, Bubbles!" I say, teary-eyed. "*Te juro.* I swear. You and I were standing under an umbrella together—"

"You shoulda known that dream was a fake, because I never stand under an umbrella with you—you always make the umbrella bop up and down and get my hair wet!"

Now I'm really crying. "I'm not going to write any more songs with you!"

"Is that a promise?" Bubbles asks, not backing down. She hates it when I start crying, because it makes her feel like a bully—which she is. Bubbles the bully!

Now the peeps on the steps are staring at us. I turn and see this lady holding a big black cat. The cat starts meowing right in my face. *Ay, Dios mío,* his teeth look like fangs! That is a bad omen. I can tell something bad is going to happen. I gulp really hard and turn quickly from the black cat. Why does the lady with her stupid cat have to stand in back of *me*? This is not what I need right now!

All of sudden Bubbles blurts out, "How are you gonna have time for it?"

"Time for what?" I ask, still scared by the black cat and his meowing.

He won't shut up. *Cáyate!*

"Time to go to school, work in my mom's store to pay off what you still owe your mom, rehearse with the Cheetah Girls, *and* practice ballet?"

"Well, it's not like we're doing anything with the Cheetah Girls right now," I say wincing.

Bubbles shoots me a look, like, "Who says?"

"What happened?"

"That's what I wanted to tell you," Bubbles shoots back, sounding like Miss Clucky, the gossip lady on television. "My mom is going to call Def Duck Records, and ask them if we can put on an informal showcase for the New York staff—you know, give them a taste of our flava, so they can get with the program—and maybe the producer they've assigned us to—Mouse Almighty—will get excited, alrighty."

"That's a good idea," I say, my eyes opening wide.

"So, you'd better stick around for the cause, whenever it goes down," Bubbles says, licking her lips.

"*Claro que sí*, Bubbles! Of course, I will. But I'm still going to try to get into American Ballet Theatre—this is my last chance, last dance."

Bubbles just eyes me, then blurts out, "I don't know how you can do it. Remember our ballet teacher, Mrs. Bermudez?"

"Yeah," I say, chuckling. "She used to tell you, '*Plié* like a swan, Galleria, not like an ugly duckling!'"

Bubbles winces at this memory, which makes me feel like *una babosa* for even bringing it up. I'm so stupid sometimes!

At last we are inside the cathedral. Carefully, I take Mr. Cuckoo out of my backpack so he can breathe. I cup my palms together, so he has a little place to hang out.

We're just in time, because the service is about to begin. "Ladies and gentlemen, girls and boys, may I introduce the Paul Winter Consort jazz group," says a lady into the microphone. Everyone starts clapping. "They will be doing a special perfomance piece—'Earth Mass'—for this joyous occasion. And please welcome our featured dancers, from the Omega and Forces of Nature troupes. Today, Reverend Harry Pritchett will officiate over our blessing ceremony, to promote harmony and peace between man, animal, and *bug*!"

My eyes are glued to the dancers, who prance in the front of the high altar and do a beautiful routine. The ceilings in the cathedral are so high that the sound of meows and barks echoes over the music, making the whole place sound like a haunted castle. I whisper to Bubbles that I want to move closer. I don't want to miss one movement, one *grande battement,* from this troupe of dancers.

Suddenly, we hear the sound of the trumpet. *Oh, no*—the elephant is now being brought to the front of the high altar from the side entrance. He takes up all the room in front of us. I let out a sigh of disappointment. Bubbles shrugs her shoulders, like, "You know the way things flow in the Big Apple."

Sometimes I just hate everyone—and now, I'm even angry at all the animals. I just want to see the dancers! Mr. Cuckoo starts squiggling around in my palms. I look at him and stroke his head, then remember why I'm here—so he can have a blessed life, and be protected from the evil forces in the world. "St. Cucaracha will look over you, *precioso,*" I coo to him. I wish he was *my* pet, not Pucci's.

Now the lady leading the service is instructing us to stand in line, so that Reverend Pritchett can bless each and every animal. At this rate, we will be here till midnight—especially since Bubbles and I are so far back in the line.

With all this time to spare, I figure it won't hurt to say a prayer for myself. I put Mr. Cuckoo back in my backpack for a second, then cross myself and close my eyes. *Por favor, Dios,* I think, *please let me get into the American Ballet Theatre. And please protect the Cheetah Girls, and let us become famous, so we can travel all over the world, and sing to all of the creatures that you created. Amen.*

When I open my eyes, I see that Bubbles is staring at me. "I hope you said a prayer for me, too, Miss Cuchifrita Ballerina!"

"I did," I tell Bubbles, and smile at her.

Bubbles giggles. I feel like I can take a deep breath, because someone let the air out of the hot-air balloon. "I like that," I whisper to her.

"Like what?" Bubbles whispers.

"Miss Cuchifrita Ballerina," I say, beaming. I know Bubbles doesn't think I can get into the ballet company, and I know she doesn't understand why I have to do this, but I do know that she is the only sister I have—even if we aren't real sisters. Like Bubbles says, we are the dynamic duo, bound till death!

"I just hope you don't leap into the great beyond and land on your head, like you did in the twins' bedroom down in Houston," Bubbles says, bringing up that painful memory again.

"The area rug slipped," I protest.

"Don't get flippy with me, Miss Slippy," Bubbles retorts.

"I like my other nickname better." I wince.

Bubbles smirks, and says, "Okay, Miss Cuchifrita Ballerina—pirouette till payday!"

I can't believe Bubbles read my mind—but why am I surprised? Like I said, we are the dynamic duo, flapping in the wind with or without our capes!

Chapter 5

It is so cold, icicles are hanging off trees. Pursued by a magic troop of leaden soldiers, a handsome prince appears out of the darkness. Recognizing my true love, the Lilac Fairy shows Krusher—who is wearing a black cape and eye patch—a hologramma vision of me sleeping in the enchanted forest. Krusher begs the Lilac Fairy to show him where the real me lies. He smiles, and serenades the Lilac Fairy with an a capella version of his song, "She's My Girl."

The Lilac Fairy is captivated, and agrees to guide Krusher through the wicked fairy Carabosse's magic world—past the rats and the captive fairy children that were stolen from their homeland, to the place where I'm lying, in the new pink tutu Mom just bought me, asleep in a bed of pink flowers. Krusher does his famous double-neck move and supa-dupa split—snowflakes melting off his leather pants in the process—then kisses me gently on the lips. . . .

Which wakes me up. At first, I have sleep in my eyes, and rub them hard, but I recognize Krusher from his new album cover, and gaspitate because I cannot believe my eyes. I think the wicked fairy Carabosse is playing another trick on me. After all, it was she, disguised as a handsome suitor, who put the spell on me in the first place! Krusher smiles, and I recognize his big, beautiful teeth, and know that it is not Carabosse pretending to be him.

I smile back, my heart melting. Krusher whips me into his arms and we dance through the forest. I didn't know Krusher could dance ballet, but he leaps and pirouettes like the true prince he is. Suddenly, Krusher pulls me up on his shoulders, like I weigh no more than a feather. I hold my head up to the clouds, and extend my legs in a perfect split as he swirls and twirls.

Spinning round and round, I suddenly fall from his arms onto the ground, because Carabosse's evil spell has not been broken! The animals run from the forest, because there is a loud buzzing noise filling the air, a noise that is louder than my scream. . . .

Suddenly, I realize that the buzzing noise is

the sound of my stupid alarm clock going off, and that my beautiful dream has turned into a Nightmare in the Enchanted Forest. I fight off the breathless feeling in my chest. *Ay, Dios*, another omen—the *brujas* are trying to tell me something. . . .

I sit on the edge of my bed, frozen, then suddenly it dawns on me. *La bruja*—the good witch—is trying to guide me out of the forest and away from danger. She's trying to tell me that I am not Princess Aurora yet, that I'd better go practice so I can become her one day for real!

I turn and look at my alarm clock—the neon-lit numbers are shining bright and steady. It is six o'clock in the morning. I have an hour and a half to practice and get ready for school. I don't want to practice. *Yo quiero dormir más!* Sleeping Beauty is calling me.

Coming out of my dream haze, I get frozen with fear. I know in my heart that soon it will be too late for me to pursue my dream. I jump off my bed and quietly slip on my unitard, then tiptoe to the studio and turn on the lights. Yes, I'm yawning the whole time, but doing my ballet warm-up will wake me up out of my trance.

I have to write a letter to Krusher, I think,

smiling to my reflection in the mirror as I begin my pliés at the barre, bending my knees as deep as I can while keeping my posture perfect.

What if Krusher doesn't write me back? I do my stretches, alternating legs and bending over, taking deep sighs.

If I don't get into the Junior Corps, then I don't want to live. I won't even care about meeting Krusher. By the time I get to my *frappés*—bending the knee and flexing my foot so it's at a perfect right angle to my leg, I have forgotten about my fears. This is what I love about ballet. It takes me to *un otro mundo,* another world, in which I am the star—like Giselle, Raymonda, or Princess Aurora—a star whom everybody wants to kiss and love forever.

Now I feel excited, because I'm going to buy new pointe shoes after school today. I also have to go to the American Ballet Theatre, and find out if I get to audition for the Junior Corps Division. Suddenly, I get a squiggle in my stomach again. What am I going to wear? I know I'm only going to see the registrar, but every impression counts.

Red—*rojo*—my favorite color. That's what I'll wear, from head to toe. It always makes me feel my "growl power," and people always stop to look at me, because red makes everybody feel happy.

Looking down at my nails, I see that they are chipped. I'd better put on a coat of S.N.A.P.S. "Maui Wowie" Nail Polish for good measure. It's a pretty shade of Frosted Lime Green. I love it because it's not too dark, so it doesn't draw too much attention to my short, stubby nails.

After I shower and dress, I go to the kitchen to get my breakfast. I hear Mom yelling at Pucci, "No—you eat a bowl of cereal with one English muffin or one Pop Tart, but you are not going to eat both, *entiendes?*"

Just swell-io. Mom is in a bad mood. But when I walk into the dining room where she and Pucci are sitting eating breakfast, I can see why—her face looks like the girl's in *The Exorcist*. It's covered with little red bumps!

"What are you looking at?" Mom says, teary-eyed.

"What happened? *Qué pasó?*" I ask, staring at the pimply *pobrecita* who used to be my beautiful mom.

"Don't worry, I'm going to sue those charlatans who manufacture that *Vivre de Glamour* vibrating contraption!" Mom says, her voice squeaking.

I feel so bad for Mom that I don't even ask for my lunch money. I'm not going to eat lunch today anyway. Gotta lose some more weight before my big audition—*if* I get it.

"What's that on your nails, Chanel? You look like you have ten green thumbs!" Mom snaps at me.

"Um, it's a shade called 'Maui Wowie,' *Mamí,*" I stammer.

"*Mamí,* can I ride my scooter to school?" Pucci asks, interrupting us.

"No! You walk to school just like everybody else!" Mom yells.

"Moham's mother lets him take *his* to school," Pucci blurts out.

"Moham's mother is a—" Mom says, then stops herself.

Knowing Mom, she was gonna say something nasty, and bigmouthed Pucci would go to school and blurt it out to Moham, who would get hurt feelings. Ever since Daddy moved out, Pucci doesn't care about anybody else's feelings but his own, and his *boca grande*—big mouth—has gotten even bigger.

He sits there sulking, then says to me, "Mr. Cuckoo doesn't seem any different."

"Why should he?" I respond without thinking.

"You took him to get a stupid blessing, that's why," Pucci moans.

Mom grabs Pucci's arm hard, and the cereal box he's holding drops, scattering Cheerios everywhere. "Don't you ever blaspheme the church!"

I wonder what blaspheme means. I'll ask the twins, because they are very religious, but I think it has something to do with saying bad things about the church or something.

Thinking of the twins puts me in mind of the Cheetah Girls. Now that we've spent Thanksgiving together in Houston, it just seems like all five of us should be together all the time. Suddenly, a lightbulb goes off in my head. American Ballet Theatre is in Lincoln Center, right near the twins' school, the Performing Arts Annex at LaGuardia. Maybe next year, the three of us—me, Dorinda and Bubbles—could transfer to the Performing Arts Annex. That way, we'd get to be together all the time—*and* I'd get to be close to the ballet company *and* school.

I feel squiggly in my stomach again. What if I don't get accepted? I pick up the Cheerios and put them back in the box, but Mom screams at Pucci, "Pick up the cereal—and next time, I'll wash your mouth out with soap!"

I say good-bye to Mom (I don't think she hears me anyway), then grab my backpack and run out the door.

When I meet Bubbles and Dorinda before first period, I tell them what happened to Mom.

"I guess Auntie Juanita had to learn the hard way," Bubbles says. "There is a sham in every city, from Paris to Pittsburgh—and that's not pillow talk either!"

"Maybe she didn't use it right?" Dorinda offers.

"Maybe," I say, shrugging my shoulders. It must be hard having a boyfriend, and having to look pretty all the time. Especially a stuffy boyfriend like Mr. Tycoon, who's always dressed like he's going to a Billionaires' Ball or something. Mom is probably afraid she'll turn into a pumpkin after midnight, or lose her slipper—and lose him. Suddenly, I remember the question I wanted to ask Dorinda, about what Mom saw in the Moose d' Horses museum, or whatever it was called.

"Dorinda, what is a bust—I mean, the kind

you see in a museum—it's not like ours, is it?"

Dorinda chuckles. "Chanel—it's sculpture—like, just the upper part," she explains, motioning at her throat. "You know, from there up."

"Why would anybody want to look at heads without bodies—unless it's a spooky museum or something?" I wonder out loud.

"'Cuz it's like, art, that's all. Bronze statues take a lot of work," Dorinda says, then her eyes light up, like she remembers something. Dorinda opens her cheetah backpack, and whips out the cheetah photo album that she bought in Houston. "Look at our scrapbook!" she says proudly.

On the cover, she has glued the letters *The Cheetah Girls,* and inside are all the pictures of us that we've taken together. Under each picture, she has written a caption using a pink pen. "Ooo," I exclaim, as I touch the picture of us in the parking lot after we performed at the Okie-Dokie Corral in Houston. The caption reads, "The Cheetah Girls Get Sassy at the Sassy-sparilla Saloon!"

"Do' Re Mi, I can't believe you did this!" I coo.

"Quiet as it's kept, you really are the brains behind the horse-and-pony show we call the

Cheetah Girls!" Bubbles quips. "You've just been designated the official keeper of our memories, Do' Re Mi."

"I think we look dope in this one," Do' Re Mi chuckles, pointing to a picture of us performing onstage at the Cheetah-Rama for the Kats and Kittys Klub Halloween Bash. It was the first time we performed together as the Cheetah Girls—and Dorinda split her costume onstage! It was *una catástrofe,* but the audience clapped anyway, because it was all of our friends and Kats and Kittys members from all over the country—well, the East Coast, anyway.

"I guess this picture was, um, taken, before you did the lickety-split onstage, right, *mamacita*?" I giggle.

"Word, I guess so," Dorinda chuckles back.

"How did you get this?" Bubbles asks, surprised.

"Batman," says Dorinda matter-of-factly. See, Derek Ulysses Hambone, who is in our homeroom class, came to the Halloween Bash dressed as Batman. We almost didn't recognize the Caped Crusader without the baggy clothes he usually wears at school. Derek joined the Kats and Kittys Klub because he is goo-goo ga-ga over Bubbles. That's why we nicknamed him the Red Snapper—because he's always snapping at Bubbles' heels, *está bien?* His family has a lot of duckets, so he could afford to join our social club—but he would never have joined if he wasn't trying to get Bubbles to be his Batgirl, *está bien?*

"Good ole Red Snapper came through, huh?" Bubbles says, wistfully staring at our picture. "Which brings me to our latest caper. My mom is gonna call Def Duck Records today, and tell them it's time they laid at least one golden egg—by giving us a little showcase, so the East Coast Big Willies can see what we can do—and maybe Mouse Almighty will get motivated to take a nibble, know what I'm saying? 'Cuz we're tired of playing."

"I heard that," Dorinda retorts.

"So let's meet after school, and I'll give you a full report—because she'll have called me by then on my Miss Wiggy StarWac Phone," Bubbles explains.

Suddenly, I realize I've got a problem—I have to run right after school to get my pointe shoes at On Your Tippytoes, which is right down the block from the American Ballet

Theatre! If I take the number one train, it'll take me half an hour to get there, what with all the crowds bum-rushing the subway stations after school.

"Está bien. Okay," I hear myself say out loud—because I don't want to upset Bubbles, now that she has forgiven me for our Houston fiasco. I'll tell her after school.

But wait—how'm I gonna do that? There's no way I can be in two places at once! If I stick around with my crew after school, I'll never make it uptown to get my pointe shoes and get to American Ballet Theatre before they close!

Ay, caramba! What am I going to do now?

Chapter 6

I'm so glad when Italian class is over, because I can talk to Melissa Hernández about my audition. She has been going to ballet school since she was five, and now splits her freshman classes between Fashion Industries East High School and Ballet Hispanico. Her parents worked it out with the principal. Next year, she has to decide if she is going to come here full-time, or go to Ballet Hispanico and commit to becoming a professional ballerina. In many ways, Melissa and I are in the same boat—we're either gonna sink or float!

"*Hola*, Chanel!" she says when she sees me. Melissa is even smaller than I am, and her legs are even more muscular.

"Hola," I respond, then blurt out, "I've gotta talk to you."

"*Qué pasa*—what's up?" she asks.

"You know the American Ballet Theatre is having tryouts for its Junior Corps, right?" I say, trying to catch my breath because I'm so excited.

"*Sí*—I heard, but I'm staying at Ballet Hispanico till I decide what to do," Melissa responds, like she thinks I'm telling her because *she* should audition.

"I'm not talking about you, *mija*—I want to try out for it," I say.

"Oh!" Melissa responds like she's really shocked. "*You* wanna try out?"

"Sí, mija!" I say. I'm so excited, I want to grab Melissa by the shoulders and jump up and down with her.

"Go for it, if you, um, think you're ready," Melissa says, hesitating.

"You don't think I can do it?" I ask, surprised. If anybody is on my side, I would have thought it would be Melissa.

"No, Chanel, you are a great ballerina—but you haven't been training that much lately, have you? Don't you think maybe you should go back to ballet school for a year or two, *then* try to get into Junior Corps?"

"I wasn't training at all, until a couple of months ago," I admit. "But ever since I started out with the Cheetah Girls, I've been practicing every day, just to make sure my dancing skills were in gear. I'll be okay."

"Then go for it," Melissa says, grabbing me for a hug. "God bless you, *mija,* that you're ready to make that decision. I'm still not ready."

"No?"

"Part of me wants to do it, but another part of me isn't sure I want to devote my whole life to dancing. There are so many other things I want to do."

It's funny, but that's exactly how I feel. I want to be a Cheetah Girl. I want to open a beauty salon—Miss Cuchifrita Curlz. I want to be a ballerina. I want to do it all!

"I'm going by there today to see if I got an audition slot," I say excitedly.

"Good luck," Melissa says, then adds, "If you want to practice together, let me know."

"Would you?" I say, my eyes brightening. "We have a big exercise studio in my apartment, you know—my mother had it built." Suddenly, I wince inside, remembering that

Melissa lives in Washington Heights, just like my *abuela*. Her parents spend every penny they have sending her to ballet school and keeping her in pointe shoes. Why did I have to open my *boca grande* again? Now she's gonna be jealous!

"I would love to. Can I come by at five o'clock today?" Melissa asks hopefully.

"Okay," I say, hugging her tight. "You can come by at five, for sure. *Estás seguro*?"

"Sí, amor."

"Okay, I've gotta go meet Galleria and Dorinda now."

"I'll walk with you," Melissa says, and we head to the front of our school, where my crew is waiting for me.

"It's Melissa—so don't dis her!" Bubbles greets Melissa when she sees us.

"Hi, Galleria!" Melissa shoots back, then turns to me and says, "Tell me what happens—and I'll see you later."

I feel my face turning red as Bubbles asks me, "What's she talking about?"

"Um, I told her that I'm going to try to get into the American Ballet Theatre—the Junior Corps—remember I told you?" I say defensively.

"Oh, yeah—I know," Bubbles says, like,

"here goes Chuchie again." She just doesn't take me seriously, no matter what I try to do—write songs, be a ballerina, even that time I tried to make a dress in fifth grade—she just laughed when the seams came out crooked. Sometimes Bubbles acts just like my mother.

"Let's go over to Mo' Betta Burger, so we can call my mom, find out what happened with Def Duck Records, and go over our strategy."

"Um, I have to go buy new pointe shoes so I can start doubling up on my pointe work," I blurt out. "And then I have to go by American Ballet Th—"

"Yeah, but Melissa said she'll see you later. I'm not dumbo, gumbo, okay?" Bubbles says interrupting me. "That can wait."

"Oh," I say in a high voice, like I forgot. "Melissa is going to practice with me—you know, she's helping me out, because she goes to Ballet Hispanico."

"I know she goes to Ballet Hispanico," Galleria says, like, "Duh, duncehead, I'm at the head of the class, so don't try it." I don't think she likes the fact that Melissa is coming over.

"Um, we weren't going to practice today, were we?" I ask timidly. Suddenly, I feel my throat getting tense. I feel overwhelmed, like my worlds are colliding, and I'm singing, dancing, and doing hair as fast as I can!

"I don't know. I have to see what Mom says," Galleria says strongly. "Maybe the Def Duck peeps will want a whiff of our riff right away, you know what I'm saying?"

I nod my head yes.

"You can go after we finish, can't you, Chuchie?"

"Um, *claro que sí*—of course," I back down, feeling totally embarrassed.

As we walk on Eighth Avenue to Mo' Betta Burger, Keisha Jackson from our homeroom class stops in our path. We're not feeling Keisha Jackson, and she's not feeling us, *está bien*? So we act like we don't see her, because we're so engrossed in our conversation. Actually, we're practically fighting. I can tell Bubbles doesn't like the idea of Melissa coming over to practice ballet with me. I guess she feels we should be spending every second outside of school doing something with the Cheetah Girls. But I want to practice ballet too. I just do!

"Yo, Galleria and Chanel," Keisha says. Galleria and I continue ignoring her, but

Dorinda sort of nods at her and says, "What's up, Keisha?"

"Yo, I was wondering if I could buy one of them Cheetah Girls chokers." Keisha holds her hands around her neck like she is choking herself.

I feel my cheeks burning. I can't believe she is still making fun of our Cheetah Girls chokers fiasco! See, when we first made them, and sold them to some peeps at school, they fell apart—the letters we glued on with Wacky Glue went kaflooey, and the snaps came off the closures in the back. I mean, it was *una tragedia*!

Bubbles stops in her tracks and looks straight at Keisha. Uh-oh—I'm getting that Showdown at the Okie-Dokie Corral feeling all over again. *Por favor, Dios, no otra vez!*

"Keisha," Bubbles says, getting that annoyed tone in her voice. "How are you gonna buy a Cheetah Girls choker from us when the word on the street is, 'You're as broke as a bottle.'"

"Ooooooo," two girls in Keisha's crew say in chorus.

"Well, I thought, since the letters keep coming off and the snaps don't snap, that maybe you were giving 'em away—you know, like they do when they're trying to get rid of damaged merchandise at the Home De-poooo."

"Oh, I see, Keisha, you're trying to show us that you do more than sleep in merchandising class. Wonder why you got a 'D' on the test then."

"How do you know what I got on the test?" Keisha asks, finally wiping the smirk off her face.

"I guess a little Red Snapper told me," Bubbles says, now satisfied that Derek Hambone was telling the truth after all. Everybody at school knows that Derek is cuckoo for Bubbles, so it doesn't take long for Keisha to figure out who the 'Red Snapper' is—since he's in her Merchandising class too.

"*Derek* told you?" Keisha asks, with enough attitude to hook a shark.

Bubbles ignores her again. Keisha finally struts away. Even though he can be a pain, I feel sorry for Derek now. I wouldn't want Keisha to be mad at *me*. She can breathe more fire than Puff the Magic Dragon—without even opening her mouth!

Once Keisha and her crew are on their way, Dorinda asks Bubbles, "When are we gonna sell some more Cheetah Girls chokers again, anyway?"

I feel my throat getting tense again. With

school, rehearsing for our group, practicing for the ballet audition, working at Toto in New York, Madrina's boutique—I don't want to think about one more thing! *No más, por favor!* I wait with bated breath for Bubbles' response.

"I think we'd better chill with the choker skills for now. I just want to get in with Mouse Almighty alrighty," Bubbles says, looking at us for support. "It makes me gaspitate to wait, you know what I'm saying?"

"Word. Me too," Dorinda says, hiking her cheetah backpack on her tiny shoulders, like her burden suddenly got heavier.

All of sudden, I trip on a crack in the sidewalk, and the sprain in my ankle starts to hurt again. "Ouch!" I wince.

"You all right, Chanel?" Dorinda asks, touching my arm.

"I hate the sidewalks here—the cracks are so big you could fall in a hole and nobody would find you for weeks." I don't want Dorinda to help me get my balance. I haven't told anybody that I've been feeling light-headed lately, and I don't want anybody asking me about it. I don't know why it's happening, but it just happened again, and that's kind of why I fell.

Whatever the reason, my ankle is bothering me again now. I limp a few steps to try and walk off the pain. I could whack Pucci for tripping me yesterday. That's probably why my ankle is still bothering me. Or maybe it's because I've been overdoing my ballet practice the last couple of days.

"Is your ankle still hurting, Chuchie?" Bubbles asks.

"No—I told you, it's fine now. I just slipped on the stupid rug that time!"

Dorinda and Bubbles look at each other like I'm getting cuckoo, which I'm not. I'm just tired of them making a big deal-io out of it. *Basta!*

Bubbles pulls out her cell phone to call *Madrina* at her boutique. While talking on the phone, she holds out her hand to Dorinda to do the Cheetah Girls' handshake. That means something good has happened. I get excited too—and then I feel suddenly nervous. What about my ballet practice?

We plop down at a bench in Mo' Betta's, and wait for Bubbles to get off the phone.

"We're in there like swimwear," Bubbles says, extending her hand to Dorinda to do the Cheetah Girls' handshake again.

Why didn't she do it to me? Suddenly, I feel jittery again.

"The Def Duck Records A&R guy on the East Coast—'member Freddy Fudge?—has agreed to let us do a showcase at the Leaping Frog Lounge downtown," Bubbles explains, chomping into her fries. "It seems they've got some new artists they want to check out, so Mom's idea was right on time."

"Why didn't they think of it themselves?" Dorinda asks, like she's our manager.

"I guess that's why *Mom's* our manager—so let's go with the flow!" Bubbles says, shrugging her shoulders. "They agreed with Mom, that maybe if Mouse Almighty sees us in action, he'll get the right honchos at the label to get on board our choo-choo train, and let him shop for some material for us—you know, look around for songs, I guess. He's got that kind of juice—that's what Freddy Fudge told Mom, anyway."

"Well then, what does Freddy Fudge do?" I ask.

"I guess buy suits and get his hair dyed daily," Bubbles chuckles. See, Freddy Fudge is this skinny guy with blond, short, fuzzy hair. When we went up to the record label to meet him and Mouse Almighty, Freddy was wearing this *tan coolio* black-and-white-checked blazer with a red handkerchief in the pocket.

"He probably does like to shop a lot," I say to my crew.

"You would know—one shopaholic to another," Bubbles riffs.

I wish she would stop saying that about me. It's not exactly true. Well, not lately.

"I wish he would spend some time 'shopping' songs for us, so we could get in the studio and make a record," Dorinda says, huffing.

"So when do we get to be in this showcase?" I ask, feeling my heart fluttering. I hope it's not before my audition for the ballet company. Please don't let it be before my audition!

"They're gonna arrange it, and get back to Mom about it," Bubbles says. "It'll be good—once Mouse Almighty gets a whiff of our flavor, he's gonna want to shop for songs till he drops!"

"Word, let's hope so," Dorinda says, chomping on her burger like a mischievous chimpanzee. I don't want to tell her that she has ketchup on her mouth again, after all the time we've spent trying to teach her table manners. Meanwhile, I'm too nervous to eat, and Bubbles notices. "Chuchie, you're not gonna eat?"

"No—I have to go now and get my pointe shoes, and see if I got the audition appointment," I say nervously. I had an apple for breakfast and a glass of juice. I don't want to eat anything else today, because then I'll be too fat for my audition!

"You sure didn't eat a lot down in Texas—I was amazed," Bubbles says, trying to figure out what's going on.

Dorinda saves me from Bubbles interrogation when she blurts out, "What audition appointment?" I can't believe she's talking with her mouth full of Chunky Funky burger!

"Remember I told you on the plane?" I remind her. "I'm going to audition for the Junior Corps Division of the American Ballet Theatre—*if* I get the appointment, that is."

"Word?" Dorinda asks. Bubbles doesn't say a word. I know what they're both thinking—after that klutzy performance at the twins' house in Houston, the only thing I should be doing is pliés in my bedroom!

I give Dorinda a look, like, "We'll talk later." Sometimes Dorinda and I talk on the phone. I feel more comfortable telling her certain things than I do Bubbles. And sometimes Do' calls me, to tell me about what's going on in her house. She lives with her foster parents, Mr. and Mrs. Bosco, and ten foster brothers and sisters, and she has a lot of problems at home. I feel so bad for her sometimes. Even when Mom is being mean to me, I know that my Abuela Florita really loves me, and so does Princess Pamela, my dad's girlfriend. That's more than Dorinda has.

"Um . . . I gotta go," I say, feeling bad that I have to leave my crew.

"Okay—but we're definitely gonna start practicing Tuesday or Wednesday, so plan on it," Bubbles says in a mean tone.

"I know," I shoot back. "We can talk later in the chat room?"

Not looking up from her plate of french fries, Bubbles moans, "Whatever makes you clever."

Ever since we became the Cheetah Girls, she's starting to get a lot like Pucci—a real pain in the you-know-what!

Chapter 7

My heart starts fluttering as soon as I gaze into the window of the dance store, On Your Tippytoes. All those tutus, pointe shoes, and tiaras—*tan coolio*! I love dance shops—even the smell of new leather soles on ballet slippers makes me intoxicated!

Once inside, I head straight for the pointe shoes. On the way, I pass the rack for tights. I might as well pick up a new pair of pink ones for my audition, I tell myself. Pink tights and pink pointe shoes always make my legs look longer, and I want my legs to look like they go all the way to my neck!

While I try to find my size—petite—I hear someone in back of me mutter, "Excuse me."

"Oh, I'm sorry," I turn and apologize to this blond girl, because I'm blocking her view of the tights rack. As she reaches over me for a pair of flesh-colored tights, I notice that her hair is pulled back so tight that her eyes are slanting like a mummy's.

Yuk, why is she buying beige tights? I ask myself as she walks away. I look at her legs to see if she is a ballerina, but I don't think so. She must be a jazz dancer or something, because those tights are very, very unprofessional. I can just see Mrs. Bermudez, my old ballet teacher at Ballet Hispanico, pulling her to the side, and telling her so. "Pink is what dancers wear onstage," I heard her tell the *pobrecita* who made the mistake of wearing beige tights in class one day.

I scan the rack of pointe shoes—first picking up a pair of satin ones, then deciding on a pair of Capezios in leather. I ask the saleslady for a pair in a size seven. Taking off my red ballet flats and red socks, I wiggle my toes so they can breathe. That's when I notice that my big toenail is purple, and the rest of my toenails are an ugly yellow color. Oh, well, that's the price I have to pay for doing pointe work. I won't be getting a pedicure for a long time. When you're training, you need all the lumps, bumps, and calluses you can develop, to protect your tootsies.

The good thing is, I have a squarish foot with short toes that are almost all the same size. They are the best feet you can have as a ballerina. I didn't know this until Mrs. Bermudez looked at my feet one day and told me so. I'm also lucky because I don't have a high arch—which looks prettier in pointe shoes, but is not as strong or easy to control.

"How do those fit?" the saleslady asks me.

"Fine," I say, smiling as I gaze starstruck at my new Cinderella slippers.

"You look so pretty in that red outfit," the lady says, beaming at me. I wish I could tell her that she would look *tan coolio* in something red too, instead of that skirt suit in drab green—or as Bubbles would call it, "tacky khaki." Red would go better with her beautiful black hair and exotic brown eyes.

Just to make sure I don't insult her or something, I ask, "Where are you from?"

"Tokyo," she says, beaming at me like she's so happy I asked.

I'm not sure where Tokyo is. The saleslady

picks up on my blank expression and says, "Japan."

"Oh!" I exclaim, suddenly remembering that word the Japanese lady said at the Blessing of the Insects, when she tried to get past me to the altar. "Do you know what, um, 'cootie say' means?"

Suddenly I feel stupid. The saleslady is probably tired of people asking her questions like that, and making her feel like a foreigner all the time. (I know Mom hates it when people can tell she is Dominican. She likes to pretend that she is French, or even just plain ole American—which, according to my history teacher, Mr. Globee, doesn't even exist anyway.)

But it looks like the saleslady is getting more excited by my question than insulted, because she starts laughing. "Oh! Maybe you mean—*kudasai?*"

"Yes!" I say, so happy that we're finally speaking the same language.

"Yes—that means 'please' in Japanese!" she exclaims, and I can tell she is happy she could help me.

Now I stand on pointe to make sure their is enough room in the toe. Contrary to what people believe, the pointe shoe doesn't hold you up—it's your foot, supported by your legs, supported by your middle.

"I wish I could do that!" the saleslady exclaims.

I smile, but try not to get distracted by how nice she's being—because I have to concentrate to make sure these are the right shoes for me. Each and every pair of pointe shoes are hand-made, and they're kinda like snowflakes—they may look alike, but they're all unique, and have all sorts of variations in the sizing.

"Which company do you dance with?" the saleslady asks.

"Oh, I'm not with a company—yet," I say nonchalantly, but I'm so flattered that she thinks I am a professional ballerina. Now I feel as proud as a peacock—and my feathers are definitely starting to spread. "I have an audition," I say. Then I realize that I'm telling a fib-eroni—because I don't even *know* yet if I have an audition — not until I leave here, and check with the American Ballet Theatre office.

Well, I *almost* have an audition. So I tell her, "I'm going to be doing 'Black Butterfly,' so I have to make sure the shoe is hard enough to do thirty-two *fouettes*." *Fouettes* are a very demanding type of turn, so I'll be *en pointe* constantly in front of the judges. Of course, I'm not going to have to do the whole piece for the audition—but still . . .

The saleslady is staring at me, waiting for me to make up my mind.

"I'll try one more pair before I decide," I tell her, hoping she doesn't get annoyed.

But I don't think she does, because she brings me three other kinds of pointe shoes, and lets me try them all on in peace.

"I'll take these," I tell the saleslady, finally deciding on the fourth pair, which seems to have the most room at the toe for padding. Once I get to the register, I ask for some ribbon and lambswool. The lambswool will protect my tootsies, and minimize the rubbing of the skin against my shoe, but still let me feel the floor.

"Which kind do you want?" the man behind the counter asks me, placing different types of lambswool on the counter so I can touch them.

"This one," I say, settling on the fluffier brand—which will wrap around my trouble spots (my big toe, the little toe, the knuckles, and the tips of my toes) without giving me grief afterward.

"How much ribbon do you want?"

Now is not the time to skimp on ribbon. "Um, six—no, make that six and a half yards," I say proudly. There has to be enough ribbon to cross over my foot at the front, and wrap twice around my ankle to tie in a neat knot (not a bow, which is very unprofessional) at the back, outside the ankle—the part that doesn't show when my feet are turned out.

"What color?" the man asks, annoyed because I'm holding him up, and he has other people to wait on. Everywhere you go in New York, there is always a line, it seems!

"Oh, I'm sorry—the flesh-colored one."

As I walk around the corner to the American Ballet Theatre, I stare closely at the sidewalk for any good omens. If I find money on the sidewalk—even a penny—in *brujería* it will mean something good is going to happen to me! Santa Maria, Sophia, and Catalina, please give me a sign—*por favor*!

Suddenly, I notice that I'm dillydallying on the sidewalk. I guess I'm nervous about going to American Ballet Theatre—what if they tell me I don't have an audition? Or that they lost my application? I'll die right there on the spot!

For the first time today, I wish Bubbles and Dorinda could be here with me. I always feel stronger when I'm around them. I smile to myself, thinking of the new nickname Bubbles gave me—Miss Cuchifrita Ballerina.

Oh, that's right. Aqua and Angie's school—the Performing Arts Annex—is right here in back of Lincoln Center too. Maybe I should try to find them? Nah—it's already four o'clock, and they've probably already left for the nearest BBQ hut. No, wait—there is one day of the week that they stay after school, and take extracurricular activities. Is it Monday or Thursday? I can't remember. I shake my head to get rid of the cobwebs—I suddenly feel so confused and light-headed.

At last, I find myself at the entrance of the American Ballet Theatre. Even though it's only three blocks away from the ballet shop, I feel like Little Red Riding Hood making her way through the forest! Taking a deep breath, I open the heavy wooden door. My heart is beating so fast when I walk up to the receptionist that I think I'm going to have a heart attack!

"Can I help you?" she asks, but she isn't smiling, which makes me even more nervous!

"I, um, filled out a form, I mean I sent in an application for the Junior Corps—"

"You want to know if you have an audition date?" the receptionist cuts me off.

"Um, *sí*—I mean, yes," I stutter. Now I'm really blushing, because I always lapse into Spanish when I'm nervous, and she must think I'm kinda slow or something!

"What is your name?"

"Chanel Simmons," I say quietly.

"Have a seat, someone will be right with you."

I always hate when people say that, because sometimes that means that you are in big trouble—like when I used to get called to the principal's office in grade school.

I look around at all the beautiful ballet posters in the office. Well, I am definitely not in grade school anymore. I'm sitting in the reception area of American Ballet Theatre—which has some of greatest ballet dancers in the world.

Ooo, look—Paulina Perez! I stare at the poster of one of my favorite ballet dancers. She is so beautiful and graceful. "There was never a more beautiful Giselle . . ."—that's what Mom said after she saw her in a production of it when she was younger.

"Chanel Simmons?" asks a lady who has stepped out from behind a door.

"Yes," I respond, snapping out of my daydream.

"Please, come in. I'm Mrs. Chavez, the Junior Corps registrar."

I follow her into a tiny, cramped office. "Please sit down," she says, motioning for me to sit in the chair directly opposite her desk. I wonder if this means I didn't get an audition.

Mrs. Chavez shuffles through some papers, then says, "Ah, yes." She sits quietly as she examines my form. I can tell it's mine, because I filled it out in red ink. Mrs. Chavez looks at me, but she isn't smiling. "I see you attended Ballet Hispanico from the age of six till twelve. Where did you go after that?"

"I, um, have been practicing at the studio in my, um, apartment, well, we live in a loft."

"Oh?"

"Um, we have a barre in the studio and everything. My mother takes, um, dancing," I say, deciding that I'm not going to tell Mrs. Chavez about Mom's latest obssession with wiggling her belly button in the mirror!

"Chanel—we received a recommendation from your teacher at Ballet Hispanico. She feels you could do the work if you put your mind to it, but it seems—"

"I'm ready to put my mind to it now," I say, feeling the heat flash around my temples, then shut my *boca grande* out of embarrassment for interrupting Mrs. Chavez in the first place.

"Like I was saying," Mrs. Chavez says slowly, making me feel embarrassed all over again, "Mrs. Bermudez felt your decision to interrupt your studies was influenced by your best friend, um—?"

"Galleria."

"Yes," Mrs. Chavez says, then pauses, which I take as my cue to explain or plead my case.

"Galleria, um, didn't want to take ballet classes anymore—and even though I wanted to continue, I didn't. See, my parents were getting a divorce around that time, and I didn't want them to have to pay for it. . . ." I'm shrieking inside, because maybe I'm talking too much.

"The divorce?" Mrs. Chavez asks, confused.

"No!" I say, turning so red I match my sweater. "I mean, they didn't want to pay for my ballet classes."

"I see," Mrs. Chavez says, softening just a lit-tle—*gracias* gooseness! "Do you think you are really ready to dedicate your life to ballet?"

I freeze inside. What does she mean by *my life*? "Well, I'm ready to work really hard practicing and rehearsing." *Por favor, Dios,* please let that answer her question!

"I'm curious, Chanel—what made you change your mind?" Mrs. Chavez asks, and now I see a little twinkle in her eyes, which means she must like me.

"I'm fourteen now—and if I don't get into a company soon, it will be too late for me." I say, trying to seem as serious as I am.

"Dedicating one's life to ballet is a serious commitment—and very few girls each year are invited from outside the school to join the company in any of the divisions." Mrs. Chavez pauses again, as if she is thinking. "In light of Mrs. Bermudez's recommendation, we are going to allow you to audition for the Junior Corps."

"Thank you, Mrs. Chavez!" I say, finally letting out a sigh of relief.

"But I just want you to know, Chanel, that if you are not accepted, you may always feel free to audition for our school, or for other schools." Mrs. Chavez sounds like she's trying to soften the blow. "It's the pursuit of ballet that is most important—not the institution."

"But I want to be with American Ballet Theatre," I protest.

Before I can tell Mrs. Chavez why—because Paulina Perez is my favorite dancer in the whole world—she is dismissing me. "Here is the information you will need for the audition on Saturday."

Mrs. Chavez hands me a form, and I want to bolt for the door. *Corra, corra!* I should just run away now—I'm not ready for an audition yet!

Taking another deep breath, I realize that I'm as ready as I'll ever be. I have been practicing for weeks. Ever since October, when Dorinda auditioned to be a backup dancer for Mo' Money Monique's tour, I secretly knew I wanted to try out for ballet again, and I started to practice whenever I got the chance. I just never told anybody.

I only have to audition for fifteen minutes—what could possibly go wrong? I could do the steps from "Black Butterfly" backward—every combination, every *grande battement*, and, most importantly, every *fouette*—those beautiful turns that I have worked so hard to do perfectly.

Walking toward the subway, I read my audition sheet over and over, to make sure I don't miss anything. "Wear comfortable clothes. Don't do a segment longer than fifteen minutes. Blah, blah . . ."

I'm not looking where I'm going. As a result, I miss the first step going down to the subway, and almost trip down the rest! Luckily, the man in front of me breaks my fall.

"You all right?" he asks, concerned.

"Yes," I respond, feeling like a *babosa*. Whenever I get nervous, I always seem to do stupid things! I clutch the plastic bag containing my beautiful new pointe shoes. Catching my breath, I get to the bottom of the subway stairs in one piece. I can't wait to get home and sew on the ribbons, then break them in during practice with Melissa.

I chuckle, thinking about what Bubbles shouted out to Melissa this afternoon: "Melissa, don't dis her!" Bubbles is so funny. Suddenly, I feel a pang in my chest. I really do think of Bubbles as my sister. I wouldn't be here if it wasn't for her. I mean, going to Fashion Industries East High School and being in the Cheetah Girls.

The only thing we don't have in common anymore is ballet. I sigh away the sadness. If I could have one wish, I would ask a fairy godmother to make Bubbles a ballerina too—then we would really be the dynamic duo, bound till death—and we could pirouette to a payday!

Chapter 8

I'm too excited to eat dinner. I run straight to the exercise studio, to sew the beautiful ribbons onto my pointe shoes. I plop down on the floor, happy that Mom and some lady I've never seen before are too busy in the den to care about me.

I rifle through my heart-shaped thread box, looking for the right thread to use. I put back the cotton thread, and settle on the crochet kind—it's stronger than cotton, which rots and snaps after being rubbed by my sweaty feet. I bend the heel so it lies flat against the side of my left pointe shoe. That way, I can find the right place to sew the ribbon.

After I finish, I sew dressmaker's tape on the

inside, to make the ribbons especially strong. This way, when I wear out these pointe shoes, I can use the ribbon over again. Sometimes I'm such a smart *señorita*! I say to myself proudly, as I sit and gaze at my pointe shoes. Then I change into my unitard and put them on.

The doorbell rings, and I jump up to get it, noticing that I'm feeling a little light-headed again. I wonder if I'm coming down with a virus, I think, panicking to myself. Maybe I'd better drink a glass of water.

"I'll get it," I yell, so Mom doesn't have to come out of the den. I want her to keep busy talking to the lady.

"*Hola*, Melissa!" I say excitedly, hugging her, then ushering her right into the exercise studio. Melissa is looking around like she is really impressed.

"Your hallway is five times bigger than my whole apartment!" she says with glee, then gasps at the exercise studio. "*Ay, Dios mío*, if I had this to practice in, I'd never leave my house!" Her eyes are moving around like pinballs.

"Well, I can't even get *in* here half the time," I protest. "My mother exercises twice a day."

"*Verdad?* Really?" Melissa asks, impressed.

"She used to be a model," I offer in explanation.

"Really?" Melissa says, sounding like a broken record.

"Really—and believe me, she works really hard to stay skinny. More than me!" I say, laughing. "Hey, guess what? I got an audition for the Junior Ballet Corps!!"

"Really?" Melissa responds, her big brown eyes opening even wider, but now even *she's* laughing at herself for saying the same thing over and over again.

"Really, *mija*—so we've got to practice hard!" I show off my new pointe shoes. "I went to Tippytoes after school."

"Well, let's break them in," Melissa says, getting serious. I can tell that she loves ballet as much as I do. She changes into her leotard and begins her warm-ups at the barre.

I can't help but notice how much smaller her butt is than mine. Suddenly, I feel insecure. *My butt sticks out too much for me to be a ballerina.*

"How is Mrs. Bermudez?" I ask. Now I miss her, since she gave me such a good recommendation to Mrs. Chavez.

"Strict as ever, but she doesn't teach the advanced classes anymore," Melissa says. "We have a new teacher, Mrs. Ferrer—she came from the Joffrey, and she's really strict."

"Really?" I respond, sounding just like Melissa. Joffrey Ballet School is in New York too, and it's just as famous as American Ballet Theatre. Maybe I should try out there, too. Their students graduate to the Joffrey Ballet Company, and to companies all over the world—sometimes even to faraway places like Eastern Europe, where Princess Pamela is from. That would be so exotic! I think dreamily to myself as I warm up.

Once we get into the meat of our ballet practice, Melissa and I aren't chatting anymore. You have to really concentrate on the *adagio* steps—preparations for turns that start out simple, but get a lot more difficult once you add the head and arm movements.

"Let's do *petit allegros* now, okay?" Melissa suggests.

I nod my head okay, and prepare for the small jumps—like the *changements* that come before the *grand allegros*—which call for bigger combinations on the diagonal. This is the stuff I have to be down on.

Now I start getting nervous, because it's time

to show Melissa what I'm gonna do for my audition. She does her cool-down—some *grand battements* and *ports de bras* with her arms—and watches me get ready to do my routine.

"Okay, *mija*—your extensions are good," Melissa says, smiling.

"I know," I say, touching my hair. "I just got them put in."

Melissa breaks out in a big smile at my joke. In ballet, an extension refers to how high you can lift your leg, in movements like the *battements* and *developpé*. I can lift my legs high, *está bien?*

Before I get too bigheaded, Melissa barks, "Okay, now let's see your *'Mariposa Negra.'*" I've already told her I'm going to audition with a piece from the *Black Butterfly*, a famous Spanish ballet.

I take a deep breath and put on my audition music—it's by Tchaikovsky, the famous Russian composer of *Sleeping Beauty*, *Swan Lake*, and *Nutcracker* fame.

Melissa beams, and nods her head for me to begin. She sits on the floor like she is one of the judges, pretending she has pen and paper in front of her, and is writing notes on my performance.

I ignore her, because that's what you're supposed to do at an audition. You have to totally concentrate on every single step you take. I take a deep breath, and suddenly I'm feeling dizzy again. I shake my head for a second.

"*Qué pasa?*" Melissa asks, concerned.

"*Nada*—I feel dizzy, but I don't know why," I mutter, trying not to pay attention to the lightheadedness.

"Have you eaten?" Melissa asks me.

"No," I respond, like, "what does that have to do with anything?" You never eat when you are rehearsing for a big performance—and this is a big performance, even if it is just an audition!

Melissa looks at me, but doesn't say anything. She nods her head again for me to begin. I start the Tchaikovsky tape, and put my hands over my head in *port de bras* position. Gingerly, I flutter my arms. I am playing one of the follower butterflies—to audition as the lead would have been too brazen, too conceited for a ballerina auditioning to get into Junior Corps Division.

I take a few steps *en pointe*—which is the easy part. It's going from flat to pointe, and coming down on one foot as well as two, that separates the *chicas* from the lead ballerinas, *entiendes*? I turn twice, then dip into a *fouette*, then turn again, maintaining my balance.

Ouch, my ankle hurts—and so does my head! I keep going—*jeté*, plié, *fouette*, and the leap that takes me halfway across the exercise studio—before I dive into a beautiful curtsy and drape my body to the floor.

"Bravo! Encore!" Melissa says, clapping loudly. I don't respond, because I cannot expect that at my audition. No one will clap. They will simply nod, and say "thank you"—and I will be expected to exit from the room immediately.

"Do I need any work?" I ask Melissa, wiping the sweat from my forehead with a hand towel.

"Yes," she responds without hesitating, and I feel the sting of rejection, even though I know she is being helpful. If there is anyone who wants me to do my best at this audition, it's definitely Melissa.

"Your *fouettes* feel forced. It looks like you don't have your balance when you come back to the center," Melissa instructs me.

"Okay," I moan, then put on the record and do the routine again. Melissa watches me carefully, and I try really hard to concentrate on my *fouettes*. I think it's because I feel dizzy that I don't quite get them. No, that isn't true—I *always* have trouble with them.

Melissa claps again when I finish, but this time she doesn't say "Bravo," or anything. I know it's stupid, but that makes me feel more nervous. Maybe I shouldn't even go to this stupid audition if I don't want to come off like a big *babosa*.

"I think you're ready," Melissa says with a sigh.

I take off my sweaty shoes and hang them over the barre, so they can dry and be ready for my big day on Saturday.

"Chanel!" I hear Mom yelling for me. Melissa and I hurry toward the kitchen. Mom is standing there with the phone in her hand. Funny, I didn't hear the phone ring. I guess I was really concentrating on my practice. I grab the receiver, and hear Bubbles's voice.

"*Mamacita*, we have a game plan," she coos. I guess she's trying to be nice to me, because she was so nasty when I wouldn't hang with her and Dorinda after school today.

"What happened?" I respond, waiting to hear the details.

"We have a showcase in two weeks—on a Friday night at seven o'clock," Bubbles says proudly.

"Really?" I respond, then catch myself, because I'm sounding like Melissa again. But I *am* surprised. I mean, *Madrina*—Bubbles's mom—can cook up things faster than Uncle Ben's Minute Rice, which is what Mom's cooking right now for dinner. (She always uses the white rice when we have company instead of the Goya yellow rice. I guess the lady with the big glasses is staying for dinner.)

"We're gonna rehearse starting Monday—you know, back to basics. We're just gonna give 'em 'Wannabe Stars in the Jiggy Jungle,'" Bubbles explains, while I stand there in my leotard, feeling dirty.

"How come you're breathing so heavy?" Bubbles asks, finally noticing that I'm panting like a puppy.

"I, um, just finished doing my ballet practice—with Melissa," I explain nervously. Why should I feel bad? I guess I don't want Bubbles to think we're having fun without her.

"You're *still* practicing?" she asks, surprised. "It's nine o'clock already. I thought you said she was coming over at five o'clock!"

"She did," I protest. "Bubbles, the audition is Saturday. I have to be ready."

"That's good," Bubbles says like she means it—but even over the phone, I can tell when she is poking her mouth out and getting an attitude. "This way, you'll have it out of the way for our rehearsal."

I can't believe Bubbles! She's not even considering the possibility that I will get into the Junior Ballet Corps! I feel myself getting angry. Bubbles can write songs better than I can. Why can't she understand that I'm a better ballerina than she is? That's why I have to do this on my own—without her.

"If I get into the company, Bubbles, then I'm gonna have to rehearse—I'm just gonna somehow find time to do both. But for right now, it's fine."

"Well that's the point to this joint, Chuchie," Galleria says, in that big sister voice I hate. "If we do a showcase for the East Coast peeps at Def Duck Records, maybe they'll get us into the studio, and start wagging instead of lollygagging."

"I know. Don't worry, Bubbles, we're gonna rehearse really hard together, and be ready for all the quacking Ducks!"

Bubbles doesn't laugh at my joke. I guess she is *caliente* that I invited Melissa over to my house to practice with. I start feeling guilty, and then I get dizzy again. My legs feel weaker than a scarecrow's, and I plop right down at the dining room table. Melissa looks at me, concerned, and sits down too. Mom has come back from the den with the lady in the big glasses, so I don't want to stay on the phone.

"Bubbles, I feel dizzy. I'd better go—I have to shower and, um, *Mamí* has company, too."

"Mr. Tycoon?" Bubbles asks nosily.

"Um, no." I don't want to say anything about the lady, since she is hovering near the table. That would be rude. I know Bubbles is annoyed that I won't stay on the phone and talk with her, but I don't want to right now. "Bubbles, I have to leave at two o'clock to go to the audition. I'll call you afterward, *está bien?*"

"Okay," Bubbles says, giving in. "Good luck tomorrow." I think she means it.

Pucci comes into the dining room, and looks at Melissa out of the corner of his eyes. I introduce him, even though I don't want to. He mumbles a hello, then plops his Pick Up Stix game box on the table. Fumbling with a pile of Stix, he blurts out to Melissa, "Are you a Cheetah Girl too?"

"No," Melissa responds.

"Good," Pucci says, making a mischievous face.

"Pucci—get that box off the dinner table," Mom tells him, then introduces me to the lady in the big glasses. "This is Lois Paté—she is going to be working with me on my book."

"Hi, Ms. Paté," I say, noticing that her name rhymes with *plié*, which I don't want to think about until tomorrow morning when I get ready for my audition. Suddenly, I realize this is who Mom has been talking about on the phone—the "ghost writer"—but she doesn't look like a ghost to me. I wonder why they use that expression.

"I have to go," Melissa whispers to me. It is already getting late, and I know she has to travel all by herself on the subway to Washington Heights, which is in the upper part of Manhattan—almost all the way to the Bronx. I feel guilty that she has to go home by herself. I walk Melissa to the door, and she gives me a hug and says, "*Buena suerte* tomorrow. Good luck at the audition."

My hands are freezing; I'm so terrified. I run to my room and lie down without even taking a shower, because I am so dizzy I can't see straight. Plopping down on my bed, I pass out—just like Sleeping Beauty.

Chapter 9

I thought I knew what it meant to be scared, but now I know what terror really is. Just the thought of seeing Mrs. Chavez and the other judges watching me at the audition is enough to send me running for the hills. Still, I am so proud of myself—because even though my stomach was growling this morning, I didn't eat anything, and now I don't feel hungry at all. I feel like I'm floating on air.

When I open the door of the American Ballet Theatre, I stand as tall as I possibly can, like I'm not nervous about anything. *Nada, está bien?* I'm going to leap into stardom, that's what I'm going to do!

Then that stupid little voice comes into my

head again. *Maybe the judges won't think I'm so good.* I start shaking as I sit down in the waiting room.

A lady with a sharp voice instructs me to change in the anteroom studio. *This is it.* Now I will know if I have what it takes to be a ballerina—or not.

I turn nervously and look at the other girl in the anteroom, who has already changed. She looks a little older than I am, and she has long black straight hair pulled back into a ponytail. I watch her as she stands and does pliés—warming up and getting ready for the big time. Then she walks over to her canvas bag to get something out. I sneak a glance at her butt. She doesn't have one at all! I start shrieking inside again. How could I be so flat-chested, yet have a butt that sticks out?

"Chanel Simmons?" says a lady, sticking her head around the door. She is holding a clipboard. I wonder how I got called before the other girl. She must be early, I guess.

"Do you have a tape?" the lady asks me.

I hand her my Tchaikovsky cassette, which is clearly marked "Blank" on Side Two, so the assistant won't have any trouble figuring it out.

I sneak one last look at myself in the mirror as I walk to the center of the exercise studio. My hair is slicked up in a ponytail, and the styling gel is holding up okay, because I don't see any frizzies trying to take over.

Standing in the center of the studio, trying not to look at the judges, I feel the strangest feeling in my life—it's as if I have left my body, and I'm watching myself from above, where I'm floating. Suddenly, I feel my hands shaking, and I hope no one notices it but me. All that matters now is, it's time to dance!

The music has begun, and I begin to do the movements from the "*Mariposa Negra*" ballet piece. I place my hands over my head in *port de bras* position and my feet in fifth—then begin my pliés and *petit allegros* before I do my first *fouette*.

All of a sudden, I feel like I'm going to faint! Not now, *Dios*, please! I pray, as I do another *fouette*, then get ready for my series of grand leaps. One, two, three—

I leap, then turn—but lose my balance instead! "Aaah!" I scream, as I fall backward onto the floor—and disappear into darkness!

When I wake up, I see Mrs. Chavez and one of

the other judges huddling over me. *Ay, Dios mío*—I must have blacked out! I feel a sinking feeling in my stomach, and then—worse—a shooting pain in my left ankle.

"Drink this," Mrs. Chavez instructs me, handing me a paper cup of water.

"I don't know what happened!" I moan, now that I am conscious and fully aware of my *catástrofe*.

I ruined my audition! Tears start streaming down my face. My left ankle feels like it's on fire!

"You, um, fell and passed out," Mrs. Chavez says, waiting patiently for me to stop moaning. "Drink this water, please."

A lady comes with a wet washcloth and puts it over my forehead. "EMS is coming. They're going to take you to the hospital," she says.

"Hospital? I don't need to go to any hospital," I say, trying to talk normally between grimaces.

"Can you move?" Mrs. Chavez asks me.

I try to lift myself up without putting any weight on my left foot—but as soon as I get midway off the ground, I feel a shooting pain in my butt.

"Mr. Herrera, we'd better put her in the wheelchair," Mrs. Chavez says.

"We're gonna lift you up, Chanel," Mr. Herrera informs me. "Hector, can you come here, please?"

I don't want to be lifted up—I want to walk, but I'm too scared to try. Mr. Herrera and Hector get on each side of me and pick me up.

"Oouch!" I scream. My left ankle, dangling in midair, burns.

"Just one more second, Chanel. Can you sit like this in the wheelchair?"

"NO!" I cry out.

"Okay, then, we'll wait for the stretcher," Mr. Herrera says, as they put me back down on an outstretched blanket.

When the ambulance people arrive, Mrs. Chavez instructs them, "She's gonna need a stretcher."

I feel like such a *babosa*. What happened? I don't remember! Suddenly everything just went blank. . . . I guess the dizzy spells were an omen that something bad was gonna happen. I should have listened!

"I'm sorry I ruined your auditions," I say to Mrs. Chavez earnestly.

"That's okay, Chanel, we'll be fine," she says, and I notice the tiny furrows in her forehead get deeper. She is probably worried that they'll get in trouble or something.

The ambulance people return with a stretcher. "Okay, one, two, three." I feel the shooting pain in my butt as they pick me up, but I try not to yelp anymore.

"Where does it hurt?" asks one of the ambulance attendants.

"In my, um, near my backside, and my left ankle," I explain, trying to be mature.

Inside the ambulance, an attendant puts an oxygen mask over my face. I start to panic. What if I don't wake up? Fresh, hot tears roll down my cheeks. Not waking up would be better than living through this!

The attendant takes a tissue and wipes my face, then secures the oxygen mask, covering my nose. I close my eyes, and listen to the whirring sound of the siren. This is the first time I've ever been in an ambulance.

Suddenly I see Abuela's face before my eyes. She had to be taken to the hospital once, when she fell on the icy sidewalk in her neighborhood. Abuela is going to be so disappointed in me, I think, breathing in the oxygen and drifting off to sleep.

As I'm carted into the Lincoln Hospital Emergency Room, I try to decide who I would least want to see now—Mom, Abuela, or Bubbles. When I wake up and see Mom's face, I finally decide—it's Mom.

The attendant wheels me into a small room with a white curtain. "A nurse will be with you shortly," he says, and leaves. Mom stands next to me until another attendant comes in, and gives me a paper gown to put on. Mom tries to help me get out of my leotard.

"I can't," I scream. The attendant gets some scissors, and starts to cut off my leotard! Tears are streaming down my face.

"Don't cut my shoes!" I beg.

"We won't have to if we can get them off," he replies.

Mom hurriedly unties my pointe shoes. I know she doesn't want to waste the fifty dollars. "No duckets down the bucket," as Bubbles would say. Now I wish Bubbles was here to comfort me.

"Did you call Bubbles?" I ask Mom. I'm happy to see that the rash on her face is clearing up. Still, when I look at her, I see this image of her wearing that scary hockey mask.

"Don't worry about Bubbles now, okay?" Mom says sternly.

My ankle feels like a football. The attendant takes my pointe shoes and cut leotard, and puts them in a paper bag, then staples it closed. "You can get these when she's being released."

"Thank you," Mom tells him.

After the attendant leaves, we sit there in silence. I'm so relieved that Mom doesn't say anything to me while we're waiting for a nurse, doctor, or the Boogie Man to come see me. *Please, somebody come!* I lie there, resigned, with my eyes closed. The throbbing pain doesn't matter anymore. Nothing matters now, because I didn't get into the Junior Corps, and I'll be lucky if anybody ever lets me audition again!

Gracias gooseness, a nurse comes right in and starts poking around. "We have to take some blood samples," she says nicely. "And if you could fill out these forms—and make sure to include your insurance card."

Mom takes the clipboard and starts scribbling stuff.

The nurse takes out the needle and sticks me in the arm. I keep my eyes closed real tight.

Even though I hate needles, I'm not going to show Mom that I'm afraid.

While we're waiting for the doctor to come into the room, I watch the solution dripping into my IV bottle. It puts me into a trance. It seems like a thousand years before the doctor finally comes into the little room to see me.

"Hi, I'm Dr. Reuben," she says, looking at me curtly, then checking the chart at the foot of my bed. "Okay, I see we have swelling in your left ankle. Let me examine it. I'm going to touch your leg and ankle, Chanel, to determine the range of motion. You tell me where it hurts."

Every way the doctor touches, I scream, "Ouch!!!"

"We're going to have to take X rays now, to see if her ankle is broken. Mrs.—"

"Simmons," Mom says.

The doctor then turns me over on my stomach, with the help of the nurse.

"Tell me where it hurts," Dr. Reuben says, moving her hands on different parts of my back.

"Lower," I instruct her. "Ouch!!" I wince, when she touches the top of my backside.

When Dr. Reuben finishes, the nurse informs

Mom, "Just have a seat and wait here until we come back."

Mom sits in a chair, and doesn't even look at me while I'm being wheeled out to the X-ray room. But when I get back, there is a flicker of warmth in Mom's eyes like she is happy to see me.

After the attendant leaves, I moan to Mom, "I didn't do so well at the audition."

"What happened. *Qué pasó?"*

"I don't know," I stutter, then start crying again, which makes me feel so stupid!

After that, Mom doesn't say a word, and I'm staring at the ceiling. It seems like a thousand more years before Doctor Reuben comes back in.

"Okay. From your X rays, Chanel, it looks like you have a broken tailbone and a Grade II ankle sprain in your left ankle. Have you sprained your ankle before?" Dr. Reuben asks me, shoving her hands in the pocket of her lab coat.

"Um, yes—last week, in Houston," I confess. Mom looks at me surprised. "But, it was just a little sprain. Nothing like this."

"That's probably why there is so much inflammation and purple shading," Dr. Reuben continues. "Well, it's going to take six months or longer to heal completely."

"Six months!" I say, squeaking. *Bubbles is gonna kill me!* What about our showcase?

"But, it will improve tremendously after a three- to four-week healing period," Dr. Reuben adds, upon seeing the alarmed look on my face.

"Am I going to be able to dance again?" I ask.

"Once an ankle sprain occurs, the joint itself may never be as strong as it was before the injury. But you'll regain strength in time," Dr. Reuben says. She is a very serious lady, so I can't tell if she is just being nice and trying not to scare me. "Are you a dancer?"

"Yes," I say, and it's hard to believe my own ears. "But not a professional one."

"Well, if all goes well, you'll be able to bear full weight on your ankle within a four-week healing period," Dr. Reuben continues. "The initial treatment is what I call RICE—Rest, Ice, Compression, and Elevation."

I sink into the bed, feeling hopeless. I don't want any RICE treatment!

"You're going to have to apply ice packs to the sprained ankle for thirty-minute periods, every three to four hours," Dr. Reuben tells Mom. "You should also apply compression with an elastic wrap, but don't wrap it so tightly that her circulation is blocked. And while she's resting, elevate the ankle by propping up the leg with pillows."

"What about the tailbone?" I ask, wondering what concoctions Dr. Reuben has for that.

"Oh, there's not much you can do for that. The tailbone is very delicate, and it heals itself naturally. Just put on ice packs and some arnica—rub it on like a balm."

"How long does she have to stay here?" Mom asks.

"She can leave now. She'll be much more comfortable at home. There's no need to keep her here," Dr. Reuben says assuredly.

I don't wanna go home! I want to shriek to Dr. Reuben, but I don't say anything.

"Here are your crutches. You should use them until you can walk without pain," Dr. Reuben says, instructing the nurse to place the crutches near me by the bed.

"Don't you have to wrap her ankle?" Mom asks. I guess she doesn't want the doctor to think she means my tailbone.

How am I going to tell my crew that I broke my tailbone at the audition? I would rather have suffered a head concussion!

"No, Mrs. Simmons. After a few weeks, we're gonna put a brace on it if it doesn't heal properly. It should, though, if she completely stays off it for the first week."

One week in prison. That's all I can think of.

"One more thing," the doctor says, her face growing more serious. "About the dizzy spells you were having? Chanel, have you been going without eating?"

"I . . . well, I . . ." She can tell I have, and so can Mom, who looks at me in horror, her eyes wide. "I didn't want my butt sticking out at the audition. . . ." I say meekly, sounding lame even to myself.

"Chanel, have you ever heard of anorexia?" the doctor asks. When I don't answer, she says, "It's when people starve themselves because they think they're too fat. Now, you are definitely in the normal weight range. You do not need to diet, and you certainly shouldn't be starving yourself. That's why you passed out—and if you'd kept it up much longer, you could have done serious long-term damage to yourself."

"Really?" I say, in a voice so meek it's almost a whisper.

"Really. People die of anorexia, Chanel. Young girls die. Now you've got to get your strength back up. I suggest you eat whenever you're hungry, as long as it's healthy food."

"Yes, ma'am," I say. "I mean, yes, Doctor."

As I am being wheeled out of the emergency room and into a fancy van, all I can think about is what a stupid *babosa* I've been. If I hadn't been so concerned about my butt that I stopped eating, it wouldn't be broken right now. Maybe I'd even be in American Ballet Theatre Junior Corps Division! And my ankle wouldn't look like a purple grapefruit. When that doctor said I could have died, I got really scared, and I'm still shaking as Mom wheels me outside, where a big, fancy van is waiting for us.

"Kashmir arranged for the van," Mom explains to me. I wince. It figures that Mom called Mr. Tycoon for help, and not Daddy.

That's okay. I'm going to call Daddy myself when I get home.

As soon as I'm all propped up in my bed, Bubbles calls—before I get a chance to call Daddy. Mom takes the phone from me, and tells Bubbles to call back tomorrow. I'm so relieved. I know Bubbles will be upset with me when she finds out we won't be able to do our showcase in two weeks for Def Duck Records.

"You can come by tomorrow," Mom explains sternly to Bubbles.

For once I am happy that Mom is related to Puff the Magic Dragon. Nobody can breathe more fire than her—except maybe *Madrina*, Bubbles's mom. . . .

I don't know what time it is when I wake up, but the sun is shining through my bedroom window. I look down, and see that I'm wearing my pink flowered nightgown. Now I remember Mom putting it on me, but that's the last thing I remember. I look over at my alarm clock—the neon numbers say it's 9:00 A.M.

Nine o'clock in the morning! Why didn't anybody wake me up?! Suddenly, when I feel the shooting pain in my lower back, I remember why—because I'm not going to school today.

I can't believe I slept the whole night without waking up! Shaking my head some more, I realize that today is Sunday. There's no school anyway.

Then I smell something cooking in the kitchen, and notice that my stomach is growling really loud.

"Mamí!" I yell.

Pucci peeks his head in the door. "*Mamí* wants to know if you're hungry."

"Yes!" I exclaim. He runs out, without even saying anything nasty. I feel really weak—like I haven't eaten for a thousand years.

Mom comes into the bedroom with breakfast on a tray. I can't remember the last time she did that! "Don't tell me you're not going to eat anything again," Mom huffs. "Remember what that doctor told you."

"Don't worry," I say, biting off a sausage. "I'm going to eat everything on this plate. I've never been so hungry in my whole life!"

"Galleria and her mother are coming over at ten o'clock. After you finish eating, I can bring a pan and some water to give you a sponge bath," Mom says.

"A sponge bath?" I squeal. "I can—" I stop myself, because I realize that I can't, so I just sigh and say, "Okay."

Four sausages, two English muffins, and four scrambled eggs later, Mom gives me a sponge bath, which makes me feel like a little girl again. I feel so humiliated, but I don't want to start crying again.

"I'm going to get better real quick," I say to Mom. She doesn't say anything—not even "I told you so." She didn't want me to try out for the Junior Corps, because she knew I wasn't ready. That's probably why I got so nervous and ruined everything. I feel so stupid now—I probably dieted myself right out of a place in American Ballet Theatre's Junior Corps Division!

"Which nightgown do you want to wear?" Mom asks me.

"The cheetah one," I say with a sigh. If my friends are coming over, I want to let them know I'm still a Cheetah Girl—even if this cheetah is a hurting kitty.

Mom brings in a bucket of ice, to do the ice packs on my ankle and tailbone.

"It's so cold," I say, shivering. "I can't believe I have to do this fifty times a day!"

"You're lucky your ankle isn't broken," is all Mom says, but I know she wants to say more.

Luckily, the doorbell brings. I motion to Mom for her to hurry up.

"Don't worry," she says. "I'm sure they've seen ice packs before!"

For once, I keep my *boca grande* shut. Pucci

opens the door, and I hear everyone talking in the hallway.

"In here!" Mom yells, but Pucci is already bringing them into my bedroom. He comes in first, and stands at the edge of my bed with his box of Pick Up Stix.

Madrina looks even taller than usual. With her big Cheetah hat on her head and high heels, she almost touches the ceiling!

"Chanel, you look swell," *Madrina* says, bending over to kiss me. "We brought you something from all of us."

Bubbles comes from behind her, and puts a big box with a big cheetah bow on top of me on the bed.

"Oooo!" I coo. "What is this?"

"Open it and you'll see," Pucci says, like a smarty-pants.

"He's right, darling," *Madrina* says, sitting on the edge of my bed. "You won't know unless you open it."

Then I see that the rest of the Cheetah Girls are here, too. "Hi, Do' Re Mi!" I exclaim, as Dorinda comes into the room and bends over to kiss me. "Hi, Aqua. Hi, Angie!" The twins come over and kiss me, too.

"Does it hurt?" Bubbles asks.

"Yeah."

"Lemme put some more pillows under your head," Mom says, propping me up some more.

"Gracias, Mamí," I say, intent on unwrapping the bow on the big, beautiful box. "Aaah!" I exclaim when I see the layers of cheetah tissue paper inside.

Inside the box is a tutu covered with cheetah ribbons! "Ooo, this is *tan coolio,*" I say, tears coming to my eyes. "Where did you find this?"

"It's just a tutu," Madrina explains.

"Bubbles and I sewed on the ribbons," Dorinda says, chuckling. "Look underneath, too."

"Oh!" I say, realizing there is more. Under more tissue paper, there is a cheetah leotard! "Ooo!"

"We thought if you want to be a cheetah ballerina—maybe sometimes when we do our shows, you could do ballet moves or something," Dorinda explains carefully.

The tears overflow from my eyes. And I thought my crew would be so mad at me!

"Chuchie, I think that would be sort of cheetah-licious. You know, as usual, the Cheetah Girls are coming with their own flavor. Miss Cuchifrita Ballerina isn't gonna sleep on her leaps," Bubbles says proudly.

"I think it would be dope—you know, we could be leaping at the Leaping Frog," Dorinda explains earnestly.

"But we're not going to be able to do the showcase in two weeks," I say sadly.

"I know." Bubbles sighs, then turns to leave.

"Where ya going?" Pucci asks her.

"I wanna get some Dominican punch—I know Auntie Juanita has made some," Bubbles jokes. Mom's idea of Dominican punch is mixing tropical punch with diet orange soda and root beer. I think it tastes yucky, but Bubbles likes it.

"I'll get it," Pucci volunteers, surprising us all.

"Get me one too, Pucci darling," *Madrina* coos proudly at Pucci. Then she takes my hand and says assuringly, "Don't worry, Chanel. I called Freddy Fudge at Def Duck Records, and told him to push the showcase back by another week. God knows they've done enough quacking about nothing, so one more week isn't going to make a difference in that little pond."

"They're still panting like puppies, don't you worry!" Aqua pipes up, then opens up her Cheetah backpack, and pulls out our Miss

Sassy trophy! "We think you should keep Miss Sassy for a while."

I start boohooing some more. "Thank you. She'll be very happy here. I'm going to put her right next to Mr. Smoochy-Poochy Hugs and Kisses," I coo, pointing to my stuffed dog on the shelf.

"I thought his name was Snuggly Wiggly?" Bubbles says smirking.

"I'm still dizzy, *mija.*"

Everybody smiles at me. I feel so much better, now that I know they care about me.

"If we do the Def Duck showcase in three weeks, do you think they still wanna do it at the Leaping Frog?" I ask *Madrina,* squinching up my nose.

"Why? You don't want it there?" *Madrina* asks, ever the manager.

"Well, if it's okay with you, I would rather not hear the word 'leaping' for a while."

Angie, Aqua, Bubbles, and Dorinda start giggling. "Leapin' lizards, why on earth not?" Aqua asks.

"Because—I don't think I'll be leaping into stardom anytime soon, okay?" I say, giggling.

"No?" Bubbles asks, not believing her ears.

"No," I say, smiling and wiping away my tears. "No pirouettes till payday!"

Bubbles kisses me on the cheeks and says, "Now that's a song, Miss Cuchifrita Ballerina!!!"

Miss Cuchifrita, Ballerina!

Chanel's so swell
'cuz she's got the moves
Plié, sashay
Pirouette till payday!

Plié, sashay
Pirouette 'till hey day.
That's what we say
So don't shout né né
Hey,
Ho,
Go with the flow
And act like you know!

The Cheetah Girls Glossary

Adagio: In Italian it means slow; in ballet class, it refers to slow, stretchy exercises at the barre or in the center which have to do with balance, extension, and long lines in the body.

Allegro: The part of the ballet class when you learn small jumps.

Attitude: Working a situation. In ballet, it's a position in which the working leg is bent, not straight, and may be raised to the front, the side, or the back.

Babosa: Spanish for cuckoo head; idiot.

Barre: The barre is the wooden or metal railing that is either attached to the wall of the classroom or exercise studio, or moved to the center and used as a support. You rest your hand gently on it and don't clutch it for dear life!

Cáyate la boca: Spanish for "Shut your trap!"

Claro que sí!: Spanish for "Of course, you silly nilly."

Clunkheads: Dodo birds. Dunces.

Copyright infringement: When you bite someone else's flavor—like their music or lyrics—and act like it's your own—without giving them credit or duckets.

Corra, corra!: Run like a hyena!

Ding, ding: Exactly, duncehead.

Down in the Dumpster: Sad.

Gracias gooseness: Thank goodness.

Grand allegro: The large, diagonal combination at the end of ballet class where the jumps get more "grand," or bigger.

Extension: Hair weave; in ballet, it refers to how high you can lift your leg in movements like *battements* and *developpé*.

Howdy do: A common greeting in Houston that really means, "Wazzup?"

La culpa mía: Spanish for "my fault" or "my boo-boo."

Mackin': Sweatin' or swooning for someone or even daydreamin' about them all the time.

Mariposa negra: Black Butterfly.

Párate!: Spanish for "Stop, you cuckoo bird!"

Perpetrate: To do something shady or pretend that you're something you aren't.

Petit allegro: Any jump in ballet from one leg to another.

Pirouette till payday: Dancing till the duckets fall from the sky.

Pliés: Deep knee bends as performed in ballet warm-up exercises.

Port de bras: How you move your arms in different positions in ballet class.

Silly mono: Silly monkey. As in, "Stop acting like a silly *mono*!"

Terminado: Spanish for "finished." Kaput.

Tight: Dope. Brilliant.

Youston: The way some peeps down south pronounce "Houston."

Dorinda Gets a Groove

For my Hollywood peeps, Walter Franks,
who puts duckets in the banks
while always giving thanks
to the creator and initiator
of his theatrical flow,
which makes imitators take notice
of his comedy show
and act like they know
that this is one hot dog
who ain't full of beans and schemes
in the land of dreams!

Chapter 1

Today is the first day Chanel is out of her house since her ballerina audition, when she broke her tailbone and sprained her ankle. I can tell she is so excited she could do a pirouette right here on Thirty-ninth Street. I don't know how Chanel managed to stay home for a week—getting ice packs on her butt and resting with her ankle elevated on a pillow—because she can be really restless. I mean, Chanel probably has more energy than all the dancers in the American Ballet Theatre put together! Of course, now that she's really messed up her ankle, the doctor says the only pirouettes she'll be doing are in her daydreams.

Well, Chanel's not the only one glad to be out of the house. When I left for school this morning, I heard my foster mother, Mrs. Bosco, talking on the phone with someone down at the foster care agency. So I know something is about to go down, and I'm in no hurry to go home and find out what it is. See, with ten foster brothers and sisters, there is *always* some new drama unfolding at my house.

Right now, though, we're waiting outside this fancy-schmancy restaurant for Ms. Dorothea, who is Galleria's mom, Chanel's godmother, *and* the Cheetah Girls' manager. I guess you could say we are triple lucky. The Cheetah Girls, of course, is the name of our singing group—but we are as tight as a crew can be: besides little ole me—Dorinda "Do' Re Mi" Rogers—there's our ringleader, Galleria "Bubbles" Garibaldi; Chanel "Chuchie" Simmons (also known as Miss Cuchifrita Ballerina); and the "boostin' Houston twins," Aquanette and Anginette Walker.

We're getting together tonight because Ms. Dorothea is treating us to dinner. She knows how hard it's been for Chanel to stay off her feet—and for us, too, because we can't rehearse until Chanel gets better.

Looking up at the awning, I try to pronounce the restaurant's name but keep bumbling the last word. *"Le Kosher Cha-too?"*

"No, Do', it's Cha*teau*—as in 'act like you *know*,'" Galleria says, with emphasis, so I'll get the drift. "Mom must be pulling a Rapunzel, and weaving the fabrics herself on a loom," she hisses in between loud pops of bubble gum—the habit that earned Bubbles her nickname to the max.

Ms. Dorothea left early this morning to shop for fabrics for her spring collection. See, Ms. Dorothea has this dope boutique, called Toto in New York . . . Fun in Diva Sizes, down in SoHo near where Chanel lives. Ms. Dorothea is definitely my inspiration, because I love designing clothes—as much as I love dancing and being in the Cheetah Girls.

"Miss Cuchifrita Ballerina, are you getting tired?" Galleria asks, concerned. We gave Chanel her second nickname *before* her pirouette caper backfired and landed her in the emergency room. See, when we got back from Houston, Chanel decided to give her ballerina moves a test run by auditioning for the Junior Corps Division of American Ballet Theatre. She got so nervous at the audition, though, that she went leaping across the floor and landed right on her back!

I think Chanel is relieved that she has to hang up her pointe shoes for good, because now she has to face the fact that she's stuck with *us*. I mean, we're *all* kinda scared about being in a singing group. It's not an easy-breezy ride on Hit Records Street, you know—it's a lot harder than we thought it was gonna be.

"Coming through, ladies, coming through!" yells this big, gruffy guy, startling me out of my thoughts. I turn to see Mr. Gruffy and two other tough-looking men, all wearing the same blue jumpsuit uniform and wheeling a huge cart filled with big rolls of fabric right in our direction.

Aqua is so busy gabbing to her sister, Angie, that she isn't paying attention. I push her aside gently, so she won't get knocked off the sidewalk and end up with "street gravy" splattered all over her nice powder-blue skirt and white blouse.

The men roll past us like they're maneuvering a Mack truck in a war zone. I turn to the twins and chuckle, "Now you *know* we're back in New York."

"You're sure enough right, Miss Dorinda," Aqua says, rolling her eyes in the direction of the "three gruffateers."

I look up at all the gloomy gray buildings with dusty windows and wonder what the people inside are doing—cutting patterns, sewing on sleeves, fitting clothes on mannequin figures. See, this is the heart of the Garment District, and buyers from all over the world come here to see what the Big Apple has to offer in the fashion department. Yup, the Big Apple has got it like that.

When I look down, I see a big cheetah hat sticking up from the crowd of people rushing to get home from work. "There she is!" I say to Galleria, pointing down the block. "I can spot your mom's spots anywhere."

When she gets close, I can see that Ms. Dorothea's face is shiny with perspiration. "Sorry I'm late, darlings, but I've just been haggling for dear life with these sales reps. You wouldn't believe what they were trying to charge for wool—*blend*." Ms. Dorothea takes a deep breath.

"Hi, *Madrina*!" Chanel says excitedly. She bends over to kiss her godmother, while trying to balance her pink plastic pocketbook and pair of crutches at the same time. Chanel loves purses, but I love the cheetah backpacks Ms. Dorothea gave all of us when we became the Cheetah Girls. That's what I always carry when I'm rolling.

"Hi, *Madrina*," yells Pucci, Chanel's younger brother, who has also come along for the supa-dupa dinner.

"Hello, Pucci. After you, Monsieur and Mademoiselle," says Ms. Dorothea. She opens the door of the restaurant, and makes a grand gesture with her arm for Pucci and Chanel to enter first—like they're Prince Charming and Cinderella walking down the red carpet to the Ball. I guess it is kinda special, since this is the first time the Cheetah Girls have all been out together since we got back from Houston.

"This is really nice!" Pucci exclaims when we walk inside. Ms. Dorothea picked this restaurant, and she has diva-size taste, if you know what I'm saying.

"Juanita, I think you're going to owe me one after this," Ms. Dorothea says to Chanel's mom,

Mrs. Simmons, who has also been invited for dinner. I can tell Ms. Dorothea is really proud of her restaurant selection.

Pucci looks so cute, strutting ahead of me in his three-piece burgundy corduroy suit. "Pucci, you look really nice," I exclaim, gently touching his shoulder.

"This is the suit *Madrina* gave me for my birthday," Pucci says proudly, sticking out his chest like a peacock.

"I love pinwale," I say, rubbing his shoulder and looking admiringly at Ms. Dorothea. We both could spend hours looking at fabrics and touching them.

"But I'm not a pin-whale!" Pucci blurts back at me, grinning, then looks at Galleria for approval. I can tell Pucci really likes Galleria, and really looks up to her in the snaps department.

"I know, Pucci," I say, humoring him. "I was talking about the fabric—pinwale means small-ribbed corduroy."

"*I* know that," Pucci shoots back, raising his left eyebrow and cocking his head.

"You did not," Galleria says, rubbing his bald head. Pucci's head really does look like a pool ball, now that he's had it shaved clean again.

As the hostess shows us to our table, I can't help but notice that we look, well, different from the other people in the restaurant—and that's not because of Chanel's crutches, if you know what I'm saying. Ms. Dorothea doesn't seem to notice, because she waltzes by the tables with her head held so high it almost touches the ceiling. She's like the head cheetah in an empty desert—there's no way she could hide her spots! I wish I was tall like her—then everybody would respect me, too. I guess I'm still a cub, because I put my head down as we walk by this big round table, with ladies wearing pearl necklaces and matching earrings. Then I shove my hands in my jacket, and fidget with my fingers inside the deep pockets.

The hostess seats us at a big round table, too, with a nice white linen tablecloth—not paper or plastic, okay? I get nervous again, because I don't want to spill anything on it. Even the napkins are linen. I wonder how they keep everything so clean. Daintily unfolding the linen napkin, I place it carefully over my lap. Chanel taught me that little "magic trick." Well, it was a magic trick to me, because I didn't have any table manners until the rest of the Cheetah

Girls taught me how to "slice on the nice tip"!

I glance at the table next to us and notice that the boys are wearing some sort of beanies on their heads. I wonder what those are? Then I look around and notice that almost *all* the boys in the restaurant are wearing the *same* thing on their heads, pinned in place with bobby pins.

Angie and Aqua whisper something to each other, which is probably why Ms. Dorothea pipes up. "I wanted to treat you girls to something different. This is what you call a kosher French restaurant."

We all look at each other, and I can tell that none of us knows what she's talking about. At least Pucci has the nerve to speak up. "How come all the boys are wearing those things on their heads?"

Ms. Dorothea chuckles at Pucci, so I relax into my chair. "Those are yarmulkes, Pucci. It's a sign of reverence for males of the Jewish faith to wear them in public."

"Oh," Pucci replies, then shrugs his shoulders. "How come the girls don't wear them, too?"

"That's a good question, and one I don't know the answer to," Ms. Dorothea explains, smiling at the lady next to us with all the kids.

Now that Pucci has broken the ice, I decide to ask a question too. "So, um, what does kosher mean?"

"Well, it means that the restaurant serves food according to Jewish dietary laws, such as, they don't serve meat and dairy products in the same meal, or sometimes not even in the same restaurant, and the meat is only from birds, or animals that have split hooves and chew their cud, like cows—but definitely not pigs."

We all look at Ms. Dorothea like she's suddenly become a farmer.

"You mean like giraffes, too?" Pucci asks giggling.

"Exactly, Pucci—except I don't think you'll find any giraffe dishes on the menu. But you will find duck, steak, bison."

I wonder what a bison is, but I'm certainly not going to ask. I'll look it up tomorrow in school. As if reading my mind, though, Ms. Dorothea adds quickly, "Bison, of course, is buffalo meat."

"Buffalo meat?" Pucci says, squinching up his nose. "Yuck."

Mrs. Simmons throws Pucci a look.

"Nonetheless, you will find the food quite

fabulous here," Ms. Dorothea says, looking over her menu at Mrs. Simmons.

Taking her cue, we each pick up our menus and gaze upon the goodies. *Everything on the menu is in French!* I realize, staring at the type and panicking, until I look closer and notice that the English version is in tiny letters below each selection. Whew! I sure wasn't gonna try to pronounce anything to the waiter in French, if you know what I'm saying.

"So, Chanel, how are you feeling?" Ms. Dorothea asks her goddaughter.

"Fine! I'm so happy to be out of the house!" Chanel says cheerfully.

"I caught her trying to do leg lifts in the exercise studio this morning," Mrs. Simmons announces to all of us.

"Keep it up and you won't be able to perform in the Def Duck showcase that I'm setting up—again," Ms. Dorothea warns her. See, when Chanel sprained her ankle, we had to postpone doing a showcase for the East Coast executives at Def Duck Records. Ms. Dorothea was gonna hook us up with a showcase at the Leaping Frog Lounge downtown.

"So, Dorinda—how's your sister, Tiffany?"

Ms. Dorothea suddenly asks me. Now why did she have to bring that up? See, not too long ago, I didn't even know I had a half sister named Tiffany. She and I have the same birth mother, but Tiffany was adopted as a baby, and I was sent to foster care. Then, last month, Tiffany came and found me—and now I'm not sure I want to deal with this new drama, you know what I'm saying?

"Oh, she's okay," I say quickly, then change the subject back again and fidget with the menu. "When are we going to do that Cheetah Girls showcase, Ms. Dorothea?"

"As soon as Chanel's able to walk on stage without a crutch. Don't worry—the A&R people are panting like puppies over the idea." Ms. Dorothea sips from her glass with a satisfied smirk. *She* was the one who thought of approaching Def Duck Records with the idea of putting together a showcase, so the East Coast executives could get a whiff of our flavor. Then maybe they'll be motivated to put us in the studio with big-cheese producer Mouse Almighty—the man who holds the key to our future. See, if such an important producer picks the right tracks for us, then we sound good—

and if we sound good, then the tracks will test well, and Def Duck will give us a record deal—that's what I'm talking about.

"I sure hope Chanel's ankle heals fast," I say, chuckling. Then I get embarrassed, because I don't want her to think I'm being insensitive about her situation. Chanel and I are really tight, you know what I'm saying? I smile at her, and she smiles back, so I guess everything's cool.

"Don't you worry, Do' Re Mi, I'm gonna be back in Cheetah Girl form in no time," Chanel says, then looks cautiously at her mother. "You'll see, *Mamí*."

Uh-oh. I hope we're not going to spin *that* record again. See, Chanel's mom is looking for any reason to yank her out of the Cheetah Girls because she doesn't approve of this whole girl-group thing. She thinks we'll ruin our futures or something.

Luckily, something catches Mrs. Simmons's attention. I turn to see what she's looking at—it's the waiter, who has returned and is ready to take our orders.

Afterward, the conversation turns back to the Cheetah Girls—only this time, it's Ms.

Dorothea who's bringing in the noise. "Have you girls heard any more ruckus from that group in Houston?" she asks innocently as we chomp on our food.

"What group?" Mrs. Simmons asks, concerned. *Uh-oh.* Judging from the way Chanel is squirming in her chair, I guess she didn't tell her mother about what happened. Why would she?

We all look at each other, and finally Galleria realizes that someone is gonna have to fill Mrs. Simmons in on the showdown that took place at the Okie-Dokie Corral. "See, Auntie Juanita, we performed with this group called Cash Money Girls, in the Miss Sassy-sparilla contest, and they said that we stole the words from *their* song for *our* song," she explains.

Mrs. Simmons daintily cuts her meat with a knife and fork, and I can tell that she is trying not to say anything. I watch her closely, and cut my steak the same way, but I guess I'm trying too hard, because one of the little red beans flies off the plate and plops onto the pretty white tablecloth! "Sorry," I say, my face turning red. Now I don't know if I'm supposed to pick up the bean or just leave it there.

Chanel beats me to it, sticking her fork into it

and plopping it back on my plate. "It's okay, *mija*," she whispers, then winks at me.

"Copyright infringement. Hmm," Mrs. Simmons finally says.

"Well, I guess you girls learned a new word in your vocabulary—plagiarism." Ms. Dorothea chuckles, then winks.

I know she's right. Galleria and Chanel should have known better than to crib another group's lyrics—'cuz it just looks like we're trying to bite *their* flavor.

All of a sudden, the twins let out a scream in unison: "*AAAAHHH!*" Aqua lifts her feet in the air and looks over in the corner. "We just saw a mouse run by!"

"A mouse?" Mrs. Simmons asks in disbelief.

"*Sí*—a mouse, I saw it too!" Chanel shrieks.

I just sit quiet and be chill. I've seen a lot of mice up in the projects where I live, so I'm not afraid of them at all—but it is kinda strange that a mouse would be hanging out in a nice restaurant like this, you know what I'm saying?

The hostess and the waiter scurry over to our table with a million apologies. "We are terribly sorry. We can't believe that happened. Are you okay?"

"We're fine, darlings," Ms. Dorothea says, trying to take control of the situation.

"Well, please—desserts and after-dinner drinks will be complimentary," the hostess says.

After we accept, Galleria quips, "I wonder if that was Mouse Almighty, trying to find us some tracks for our test demo!"

"I wish it was!" Aqua says, trying not to act scared anymore. "Then at least we could offer *him* a complimentary dessert, too!"

Chapter 2

Even though it's already dark by the time I hit the courtyard in front of my building, Ms. Keisha is still sitting there with her children, Pookie and Tamela. I can see Ms. Keisha's pink-flowered housecoat peeking out from under her gray plaid overcoat, and her pink bedroom slippers are so fluffy it looks like she's wearing Martian-sized marshmallows on her feet. As I walk up to the bench they're sitting on, I can feel a bad case of the squigglies coming on, because I know she is dying to tell me *something*.

"Betty sure has her hands full now," Ms. Keisha starts in on her story. Betty is the first name of my foster mother, Mrs. Bosco, who doesn't like Ms. Keisha a whole lot. "You didn't come home today after school, did you?" Ms. Keisha asks, but I can tell she already knows the answer.

"No I didn't. 'Member Ms. Dorothea, our manager?"

"Yeah—that lady who was up here dressed like a tiger, at your 'adoption' party—I mean, well you know what I mean," Ms. Keisha says loudly.

"She wears cheetah stuff," I correct her, my cheeks burning from embarrassment. It figures Ms. Keisha found out that my 'adoption' didn't go through.

"Um, she took us out to dinner to this fancy restaurant, and some mouse decided to get in on the action, too," I babble, because I'm scared about what Ms. Keisha is gonna tell me.

"At least he didn't go home hungry—'cuz he sure wouldn't have found anything to eat in my house!" Ms. Keisha snarkles like a hyena. Then Tamela and Pookie let out little hyena snarkles, which is kinda scary, because they sound just like their mother.

"Well, you got a new sister," Ms. Keisha pipes up, finally getting to the point of this joint.

Now I've got a pain in my chest. How does Ms. Keisha know about Tiffany? I can't believe Mrs. Bosco told her! Now Ms. Keisha will tell everybody in the projects that I have an adopted sister! I'll bet Mrs. Bosco invited Tiffany over here behind my back, so she can see how messy and tiny our apartment is!

"You should have seen that child crying—she cried all the way upstairs," Ms. Keisha says, nodding her head.

Why would Tiffany be crying? Why was she *here*? Well, I guess it figures that she would be a big crybaby. She probably gets her way all the time, what with her parents living over on Park Avenue.

"Annie Buckus in 3C says that's the same child that was on the news last week. That's what she said, all right." Ms. Keisha folds her hands in her lap and rocks back and forth. When she sees the alarmed look on my face, she quickly babbles, "I don't know how Annie could remember something like that, but she swears it's the same child. But you know Annie—she never gets anything right."

"Yeah," I say, completely dumbfounded. What could be wrong with Tiffany that she would be on the news?

"'Member when Gus got robbed across the street, and Annie swore up and down she saw the guy—and that he was a big ole tall guy with an Afro? When the police caught the thief, he looked like a little beady-eyed raccoon—he wasn't nothing like Annie said!"

"No, I don't remember that," I respond, but I'm not really listening to Ms. Keisha. I'm lost in my own thoughts, trying to catch my breath, because it feels like somebody is standing on my chest or something.

"Yeah—that's right, you was too young to 'member that. You're so mature, sometimes I forget you're just a little bitty thing," Ms. Keisha says, chuckling.

I wish Ms. Keisha wouldn't call me little. I *hate* being called little—but now I've gotta find out what's going on, so I ask her nicely, "What was the girl on television for?"

"Annie says that they found the child wandering by herself in Coney Island, over there in Brooklyn. Now you know her mother went and left her there. The child was sitting on the bench wailing for so long, that finally one of the security guards took her to the police station."

Ms. Keisha wraps her coat tighter around her chest. "She got a West Indian accent, too. I could tell, even though she was carrying on and screaming all the way to the elevator."

Now I think Ms. Keisha doesn't know what she's talking about. At least, not Tiffany. "Um, what did the girl look like?" I ask hesitantly.

"Oh, little ole thing with pigtails and a big pout on her face," Ms. Keisha responds.

"Her sneakers were dirty!" Tamela blurts out. "They had holes in them, too."

"Hush up, Tamela—the poor child was probably scared to death, and all you talking about is her sneakers!

Now I *know* she isn't talking about Tiffany. I feel so relieved! "Well, I'd better be going," I say, turning so red I can't even look at Pookie and Tamela.

Ms. Keisha yells after me, "Dorinda, let me know tomorrow if it's the same child Annie saw on the news."

"Oh, right," I say, but now I'm wondering what really is going on upstairs. This must have something to do with what Mrs. Bosco was talking about on the phone this morning.

When I open the apartment door, Twinkie

greets me as usual. Her blond, fuzzy hair is plopping all over the place, and her cheeks are more red than usual. "We got a new sister," she whispers to me, grabbing my arm. "Mr. Bosco is home, too."

I feel the squigglies in my stomach again. I should have known Ms. Keisha was right. She seems to be the only one around here who knows what's going on—because I sure don't!

"That's her," Twinkie says, pointing into the living room at this sad, pouty-faced girl. "She doesn't like us. I don't think she wants to be here."

Neither do I, shrieks a voice inside me, but I give Twinkie a hug and whisper back, "Don't say that, Twinkie. Don't you remember how sad you were when you came here?"

Twinkie nods, and says, "You let me eat all your pretzels."

"That's right," I chuckle. Twinkie's real name is Rita. She has lived with Mrs. Bosco for almost two years, and we have grown very close. I don't know what I would do if I didn't have Twinkie's fat cheeks to squeeze every day. But now I have to deal with this new situation. Why didn't Mrs. Bosco ask *me* if I wanted another foster sister? Nobody ever asks me anything!

I heave a deep sigh and walk into the living room. My foster brothers Nestor and Khalil are helping Mrs. Bosco fold the laundry. One good thing about Mrs. Bosco is, she makes the boys do as much housework as the girls, or they don't get to go outside and play.

Mr. Bosco is sitting on the end of the couch that isn't covered with clothes. I wonder why he isn't at work, even though he is wearing his security-guard uniform.

"Hi, Mr. Bosco," I say, trying to act normal. See, I'm not used to seeing him that much, because he's either working, sleeping, or hanging out at the Lenox Café down the block, where he can smoke his cigarettes in peace. Mr. Bosco isn't allowed to smoke in the living room, and sometimes I hear Mrs. Bosco fussing with him to clean the butts out of the ashtray in their bedroom.

"Oh, you got yourself a nice bag for school," Mr. Bosco says to me as I drop my cheetah backpack on the floor.

"Yeah," I reply. "Ms. Dorothea, um, the manager of the Cheetah Girls, gave it to me." I already told him where I got it, but I know he has a lot of stuff on his mind.

I wish Mr. Bosco would keep talking, so I could avoid dealing with the situation at hand, but he's gone back to watching TV.

"See the new butterfly I made?" Twinkie says to Mr. Bosco, holding up a butterfly she cut out of paper. She loves butterflies more than anything.

"That's nice—lemme see that," he says, and Twinkie moves closer.

I wish I could fly a million miles away, like one of Twinkie's butterflies. Without seeming obvious, I glance over at the new girl. She is sitting frozen like an angry statue on the faded orange couch. Her pretty face is covered with dried tears, and her eyebrows are squinched into a scowl. She is a real pretty caramel color, and I can tell, even though it's kinda dark in the living room, that her skin is smooth, and she doesn't have any scars on her face. She looks well taken care of—unlike Kenya. When Kenya first came here, her whole face was covered with white spots and scabs. The doctor said it was from a vitamin deficiency.

Suddenly I realize I'm staring, so I look away, just as part of the chocolate-chip cookie the new girl is holding in her hand drops on the floor.

"She doesn't want the cookie—I'll take it!"

volunteers Kenya, trying to take the rest of the cookie out of the girl's hand. The girl lets out a piercing scream.

"Kenya, I've told you to please leave her alone!" Mrs. Bosco snaps in her gruff, cracked voice.

I go over and pick the cookie crumbs off the floor, right by the girl's legs. Looking up at her, I smile and say, "Hi."

But she doesn't respond. She sits like a stone, and stares at me with her big, black, intense eyes, which are filled with so many feelings that it almost scares me.

"Dorinda, can you come in the kitchen for a second?" Mrs. Bosco says suddenly, getting out of her chair and picking up a pile of kitchen towels.

"Okay," I say, following her into the kitchen, and waiting to hear what she has to say.

"Gaye is going to be staying with us for—I don't know how long," Mrs. Bosco starts in, stuffing the hand towels into the kitchen drawer. Then she pauses, like she's uncomfortable. "So I guess you got yourself a new sister."

I don't want another sister! I shriek inside, but I hear myself say, "Okay."

"They found her wandering around in

Coney Island," Mrs. Bosco continues. "Nobody seems to know how she got there, or nothing. I know we don't have the room, but we'll just have to make do."

"Ms. Keisha says somebody saw her—um, *Gaye*—on the news," I tell her.

"Well, she's probably right, 'cuz if anybody knows everybody's business, it's Ms. Keisha."

Suddenly, I feel so sad for little Gaye. I remember when a strange lady came and took me from Mrs. Parkay's house—the first home I remember—without telling me why.

"I'll see you soon," Mrs. Parkay said to me, and waved good-bye. Even though I was only five, I remember thinking she was lying, because she had packed up all my clothes and handed them to the lady, who told me to get into her car. I remember asking the lady why my foster sister Jazmine wasn't coming with us. Now I know why, of course—Mrs. Parkay gave me away, and Jazmine wasn't my real sister—but someone named Tiffany is!

My legs feel weak, like spaghetti—so I sit down at the kitchen table.

"Are you okay, Dorinda?" Mrs. Bosco asks me.

"Yeah, I'm okay. How come Mr. Bosco didn't

go to work?" I ask, curious.

"Oh, he wanted to help out with Gaye and all. She was carrying on like a hurricane." Mrs. Bosco wipes her forehead with a tissue. "But she done settled down now, so he's gonna go to work late."

Suddenly I feel tears trickling down my cheeks. Mrs. Bosco is silent, then tells me, "Dorinda, we'll get through. She'll be all right. We'll *all* be all right."

"Yeah," I reply, wiping away the tears.

I sure hope so. But I can't help thinking of my half sister Tiffany, who was lucky enough to get adopted, and by rich folks, at that. Why do some people have all the luck, and others —like me and Gaye—have none?

Chapter 3

Going to school in the morning is a big production in my house on a *normal* day. But today, everybody is on edge, because our new foster sister Gaye stayed up the whole night crying. She is sitting at the table, staring at her breakfast, and I don't think there is much hope of getting her to eat it.

"Here," Mrs. Bosco says, placing a bowl of ice cream in front of her. It reminds me that Mrs. Bosco gave me ice cream the first day I came to live here, too.

At first, Gaye just stares at the bowl. Then, slowly, she picks up her spoon and starts fiddling with it. Finally, she starts wolfing down spoonfuls of ice cream.

"Why can't I have some?" Kenya asks, moaning like a big baby.

"No, Kenya. Can ya just eat your breakfast?" Mrs. Bosco snaps.

"Kenya, can ya please just shut up!" snipes Nestor.

"That's enough, Nestor," Mrs. Bosco says, then stands over Kenya. "I found some candy wrappers in your pants pocket when I was doing the laundry. Keep it up and you won't have a tooth left in your—"

Mrs. Bosco stops talking because the phone is ringing. Maybe someone from the agency is calling, because they found out more about Gaye's mother or something.

"Yes! Hi, Tiffany," Mrs. Bosco says warmly into the receiver.

Oh, no, not Tiffany! Why is she calling here before school?

"Yes, you just caught her," Mrs. Bosco says. "Uh-huh. Uh-huh. She's gotta leave by seven-fifteen to get to school on time—you know, with the trains and all. Uh-huh. Uh-huh. Uh-huh."

What is Tiffany gonna do, talk Mrs. Bosco's ear off? Finally, Mrs. Bosco hands me the receiver, even though I wish I could do a Houdini and disappear.

"Hi, Dorinda—remember me?" Tiffany asks, then lets out a nervous giggle.

"Of course I remember you," I respond, even though I can hear how stupid it sounds. I wonder if Tiffany's parents know she's running up their phone bill. They probably wouldn't care, with all the money they have.

"Well, I hadn't heard from you, so I thought I would give you a call. What's the deal-io?" Tiffany asks, giggling again.

"Um, nothing," I say, noticing that Tiffany is trying to talk like me.

"Um, I was wondering if you wanted to meet today after school?"

"Well, I'm not sure—I have to check and see if we have rehearsal today—you know, my group, the Cheetah Girls." I turn to see if Mrs. Bosco is within earshot, and she is—so I turn my back to her quickly.

"Um, I've gotta go to school now, so I can meet Chanel and Galleria," I say, hoping Tiffany will get off the phone.

"Oh, okay—so, you'll let me know if you can come over after school?" Tiffany is like a dog with a bone who won't leave it alone.

"Come over?" I ask, surprised.

"Yeah—my parents won't be here, and we can just hang out. 'Member I told you I wanted you to play my new keyboard?" Tiffany says, like she's dangling a carrot.

"Um, I don't know how to play keyboard," I say, unsure.

"It's fun—I'll show you," Tiffany says, not taking no for an answer.

"Um—I'll call you later and let you know."

After I hang up the phone, I wolf down the rest of my cereal, but Mrs. Bosco is staring at me. "You know, it's one thing when family leaves you, but it's another when they *find* you. You don't look a gift horse in the mouth, Dorinda—just check to make sure it has hooves."

I'm sure this is another one of Mrs. Bosco's Southern expressions. Thanks to her and the twins, I know a lot of them now—except for this one.

"I didn't say I wasn't going to see her," I protest, wiping the milk from the corner of my mouth with a paper napkin.

"I heard you tell that poor child that you have rehearsal. How you gonna rehearse when one of you has lost a hoof?" Mrs. Bosco snaps.

I chuckle involuntarily. Mrs. Bosco is funny sometimes, and she doesn't even know it. Now I feel stupid for telling a lie in front of her.

My brother Topwe drops his bowl on the floor, and I'm so relieved for the distraction. "I'll get it."

Topwe coughs, spitting a mouthful of cereal onto the table.

"Cover your mouth next time," Mrs. Bosco says softly.

"His cough doesn't sound good," I say, concerned. Topwe was born HIV-positive. Now he's seven, but he still gets bad colds sometimes.

"I'm gonna keep him home from school today," Mrs. Bosco says, like she has just decided it. "Dorinda, before you leave, get me the number for his school."

I dial the number for Mrs. Bosco and hand her the phone instead. This way I can leave without talking any more about Tiffany.

When I open the door downstairs in the lobby, I accidentally step in something really mushy and disgusting, that almost makes me slip. Someone has taken the garbage out of the cans and strewn it all over the courtyard—

again. During the night, a lot of homeless people tear open the garbage bags that sit tied and ready for collection.

Once I close the door, I notice that our super, Mr. Hammer, is behind the railing trying to clean up some of the strewn garbage.

"We're gonna get another ticket from the Sanitation Department," Mr. Hammer says gruffly, shaking his head in disgust. "I don't know why they don't just take the cans and sell them, instead of going through all the garbage and making this mess. Say, how's that computer working, Dorinda?" Mr. Hammer yells after me.

"Still clicking!" I say, smiling back. Last year, right after Christmas, someone threw out this really good computer, and Mr. Hammer fixed it up and gave it to me. It makes doing my homework a lot easier, and now I can talk to my crew on the Internet, you know what I'm saying? That reminds me, I was supposed to go online last night and say good night to Chanel, but I forgot, with all the drama going on in my house.

The trains are running on time—which is good, because I want to get to school early, so I can help Chanel if she needs it. Today is her first day back at school since her accident, and she may have a hard time getting around.

When I finally get to school, I head for the lockers, where I meet my crew before homeroom. A whole bunch of people are there, crowded around Chanel. I should have known she would be milking her crutches for points. She smiles at me like she's in a beauty contest, and stands there posing by the lockers, like she's holding a pair of designer crutches or something.

"Hey, wazzup?" I say to Galleria, since Chanel is busy holding court.

Before Galleria even says hello, she shoves a newspaper right in my face. "My mom saved this for us from the newspaper, so we could see it when we got back from Houston," she says, smirking.

My stomach flutters as I read the article with Galleria. Chanel stops holding court to join us, and balances herself by leaning on my shoulder. I read the article out loud, while Galleria looks over one of my shoulders and Chanel leans on the other one:

"'A copyright infringement suit was filed in L.A. on November 15 against pop star Kahlua Alexander, 19, by songwriter Mon' E Richardz.

Richardz claims that Alexander's song "Plucked by Def Duck" borrows too heavily from one of his own, "Goose on the Loose," recorded by In the Dark on 1999's *Struck by a Monkey Cane.* The lawsuit claims Alexander wrongfully gave songwriting credit to herself and producer Mouse Almighty, a.k.a. Sean Johnson. Richardz seeks undisclosed damages. Alexander's publicist contends, "Several musicologists have stated there is no copyright infringement. Kahlua, Mon' E, and Def Duck Records did not copy the song."'"

"Wow—a musicologist. That sounds deep, right?" Galleria riffs. "See, this goes to show it's not so easy to call something copyright infringement right out of the box."

"What does 'undisclosed damages' mean?" I ask, still staring at the article.

"A lot of duckets in the bucket, that's for sure," Galleria says, like she's an expert. "That's what my mom says. I bet Mon' E Richardz would probably settle for whatever royalty juice he could squeeze out of Kahlua's songwriting oranges, huh?"

"I guess," I say, not really sure.

"Mom says a lot of artists fight over this all

the time. But it costs a lot of money to sue somebody, because then you've got to prove that they stole your flavor." Galleria ponders for a moment. "I guess it wouldn't hurt if we tried to write original songs in the future, though."

Wow—that's the first time I heard Galleria say "we." I wonder if she means that she and Chanel will be writing another song together. Not that I'm asking, okay?

"Then again, being in the studio with Mouse Almighty singing *anybody's* songs would be like music to my ears," Galleria says, heaving a deep sigh.

"I hear that," I moan. "I wish we could start rehearsing again."

"*I* wish we could go to Mariah Carey's concert tomorrow," Chanel moans.

"Well, we don't have Mariah Carey money for the tickets—I mean, fifty duckets in the bucket is kinda steep, *mamacita,*" Galleria counters.

"I hear that," I moan again. "I'd love to go to see Mariah Carey, too, you know what I'm saying? But I'm not paying!"

We crack up, and help Chanel go upstairs to her homeroom. Galleria and Chanel are in the same homeroom class, since they both major in Fashion Merchandising. I major in Fashion Design, so I have to go to the fourth floor by myself.

"How come you didn't log on to the chat room last night?" Chuchie asks me, still hanging on my shoulder.

"I couldn't," I answer softly. I guess it's time to tell my crew about Gaye. I take a deep breath, and tell them everything that's happened so far.

"You mean someone just left her by herself in the *street*?" Chanel asks in disbelief.

"Yeah—I guess so," I say, shrugging my shoulders. "Mrs. Bosco says the police have put up flyers all around Coney Island, where she was found, but nobody has come forward with any information."

Chanel gets tears in her eyes, so I pull out a tissue, just in case she needs it.

Galleria puts out her hand and does the Cheetah Girls handshake with me, but she seems dazed and confused, too. "Maybe someone will come and get her. If not, maybe *we* can figure something out."

"Maybe." I part ways with my crew. Taking the stairway up to the fourth floor, I think about what Galleria said. If anyone could track down a missing person, it would definitely be Bubbles. I mean, when the twins' uncle Skeeter was missing while we were in Houston, *she's* the one who figured out how to find him—or else he might have stayed missing for a whole lot longer. Maybe we *could* find Gaye's mother. On the other hand, what's the use of finding a mother who doesn't want her?

By the time I get to my last class of the day—sociology—I've forgotten all about my problems at home. That is, until the teacher, Mrs. Garber, tells us our class project: "Although most of you were born in this country, you'll discover that many of your great-grandparents, or even your grandparents, weren't. I want you to create a time line for one of your parents, tracing their origins, and making them parallel whatever historical events were happening in this country at the time. You don't have to account for every year of your parent's life, but most of them." Mrs. Garber draws a diagram of a time line on the board, and puts years next to the lines on the graph.

I can't do this! I want to yell. *I don't even know*

where my parents are! I don't even know who *they are*!

Mrs. Garber isn't finished giving me a headache. "After the time line, I want you to write an essay about your parent's migration pattern—describing in detail why they moved, what city in the United States they moved to, and what year. Don't go overboard, giving every detail of your parent's life. For example, we don't want to know what your mother ate for breakfast on the day you were born, okay?"

Some of the students in the class laugh at Mrs. Garber's joke. I just want to cry. I'll bet they know what their mother had for breakfast on the day they were born. I don't even know *where* I was born. Sinking into my chair, I just wish I could do a Houdini and disappear on the spot. How am I supposed to find out all this stuff, huh? By snapping my fingers?

"The migration essay should only be about three to four typewritten pages," Mrs. Garber continues. "We're not looking for *Roots*. Just have fun with it. If you do this assignment properly, you'll get a greater sense of the history that's living right under your noses. Everyone understand?"

I stare at Mrs. Garber's bright red blazer until

it becomes a blur. What am I going to do? I decide to wait until after everyone leaves the classroom, then talk to Mrs. Garber on the D.D.L. I would be embarrassed if anybody overheard my conversation, you know what I'm saying?

"Um, Mrs. Garber, can I speak to you?" I finally ask, my voice cracking.

"Yes, Dorinda, I'll be right with you," she says, scribbling something on some papers, then closing her folder. She looks me straight in the face, and asks, "Are you having trouble understanding the assignment for the class project?"

"Um, yeah. I, um, don't know how I'm going to do it," I say, shaking my head.

"Why not?" she asks.

"I don't, um, know much about my parents, so I don't know how I'm gonna complete—I mean—even *do* the project." I hope Mrs. Garber will get the drift without me having to spell it out.

"Who do you live with?" Mrs. Garber asks, concerned.

Now I guess I do have to tell her. "My foster parents," I say, and I feel myself getting embarrassed again.

"Okay—well then, ask one of your foster

parents if you can do a time line on one of them," Mrs. Garber says cheerfully.

I just stand there like a statue, so I guess Mrs. Garber figures something is still wrong—and it is. I don't want to ask Mrs. or Mr. Bosco so much stuff about their business. If they wanted me to know, they would have told me. I don't really know that much about them, except that Mrs. Bosco was born in North Carolina, and her grandfather worked as a tobacco sharecropper.

"I understand what you're going through, Dorinda," Mrs. Garber says, putting her arm on my shoulder.

Yeah, that's what a lot of people tell me so I don't feel bad, but they don't really understand what I'm going through.

"My grandparents were killed in the Holocaust, like many other Jews. After the war, many kids were placed in foster homes—including my mother," Mrs. Garber says, putting her arm around me.

"Really?" I ask, surprised. I guess she *does* understand—a little.

"There are so many stories in my family tree that are missing, that I would never be able to complete this assignment either. Do the best you can, Dorinda," Mrs. Garber tells me.

"Um—did they kill a lot of Jewish people in the Holo—"

"The Holocaust? Yes. Millions were killed, but the human spirit cannot be stopped. I think tragedy makes you appreciate the people in your life—the ones who really do care about you. I'm sure your foster mother will be happy to provide you with enough information for your time line."

"Thanks, Mrs. Garber," I say, then walk downstairs to meet my crew. Without even thinking, I go instead to the telephone booths by the cafeteria, and call my half sister Tiffany. "Um, you still want me to come over?"

"Yeah!" Tiffany responds, sounding really excited to hear my voice.

Walking toward the school exit, I take a deep breath, and find myself smiling. Mrs. Bosco was right. I shouldn't look a gift horse in the mouth—but I *am* gonna check to see if Tiffany has hooves!

Chapter 4

To get to Tiffany's house, on Eighty-second Street off Park Avenue, I have to take two trains, then walk. I can't believe all the kids I see walking around in private-school uniforms—they look like they're in an army or something, except for all the giggling. And the uniforms are all different, too—plaid and solid, gray, red, blue, navy—which means there are a lot of private schools in this neighborhood. I can tell some of the girls are rolling up their skirts at the waistband on the sneak tip, because their skirts look a little too short around their knobby knees, if you know what I'm saying. And some of the boys have mad funny haircuts, too.

Even with all the gangs of kids walking

around, it's a lot quieter in this neighborhood than mine. I can even hear some birds chirping. I open the door to Tiffany's building, but a doorman wearing white gloves beats me to it. Wow, I've never been in a building with a doorman! His uniform is green, with black and gold trim. He's wearing a hat with trim around it, too. I get a little nervous, and straighten my back so I seem taller—which is still a *lot* shorter than the doorman.

I feel strange asking for Tiffany Twitty, but I guess the doorman must be used to hearing her funny last name by now. He just asks for my name, without cracking a smile.

"Miss Rogers," I say, being polite, and standing aside so people can walk by me. See, Tiffany's real name, before she got adopted by the Twittys, was Karina Farber. That's what she told me, anyway. She said she found a baby picture of herself, that her parents kept in a locked safety box, and that her real name was written on the back. Tiffany seems like a supa sleuth, even if it took her eleven years to figure out she was adopted—which was something the Twittys didn't want her to know.

The doorman rings Tiffany's apartment, then

directs me to a bank of gilded elevators. They even have furniture in the lobby—a big burgundy couch, chairs, and a statue spouting water! Wow, I knew her parents were rich, but I didn't know Tiffany had it like *that*!

When the elevator door opens, there's already a lady inside, with a little white poodle. I don't mean to stare at the lady, but the beady eyes on the head of the fox stole around her neck are staring right at me! Then her dog sniffs at my legs, and suddenly I get embarrassed. The lady sees the look on my face, then asks me, "Do you have a dog?"

"No."

"Oh. Well, he's sniffing at something."

Oh, no. Maybe he's sniffing at the garbage from the courtyard of our building that I stepped in this morning! Suddenly I feel really dirty. I wonder if it's such a good idea that I came here. Maybe Tiffany's parents don't know I'm coming over, and they wouldn't like it if they found out.

"Come on, Baubles, let's go," the lady says, pulling her dog's shiny leash. I wonder if those are diamonds. Nah, they're probably rhinestones. The lady doesn't say good-bye to me when she gets out of the elevator. So I shout after her, "Have a nice day."

"Oh—yes, you too, dear," the startled lady says, turning around abruptly.

When Tiffany opens her apartment door, I greet her the same way. "Hello, dear!"

"Wazzup with you?" Tiffany says, her big blue eyes brightening when she sees me. I wonder why she's talking differently than when I first met her in Central Park. She's even wearing a cheetah turtleneck over her gray sweatpants.

"Check out your spots," I say, chuckling. I think Tiffany needs a little fashion coordination, but I don't want to hurt her feelings. "I met one of your neighbors in the elevator," I say, leaving the fashion bone alone for a sec.

"Who?"

"This, um, foxy lady with a white poodle," I say, then start to laugh. Whenever I get around Tiffany, I seem to get a case of the giggles.

"Oh, Mrs. Chirpy," Tiffany says, covering her mouth.

"That's not her *real* name!"

"Yes, it is! Her husband owns Chirpy Cheapies catalog, and her dog, Baubles, has bad breath."

Now I double over laughing, wondering how Tiffany makes up all these tall tales she tells. "How do you know he has bad breath—did you kiss him?"

"No!" Tiffany says, falling into me. "One day, this lady with a German shepherd got into the elevator, and Baubles went to kiss him, and the German shepherd barked."

"How do you know it wasn't a her?" I challenge her.

"Who?"

"The German shepherd—maybe it was a girl?"

"Maybe—but she sure didn't like Baubles sniffing her butt, 'cuz she whacked Baubles in the face with her big black tail!" Tiffany giggles, then plops down on the couch, sticking her shoeless feet under her.

We could never do that at my house—even though both the couches are so raggedy, Mrs. Bosco says she doesn't want them to get more messed up than they already are. "You stay home by yourself?" I ask.

"Yeah," Tiffany says, but when she hears a noise down the hallway, she quickly adds, "sometimes—when my brother isn't here."

"Oh," I say, 'cuz I don't want her to feel bad for exaggerating.

"He's in tenth grade—his name is Eric the Ferret."

I wonder if Tiffany's brother is adopted, like she is, but I decide it would be rude to ask, so I don't. Looking around the living room, I notice there are lots of Lucite boxes with dead butterflies hanging on the walls. "I wish Twinkie could see those," I say.

"Oh, those are my father's. Wanna see the pictures from Thanksgiving?" Tiffany asks excitedly.

"Yeah," I say, then put my backpack down on the carpet. Looking around at all the beautiful furniture and flowers in vases, I exclaim, "Wow, your house is nice." The living room almost looks like it's out of a magazine or something. They probably have a maid who comes in to clean the house every day.

Tiffany proudly hands me a stack of photos. In the first one, she is standing outside of a log cabin with her parents, and a tall boy with blond hair and big white teeth.

"That's Eric the Ferret—see, his teeth are really big."

"Oh. Where is this at?"

"It's our house in Massachusetts. We go there on weekends, and Thanksgiving and Christmas, too. In the summer it's cool, because there is a big lake to go swimming in."

"Well . . . I got to go to Houston for Thanksgiving."

"Really?" Tiffany acts like she's really interested, so I tell her all about the Cheetah Girls' adventures in H'Town—leaving out the showdown at the Okie-Dokie Corral, of course—with those fake wannabe Cash Money Girls, who tried to run us out of Dodge over some stupid beef jerky.

"You got any pictures?" Tiffany asks excitedly.

"We bought a cheetah photo album when we were there, and now I'm gonna keep all the pictures we take," I announce proudly. Then I realize she wants to see them now. "Um, but I didn't bring it with me."

"Oh," Tiffany says, disappointed.

I tell Tiffany about the mouse in the kosher restaurant. She breaks out in a fit of giggles. "Oooo!" she squeaks, her eyes lighting up. "You wanna see my hamster, Miggy? He's in my bedroom."

Tiffany's bedroom is just like I expected it to be—frilly, pink, and filled with stuffed animals, CDs, and posters of singers—everybody from Mariah Carey to Kahlua Alexander to Limp Bizkit.

"Oh—you like Kahlua?" I ask, standing in front of the big poster of my favorite singer. Kahlua is responsible for the Cheetah Girls getting the hookup with Def Duck Records—even though nothing has happened yet. I explain this all to Tiffany, almost knocking into her fancy scooter, which is propped up against the wall.

"I wish I could put my hair in braids like Kahlua's," she says.

"She doesn't have braids anymore," I tell her. "We met her at Churl It's You! salon when she was getting her hair done for this movie."

"Really?" Tiffany asks, impressed. "But I like her hair better with braids." Tiffany smooths down her fine, blond hair, then adds, "My hair is more like Mariah's when she straightens it."

"You like Mariah, too." I smile.

"Are you kidding? I want to see her in concert this Friday, but my parents won't let me go," Tiffany says, annoyed.

I wonder why they won't. I'll bet they could

afford the fifty dollars for the cheapest tickets. Maybe they think she's too young or something.

"Is the record company really going to let you go in the studio and record songs?" Tiffany asks excitedly.

"I guess—they said they would team us with producer Mouse Almighty—you know, he worked on Karma's Children, Kahlua, and Sista Fudge's records, too."

"Really?" Tiffany asks with bugged eyes. Every time I tell her anything about the Cheetah Girls, she acts like a kid in a candy store. Soon I get to hear why.

"I want to be a singer too," she confesses, kind of self-consciously.

"Let me hear you sing," I say, egging her on so I can see if she has the skills to pay the bills.

"Not now," she says, getting all coy and blushing. She walks over to a pink trunk in the corner of the room and says, "See? Look in my glamor trunk. I was a Cheetah Girl, too—even when I was little." Holding up a tiny cheetah skirt with a matching cape, Tiffany puts it against herself and wiggles her hips. "I used to walk around the house wearing this outfit, and singing like Mariah Carey—'I'm just your butterfly, baby!' "

I chuckle at Tiffany's squeaky voice.

"I'm just playing around—but I really do sing. When I know you better, I'll do it," she says shyly, then takes her pet hamster out of her cage. "Want to pet Miggy?"

"Okay," I say, letting Tiffany put the hamster in my palm. I keep looking around Tiffany's room, until I notice the electronic keyboard against the wall.

"That's the keyboard I got for my birthday," she brags. "My parents felt so bad about me finding out I was adopted, they let me have it. Now they're being really nice to me."

"They weren't mad at you for snooping around and finding the key to the locked box?"

"Nope—they felt too guilty about the whole thing," Tiffany says, lying back on her bed. Then her face gets sad. "I told Christine, my best friend at school, that I found out I was adopted, and she went and told Leandra, who hates me. Then Leandra went and told everybody at school. Now the kids are making fun of me. They call me an adopted Miss Piggy."

Tiffany is—well, chubby—but that sounds

really mean. I think she's kinda cute. Now I start thinking about the situation I've got at home. "I got a new foster sister yesterday."

"Really?"

"Yeah—this girl that was on the news, because her mother left her by herself in Coney Island." Suddenly, I feel uncomfortable. Why am I telling her this?

Tiffany sits up straight on the bed and stares at me. "How old is she?"

"Nobody knows. She looks about five, I guess. We don't know anything about her, except she says her name is Gaye."

"That's so sad," Tiffany responds. "Maybe somebody will come looking for her."

"Maybe—they had her picture on the news and everything. I guess somebody has to know her, right?"

"Unless she's not from New York," Tiffany says, like a divette detective.

"Wow, I never even thought of that," I say.

"Maybe her mother came all the way to New York so nobody would know her, and then left her there in Coney Island, because she knew somebody would find her," Tiffany says, her blue eyes widening.

Maybe Tiffany knows where *I* was born, I'm thinking—but I don't want to ask her. "You said you were born in California?" I ask instead, hoping maybe she'll tell me more.

"Yeah—I think our mother moved there, then left me—I mean us." Tiffany doesn't seem sad about it at all. "Where were you born?"

"I don't know," I say, disappointed that *she* doesn't know. "I guess I always thought I was born in New York, but now I'm not so sure." Suddenly, I get a pain in my chest. "I don't care where I was born," I blurt out. "I don't care where our mother is!"

"*I* do," Tiffany says. "Maybe we can find her together."

"You can go look for her yourself—because I have better things to do with my time!" I pout.

"Okay," Tiffany says, shrugging her shoulders. Then she gets up, grabs a booklet, and hands it to me. "Here's the book for the keyboard. You wanna learn how to play it?"

"Yeah. Why not—if you don't mind listening to some wack playing!"

Chapter 5

I have never played any instrument before, so I feel kind of nervous about playing the keyboard—with Tiffany, no less. But it turns out she is a really good teacher. After an hour of trying, I'm actually playing pieces of songs I know. *I can't believe I'm learning to play the keyboard!* "This is dope," I say after a while. "Let me hear *you* play something."

Tiffany starts playing, and I recognize the song instantly. Kahlua Alexander and Mo' Money Monique's duet, "The Toyz Is Mine."

Tiffany definitely has mad skills playing the keyboard. Next to me, she sounds stomping. "I'm going to get us some lemonade and cookies," Tiffany says, jumping up.

I bang around some more on the keys, and I

feel like I could do this all day. Then I feel a lump rising in my throat. I wonder how much a keyboard like this costs?

"Um, where did your parents buy the keyboard at?" I ask Tiffany when she comes back, handing me a pretty pink glass of lemonade.

"Kmart. It cost twelve hundred dollars," she says matter-of-factly.

"How do you know what your birthday present costs?" I ask, surprised.

"'Cuz when we went to Kmart to buy my school supplies, I went into the aisle where the keyboards were and I saw mine—that's how," Tiffany has that satisfied smirk on her face—the one she gets when her supa-sleuth skills pay off.

"It's going to be a long way down the yellow brick road before I can afford a keyboard," I moan. Then I start wondering why I should bother learning at all, if I'm not going to be able to afford one.

"You can come over and play it whenever you want, Dorinda," Tiffany says, putting her hand on my shoulder.

Then she goes on teaching me the keyboard like nothing happened. I get interested again, and soon I forget about whether I can afford to buy one of my own. At least when I do get one,

I'll know how to play it. "You know, you'd make a really good teacher," I tell her.

"Are you trying to tell me I'm not going to be a singer?" Tiffany says, turning to me on the bench, and giving me that earnest look with her big, blue eyes.

"I didn't say that," I respond, my cheeks turning warm.

All of sudden, Tiffany breaks out into a big smile. "Psych! I know I'm gonna be a singer, too."

I don't want to rain on Tiffany's parade, you know what I'm saying? Who am I to say she can't be a singer, even if she sounds like a hoarse hyena in a rainstorm?

"Maybe I could sing for the rest of the Cheetah Girls, and they'll let me be in the group with you!" Tiffany says, getting excited and putting her head on my shoulder. Her blond hair is so soft, and I smell the familiar baby powder scent that now reminds me of her.

"I don't know, Tiffany. It's not my group or anything," I say, because I feel bad. Here she is being nice to me, trying to be my sister and everything, and I don't want to be down with her like that.

"Please?" she says, giving me a pleading

look with her big, blue eyes. Now I can tell she's really serious. "I could sing and play the keyboard. I mean, you don't have a keyboard player, right?" I'll bet she's used to getting her way about everything.

"Well, we don't use instruments at all—you know that; you came and saw us at the Apollo, when we were in the 'Battle of the Divettes' competition. See, we use tracks, just like a lot of other groups do. It costs a lot of money to have live musicians onstage."

"I'd play the keyboard for free," Tiffany says, not letting up.

"Well, I'll ask the rest of the Cheetah Girls if you can sing for them. How's that?" I say, finally giving in, and hoping she'll leave the Cheetah Girls bone alone for a while.

"Okay—when?" Tiffany asks directly.

"I . . . have to call and ask them."

"You can call Galleria now," Tiffany suggests, handing me the phone. "She's the leader of the group, right?"

"R-right," I say, then add quickly, "but she's not home right now."

"Do the Cheetah Girls go into a chat room?" Tiffany asks, like she's getting at something.

I can't tell her what chat room we go into—then maybe she'll be trying to sweat us all the time! But how can I *not* tell her? "Um . . . Yeah."

"Well, which one?"

"Phat Planet," I say, telling her the truth, because I don't want to lie.

"My onscreen name is LimpCutie," Tiffany says, proud of herself.

I realize that it's probably a riff off of Limp Bizkit, seeing as she's got their poster on her wall.

"I can go on tonight, and see if the Cheetah Girls are in there, okay?"

I know she isn't really asking me, so I don't say anything. Tiffany walks over to her closet and opens a trunk. "Here's the safety equipment I told you I was gonna give you," she says, pulling out a pair of knee guards and a pair of elbow guards.

"Oh, that's okay," I say, suddenly feeling embarrassed again. I don't want her giving me things. I don't think it's cool.

"Take them—I told you when we first met in the park that I had an extra set. I don't need them." Tiffany shoves them into my lap.

"Okay," I say, smiling, "then I'm going to make you an outfit."

"Really?" Tiffany just gets excited about everything. Skating, singing, playing the keyboard, you name it!

"Yup, I'm gonna design an outfit and make it for you. Let me take your measurements," I say, finally feeling like I have something to give her, too. "I have a sewing machine at home."

"Really?" Tiffany says again. I guess that's the one thing she doesn't have. "I don't know how to sew anything."

"You got a tape measure?" I ask her, chuckling.

"No—wait. I think my mom has one in her room." Tiffany runs to get it.

All of a sudden, I hear the apartment door open, and some voices in the hallway. I get nervous, because I realize that it's probably her parents. I hope they don't get upset that I'm here. I can't make out what they're talking about, so I just get off the keyboard bench, and sit in the princess throne by Tiffany's bed.

Tiffany comes running back into the room and whispers, "I can't get the tape measure now, but we'll do it next time you come over. My mother's home from work, and she wants to say hello."

"Okay," I say.

Tiffany drags me by my arm back into the living room, where Mrs. Twitty is sitting on the couch, wearing a black dress with a strand of white pearls around her neck. She seems really nice and proper, just like she did when I met her at the Apollo.

"Hi," I say, smiling.

"Please sit down, Dorinda," motions Mrs. Twitty.

"Thank you. That was real nice of you, bringing Tiffany to see the Cheetah Girls at the Apollo."

"Oh, it was fun," Mrs. Twitty says. "I really enjoyed it. I think you girls are very good. You know, that's all Tiffany talks about now—being in a singing group. She just *loves* singing groups. She plays those CDs all the time, and she loves that keyboard," Mrs. Twitty says, like she's not sure if *she* likes it or not.

"I want to go to a performing arts school, like the Walker twins do," Tiffany says, putting her head on her mother's shoulder.

"Well, we won't have any of that, dear," Mrs. Twitty says. "We pay good money to send you to St. Agnes."

Tiffany pouts, and I can tell she's not happy,

but I'm not saying anything.

"Dorinda is gonna let me try out to be a Cheetah Girl!" Tiffany says suddenly.

I can't believe she said that! I didn't say she could try out for the Cheetah Girls! I decide I'd better keep my mouth shut, but Mrs. Twitty is definitely interested in hearing what I have to say about it.

"Is that right?" she asks, looking straight at me. Her eyes are really blue, just like Tiffany's. In a way, *she* looks like Tiffany's real mother, I guess—except that her hair is dark brown, and her nose is straighter than Tiffany's. "That would be really good for her."

I guess Mrs. Twitty sees the confused look on my face, because she quickly adds, "To try out, I mean."

"Yeah, um, I'm gonna ask the rest of the Cheetah Girls if she can," I say, glad that Mrs. Twitty has made it seem less scary than it is.

"I'm teaching Dorinda how to play my keyboard," Tiffany says, like she's really proud of herself. "She's really good, too!"

"Tiffany just loves that thing—she'd play it all day if we let her," Mrs. Twitty says, nodding her head at me.

I wonder if I should say good-bye, because I've been sitting here a long time. I'd better be getting uptown, to see what's cooking with my new foster sister, Gaye, if you know what I'm saying. Just thinking about going home, the heavy weight that I feel lately on my chest has come back in full force.

"The two of you sure have something in common," Mrs. Twitty continues.

"What?" I ask, suddenly realizing that I spaced out for a second.

"Well, you're both musically inclined. Tiffany plays the keyboard, and you sing. That's what I meant," Mrs. Twitty adds, like she hopes she didn't offend me or anything.

"Oh, yeah," I say, nodding. I don't think it's such a good idea for me to ask the Cheetah Girls if Tiffany can try out.

"That's all Tiffany talks about is singing. Or this singer and that singer. Did you see all the posters on her walls?"

"Yeah," I answer.

If you ask me, I think Tiffany is just trying to be in the mix 'cuz she thinks it's fun. I wonder what Tiffany sounds like when she's really singing. She seems kinda shy about singing in front of people—and Tiffany isn't shy otherwise, if you know what I'm saying.

"Would you like to stay for dinner?" Mrs. Twitty asks me.

"No, thank you," I respond quickly. I want to tell her why I have to go home, but I feel embarrassed, so I decide not to.

"I got out of work earlier today than usual," Mrs. Twitty continues, "so we won't have to eat takeout."

"Where do you work?" I ask Mrs. Twitty, since I figure I can talk about that.

"I'm the research director for The Butterfly Foundation," Mrs. Twitty says proudly.

"Oh—that's why you have all the butterflies on the wall," I say excitedly. "My fos—um, my sister Twinkie loves butterflies."

"Well, she'll have to visit sometime. My husband is the head scientist there—that's where we met, you know. I guess you could say the 'nutty professor' caught me in his net," she says chirpily.

"Wait till I tell Twinkie—she'll be so excited!" I say, chuckling at Mrs. Twitty's joke. She is a funny lady. "Well, I'd better get home." I get up and grab my backpack and the safety equipment. Suddenly, I feel self-conscious, like a bag lady or something. Mrs. Twitty notices me clutching the bag, so I quickly add, "Um, Tiffany gave me the pads—she said she didn't need them."

"Oh, yes, she must have outgrown those by now," Mrs. Twitty says, causing Tiffany to wince.

"Mom, I can still fit in them," she protests; but when Mrs. Twitty looks at her, she adds with a sheepish giggle, "Well, almost!"

I guess it *is* kinda weird that I'm smaller than Tiffany, even though I'm older.

"Well, I'm glad someone can put them to good use," Mrs. Twitty says, then gets up to show me to the door.

Once I'm in the hallway, Tiffany sticks her head out her door and says, "Sorry you have to bounce, *mamacita*!"

"Me, too," I say, chuckling at my sister. As I walk to the subway station, I'm thinking about how much fun I had learning the keyboard. Even though I'm jealous that she has so much and I have so little, I'm glad I came over to my sister Tiffany's house—she is a trip! Besides, she's my for real, forever sister—and that means a lot.

Chapter 6

Thank goodness for my crew. They may not live in foster homes, but I know they care about me. When I meet them at Riverside Church for our Kats and Kittys Klub meeting, I just start babbling about the latest drama in my house, when I didn't even plan on telling them diddly widdly.

Last night, Gaye kept me up all night, crying and screaming from nightmares. She even got out of bed and ran down the hallway, yelling that a car was chasing her. "Please don't hit me!" she kept screaming, over and over.

"Maybe she wasn't really talking about a car," Galleria says, putting her arm around my shoulders, and I can tell her mind is working on the divette detective tip.

"That is just so sad," Aqua says, and I see tears forming in her eyes. "I can't believe a mother would shame the Lord by leaving her child in the street."

I wonder where my mother left me, a voice shrieks in my head. It's something I've never thought about before, but now that Gaye is living with us, I can't get that thought out of my head. Not that I really want to know, if you know what I'm saying.

When we're climbing up the steps inside the church, Chanel almost misses one, and wobbles with her crutches into the railing, but luckily, Aqua grabs her arm. "Let me help you, Chanel," she insists.

Now I feel bad for babbling while poor Chanel is hobbling around on crutches. It seems like I'm always thinking about myself. Even though Chanel hasn't whined once about spraining her ankle, I know those crutches must be driving her loco.

"Stop it. I can help myself!" she snaps at Aqua, so I know I'm right. She must really be buggin', because Chanel is really sweet to everybody—maybe a little *too* sweet, if you know what I'm saying. See, Chanel doesn't always stand up for herself, but I guess Galleria stands up enough for both of them.

"What are we talking about tonight?" Angie asks her sister as we approach the landing. Once a month, we attend a general meeting for the Kats and Kittys Klub, this really dope social club for teens that Galleria and Chanel have belonged to since they were babies. The Kats and Kittys Klub has lots of chapters all around the country, and Aqua and Angie transferred into the metropolitan chapter when they moved to the Big Apple last summer. That was really lucky for us, because it's how we all hooked up and became the Cheetah Girls together.

"Let's see—our volunteer drive for Christmas," Aqua says. Aqua and Angie are teen advisors on the volunteer committee. Galleria and Chanel are on the party and events planning committee.

I'm just lucky they let me in the building, if you know what I'm saying. See, membership into the Kats and Kittys Klub is something like six hundred duckets a year, but Galleria and Chanel pulled a few strings so I could get a one-year scholarship for free. Actually, I think they pulled a whole ball of yarn, but just don't want me to know.

"We've also got to finish planning our Christmas bash, 'cuz the season is coming up, and we've gotta head down Candy Cane Lane with fortune and fame!"

"Don't remind me about Christmas," I snort. "I'm not so sure I want to be in my house at Christmastime this year."

Everyone gets silent for a second. Then Chanel asks, "What does your foster mother say about keeping Gaye?"

"That we are just gonna make do," I say, shrugging my shoulders. "I know she can't afford it, but I guess we'll get by."

"Do they give Mrs. Bosco money for that?" Aqua asks nervously.

"Yeah, but not much. Mrs. Bosco says that after she buys the milk and cereal, that check is long gone. I can forget about getting a keyboard, that's for sure. No way Mrs. Bosco can afford to buy me one. Do you know that a keyboard costs twelve hundred dollars?"

"What happened?" Chanel asks, puzzled.

Then I realize I should tell them about my

trip to Tiffany's crib. "My sister Tiffany is teaching me how to play her keyboard."

"We didn't know you went to see her," Galleria snorts.

"I didn't even know I was going to see her. I decided on a dime, right after last period yesterday."

"She knows how to play real good?" is all Aqua wants to know.

"Well, yeah," I respond. "She had a few grooves, but what do I know?"

I wonder if I should tell my crew that Tiffany wants to be in the group. No way, José! I decide.

As we make our way to the room where the Kats and Kittys meeting is held, Galleria heaves a deep sigh. "Well, I'd better brace myself for the Red Snapper trying to get his hooks into me again."

The Red Snapper—a.k.a. Derek Ulysses Hambone—is a student at our school, and he has a crush on Galleria. As soon as he found out she was a Kats and Kittys member, he went and joined, because he's got it like that. See, Derek's family are automotive "big Willies" in Detroit, who moved to the East Coast when his father expanded his thingamajig company—he manufactures some sort of widgets that you need to put in cars. I don't know much about cars, so I forgot the name of the part.

"I can't believe he joined," Chanel moans.

As we make our entrance, Mrs. Bugge, our chapter treasurer, gives us a shout-out: "Here come the Cheetah Girls. I guess we can start now." Everybody feels bad that Chanel is walking on crutches, so I think Mrs. Bugge is trying to blow up our spot, if you know what I'm saying.

The Kats and Kittys Klub in New York has two fund-raisers a year, so that we can donate duckets to charities. Today, we'll decide which organizations to donate the duckets to—and since Aqua and Angie are the teen advisers on that committee, they'll get to help in the voting process.

We all walk to the other end of the table, where there are empty seats. Derek bares his gold tooth as soon as he catches Galleria's eye. "Hey, wazzup, Cheetah Girl?" he says in his goofy voice. Derek is wearing a baseball cap turned backward, which makes his pinhead look even funnier.

Finally, Indigo Luther makes *her* entrance—

and I guess it would be hard to miss, considering the fact that she's six feet tall (even though she's only fourteen). The hot-pink rabbit jacket she's wearing would be hard to miss, too. Indigo Luther is our teen chapter president, and already a professional model. "Hi, everyone, sorry I'm late," she says, plopping her red rabbit pocketbook on the table like it's a trophy.

"Can I have your attention please," says Mrs. Bugge. She hands out the minutes from the last Kats and Kittys Klub meeting. "Here is our latest treasury report. We have to take a vote on which charity organizations we would like to donate money to. As you may remember, this is the money we raised from this year's Kats and Kittys Halloween Bash, where the Cheetah Girls performed for the very first time—but not the last."

Everyone applauds, and my crew and I look at each other, smiling with pride to think how far we've come, and how far we still have to go.

Mrs. Bugge clears her throat. "Aquanette and Anginette—could you take over the voting, please?"

"Our choices for donations are the Riverside Youth Fund, Pediatric Illness Fund, Sickle-Cell

Anemia Foundation," Aquanette starts in.

I wonder why she hasn't included an organization that helps foster kids. But since I'm not on the committee, it's not my place to say anything. Besides, I realize, the other organizations deserve the donations anyway.

"But what I would like to suggest," Aqua continues, "is that we consider donating the money to ACS, in the Division of Foster Care, for the specific use of the Bosco family. They're the family that has taken in the girl you may have seen on the news—the one named Gaye, who was found wandering around Coney Island and remanded into foster care."

Everyone gets real quiet, and I can feel some of the Kats and Kittys members staring at me. I stare down at the table like I'm looking for something, because I feel my ears burning with embarrassment. I can't *believe* Aquanette is saying this in front of the whole Kats and Kittys Klub! I'll bet they all already know that I live in a foster home, and that everybody's been talking about me behind my back. In fact, that must be how Galleria and Chanel got me a free membership!

I feel myself sinking lower into my chair. I can't even look at Aqua while she's talking.

"I think we should explain," Angie says, cutting in. "On Monday, Dorinda's foster mother, Mrs. Bosco, took Gaye in, after every effort was made to locate her mother, or anybody who knew her. Mrs. Bosco is already taking care of eleven foster children."

"Well, I think that's a very valid suggestion," Mrs. Bugge says. "Let's include it in our choices."

"Okay," Aqua says. "So we'll begin voting now. We'll pass around the ballots—please fill them out and return them to the basket."

All of a sudden, I feel Galleria's hand pressing down on mine. She must know how embarrassed I am. After everyone in the room finishes voting, Aqua and Angie separate the ballots into piles according to the votes marked on them, then Mrs. Bugge reads the final vote.

"For the record, this year's Kats and Kittys Klub charity donation will be sent to ACS, in the Division of Foster Care—to be allocated for the specific aid of Gaye, a foster child in the temporary custody of Mrs. Bosco." Mrs. Bugge smiles at me warmly.

All of a sudden, I burst into tears. I wish people wouldn't feel sorry for me all the time—it makes me feel totally humiliated!

I keep my head down. I can feel Galleria giving me a hug, before she gets up to speak as the teen adviser for the events planning committee. I'm relieved when she starts talking, because everybody isn't looking at me anymore.

"The time is upon us to nail down plans for our Christmas Eggnogger. Instead of throwing it at the Hound Club like we did last year, I would like to suggest that we try another place," Galleria says, like she's not taking no for an answer.

"Well, what do you suggest?" Indigo says, looking straight up at Galleria.

"We heard about this new club called the Weeping Willow," Galleria says, like she's daring Indigo to defy her.

"I know that place," Indigo says like she's bragging. "You haven't been there yet, have you?"

"No, um, Chanel and I thought we would check it out after we get the committee's approval."

"Well, when I modeled in a fashion show for Phat Farm, they threw a party there afterward. I don't think we can sell enough tickets to fill capacity—I mean, it's kinda big."

When I look up, I see the grimace on Galleria's face.

"If we get each nonsenior member to bring five guests, and senior members to bring ten, then I think we can fill and chill the club, you know what I'm saying?" Galleria asks, looking around at the other members for their opinion—including Derek's.

"Yeah!" Derek says, piping up in Galleria's defense. "And, um, are we going to invite peeps from other chapters? That could bring in the noise, you know what I'm saying?"

"That's basically up to us," Galleria retorts, waiting for Indigo to counter.

"I say we invite other chapters," Indigo agrees, surprising Galleria.

"And one parent from each chapter has to be a chaperone—no ifs or buts about it," Mrs. Bugge adds.

"Okay," Chanel pipes up, then giggles. "Can we go look at the place?"

"Agreed," says Indigo. "I move that we close the meeting, and that the advisers for the party committee report directly to me and Mrs. Bugge during the planning."

"I second!" yells Derek.

"I third that we head out of here and eat some steer," Aqua pipes up.

"That sounds finger-lickin' good to me," Galleria chuckles, happy that the meeting is over, and we can be by ourselves.

Of course, I know that Aqua is just saying we should go to McDonald's for a Big Mac. But even though I'm having a Mac attack myself, I don't want to hang with my crew right now, because they really embarrassed me. I need to figure out how I can get out of this plan, and head home to a can of Spam or something. . . .

Chapter 7

Mrs. Bosco is so happy about the Kats and Kittys Klub donation to ACS—the Administration of Children's Services—that she just dismisses my feelings about being called out as a foster child in front of my fellow Kats and Kittys. She makes me so mad, I don't want to ask if I can talk to her about her background for my school time-line project.

"Dorinda, sometimes I think you have a hard head. Your life is gonna be so much easier when you learn not to look a gift horse in the mouth." She is folding up the laundry—which it seems like she's doing all the time, because there are so many people living in our house.

"I know—and I'm supposed to check it, to

make sure it has hooves," I say, trying to go along with the program. I still don't know what Mrs. Bosco means by the last part, but I'm not gonna ask. I've had enough embarrassment for a whole year!

"I don't think God loves you any less than other children, just because you lost your mother," Mrs. Bosco continues. "And obviously, those Kats and Kittys children like you, too."

Now I feel stupid for coming home and crying in front of Mrs. Bosco. I didn't mean to, but sometimes I get so clogged up inside, everything spouts out all over the place—kinda like that girl in *The Exorcist*. I guess I don't know how to express my feelings the way other people do.

Suddenly, what Mrs. Bosco just said sinks in. What did she mean by "I lost my mother"? Maybe she knows what happened to her, and she's just not telling me. Maybe she's dead!

"Tiffany called you twice today," Mrs. Bosco says, shaking out Topwe's red corduroy pants, then folding them really carefully. I hear Topwe coughing from his bedroom. He went to bed early because he's still not feeling well—otherwise he would never miss his favorite television show, *She's All That and a Pussycat*.

At least I'm not HIV-positive like Topwe. My problems are nothing next to his, or Gaye's. So why am I being so self-conscious about everything?

"Maybe I should make him some warm milk and bring it to him in the bedroom?" I ask Mrs. Bosco, getting up to go to the kitchen.

"No, Dorinda. I gave him some cough syrup and his medicine before he went to bed. Let him sleep if he can." Mrs. Bosco looks up at me, adjusting her bifocal glasses. I know her eyesight isn't good, but sometimes I wonder if she does that because she wants to look closer inside me or something—like she has gamma-ray vision.

"Tiffany told me all about you learning the keyboard. You ain't said nothing about it." I can tell, by the tone in her voice, that she's really asking, "Wazzup with that?"

"Oh—yeah. It was a lot of fun," I respond, trying to sound kinda bubbly about it. "It's not easy or anything. I'd have to practice a lot—but I would like to learn it some more."

"Well, that sounds real good," Mrs. Bosco says. "'Member you used to want to play the piano?"

I wonder why Mrs. Bosco is bringing that up.

The only reason I never took piano lessons is because she couldn't afford it.

"Maybe Tiffany'll let you practice with her again. That'd be good for you two," she goes on.

I know I shouldn't feel disappointed, but I do when she doesn't say anything about buying me my own keyboard.

"She also said you might let her be in your group," Mrs. Bosco says, searching about the bottom of the basket for stray socks.

I can't believe Tiffany told Mrs. Bosco that! She's just not going to let up about being in the Cheetah Girls. "Let me help you with those," I say quickly. There's always a lot of socks, and sometimes it's hard to tell the blue ones from the brown ones or the black ones, especially since the light in the living room isn't really bright enough.

But Mrs. Bosco is staring at me, knowing that I'm avoiding answering her. "Well, it's not my group," I say, trying to explain. "And I didn't exactly tell Tiffany she could be in it."

Now I feel bad—again! After all, Tiffany let me practice on her keyboard. I guess the least I could do is ask the Cheetah Girls if she could audition, like she wants to. "I guess I could ask the

Cheetah Girls to hear her sing," I say, giving in.

"Well, that's all you can do, right?" she says, like she's finally going to leave me alone about it. "You know, if you keep your word, then the rest takes care of itself."

"Yes, I guess you're right," I say, folding the socks tightly into each other. Suddenly, I realize that I haven't heard one word from my new foster sister. "What's up with Gaye?" I ask.

"I guess she done finally wore herself out," Mrs. Bosco says with a heavy sigh.

"Have you, um, heard anything else?" I ask hesitantly. After what Galleria said, I'm beginning to wonder myself. Someone, somewhere, must know Gaye, or know someone who knows her.

"When people disappear, they usually don't want to be found, and they have a real good way of staying lost," Mrs. Bosco says.

From the way she looks at me, straight in the face, I suddenly realize that she *does* know something about my mother—I think she's trying to tell me that *my* mother disappeared, and doesn't want to be found.

Twinkie and the rest of the girls have finished with their baths. I can't believe that

Monie, my oldest foster sister, who is sixteen, actually gave them a bath and got them into their pajamas! Monie usually only thinks about herself.

Twinkie peeks into the living room, even though it's way past her bedtime. "Hi, Dorinda," she whispers.

"You can come on in for a second, Rita, but then you better go to bed," Mrs. Bosco says, smiling at her. "Come take y'all's clothes and put them in the drawer."

"Okay," Twinkie says, taking the folded clothes in her arms. "Dorinda, the Butterfly lady was on television."

"Oh, was she singing?" I ask Twinkie. Twinkie calls Mariah Carey the Butterfly lady, because it's the name of one of her hits.

"No," Twinkie says, "but I wish I could go see her sing!"

"I know, Twinkie, but her concert costs fifty dollars, and that's a lot of money," I say, giving her a hug.

"Fifty dollars?" Mrs. Bosco says, almost choking. "She'd better be doing a whole lot of singing for that kind of money! Where's she singing at?"

"Madison Square Garden," I add, feeling a twinge of sadness. Now that I'm in the Cheetah Girls, I spend a lot less time with Twinkie. We used to be so close. I wish I could take her to see Mariah Carey. Shoot, I can't wait till Twinkie can see me and the Cheetah Girls sing! "So what was she doing, Twinkie?"

"Oh, she was with a lot of kids, talking about foster children. Telling people to take foster children like us," Twinkie explains.

"Really?" I wonder what she's talking about.

"That's not what she means, Dorinda. She didn't say nothing about y'all or nothing. Just, it's some kinda, some new, um—"

"Program?" I ask.

"Uh, yeah," Mrs. Bosco says, then changes her mind. "No, it's not really a program, you know—it's more like a commercial, where she's trying to get people to take in foster children, and they tell you a number to call, you know."

"Oh. You mean like a public service announcement?"

"Yeah—that's exactly it," Mrs. Bosco says, finally satisfied.

"I haven't seen it," I say, surprised.

"See, Rita, when you get bigger, you gonna be

right smart like Dorinda. She don't miss a trick."

"How come she don't have us on television with her?" Twinkie asks me.

"Well, I guess—no, I *know* if she knew you, she would," I tell Twinkie. But what I really want to say is, "Why would you want to be on television, announcing to the world that you're a foster child?" I wouldn't do it, not even if Mariah Carey asked me herself, you know what I'm saying?

"Rita, there's a whole lot of kids like you in the world, and I guess she's trying to help, because she's famous and people will listen to her." Mrs. Bosco motions for Twinkie to come closer, so she can smooth down her hair. Twinkie's hair is always flying all over the place like a pinwheel or something. "If there were enough homes for foster kids, then she wouldn't have to ask people to take them in, but Lord knows those people running the agencies can barely tie their own shoelaces!"

Mrs. Bosco doesn't like dealing with the foster care agency, because she thinks they're kinda disorganized.

"If they paid those people enough money, then I'll bet they'd find homes for every child,"

Mrs. Bosco goes on, like she's just getting started. "They don't mind paying these people all kinds of money on television just to act stupid."

"Okay, Twinkie, it's time for bed," I say, kissing her good night. I decide not to tell her about Tiffany's parents and The Butterfly Foundation—yet. I don't want to get her hopes up, and then find out I can't really bring her there.

Now that Mrs. Bosco and I are alone, I ask her about doing the time-line project for my sociology class.

"Well," Mrs. Bosco chuckles, "I have a hard enough time remembering what happened yesterday, let alone forty years ago, but I guess I could try."

"Thank you, Mom," I say, because I know she likes me to call her that. "I'll probably start it next week."

"That'll be something telling you about all my kin—there's a whole lot of us still down in North Cadilakky," Mrs. Bosco chuckles, making fun of her home state, North Carolina. "Believe me when I tell you, when you have a little kin, you should pay some mind to keeping them around."

"Yeah," I say turning around and smiling

because I know what Mrs. Bosco is getting at—that I should be happy my sister Tiffany found me. Right now, though, I'd better at least see if my crew is in the chat room, so I can ask them about hearing Tiffany sing.

First I go into Rita's bedroom, to take a look at Gaye. It's hard for me to imagine her sleeping, after all that drama she caused last night. I tiptoe closer, and see her curled up in a ball, with her thumb stuck in her mouth. She seems kinda old to be doing that, but I guess that's all she has that she can call her own. I wonder what she likes—maybe she likes teddy bears, like Arba does. Or butterflies, like Twinkie. Or DIVA dolls, like Kenya. All of a sudden, I feel excited about getting to know Gaye. Maybe it won't be so bad having her here.

"Good night, Doreety," Twinkie says, imitating the way Arba says my name. Arba is from Albania, and she has her own way of talking. I look over at Arba, and see her long, dark hair spread out on the pillow, and her favorite teddy bear sleeping next to her.

As I walk into the bedroom that I share with Monie and Chantelle, I see Monie sitting at my computer. Why did she have to come home tonight? I want to tell her to go talk on the phone or something, like she always does. I need to check my e-mail, and see if any of the Cheetah Girls are in the Phat Planet chat room.

Why is she always hogging *my* computer? When our super, Mr. Hammer, gave me the computer, Mrs. Bosco said that I should share it with Monie and Chantelle. Well, I don't want to!

"Are you gonna be a long time?" I ask, hoping Monie doesn't give me a hard time.

"Nah, I just gotta finish this letter for my nurse's aide application," she says, taking her bubble gum out of her mouth and twirling it around her finger, then putting it back in.

"Everybody in the building's heard about Gaye, so I thought I'd better come home and help Mrs. Bosco if she needed it," Monie says without turning her head. "I saw the thing on the news about her, too."

"Yeah, I heard about it—she was really on the news?" I ask, curious.

"No, Dorinda, *she* wasn't on the news—they were just talking about her. They showed her picture, and left a number if anybody had information, that type of thing," Monie says, getting an attitude.

"Oh. That's what Ms. Keisha said."

"What would Ms. Keisha know? She can't even get a job."

I guess now that Monie is applying for a nurse's aide position, she thinks someone is gonna hire her with that nasty attitude? If you ask me, she might as well head down to the unemployment line, and fill out an application early, you know what I'm saying?

"You gonna get a job?" I ask, curious to see what she's gonna say. I can't imagine her being anybody's nurse's aide. She didn't even know what to do when Mrs. Bosco got a bronchitis attack last winter. *I* was the one to call for an ambulance to take her to the hospital. Monie just stood around, acting all scared. *I'd* be scared to see Monie with a thermometer, trying to take someone's temperature—she'd probably stick the patient in the eye with it or something!

"I don't know, Dorinda, but I'm sure gonna do something to get outta here, that's all I know," she snorts at me. "There. I'm finished. Go on and use the computer."

I feel angry that she doesn't say *your* computer, but I don't say anything, because I don't want to get into a fight with her. I decide to go into the Phat Planet chat room first, because somebody from my crew is probably there. Knowing Chanel, she probably needs someone to talk to, sitting up there in bed with her ankle elevated on a pillow, or getting treated to an ice pack on her butt!

The first person I see, typing madly in the chat room, is supa-tasty "LimpCutie." I should have known Tiffany wouldn't have wasted any time hogging up the chat room! Why did I even tell her about it? Of course, Tiffany recognizes my log-on name, "Uptown Hoodie"—and I can almost hear her squealing with delight, just by her greeting.

UPTOWN HOODIE—IT'S ME, HANGING WITH THE POSSE!

HI, LIMPCUTIE, I type back, so I don't bust her cover, but I really would like to tell her to "scram and take the Spam"—or something that Galleria would riff when she gets mad.

I GOTTA TELL YOU SOMETHING, she types on the screen. GUESS WHO WAS ON TELEVISION TONIGHT, TALKING ABOUT FOSTER CHILDREN?

I KNOW—MARIAH CAREY, I type back.

YES, MAMACITA—MAYBE WE CAN GET TO MEET HER?

I can't believe it, but Tiffany is always

angling for *something*. She's worse than Galleria! What does she think—just because Mariah Carey does a public service announcement for foster children, we're gonna get to meet her? I wanna scream at my clueless sister, "Get a grip, Tiff!"

All of a sudden, I notice that Galleria is online. WAZZUP, UPTOWN HOODIE? she types. I SEE YOU HANGING WITH SOME NEW CREW, RIGHT?

IT'S MY SISTER, I type back.

YOU'RE JOKING OR SMOKING? Galleria types on the screen.

NO, I'M NOT.

SEEMS LIKE THE TWO OF YOU ARE HANGING TIGHT LATELY, DON'T YOU THINK? Galleria types—and knowing her, there is more to that nibble than a piece of cheese.

NOT EXACTLY, I explain, then realize that Tiffany is "seeing" everything I say, so I'd better mention that she wants to audition for the Cheetah Girls. LISTEN, WHAT TIFFANY WANTS TO KNOW IS, CAN SHE SING FOR US?

SOMEONE MUST'VE CHANGED THE CHANNEL TO A TELEMONDO STATION! types Chanel, who is also in the chat room. Galleria must've beeped her. I know they have a secret code when they want to talk online. I'm gonna get a beeper soon, too.

SHE WANTS TO TRY OUT FOR THE GROUP, THAT'S ALL I'M TALKING ABOUT.

WHY DIDN'T YOU TELL US BEFORE? Galleria challenges me.

I KNOW, BUT WITH EVERYTHING GOING ON, I THOUGHT I SHOULD ASK NOW.

HI, GALLERIA! LimpCutie types, breaking into the conversation.

YOU WANNA RIFF WITH US SOMETIME? Galleria asks Tiffany.

YES!

CHANEL NO. 5, YOU WANNA HAVE SOME COMPANY TOMORROW NIGHT? Galleria asks, using Chuchie's onscreen name.

ESTÁ BIEN WITH ME!

When I sign off to Tiffany, I can't help but crack a joke. SEE YOU TOMORROW NITE AT CHANEL'S CRIB, LIMPCUTIE—BUT DON'T EXPECT MARIAH CAREY TO BE IN THE HOUSE CHECKING OUT YOUR AUDITION!

HEY, UPTOWN HOODIE, YOU NEVER KNOW! IF MAMACITA MARIAH KNEW HOW DOPE I WUZ, SHE WOULD FLUTTER HER WINGS LIKE A BUTTERFLY JUST TO SEE ME! SO WHY DON'T YOU CALL HER AND INVITE HER?

What was I thinking, inviting Tiffany to sing for the Cheetah Girls? Well, I didn't exactly invite her—Galleria did. I think Bubbles's invitation was more like a challenge to her, though.

My biology teacher, Mr. Roundworm, says genes have a mind of their own, and they do exactly as they please. Maybe he's right, 'cuz my sister Tiffany is definitely popping kernels in her own microwave, if you know what I'm saying!

Chapter 8

I haven't said anything about the Kats and Kittys drama to my crew, and I hope none of them bring it up. Mrs. Bosco is right—I shouldn't look any gift horse in the mouth, just check to make sure it has hooves. I know that my crew is down with me, so I shouldn't sweat it.

Oh, now I get it—maybe that's what Mrs. Bosco meant about the hooves part. Just make sure your friends—or the "gift horse"—are for *real*. Yeah, well my crew still blabbed their big mouths—and told *everybody* in the Kats and Kittys Klub that I'm a foster child—like *my* face should be on a poster, begging for donations or something!

Well, now I'm about to be face-to-face with my crew. They arrived at Chanel's house before I did, since I had to work my three-hour shift at the YMCA, then come back downtown to SoHo, where Chanel lives. Believe me, I was real glad to get some duckets in my pocket, though.

Aqua beams when she sees me—which makes me feel good to see my crew. That is, until Galleria asks, "What did Mrs. Bosco say about the donation?"

"You know, she thought it was cool," I say, but I can hear how choked my voice sounds.

"Dorinda . . . I, um, we thought it was okay to tell everybody about your situation," Aqua says earnestly. "It was Indigo's idea to put ACS on the charity voting ballot, because she saw Gaye on the news, too."

No wonder Indigo was so nice to me! The whole world saw Gaye on the news but me! Now my crew is standing around the living room, looking at me like I'm a lost puppy who needs a bone—and a home.

"I just wish you didn't tell *everybody*!" I blurt out, tears springing to my eyes.

"We're real sorry," Angie pipes up.

"Okay, squash it," I say, when I hear Pucci's footsteps running down the hallway.

"*Mamí* made stuff for your friends," Pucci says to Chanel. His eyes twinkling, he motions for us to come into the dining room.

Chanel hobbles in first. The table is covered with a pretty pink flowered tablecloth, and matching paper cups, napkins, and plates. From the looks of the food on the table, I can tell Chanel is definitely milking her sprained ankle for points. She even got Mrs. Simmons to make *plántanos* (fried plantains) and Dominican-style *pollo caliente* (spicy chicken wings and drumsticks) for us to snack on.

Now, looking at the food, I realize how hungry I am. I'm not sure if you're supposed to eat these things with your fingers or a knife and fork, so I wait until I see Galleria take one of the legs, put it daintily on her paper napkin, then eat it with her fingers. I do exactly as she does, including lifting my pinkie finger higher for effect.

Galleria, Chanel, Aqua, and Angie decide to sit down at the dining room table, while we wait for Tiffany to get here. After we get our grub on, the plan is that we are gonna hang out in Mrs. Simmons's big exercise studio, and sing a little with Tiffany. Pucci has already put a folding chair in the studio so Chanel can sit down. Even though her tailbone is healed, Chanel still has to stay off her badly sprained ankle as much as possible.

I think Chanel feels kinda lonely that we didn't come over and rehearse at her house last week. Pucci is being nice to Chanel too, which I can't believe! "Chanel, you want something to drink?" he asks.

"A Dominican cocktail, *por favor*!" Chanel says, milking Pucci for more points. Even though the pitcher of Mrs. Simmons's Dominican cocktail (I think it's mango and cranberry juice with tropical punch) is right in the middle of the table, Pucci pours it for Chanel.

Mrs. Simmons turns on the radio, then places some pretty crystal glasses back in the breakfront. Wow, all the crystal sparkling in the breakfront makes the room look really fancy!

"You girls have fun, but I've got to get back to work, because I'm on deadline," Mrs. Simmons says. But she keeps lingering in the dining room, doing things.

The radio deejay announces the Mariah Carey concert on Friday night.

"I wish they were giving away some free tickets, shoot," Angie blurts out.

"I wish we could just pay and go!" Chanel pipes up, loud enough for her mother to hear.

"Chanel, how are you going to go to a concert on crutches? *Dígame!*" Mrs. Simmons snaps. "Tell me that—even if you had the money?"

"What happened?" Chanel counters, getting that innocent look on her face, like she doesn't know what she said. "Disabled people get to go places too, *Mamí*!"

"I know, Chanel," Mrs. Simmons shoots back, like she's embarrassed. I wonder why Mrs. Simmons keeps lingering in the dining room area, even though she says she has work to do on that book she's writing. I think she wants to see what my sister Tiffany looks like or something, because she turns and asks me, "Where does your sister go to school?"

I freeze for a second, because I can't remember. Then it pops back into my head. "Um, St. Agnes of the Peril."

"Oh, private Catholic school," Mrs. Simmons says, like she's impressed.

"Uh-huh."

Pushing up the sleeves on her pretty pink

furry cardigan sweater, Mrs. Simmons keeps at it. "So how much younger is she than you?"

I almost choke on my chicken wing! Why is Mrs. Simmons being so nosy? Even Galleria pauses her chomp and looks up at me!

"Um, a year," I say, my stomach starting to get a bad case of the squigglies. Inside, I'm shrieking, *Please don't ask me any more questions about Tiffany!*

"So . . . she's thirteen?" Mrs. Simmons continues absentmindedly, now arranging some silver knives in the breakfront drawer.

For a split second, I wonder if I should tell a fib-eroni. Then I realize that eventually my crew is gonna find out that I'm only twelve years old, and not fourteen like they are—even though I'm in the ninth grade, too. "No, um, she's eleven," I say. Then I wait for the sky to fall on my head like Chicken Little.

Everybody stops and looks at me. I guess Chanel is better at math than she thinks, because she's the first one to say, "What happened? Do' Re Mi, how old are you?"

"T-twelve," I say, fighting back the tears.

"How could you be twelve years old!?" Aqua asks, so shocked that her eyes are bugging out.

The twins are still thirteen, see. Their grandmother sent them to school early, because she thought they were so smart. Well, now my crew knows how smart *I* am—or how *stupid*, for trying to tell a fib-eroni on the sneak tip!

"I got skipped twice already," I say apologetically.

"That's nothing to be ashamed of, Dorinda," Mrs. Simmons says, surprised.

"I'm sorry I didn't tell you before," I say, looking straight at Galleria, then Chanel, then Aqua and Angie. "I was embarrassed."

"You *should* be sorry for telling us a fib-eroni," Galleria snorts. "We tell you *everything*."

"Well, you didn't tell me you were going to blab to everybody in the whole world that I live in a foster home!" I blurt out. Just then, the doorbell rings. Galleria and I lock stares for a sec, before we're distracted by loud giggling coming from the hallway.

"*Mamí*, she has a Flammerstein Schwimmer scooter like I do!" Pucci says excitedly, riding his fancy-schmancy scooter into the dining area. It looks just like the one I saw in Tiffany's bedroom, except the knobs on Pucci's are acid green, and Tiffany's are neon pink.

"Pucci—don't make me take that thing away from you!" Mrs. Simmons yells. Then she notices Tiffany, and smiles a big, phony smile.

I feel so embarrassed when I see how corny Tiffany's outfit is. Now she's wearing a cheetah knit cap with a pom-pom on top, a matching cheetah sweat jacket, and a white skort—you know, the kind with shorts underneath. I notice how red her thighs are—probably because they're freezing to death. I look down at her feet to see why she looks so tall. I can't believe it—she went and got black Madd Monster shoes, just like mine!

"Aren't your legs cold?" Mrs. Simmons asks Tiffany, causing *everybody* to notice how short her skirt is, and making me more embarrassed than I already am!

"No," Tiffany says, giggling nervously.

"You have a funny giggle!" Pucci blurts out.

"I do," Tiffany says, giggling even more!

Chanel says something in Spanish to Pucci, which I don't understand, and he runs out of the dining room area.

"I like your shoes," Chanel coos to Tiffany.

"Thanks," she says, and now she's blushing. "I got the same ones Dorinda has."

"Come get your grub on," Galleria says, chuckling to Tiffany.

"Oh, thanks," she says, licking her lips.

"Of course. It ain't no thing but a chicken wing!" Galleria riffs, handing her a paper plate.

"You're the one who rhymes all the time, right?" Tiffany asks Galleria, like she's a famous singer or something.

Galleria giggles, but at least she doesn't snarkle the way Tiffany does. I'm trying to check out Galleria, Chanel, and the twins on the sneak tip, to see how they're feeling Tiffany. I can't believe Galleria hasn't said anything about Tiffany's outfit! Galleria's motto is, "You definitely don't wear white after Labor Day, or before Memorial Day." But Galleria is definitely on her best behavior tonight.

After we finish our munch, my crew starts "chatting" with Tiffany. Please don't let them ask her anything about this adoption situation, or our mother!

But I can tell that Galleria is angling for some info about our situation. And just like I thought would happen, Galleria asks Tiffany how she found out she was adopted!

"I found the key to my parents' safe-deposit

box!" Tiffany squeals with delight. "It took me two Saturday afternoons."

"You work fast, girlina," Galleria squeals back. "I'll make sure to keep you away from the jewel vault when I get one!"

I should have known those two would hit it off. Tiffany tells Bubbles every last detail, and Galleria just pries it out of her, like clues to an unsolved mystery.

"Dorinda, you know I've been hearing melodies all day to that song I wrote about you—'Do' Re Mi on the Q.T.'"

Why would Galleria bring that song up now? That's the one she wrote when she found out Tiffany was my sister. See, at first, I didn't tell my crew about Tiffany coming to find me. But when she showed up at the Apollo Theatre with her parents, to watch us compete in the Battle of the Divettes, I was busted—cold!

Afterward, Galleria wrote a song about it, because she said I'm the most secretive person she's ever met. Now she wants to sing the song in front of Tiffany! Where's the Sandman from the Apollo when you need him to drag her away, huh?

"Tiffany, why don't we all sing the song

together?" Galleria says, popping a track into the cassette.

"This is a master jammy whammy," Galleria explains. "See, Ms. Dorothea gets these phat club tapes made by some deejay, and we use them for rehearsing and performing."

"I know what this song is!" Tiffany says, excited. "It's from Mariah Carey's *Rainbow* album."

"Yeah, you're right," Aqua says, then looks at Tiffany. "Dorinda said you've got a real nice keyboard. How'd you learn to play?"

"I taught myself," Tiffany says proudly.

"You didn't know how to play the piano or anything?" Aqua asks, impressed. The twins go to LaGuardia Performing Arts High School, and even though they don't play any instruments, there are a lot of music majors in the mix at their school.

"No," Tiffany says proudly. "I didn't."

"Well, we've gotta come over sometime, and see your magic keyboard!" Angie jokes.

Tiffany takes her seriously, and says, "When do you wanna come?"

"Girlinas, we have to get back to the beat," Galleria cuts in. We all go stand next to Chanel, so she doesn't have to move her chair, and get ready to harmonize. This is what I love most about being in a singing group—just riffing together in rehearsal. When you're onstage, it's a lot more scary.

"Okay, let's sing the part, right after the lead, in C minor, and the chorus in B flat."

"Okay!" Tiffany says excitedly.

Galleria hands us each a copy of the song, then starts the intro. Chanel joins in, and then we're all supposed to sing the rest of the lead together:

"This is Galleria
and this is Chanel
coming to you live
From Cheetah Girls Central.
Where we process data that matters
And even mad chatter
But today we're here to tell you
About our friend, Do' Re Mi
(That's Miss Dorinda to you)
Kats and Kittys, the drama
Has gotten so radikkio
Just when we thought we knew our crew
Bam! The scandal was told!"

Finally, Galleria makes the motion for us to stop singing.

I know exactly why, too. Tiffany sings like a daffy dolphin—you know, Flipper, under water! Galleria looks at her and says, "Tiffany, sing the lead by yourself."

Tiffany gets all shy, and says, "I don't want to."

"Come on, Tiffany, we're just flowing!" Galleria says, prodding her along.

"Okay," Tiffany finally agrees, then giggles some more. "'But today we're here to tell you/About our friend, Do' Re Mi/That's Miss Dorinda to you!'" Tiffany sings, but then stops.

I take back what I said earlier—Tiffany sings *worse* than Flipper.

"Tiffany—you're um, gonna need a lot of vocal training to be able to sing with us," Galleria says slowly.

All of a sudden, I feel protective toward Tiffany. Please don't let Galleria go off on my sister!

"Um, yeah, I know," Tiffany says, smiling in that innocent way that she does. "But maybe I could play the keyboard in the group?"

Tiffany just won't quit.

"Tiffany, the Cheetah Girls are all singers," Galleria says. "I mean, Chanel, Dorinda, and I don't sing as well as Aqua and Angie do, but we've still had a lot of training." I can't believe how nice she's being to Tiffany! "I mean, we could play the keyboard together sometimes, for fun and stuff. That would be cool, right?" Galleria looks around at all of us for approval.

"Yeah, maybe that would help our rehearsals and stuff," I say, sticking up for Tiffany.

"Yeah," Chanel pipes up. "I wanna learn it, too!"

"But I wanna be *in* the Cheetah Girls," Tiffany says, pouting.

"Well, let's just wait and see," Galleria says finally.

Tiffany beams, like she's accepting an award or something. Then she lets out that hyena snarkle that makes everybody giggle, and we goof around for a while before Mrs. Simmons comes inside the studio and tells us it's time to go home.

We all burst into another round of giggles before we wiggle our separate ways home. Thank God for my crew—and Tiffany, too. I can't believe they found such a dope way out of this sticky situation! Letting Tiffany hang and play keyboard with us at rehearsals without letting her be in the group is a stroke of genius!

Chapter 9

I sneak into my apartment like a mouse on the nibble tip, because it's *really* late, and I don't want to wake my foster mother or my brothers and sisters, who are usually snoozing by this time. Mr. Bosco has probably already left. He usually stops by the Lenox Café before he heads up to the Bronx to his job and begins his graveyard shift at the stroke of midnight.

My heart starts pounding when I open the door—and see Mrs. Bosco and most of my foster brothers and sisters, all sitting in the living room! They're obviously waiting for me—everybody except for Arba, who is probably sleeping.

"What are y'all doing up?" I ask, trying to act

supa cool, even though my voice is squeaking even more than the front door.

Something must be wrong. I look over at Gaye, to see if I can peep this situation, but she is sitting quietly on the couch next to Mrs. Bosco, sucking her thumb. Maybe they found Gaye's mother, and she's gonna be leaving us pretty soon or something.

Twinkie runs over to me and gives me a supa-dupa hug. "We're gonna see the Butterfly lady tomorrow!" she squeals.

"Really?" I say, humoring Twinkie. Next she'll be telling me that Dorothy from *The Wizard of Oz* called and invited us to a picnic over the rainbow, you know what I'm saying?

"We're *all* going to see her!" Twinkie adds adamantly.

"Now, Rita, why you telling Dorinda that?" Mrs. Bosco says. Then she stops abruptly, because she's gonna break into one of her coughing spells. Her bronchitis is acting up again, now that it's getting cold outside. "I told you, we're gonna let Dorinda de—"

Finally, a cough catches up with Mrs. Bosco and she starts hacking. Then she tries to finish her sentence before it subsides—"decide how we gonna split up the t-t-t-ickets."

Did I hear her right?

Mrs. Bosco reaches over to the end table—but Nestor yells, "I got it, Mrs. Bosco!" He hops off the living room floor where he was perched, grabs the newspaper off the end table, and hands it to her with a big smile. *He* seems really excited, too, just like Twinkie.

Mrs. Bosco rests the newspaper on her lap, then takes out her wrinkled handkerchief—the one she always keeps in her dress pocket. I feel stupid standing there in the middle of the living room floor—like I've been called down to detention or something in school. I just can't wait until someone tells me what's going on! Finally, Mrs. Bosco opens up the newspaper, and points to a photo that I can't make out from where I'm standing.

"Go ahead and read it yourself, Dorinda," Mrs. Bosco says, handing me the newspaper. "It's too dark in here for me to read it to you, even with my glasses on."

"Okay." I move closer, and take the newspaper from her hand. This is one of the games we play—see, I know she's illiterate, even though I pretend I don't.

I stand next to the lamp by the end table and look at the photo Mrs. Bosco pointed to. It's a head shot of Mariah Carey, just sorta smiling. Then I read the small caption below her picture: "'Pop star Mariah Carey, a longtime spokesperson for New York City foster children, was so moved by the Eyewitness News report on the abandoned child found in Coney Island, that she has provided tickets to her Madison Square Concert tomorrow night for the foster family that took in the toddler. Ms. Carey could not be reached at press time, but her spokesperson says the Administration of Children's Services will be handling arrangements for the family to attend the sold-out concert.'"

"Are they talking about *us*?" I ask in disbelief.

"I guess so," Mrs. Bosco says with a satisfied smile, shifting her weight on the couch. Gaye peers up at me quickly with her intense black eyes, then quickly hides her face behind Mrs. Bosco's ample arm.

"Ms. Keisha saw the paper first—and by the time she came into the laundry room and told me, she'd already told everybody in the building about it. She wouldn't even let me keep her paper!" Mrs. Bosco says, shaking her head.

I can feel my cheeks burning. How come nobody told me about the article in the newspaper?

"Of course, Skip didn't have any more newspapers left," Mrs. Bosco says, rubbing her legs. "'Cuz those knuckleheads on the corner done stole half of them from him at the crack of dawn. So I had to go all the way over to the Korean place on Malcolm X Boulevard and buy one. You'd think Ms. Keisha coulda bothered to tell me that before I went all the way over to Skip's, but she's too busy acting like she *is* the newspaper!"

"How—?" I start to ask, but Mrs. Bosco is just getting started.

"Of course, Manty Clarke was over there buying a Lotto ticket, and he had the nerve to invite *himself* to the concert," Mrs. Bosco says, sounding pleased with herself. "I told that toothless fool he'd have more luck striking a deal with the tooth fairy to get tickets—and he just might get some new front teeth in the bargain!"

Khalil cracks up at Mrs. Bosco's joke, which snaps me out of my daze. I don't know why I'm upset, anyway. It figures that nosy Ms. Keisha—and everybody in the building—already knew about this before I found out.

Nobody cares enough to tell me anything first.

"And then Mrs. Tattle called here after you had already left for school," Mrs. Bosco says, yawning. She's probably been telling this story all day. "She sounded real pleased with herself, that's for sure. She said everybody down at the agency was real excited. I figured they would be—anything that gets their names in the papers when they ain't been accused of doing something wrong, like they always do."

"I wish somebody had told me before now," I say, disappointed that I wasn't here when the whole thing jumped off.

"Ain't you glad we're going to see Mariah Carey?" Khalil blurts out, making me feel embarrassed again.

"Of course I am," I say, trying to sound more excited about the whole situation. "What did Mrs. Tattle say when she called?"

"Just what it says there in the newspaper," Mrs. Bosco says, scratching her wig. "What's that you call her, Rita?"

"The Butterfly lady!" Twinkie says proudly, twirling herself on the couch.

"That's right—she said that the Butterfly lady gave us some tickets to go to her concert—

free tickets—otherwise I woulda told Mrs. Tattle she could keep them, 'cuz Mariah ain't paying no bills around here," Mrs. Bosco says, nodding her head.

I guess Mrs. Bosco sees the confused look on my face, because she adds, "I told her I was gonna put you in charge of the situation, 'cause you're the musical one around here. So I said to leave those tickets in an envelope at the box office with your name on it. Don't worry, ain't nobody can touch those tickets but you. I figured you'd wanna invite your friends."

"Oh, okay!" I say, my face lighting up. This is gonna be so dope—*me,* finally doing something for my crew! Now I feel stupid for getting upset. I guess Mrs. Bosco couldn't call me at school, because I don't have a cell phone or beeper, like Galleria and Chanel have. I wish I did have one—then I would know about things right when they're jumping off, like they do. But I'm just so excited—for the first time in my life, I've got something nobody else has! Finally, I get to be the lucky one!

"You know, it would be nice if you invited your sister, too," Mrs. Bosco says. She turns to Chantelle, who is sitting by the edge of the end table, fiddling with something. "Stop playing with the coasters—they're already raggedy enough as it is."

I wonder which sister she's talking about. I don't want to be sitting at a Mariah Carey concert with Monie the Meanie, acting like she's not having a good time, the way she always does. She thinks everything is corny—including me being in the Cheetah Girls.

"Um, you mean Monie?" I ask, waiting for the response.

"No, Dorinda. I mean that child Tiffany," Mrs. Bosco says, peering at me over her bifocals as if she's wondering why I'm being so dimwitty or something.

Why should I invite Tiffany? Mrs. Bosco must realize that I've gotta invite my whole crew before I invite anyone else. It's not like Mariah Carey's peeps have given us a dozen tickets or something like that, you know what I'm saying?

"But I should invite Twinkie—um, Rita, and—" I start in, getting defensive.

"I wanna go!" Nestor blurts out, cutting me off.

"I wanna go, too," says Khalil, sulking.

"How you divide the twenty-five tickets,

Dorinda, is your business," Mrs. Bosco says matter-of-factly.

"Did you say *twenty-five* tickets?" I ask, dumbfounded.

"That's what I been trying to tell you this whole time. Mrs. Tattle says they left twenty-five tickets for you at the box office," Mrs. Bosco says, like I should get with the program.

"That's so dope!" I say, finally getting excited. I plop down my backpack and take out my notebook and a pencil, so I can make a list of everyone I'm going to invite. "O-kay," I say out loud, flipping to an empty page.

Nestor, Khalil, and Kenya are pushing at each other, trying to get a look, but then I stop and look down at Mrs. Bosco. "Are you *sure* they said *twenty-five* tickets?"

"Dorinda, if you ask me again, I'm gonna tell Mrs. Tattle to give those tickets to somebody else, 'cuz you don't want 'em," Mrs. Bosco says, chuckling. "As a matter of fact, I'm gonna tell her to give them to Ms. Keisha!"

"Awright!" I say, jumping up and down. Twinkie grabs my waist and jumps up and down, too. "Okay!" I say again, looking around at all my foster brothers and sisters. "Who wants to go see Mariah Carey?"

"Me!" screams Twinkie.

At the top of the list, I write: Twinkie. Galleria. Chanel. Aqua. Angie. Tiffany. Me. That makes seven. I can't believe I still have eighteen tickets left! "Do *you* wanna go?" I ask Mrs. Bosco, embarrassed because I didn't even think of asking her first.

"Oh, no, that's for you younguns'—first fool that stepped on my foot, or pushed into me, and I'd be outta there," Mrs. Bosco says.

"But you're the one they gave the tickets to," I protest. If it wasn't for Mrs. Bosco taking in Gaye, we wouldn't be getting to go see Mariah Carey, you know what I'm saying? Suddenly I feel bad. I'll bet Mrs. Bosco doesn't want to come because she's not feeling well.

"No, Dorinda. I'm not going to be sitting up there with all those screaming fools. Now you know I can't let you go without an adult chaperone, so I figured you'd invite Galleria's mother. She is you girls' manager, after all," Mrs. Bosco says proudly. For the first time, I realize Mrs. Bosco really is proud that I'm in a singing group.

"You sure you don't want to go?" I ask her

again, ignoring Khalil, Nestor, and now Kenya's whining.

"Dorinda," Mrs. Bosco starts in, but I already know what she's gonna say, so I cut her off before she finishes.

"I know, if I ask you one more time," I say, finishing her sentence.

"That's right."

"Okay. Ms. Dorothea and Mr. Garibaldi will be our chaperones, and maybe Ms. Simmons, too." I write down their names, and then I think maybe I should invite Pucci, too. I'll ask Chanel. She may not want her mom hanging out with us, 'cuz now that she's been cooped up in the house with a sprained ankle, Chanel wants to get away from her.

This whole thing is so dope, I can't believe it's happening! Wait till I get online and talk to my crew! I feel so excited that I look over at Gaye and smile, even though I think she is probably scared of me. I wonder if I should bring her, too? Maybe not. What if she throws a fit in public? She would probably be frightened by all those people anyway.

As if reading my mind, Mrs. Bosco says, "I don't think it would be a good idea to bring

Gaye. You go on and have a good time."

"Okay," I say, writing down Pucci's name next.

"I wanna come!" Twinkie says for the fiftieth time.

"Rita, you're going—now go on to bed," Mrs. Bosco says, yawning. "I let you stay up so we could tell Dorinda, but it's time for *all of y'all* to go to bed."

Twinkie kisses me good night, and Mrs. Bosco takes Gaye by the arm to bring her into her bedroom. I say good-bye to Gaye, but she doesn't answer. I feel so bad for her. I know how mad she's gonna be when she's old enough to figure out what happened to her. Just like I was.

After Pucci's name, I write: Khalil. Nestor. Shawn. Okay, that makes fourteen people so far. I might invite Kenya—even though she's only six, and this is a concert for grown-ups. Topwe, Arba, and Corky are also pretty young.

Even though it kills me, I write down Chantelle and Monie. I know Monie's gonna want to bring her boyfriend—but that's too bad, 'cuz I can't invite everybody. Maybe I should go see if she's here.

Before I even walk into the bedroom, Monie,

who is propped on her bed like she's been waiting for me, blurts out, "I'm not going if you don't invite Hector, too."

"Okay," I say, giving in right away, because I don't want to fight with her. I don't want to be with her at the concert anyway, and if Hector is with her, she won't be on my case, you know what I'm saying?

Monie throws me a fake smile, then decides to pick a fight with me anyway. "I don't understand why Mrs. Bosco put *you* in charge of the tickets. *I'm* the oldest—she shoulda given them to *me*."

I can't believe Monie is trying to start a beef jerky about *that*. Where is she when Mrs. Bosco needs to pay bills, write letters to her sisters and brothers in North Carolina, or has to fill out reports for the foster care agency, huh? Mrs. Bosco doesn't ask Monie to write stuff for her—she asks *me*.

But right now, I don't have time to deal with Monie the Meanie, who is definitely earning her nickname to the max. All I can think of right now is getting online and talking with my crew.

"I didn't ask to be in charge of the tickets, okay?" I turn and say without thinking.

"Yeah, well, as long as you give me two, I don't care," Monie says. Propping herself up on her elbows, she adds, "I want you to give me the tickets, too, 'cuz I don't want to go with y'all. I'm gonna be over at Hector's house—and I'll leave from there."

"Um, that's cool with me, except the tickets are at the box office with my name on them," I reply matter-of-factly. That should squash this situation for real. Like it or not, the least Monie can do is come with us as a family.

"Awright, but don't expect me to be hanging with y'all," Monie says, sucking her teeth. Then she reaches under her pillow and puts on her Walkman headphones. I wonder where she got that from?

Probably Hector bought it for her. He's seventeen, and works full-time at Radio Shack 'cuz he dropped out of school. Monie told us about it like it was something to brag about, you know what I'm saying? No way would I drop out of high school. I'm gonna go to college, too—even if the Cheetah Girls blow up.

"That's cool with me," I say, trying to be chill. I open up the third drawer in the bureau, which is my drawer, and pull out my checkered pajamas. "Just meet us outside of Madison Square Garden at six-thirty."

"Six-thirty?" Monie says, getting an attitude. "Why so early?"

"'Cuz you never know if there's gonna be a long line or something," I say, feeling stupid. Maybe it is too early to go there, but I don't want to mess this up. "It is a Mariah Carey concert, Monie."

Monie acts like she doesn't hear me, but that's okay. If she isn't there at six-thirty, then we're gonna go inside without her. The heck with it, I decide. Mariah Carey invited the *family* that took in Gaye, so that means we're *all* going. I open my notebook again, and write down some more names: Hector. 17. Kenya. 18. Topwe. 19. Corky. 20. Arba. 21. Looking at all the names on the list again, I feel satisfied, so I close my notebook and put in on my nightstand.

I try to listen if Mrs. Bosco is still up, but I don't hear anything, so I tiptoe into the living room again. I don't think she'll mind if I use the telephone to call Galleria and Chanel. I have to beep them—putting 911 after their phone number, so they'll know to answer the page 'cuz it's important. Then they'll contact the twins.

I realize that maybe I should wait till tomorrow. But as I get near the telephone, and see that the coast is clear, I decide to call them anyway. Why should I wait? No way, José! My crew is gonna want the lowdown to this showdown—even if the crows are crowing, and the roosters are up singing cock-a-doodle-doo!

Chapter 10

I was so glad when school was over today, because Galleria and Chanel went around telling *everybody*—even Teqwuila and Kadeesha, whom they *never* talk to unless it's to squash a beef jerky—that I got twenty-five free tickets to the Mariah Carey concert tonight! Fashion Industries peeps were having Gucci Envy attacks all over the place!

Then I started feeling bad, because I couldn't invite everybody I'm cool with at school. In the end, I did invite LaRonda Jones from math class on the sneak tip. I *had* to hook her up, because she hooked me up once.

See, when we made our Cheetah Girls chokers, we sold them to peeps at school—but they ended up falling apart before first period was over—and LaRonda was the only one who was cool about the situation. I made LaRonda *promise* that she wouldn't go around telling everybody I invited her to Mariah's concert.

I'm sorry, but I can't help it if I'm a little superstitious. What if I drag all these people to Madison Square Garden, and there is no envelope with my name on it, huh? All I'm saying is, it wouldn't be the first time Mrs. Bosco got things mixed up. I'll never forget how embarrassed I was when I had to finally tell my crew that my adoption didn't go through, because Mrs. Bosco didn't understand the paperwork and the whole adoption procedure.

Just after I finish getting dressed up for the concert, someone knocks on my open bedroom door, and I turn to see who it is.

"How do I *loook,* Dorinda?" Topwe asks me in his funny African accent. He grins, showing off that big gap in his front teeth that always always makes me smile. Topwe then strikes a pose in the doorway, fingering the burgundy bow tie he's wearing with his white shirt and gray pants.

"You look dope!" I say, noticing that the sores

by his mouth look like crusty critters. Topwe's HIV virus has been acting up lately, and he even had to stay home from school all week. But he's been feeling better since yesterday, and anyhow, nothing was gonna keep him from going to the Mariah Carey concert. Not even HIV!

"Come here, lemme put a little lotion on that handsome face." I grab the bottle of Magik Potion lotion, and rub some all over Topwe's face. I don't think the stuff is magic as much as it's just plain greasy.

I'm so glad I decided to invite all my brothers and sisters to the concert, even if they don't know who Mariah Carey is. I can tell they are just happy to be going somewhere, because we never really do stuff together like a real family, you know what I'm saying?

I put on my cheetah bell-bottoms and matching jacket, then look at myself in the mirror on the back of the closet door. Today, *I'm* the cheetah who's got something to growl about! Taking another long look, I decide that I need a few sparkles around my eyes, then I'm good to go. I open a pot of Manic Panic gold glitter and dab it on.

Twinkie runs into my bedroom without

knocking first, but I don't say anything, even though she knows she's not supposed to do that. "Can I have some?" she asks, eyeing my glitter. She reaches for the jar, dropping a candy wrapper on the floor.

"Go ahead," I tell her, but I dab on the gel for her. Twinkie turns to run out of my bedroom, but I yell after her, "Pick up the wrapper you dropped. You know Cheetah Girls don't litter, they glitter!"

"Yes, Cheetah Bunny," Twinkie squeals, throwing the wrapper into my garbage can and running out again. "I'll go get everybody."

When I come out of my bedroom, I'm surprised that Mrs. Bosco is wearing her nice brown corduroy jumper and her "good wig."

"I guess I might as well see what all this ruckus is about," she says, still brushing her wig into place.

"Of course," I chuckle. Now I realize that I was right. She *wasn't* feeling well yesterday. As if she's reading my mind, Mrs. Bosco goes on to say, "I must say I'm feeling pretty good today."

"You look good, too," I chuckle, helping her on with her jacket.

Now I'm wondering what we're gonna do

about Gaye. "Is Gaye, um, coming with us?"

"Yes, indeed—unless you done gave away all the tickets," Mrs. Bosco asks.

"No," I say, feeling embarrassed. I'm not going to tell her that I didn't invite twenty-five people because I felt kinda scared about this whole thing not coming off.

"I think Gaye will be fine. I'll just stay close to her," Mrs. Bosco explains, like she's trying to reassure me or something. Then she goes into the kitchen.

Gaye is sitting quietly on the couch, waiting. She is wearing one of Arba's pink jumpers, and a pretty pink bow in her braid on top.

"You look pretty, Gaye," I say, but I don't expect her to answer me, so I just turn to go back in my bedroom and get my backpack.

"*Tank* you," she says quietly.

At first, I'm startled that Gaye has actually said something to me, but I try not to make a big deal out of it. I smile at her again, but she quickly puts her head down. Walking into my bedroom, I realize that Ms. Keisha is right as usual—Gaye *does* have a West Indian accent.

"Monie's gonna meet us at the Garden, so we should all go downstairs to wait for Mr.

Garibaldi," I yell to Mrs. Bosco from the front door. I get everyone out the door, and we're off to the concert!

I'm so glad that Ms. Dorothea and Mr. Garibaldi are coming. Mr. Garibaldi, or Franco, as he insists I call him, even volunteered to pick up my family and drive us down to Madison Square Garden, since he has a big van that he uses to bring clothes from his factory in Brooklyn to their boutique in SoHo.

Mr. Walker, the twins' father, is gonna pick up Ms. Dorothea, Galleria, and Chanel and bring them to the Garden with the twins. Mr. Walker has a Bronco, and sometimes he and Mr. Garibaldi try to outdo each other over who's driving who, if you know what I'm saying.

While we stand outside our building, waiting for Mr. Garibaldi, some of our neighbors give us a shout-out. You'd think we won the lottery or something!

"I can't believe y'all are going to see Miss Mariah. I wish I was going. Don't forget to bring me back a CD, or a T-shirt, or *something*," yells Ms. Keisha, sticking her head out the window, her bright pink hair rollers bobbing all over the place as she laughs.

"Well, you'd better settle for an empty popcorn container, 'cuz that's all you'll be getting," Mrs. Bosco mumbles under her breath.

We get to the Garden, and wait outside for everybody I've invited. Pretty soon, I start getting a bad case of the squigglies. People are shoving each other, and crowding around the entrance like it's Christmas or something.

"Tickets, tickets," whispers this scary-looking guy right in my ear. I look at him, startled, and he says, "You need tickets?"

"Um, no," I say, feeling scared.

"What's he want?" Chantelle asks me.

"He's a scalper," I explain.

"What's that?"

"That's people who sell tickets at a higher price," I explain to her, trying to calm down. Please, God, let our tickets be at the box office. Don't let this turn into Madison "Scare" Garden or something! If it's all a mistake, or if there's a mix-up and the tickets aren't there, I'll never live it down—I'll just sink into the ground and die of embarrassment!

"Look at all these people—they got free tickets, too?" Shawn asks me. I can tell he's kinda uncomfortable standing around.

"No, they didn't get free tickets—we did!" yells Twinkie loudly.

"Shhh, Twinkie," I say, holding her close.

"There's Monie!" yells Chantelle as my older sister approaches with her boyfriend, Hector.

"Heh, wazzup, Dorinda," he says, giving me a kiss on the cheek. "Thanks for inviting me." At least *he* has some manners. Maybe he should give Monie lessons.

I'm so happy when I see Galleria, Ms. Dorothea, Chanel, and Pucci walking through the crowd that I could jump up and down.

"Do' Re Mi, you are definitely pos-seeee!" riffs Galleria when she sees me. She puts out her hand so we can do the Cheetah Girls handshake.

Chanel is smiling as she walks through the crowd on her crutches.

"Coming through—can't you see she's on crutches?" Ms. Dorothea says sternly to the rowdy posse that's blocking their way.

Where is Tiffany, I wonder? She said her parents were gonna drop her off, but maybe they went to the wrong entrance or something. I mean, Madison Square Garden is supa-dupa big.

"You should've seen my mom's face this

morning when I told her," Chanel heckles when she's finally standing next to me. "She almost lost her balance belly dancing!"

"She practices so early in the morning?" I act surprised.

"*Sí, mamacita*—sometimes she gets up at six o'clock to exercise!" Chanel says, her eyes bugging wide.

"She's not coming?" I ask.

"No way, José! Her boyfriend is in town, and they're going to see *La Boheme*."

"Wow," I say, wondering what that is—probably something French, knowing Mrs. Simmons.

"Um, Mrs. Bosco, can you wait here with everybody while I go get the tickets?" I ask. See, I'm getting more and more scared and scared that the tickets won't really be there—and until I'm holding them in my hot little hand, I won't rest easy.

"Go ahead," Mrs. Bosco says.

"I'll go with you, Do'," Galleria volunteers.

When we see how long the line is at the box office, I get even more nervous. "We're gonna be here all day," I moan to Galleria.

"Hang tight," she says, running over to a

security guard. I can tell by the way she's giggling that she's angling for something. "This is the wrong line," she says when she returns, wearing a satisfied grin. "We've gotta go to the Will Call window."

"Word?" I say, impressed, because Will Call sounds kinda important.

"Will Call is where they keep all the Press and VIP tickets," Galleria informs me.

I'm still nervous as I walk up to the Will Call window and ask for the tickets. "Um, they should be under Dorinda Rogers," I say to the attendant.

"Excuse me," she says, not smiling, "you gotta talk louder."

"I said, *Dorinda Rogers,*" I say, speaking up louder this time.

It seems like a thousand years are going by as we wait for her to flip through stacks of envelopes looking for our tickets. I can feel the sweat breaking out on my forehead and under my arms.

"Here you go," the attendant says, shoving an envelope through the window slot.

"Yippee-yi-yay!" Galleria shrieks, pinching my arm as I open the envelope and count the tickets.

"Don't let people see them!" Galleria adds, standing in front of me. "That guy over there is peeping the situation. This is the Big Apple—you know, they've got scalpers and pickpockets everywhere!"

"I know," I reply, embarrassed because I should know better. I shove the tickets into my backpack.

"Are we in business?" Galleria asks.

"Yeah!" Quickly, I count in my head all the people I invited, and the number of tickets I have in my backpack. Now I feel bad, because we still have some tickets left.

LaRonda and Tiffany are waiting with Chanel when Galleria and I get back. Tiffany is wearing the same white skort she had on the other day, but I don't say anything. I'm just glad to see her.

"Hi, Dorinda *mamacita*!" she says excitedly.

Chanel and Twinkie giggle at her Spanish.

"Wow, I like your hair," Tiffany exclaims to Twinkie.

"Thank you," my little sister says, beaming back. "You're Dorinda's sister?"

"Yeah," Tiffany says, looking at me for approval.

"You're the one with the keyboard?" Twinkie asks her.

"Yeah."

"Can I play it too?" Twinkie says, squinching up her nose.

"Oh, yeah—you wanna come over?"

"Can I?" Twinkie says, looking over at me.

"Don't look at me, Twinkie—she invited you," I say, chuckling. Now I can see that Twinkie and Tiffany are sort of alike, too—they both wanna get into the mix any way they can.

"Can I come over your house, for real?" Twinkie asks her.

"Yeah—you can come over for real!" Tiffany says excitedly.

Now I feel good that I'm not the only one who's got a new groove—it seems like my whole family, and the rest of the Cheetah Girls, are gonna get one, too.

"Girl, I can't believe we're going to see Mariah!" LaRonda pipes up outta nowhere. "You shoulda seen Derek's face when I told him."

"What did he say?" Galleria asks, chuckling. Even though she pretends she doesn't like the Red Snapper, we all know she does.

"His face was crushed, okay?" LaRonda

says, rolling her neck and pointing her index finger at the same time.

"I can't believe it, but I've still got tickets left," I say to Ms. Dorothea.

"That's fabulous—at least we'll have an empty seat to put our jackets on!" Ms. Dorothea says, satisfied.

"That's a real good idea, Ms. Dorothea!" Aqua says excitedly as we push our way through the entrance.

"Don't get *too* excited, darling, because my hat had better not get crushed!" Ms. Dorothea removes her big cheetah fake-fur hat.

"You should make those for your store," I yell to her.

"Are you kidding, Dorinda? I've gotta save a few head-turning designs for my private collection, or else I'd see myself going and coming all day!"

"You're right about that!" I chuckle back. Everybody copies Ms. Dorothea's designs, and some of her customers like to dress exactly like her—because Ms. Dorothea has the flavor that everybody savors, you know what I'm saying?

"Isn't this blazin' amazin', that *we're* at a

Mariah Carey concert?" Galleria riffs to Aqua as we make our way to our seats.

"Yes, indeed. We definitely have to give thanks to the Lord above," Aqua says, her big eyes popping.

"Well, I think the Lord would appreciate you giving thanks to Mrs. Bosco down here first!" Ms. Dorothea snipes.

We take our seats—which are about halfway back from the stage in the orchestra section. Soon, the place fills up, and we can all feel the electricity in the Garden as the lights go down, and the spotlights start roaming the walls.

"She's coming!" Twinkie yells in a shrilly voice, clapping excitedly.

The crowd starts chanting, "Mariah! Mariah! Mariah!"

"Do you think we should stick around to meet her afterward?" Galleria yells to me and Chanel as the crowd starts screaming with anticipation.

"It's worth a try!" Chanel says. "I mean, after all, Do' Re Mi and her family are VIPs—*está bien?*"

"You know who else are VIPs?" I say. "The Cheetah Girls!"

Galleria's eyes light up, and I can see how amped she gets by my attitude. "That's right, baby," she says. "Mariah's gonna help us fly—'cuz the Cheetah Girls are gonna *do* or *die*!"

Who's Got the Groove

We thought we had it goin' on
writing songs and gettin' along
that's Miss Chanel acting swell
and Galleria always freer
popping gum and acting glum
when the groove ain't right
and Toto bites with all his might!

Got a new member in our crew
Now she's got the rhymes
That's Miss Dorinda to you
Always true and
definitely crew
on the new school tip
without a slip

Who's got the groove?
Who's got the moves?
Miss Dorinda got it goin on'
till the break of dawn
she's riffing songs
or doing rhymes
on the banjo chords
and the mighty keyboard!

Who's got the groove?
Who's got the moves?
Miss Dorinda got it goin' on
till the break of dawn
So can't we all get along?
(I told you Tiffany is dope so let's cope and make her crew)
(Shut up, Chanel, before the copyright police come and get you, mamacita!*)*

The Cheetah Girls Glossary

Angling for info: Being nosy.

Beef jerky: Static. A fight. A beef. As in, "Why she always trying to start a beef jerky with me? I'm not the one wearing a weava-lus hairdo, she is!"

Blazin' amazin': Phat. Dopa-licious.

Blow up your spot: When someone is trying to make you feel large or important. As in, "Did you see the way Loquanda was talking about you to Rerun? She was definitely trying to blow up your spot."

Bringing in the noise: Causing trouble. Acting rowdy. Or, having a good time and showing off your skills.

Brouhaha: A fight in a restaurant or a public place.

Buggin': Getting upset or acting cuckoo.

Diddly widdly: Nada. Nothing. Not even a

crumb. As in, "I'm not giving her diddly widdly, 'cuz she wrecked my flow."

Dim-witty: Someone who needs to change the lightbulb in their brain. Clueless, but definitely not a dum-dum.

Fib-eronis: Teeny-weeny fibs. Purple lies and alibis!

Get with the program: Figure something out. Go along with something. As in, "Loquanda and I are trying out for the track team—so you'd better get with the program, or you'll be hanging by yourself after school, okay?"

Good to go: Ready for Freddy. Ready for any thing!

Graveyard shift: That spooky time of night between midnight and eight o'clock in the morning, when most people are sleeping, except for "night owls," mummies, and vampires, or people who are working the graveyard shift. It is not to be confused with "Frankenstein Hour," however, which is when most mummies—alive or dead—come out of their grave for a little fresh air, 'cuz they've got time to spare!

Gunky: Dirty. Yukky. Like muddy water.

It ain't no thing but a chicken wing: It's cool.

Everything's cool. Or, it could simply mean, *mamacita*, don't get too excited, it's just chicken!

Loco: Crazy. Cuckoo.

Lyrical flow: Someone who is good with words and writing songs, raps, or poems.

Milking for points: Taking advantage. Working it. As in, "Just 'cuz she got an A on the algebra quiz, she is definitely milking our math teacher for points."

My bad: Excuse me, I made a mistake. Oopsy, doopsy, this one's on me.

On the D.D.L.: On the down, down low. To do something without other people knowing about it. For example, "I want to make my mom a beaded necklace for her birthday, so I'm gonna have to do it on the D.D.L. so my brother won't give away the surprise." Can also mean, on the divette duckets license, which means buying something on the cheap.

Peeped: To catch on to something or pull someone's sleeve about something. As in, "I peeped Janessa cheating on the math test!"

Peep the situation: To try to figure out something. To look for clues to a situation.

Pickpocket: A sneaky bozo who goes around stealing wallets out of people's purses and pockets without them knowing it, then disappears faster than Houdini.

Plagiarism: Using someone else's words without giving them credit. In the case of songs, it can be very few words. For example, using the words *Living la vida loca* would qualify as plagiarism, since Ricky Martin already made that phrase famous in his song.

Radikkio: Ridiculous.

Right on the duckets: Right about something. As in, "You were right on the duckets. Crystal just told me that Tiara is not gonna show up. She left us hanging!"

Snarkle: A cross between a cackle and a giggle.

Stomping: Good. Dope. Tight. As in, "That song is stomping."

Street gravy: Gunky, dirty mud-filled water from the sewers.

What's the deal-io: What's the deal?

In the House with Mouse!

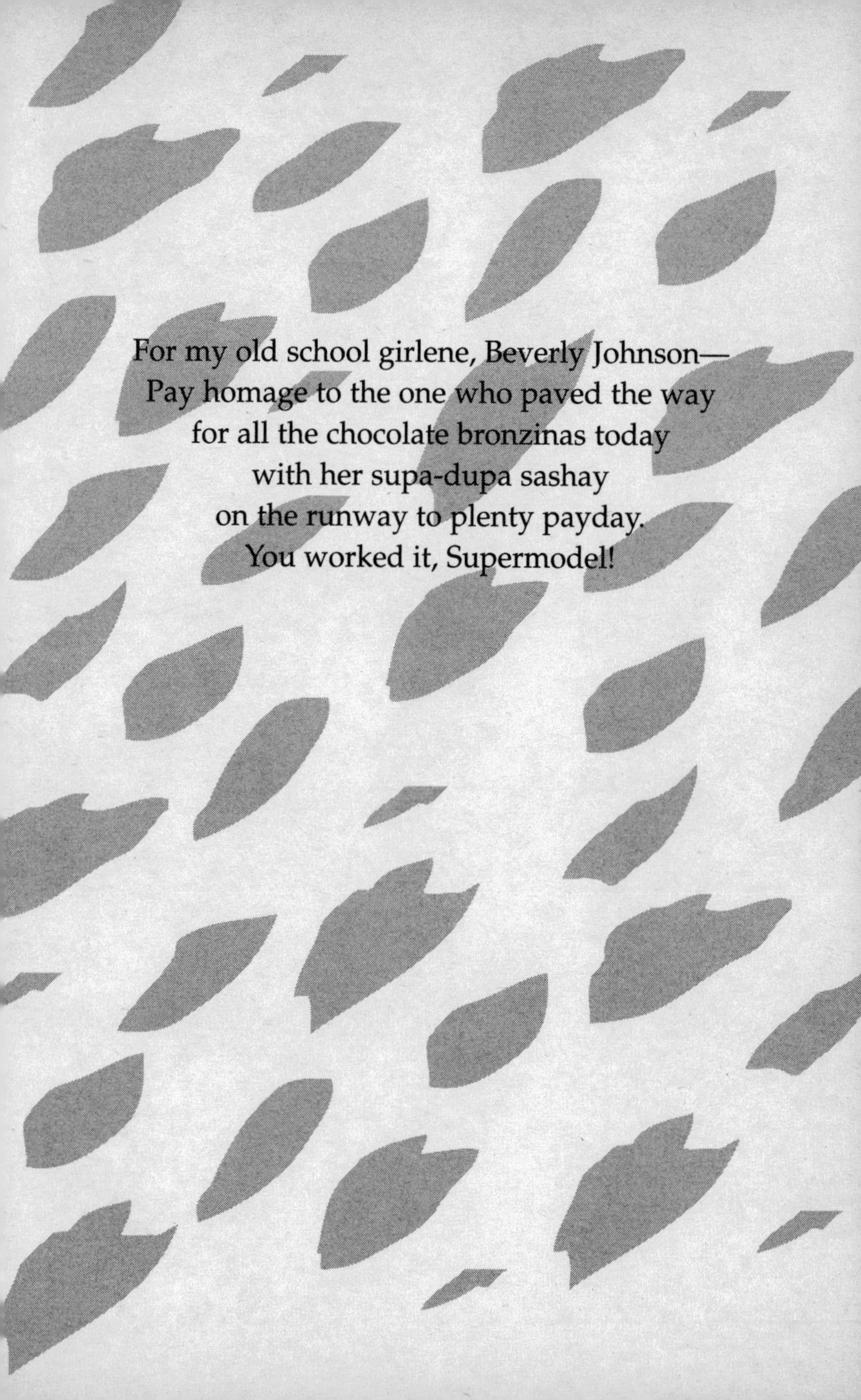

For my old school girlene, Beverly Johnson—
Pay homage to the one who paved the way
for all the chocolate bronzinas today
with her supa-dupa sashay
on the runway to plenty payday.
You worked it, Supermodel!

Chapter 1

We cannot believe how big Madison Square Garden is—a whole lot bigger than the Astrodome back home. It feels like everybody in New York is sitting right here with us at the Mariah Carey concert!

That's right, the Cheetah Girls are waiting for the "Butterfly" diva to come onstage and sing up a storm—along with about 70,000 other people who are packed into the arena, screaming at the top of their lungs, "Mariah, Mariah, Mariah!"

My twin sister, Angie, puts her hands over her ears because this is more noise than we're used to, but I'm having too much fun to mind. See, we usually feel the same way about things, because we're identical twins in every way. The only way you can tell us apart is that Angie has a beauty mark on her left cheek.

The rest of the Cheetah Girls don't mind the noise or big crowds, because they grew up in New York City and are used to its hectic, rowdy ways.

The Cheetah Girls, of course, are: Galleria "Bubbles" Garibaldi, Chanel "Miss Cuchifrita" Simmons (she got her new nickname because of her latest ballet capers, which have landed her on crutches, thank you, ma'am!), Dorinda "Do' Re Mi" Rogers, and, of course, your favorite singing twins from Houston—little ol' me, Aquanette Walker, and my other half, Anginette. (Obviously, it's no secret which one has the bigger mouth, and tends to hog all the attention. Angie is quieter than I am—and sneakier, too!)

We still cannot believe how we got to be sitting in these too-small-for-our-butts seats tonight. It's all because Dorinda got twenty-five free tickets. (Yes, ma'am, from our mouths to God's ears!) Actually, Dorinda got to be *in charge* of the twenty-five tickets, because they were given to her foster mother, Mrs. Bosco.

What happened was, the foster care agency contacted Mrs. Bosco to take in an abandoned toddler named Gaye who was left by her little self to wander around the Coney Island projects. The police department tried really hard to find Gaye's family—they put up big posters all over the city and everything. Even the local TV news stations ran stories showing her picture, but nobody came forward with any information. (New York is sooo big, you cannot imagine all the people who live here and don't even know each other's business, like they do back home.) Anyway, even though Mrs. Bosco already had eleven mouths to feed, she took Gaye in all the same.

I look over at Gaye, who has the cutest little dimples and the biggest, saddest brown eyes. She's sitting very still in her seat, with her hands folded in her lap and her legs dangling back and forth.

"I'll bet she must be around four years old," I whisper in Angie's ear, even though she can't hear me—but she figures it out when I flash four fingers under her nose. (Twins can read each other's minds, too.)

It's still hard to believe that a mother would

do something as evil as abandoning her child. But Big Momma, our grandmother back home in Houston, says, "Sometimes people lose their way, then lose their minds." We put Gaye in our prayers now, and we're never gonna take *our* parents for granted again—even if they are dee-vorced. And even though Daddy is acting stranger than ever—which I'll tell you more about in a minute.

But first, I know you must be wondering what any of this has to do with Mariah Carey. Well, when Mariah heard about Gaye on the news, she was so touched by the story that she had her record company contact the foster care agency, and provide free tickets to her concert for Mrs. Bosco and all her foster kids. There were more than enough tickets to go around—which is how the Cheetah Girls came to be here, too.

It's funny how things work out. For Thanksgiving, Angie and I pulled a few strings to get the rest of the Cheetah Girls to come down to Houston and spend Thanksgiving with our family—*and* to perform with us in the "Houston Helps Its Own" charity concert. (Yes, ma'am, the concert folks actually paid for the rest of the Cheetah Girls to fly down!) Now, Dorinda has pulled *her* strings to make sure we're here with her and her family—taking up twenty-five seats in a row. One of the seats is just for our coats and Ms. Dorothea's hat—how do you like *that* peach cobbler?

Who's Ms. Dorothea? Why she's the manager of our group. She's also Galleria's mom, *and* the most original person we've ever met. With her is Galleria's dad, Francobollo Garibaldi. He's Eye-talian—from Italy!—and he just loves my holiday eggnog. Mr. Garibaldi speaks with this Italian accent that makes everything sound like a *hoot*. He is even funnier than our uncle Skeeter back in Houston, if you can believe that.

Our daddy is here, too—even though he seems a little peaked lately. Maybe it's because he wants to be with his girlfriend—High Priestess Abala Shaballa Bogo Hexagone. No, you're not seeing things. That's her name! And as strange as it is, she is even stranger. Angie and I don't like her one bit. Ever since she came into our daddy's life, he hasn't been the same—and we wish she would get on her broomstick and ride right out of it again! Luckily, tonight she had to go to a special coven meeting with her kooky flock of followers, so she isn't here at the concert.

Most of Dorinda's family is here with us—her foster mother, Mrs. Bosco, and her eleven foster brothers and sisters—including Gaye, who I told you about earlier. I can't remember all their names—except for Shawn, Nestor, Twinkie, Kenya, Chantelle, Topwe, and the oldest of the Bosco bunch—Monie (if she pokes her mouth out any farther, it's gonna drop on the floor like a platter!), who has brought along her boyfriend, Hector. Dorinda also invited her half sister, Tiffany (who wants to be in our group, but can't sing a lick!). Last but not least, LaRonda, who goes to school at Fashion Industries East with Dorinda, Galleria, and Chanel, is also here. (Next year, we hope the rest of the Cheetah Girls will transfer to our school—LaGuardia Performing Arts Annex, which is the most competitive performing arts school in the city, and filled with Mariah wannabes.) LaRonda is here because we owed her a big favor, but that's a whole 'nother story.

The only person who *isn't* here at the concert with us (and should be) is Chanel's mom, Mrs. Juanita Simmons. Her boyfriend, Mr. Tycoon, is in town, and they went to an opera at Lincoln Center. Nonetheless, Chanel is obviously tickled pink about being out with us and having fun. Like I said earlier, she is walking on crutches, because she fell on her tailbone during a ballet school audition.

Yes ma'am, we should have seen that one coming. When we were in Houston for Thanksgiving, Chanel was practicing ballet at our mother's, and fell on her butt, spraining her ankle a little. Then, at the audition, she sprained it much worse, 'cuz there was no carpet on the floor to protect her. She fell on her butt, like I said—right in front of the people who were auditioning her. As bad as she hurt herself, I think the embarrassment hurt worst of all. Ever since then, we've been trying to help her get better. We even had to postpone putting on a showcase for Def Duck Records until Chanel's ankle heals.

"When is Mariah coming on? It seems like we've been waiting forever!" whines Nestor, Dorinda's eight-year-old foster brother. Finally, the lights go down, but we see that it's not Mariah Carey at all, but the opening act assembling onstage. Now I want to whine like

Nestor, because I feel so disappointed. It seems like we've been waiting forever for the "Rainbow Diva" to come onstage. (*Rainbow* is the name of one of her albums.)

The opening act is none other than that very "last year" group, The LoveBabiez, whose first single off their debut album—*Sweet Lullaby*—makes me wanna boohoo for Mariah. I just don't like this song at all—the lyrics are not original, and the harmony is too loud. All of us clap along to the LoveBabiez music anyway, because we are here to have a good time.

"Didn't that song go lead?" I scream into Galleria's ear.

"Actually, it went gold," Galleria screams back, correcting my mistake. "But we'll see if they still have the Midas touch next year, or if they end up somewhere sucking on their pacifiers."

Galleria is right. It seems like it's real hard to keep a music career going in this business, and that makes all of us real scared. We could get left out in the cold, like a bunch of wannabe cheetah cubs searching for our next meal!

See, you have to understand the music business—every day there is a new singing group with a new batch of songs, climbing up the charts because they had a really good producer working with them. Then, just as soon as the song leaves the charts, people forget all about the group. That is, unless you have pipes like Mariah, or Christina Aguilera, or really know how to make an impression because you're so original—which is what I hope happens to the Cheetah Girls.

I mean, I think we sing real well, but the other thing we have on our side is that Galleria and her mom, Ms. Dorothea, know how to stick out in a crowd, so our whole image is real original. But we'll see what happens—it's still too early to tell.

"Those shorts they're wearing look like *Pampers*," Galleria shrieks in my ear. I chuckle along, but I don't want Galleria to strain her voice yelling like that. Our vocal coach, Drinka Champagne, is always on us about "carrying on," as she calls it, "for no reason."

After twenty minutes, the LoveBabiez finish their set and hop into their oversized strollers, which are pushed off the stage by nannies in short skirts.

"Well, they sure had a lot of gimmicks for their show is all I can say," I humph to my sister.

Angie throws me a look, like, "When is Mariah Carey coming on?"

The lights go down again, and everybody in the audience screams. This time, I hope the "Rainbow Diva" herself will appear, so that the amateurs can go home. We are so excited we can hardly stay in our seats. Galleria jumps up, clapping, and the rowdy boys in back of us scream, "Sit down, Tony the Tiger!"

I see the look on Galleria's face, and I know she is mad. We hate when people make fun of our cheetah outfits—especially Galleria, because she isn't having it. I grab her hand and motion for her to sit down, because I don't want her getting upset or causing a scene. I mean, Galleria is very outspoken. She would do something like stick her tongue out at the rowdy boys and snarl like a wildcat, even though I don't think she would embarrass us in front of Mrs. Bosco and our Daddy. Luckily, the "Rainbow Diva" *finally* floats onto the stage.

"Oooh, look at her gown," I moan out loud, because I'm so caught by surprise. Mariah is wearing a white, sparkly, sequin gown to the floor—the spotlight follows her onstage, and it makes her look just like a beautiful angel. Her hair is so long and pretty—like Galleria's, except she straightens it more than Galleria does.

Now Galleria is happy again. She flashes her braces and puts her hands in the air, pushing her palms to the sky to the beat of the intro music. I look down the row at Daddy and smile, just to make sure he's all right—and he smiles back. I'm so glad he came with us. I know he usually just likes to relax with his pipe after work, sitting in his reclining chair, listening to jazz music—that is, when he isn't spending time with his High Priestess, the most original "pecan nut" we've ever met!

When Mariah starts to sing, Angie grabs my hand. Mariah's voice just sends chills down my spine, because she can really work her range to upper registers that we don't even have! Sure, we have sung in church choirs since we were seven, but we don't have voices like hers. Actually, no pop singer in the whole world has a voice like Mariah's—except maybe old-school singers like Minnie Riperton, Sista Fudge, and Whitney Houston.

Galleria grabs my right hand and squeezes it. Now we all sing along to Mariah's opening song—"Heartbreaker"—which is from her

Rainbow album. Of course, we know each and every word to *all* her songs, because we listen to the radio all the time—which drives Daddy crazy. We try to explain to Daddy that we're not listening just for fun. Now that we're in a singing group, we have to stay on top of the game, and keep up with the latest songs. Daddy just shakes his head—if it isn't jazz or gospel, he thinks it sounds like "a whole lotta noise."

I look over at Mr. Garibaldi, and he is just beaming and clapping along. We wish Daddy could have a good time like that, but he doesn't—especially not since he and our mother have been dee-vorced. You'd think he would be happy that we came up here to live with him—and maybe he is, but Daddy has a strange way of showing his feelings.

An hour or more goes by, but it seems like five minutes. Mariah belts out song after beautiful song, and I'm in heaven just to be here.

"I wish our seats were closer to the stage," Angie mumbles in my ear. I throw her a look. Of course, I'm thinking the same thing, but I'm just grateful to be here—even if we are sitting way up in the third tier of seats.

"Yeah, I wish we could see her up close," I yell back, checking out all the musicians in her band—thirteen of them—and the beautiful, glittering balls suspended on the stage. "Maybe one day, we'll get to sit in the front row of a concert, but you've gotta admit, this beats the Karma's Children concert in Houston any old day!"

"Go, Mariah!" I scream for good measure, as she announces the last song she is going to sing. It's one of my favorites—"When You Believe"—the duet she did with Whitney Houston for the *Prince of Egypt* movie. All of a sudden, I realize that *my* voice is getting hoarse from yelling all night.

"I'm gonna have to drink hot tea with lemon as soon as we get home," I mumble to Angie, thinking about our vocal practice in the morning. Every Saturday, the Cheetah Girls take vocal and dance lessons at Drinka Champagne's Conservatory. And believe me, Drinka doesn't play, either—she can tell if we're not singing up to speed, or just being plain lazy—and she'll call us out in front of everybody!

After clapping a thousand times (my hands are sore, too), the lights go up, and we all stand up and start putting on our coats. I beam at Galleria, and I know we're thinking the same thing—and we're not even twins!

"I wonder how we're gonna get backstage?" Galleria ponders out loud. "I guess it can't go any worse than our Karma's Children dis-miss." After that concert, the security guards gave us the bum's rush, not even letting us near Karma's Children's dressing room—even though we were one of the opening acts!

"I know that's right," I say, shrugging my shoulders.

"Well, I don't care. I swear this time we're gonna 'bum rush' the situation into a celebration," Galleria says, beaming her big smile.

"That's fine with me, too," I reply, wondering how I'm gonna explain this to Daddy.

"That's fine with me three," Dorinda adds, now that she's in on our conversation.

"Was that off the hook, snook, or what?" Galleria says, beaming again.

"You can say that again," Angie says, putting her arm through mine.

"I hope we get to perform here one day—the Cheetah Girls at Madison Square Garden." Galleria has that starry-eyed look that makes her, well, someone special. "And wait till you see the security guards who'll be guarding *us*—they're gonna make those Mighty Men in Houston look like lunch meat!"

"I know that's right," I say again. When Galleria gets that look in her eyes, you know something good is about to happen, because there is no stopping her determined ways.

I just wonder when something is gonna happen with our group. With Chanel being on crutches, we don't want to push anything, but Def Duck Records did say they were going to put us in the studio with producer Mouse Almighty to cut a few songs for a demo. It's been a long time since we got a call from them—and we've all been getting anxious that they've forgotten about us.

"Have you heard a little something from Mouse Almighty?" I ask hesitantly, because I'm not sure if I even want to hear the answer.

"No. Just a whole lot of nothing," Galleria says, smirking like she's unhappy. "He's in the studio with Kahlua, working on her new album. Let's hope when he finishes, he won't forget about the five hungry cheetah cubs he promised to work with."

"Well, darling, people only remember the last bread crumbs you threw on the pond," Ms. Dorothea pipes up. "So you can bet Kahlua Alexander is putting every producing morsel that Mouse Almighty has to offer into her platinum-selling beak."

"I heard that," I chuckle. Ms. Dorothea always has a real interesting way of putting things. Maybe Mouse Almighty will be ready to work with some new talent after filling Kahlua's beak. We sure hope so.

"*Madonna*, what a voice. *Ché voce!*" Mr. Garibaldi says, putting his beaver hat on his head and prancing around happily.

"Madonna doesn't have a voice like that," Dorinda replies, thinking Mr. Garibaldi was comparing Mariah's voice to Madonna's.

"No, silly willy—'*Madonna*' is just an Italian expression," Galleria says, correcting Dorinda's blunder. "You know, like, 'Holy cannoli'—that type of shout-out."

"Word?" Dorinda says, scrunching up her cute nose in amusement. "I didn't know that—is that how Madonna got her name, then?"

"Absolutely, schnooky—she's Italian-American," Galleria says, grabbing Dorinda by the shoulders and practically picking her up off the floor. "Man, you hooked us up. We can't thank you enough—Do' Re Mi hooked up her posse!"

Galleria twirls poor little Dorinda right into this couple, but they just beam at us, digging Galleria's energy. We walk down from the steep rows of seats, but there are so many people that the crowd is moving slower than snails stuck in a mudslide. All we want to do is figure out how to get to the backstage area.

"You never know how things flow. I mean, we might just pull this abracadabra off without even breaking a sweat," Galleria says. But I know she is just trying to reassure us. The rest of us don't have Galleria's nerve. Truthfully, we get real nervous if we feel like people are rejecting us, and it seems like there are always a whole lot of people trying to keep you from doing things, or reaching your dreams.

"You really think we're gonna get to meet Mariah?" Tiffany asks, her blue eyes getting bigger. It seems like she is the biggest Mariah fan out of all of us. Dorinda says Tiffany's whole room is covered with Mariah, Christina Aguilera, and Limp Bizkit posters. Daddy would have a proper fit if we hung up posters like that in our room!

Galleria puts her arm around Tiffany and heckles, "Well, I don't know if we're gonna meet Mariah, but she is certainly gonna meet us!"

Chapter 2

Finally, after crawling through the crowd forever, we are on the ground floor of the arena, next to the concession area. Angie and I look longingly at the Mariah posters and T-shirts that are hanging up for sale.

"Don't sleep on the Mariah posters, y'all!" yells the vendor, holding up a T-shirt of Mariah in a blue bikini.

"You girls want one?" Daddy asks, and I almost fall out of my shoes.

"Yes!" Angie replies, before I can say anything.

I can't believe Daddy is letting us buy a poster! I wonder what he thinks we're gonna do with it—keep it rolled up underneath our bed?

"I hope you know that we're going to hang the poster up in our room—on our very nice, white walls," I start in, to see how Daddy responds.

"I figured as much. Just don't go overboard—one poster on the wall is more than enough," Daddy says sternly. "I must say, I rather enjoyed her singing, though."

I think Daddy has almost cracked a smile. If I didn't know better, I'd say he has a crush on Mariah, the way he is staring at the poster! Boy, we sure are glad Dorinda invited us to this concert!

I whisper in Daddy's ear so Dorinda doesn't hear me. "Daddy, maybe we can have Dorinda's family over for dinner one night—you know, as a thank-you?"

"Well, as long as you girls are doing the cooking, I don't see why not," Daddy says. "Maybe after I finish redoing the living room."

"Redoing the living room?" I repeat, shocked right down to my shoes. Daddy just spent *six months* decorating the apartment! There's not a spot or a dot anywhere, and *nothing* is out of place. What on earth is he talking about?

"Abala felt it could use a little cultural warmth, so we're going to do it together,"

Daddy says, beaming. "She's taking me to a dealer in African arts and textiles on Sunday."

Now I *know* Daddy's been "touched by a cuckoo," because he can't possibly mean it! Angie looks at me like, "What is going on?" All of a sudden, Madison Square Garden is turning into Madison "Scare" Garden, and Halloween is long past! I mean, isn't it bad enough that we have to look at that ugly Bogo Mogo Hexagone Mask hanging in the hallway—the one Abala gave Daddy as a present?

"Daddy, are you okay?" I ask, noticing the gray cast to his complexion. I wonder why I didn't notice it before—maybe because the lights are so bright here.

"I can't say I'm feeling up to speed, but maybe it's the weather," Daddy says, wiping the tiny beads of sweat forming on his forehead. "I'm gonna get a lot of rest this weekend, that's for sure."

What I know for sure is, those herbs that High Priestess Abala Shaballa has Daddy taking aren't doing him one bit of good! I get this strange feeling in my chest, which I try to ignore. I just hope those herbs aren't hurting Daddy.

See, when Abala comes over, she has Daddy drinking all these herb drinks, to the point where he doesn't even eat regular food anymore. She gave him all these herbs to take at night, too—including frightshade, fenugreek, and some other odd names I can't pronounce!

While he is paying for our poster, I whisper into Angie's ear, "We are throwing those herbs on his nightstand right into the garbage!"

Angie nods her head, and I know we have a plan. There is no stopping us when we put our heads together.

All of a sudden, I realize we haven't paid much attention to Chanel—and we don't want her feeling left out of everything just because she's hobbling on crutches. Of course, Ms. Dorothea has that situation under control: she is tending to Chanel like she's the most delicate cabbage in the patch.

"Excuse me, sir, could you not lean over her?" Ms. Dorothea commands a man who is trying to reach a poster. "Chanel, darling, don't move—from the looks of this buffalo herd, you could become one terribly trampled cheetah!" Ms. Dorothea holds up a tiny Mariah T-shirt, and asks Galleria, "Do you think this is too small for Toto?" Toto is their precious little dog—who eats better than we do!

"His butt will stick out!" Galleria giggles.

"That's the general idea, isn't it?" Ms. Dorothea snipes, then pays for Toto's latest fashion item.

"How does your ankle feel?" I ask Chanel, concerned.

"I can't wait to get rid of these crutches!" she huffs.

"Don't worry, *mamacita,* you'll be flying like Mary Poppins in no time," Galleria says. She helps Chanel balance on her crutches while she peers at the poster near the top of the display.

"Oooh, look at the Butterfly T-shirt," Twinkie exclaims, pointing at the T-shirt stand. I feel bad that Dorinda's foster brothers and sisters can't get T-shirts—but at twenty dollars each, they can't afford them.

"You just love butterflies, don't you?" Tiffany asks Twinkie.

"I wish I was a butterfly and I could fly away!" Twinkie replies.

"Did you like the concert?" I ask her.

"Oh, yeah—can we meet the Butterfly

Lady?" Twinkie asks, her innocent blue eyes opening wider.

"Well, we're gonna try—if Mrs. Bosco doesn't mind," Galleria says firmly, grabbing Twinkie by the hand.

"That's all right with me," Mrs. Bosco says. "I think Gaye's having a good time, so let's keep going."

Gaye just stands there, quiet. I think it's the least we can do for her. She might not know who Mariah Carey is *now*, but maybe when she gets bigger, it'll be something nice to remember—instead of all the painful memories she's gonna have when she grows up and finds out that her mother abandoned her in a playground.

"Sir, how do we get backstage?" I ask the T-shirt vendor.

The vendor gives us directions. Then I squeeze Angie's arm, which is locked into mine, and yell, "Come on, y'all—this caravan is moving south!"

If we thought the security guards at the Karma's Children concert in Houston were mean, then the ones guarding the backstage area in Madison Square Garden are big ol' bull-dogs who missed their mealtime! We haven't even gotten past the backstage door when one of the security guards, with biceps the size of whole turkeys, barks out, "Please, exit to the right!"

All of sudden, Angie and I feel like the Lion in *The Wizard of Oz*—two weaselly cowards without enough courage to spread on a split-pea sandwich! We stand there, speechless, frozen in our tracks.

"Let's just leave," Dorinda's older foster sister Monie blurts out to her boyfriend, Hector. "Dorinda, we're gonna bounce."

"Why don't we just wait and see what happens?" Hector says quietly.

"What for?" Monie snaps at him, sucking her teeth. "They ain't gonna let us back there, so let's just go."

Hector whispers to her again, but this time I can't hear what he's saying.

"*No*—let's just *go*!" Monie insists, and I can tell she's gonna win this argument.

We look over at Dorinda, and she raises her eyebrows, like, "Here we go again—another showdown at another rodeo." I feel sorry for Dorinda—it must be hard, sharing a bedroom with that sourpuss Monie. At least Angie and I get along like two peas in a pod—even though she tries to sneak up in my shoes sometimes, or puts holey stockings back in our sock drawer.

"Bye, Mrs. Bosco—thank you for inviting us," Monie says to her foster mother.

"Don't thank me—thank Dorinda," Mrs. Bosco corrects her. Good for Mrs. Bosco, sticking up for poor Dorinda! See, Mrs. Bosco had told Dorinda she could invite whomever she wanted. If it was me, I sure would have run out of tickets before I picked Monie's name out of the grab bag. God would've had to forgive me for that one!

"I already told her thank you," Monie says, getting a snip of an attitude—more than Daddy would ever allow, that's for sure.

I sneak a look at Daddy, but he is engrossed in conversation with Mr. Garibaldi. Daddy looks grayer and more tired than ever, and I start feeling worried all over again. Besides, Dorinda's younger foster brothers and sisters seem like they're getting fidgety. Maybe we should all go home.

"I'll see y'all later," Monie says, waving good-bye to me and Angie without even cracking a smile.

"Good-bye, sourpuss," I want to yell after her—but of course I don't.

Now LaRonda, Dorinda's friend from school, has lost her courage too. "I told my mother I'd be home at eleven, and I gotta go all the way to the Bronx," she says, shifting her weight like she's kinda nervous.

"It's not even ten yet!" Dorinda pleads.

"I know, but I don't want to cause any problems. I really appreciate you inviting me to the concert," LaRonda says, trying to be real nice but backing out.

"Awright," Dorinda whines, kissing her good-night on the cheek instead of pulling her cowardly tail.

"Mariah was off the hook," LaRonda says, brightening. Then she turns to Galleria. "Wait till I tell Derek Hambone on Monday—he's gonna be too through with you!"

Derek is this boy at their school who likes Galleria. He joined our social club, Kats and Kittys, just so he could hang with us.

"Ooo, you're *terrible*!" Chanel says, catching LaRonda's drift.

"Now we've gotta slay this dragon," Galleria says, motioning her head in the direction of the security guard—who looks like he has had more than his share of Hungry Man dinners.

"Ladies, you cannot block the entrance, please exit door right!"

Peering up at the security guard from under her big cheetah hat, Ms. Dorothea barks back, "We're guests of Mariah Carey—which way is her dressing room?"

"That way!" the security guard motions without cracking a smile.

Whew.

"Leave it to Mom to find the yellow brick road," Galleria whispers in my ear.

"She could slay a dragon with that hat if she wanted to," Daddy says, smiling with satisfaction.

"Yes she could!" I beam back at Daddy, surprised that he cracked a joke. That's so unlike him! I'm surprised he's even going along with this whole backstage caper. Daddy doesn't like cat-and-mouse games, if you know what I mean. In other words, he's awfully strict. Ms. Dorothea, on the other hand, is more our cup of mint julep tea—she likes to have fun, but she takes care of business, too.

Snaking through the crowd and going up two flights of stairs, we find ourselves in another long hallway, with a row of security guards in business suits lined up in front of us.

"Oh, boy—just when we thought we were on the yellow brick road," hisses Galleria as we approach one of them. We all huddle together, like a swarm of nineteen bees in search of a beehive. "Maybe Mrs. Bosco'd better ask him."

"I'll ask," Mrs. Bosco offers, pulling Gaye to her side. I think Gaye is scared now, because she starts sucking her thumb. "Excuse me, would it be possible to have a word with Ms. Carey? She invited us," Mrs. Bosco tells one of the guards. "Or rather, her charity did."

Dorinda looks at me, embarrassed.

"Her charity?" the security guard says, looking puzzled. Angie and I are so embarrassed, we just look at his navy blue suit.

"Darling, we're Ms. Carey's guests—could you ask if we can see her?" Ms. Dorothea says, jumping in.

"I'm sorry, but all these other people are waiting for Ms. Carey too, and we're not letting anyone else in," the bodyguard says. I notice that he has one of those ear things on.

"Certainly—we can wait here with the other people. There's no harm in that, now, is there?

Just in case?" Ms. Dorothea continues.

"Suit yourself. I'm gonna have to ask you to please step aside, though."

I wonder how people can be so mean . . . I hope *I* never have a job where I get to be nasty to people all day!

I can tell that Dorinda is still embarrassed. "Maybe we should just go," she says to her foster mother.

Much to our surprise, Mrs. Bosco retorts, "Ms. Dorothea is right. We waited this long—what's it gonna hurt to wait a little longer? You know I ain't cooking dinner tonight when we get back home, so I'm a free agent!"

"But next Sunday night, I expect all of you at *our* dinner table," Mr. Garibaldi pipes up.

"Yeah!" Twinkie says, jumping up.

"I'll have to ask my parents," Tiffany says, looking at Dorinda.

"What are we gonna eat?" Topwe blurts out, causing the rest of the kids to giggle.

They must be awful hungry. Even though we had dinner before we left for the concert, *I* could eat another meal right now—and I'm sure I ate more for dinner than they did!

"Daddy makes lobster fra diavolo every

Sunday night—you know, it's like a family tradition," Galleria says, looking down at Topwe. He is wearing a white shirt, with a cute little burgundy bow tie that makes him look like a little gentleman. It must be so hard, dressing all these kids every morning!

"Does the lobster bite?" Nestor asks, grinning at his joke. He's a little younger than Twinkie, and has lots of pretty, curly brown hair. I wonder how he got to be in a foster home. . . . We never ask Dorinda anything about the kids unless she tells us—and she doesn't tell us much, that's for sure.

Chapter 3

We stand outside Mariah's dressing room for ages. We feel worst for Chanel, because it can't be good for her sprained ankle and tailbone to be standing so long on her crutches. Of course, she'll never admit any such thing, but that's just Chanel for you—she never lets on when she's hurting. You'd think the bodyguards outside of Mariah Carey's dressing room would have some sympathy for a poor girl on crutches!

"How long are they gonna keep us waiting in line, like wolves in the cold waiting for a Happy Meal?" Galleria hisses, then snuggles up to her mother.

As if Glinda the Good Witch heard Galleria's

whine, the dressing-room door opens, and a lady with a clipboard steps into the hallway. We look at her like she's the ticket to our next meal. Feeling our eyes on her, she turns and smiles at Ms. Dorothea. (Daddy is right, Ms. Dorothea's cheetah hat sure does come in handy for emergencies!)

"Um, Miss, do you think you could help us?" Ms. Dorothea asks the lady.

"I don't know, but I'll see," the lady responds hesitantly, like she hopes she didn't open the box with the booby prize inside.

Ms. Dorothea whispers in the lady's ear.

"Oh, I see—well, the tickets were extended through Mariah's charity organization," the lady continues, "and we can't extend any further invitation beyond that."

"Yes, yes, we understand," Ms. Dorothea says. She pauses, then adds, "Look, do you know how much it would mean to poor little Gaye, here, just to get a picture with Mariah? You know all about her situation, don't you?"

"I understand, Ms. . . ."

"Just call me Dorothea, darling. What do you think—could you give it a whirl?"

We can tell the lady is warming up to Ms.

Dorothea, just like everybody else does. "I'll see what I can do," she says. "But you see all these people on line—they're invited guests of Mariah's, so I really can't promise you anything."

The lady walks away, and Galleria starts to chuckle. "Mom, you are just shameless."

"Well, shame on *her* for not inviting us in *immediately*!" Ms. Dorothea huffs.

"Back to the waiting game," I moan, leaning on the wall and getting comfortable again.

"Sing a song for us, Tiffany," Chanel says to Dorinda's half sister.

Poor Tiffany looks like a deer caught in the headlights. Lord forgive us, but we would rather be chased by a wild pack of coyotes than have to listen to her sing another song—her voice is *terrible*!

"Why don't *you* sing the new song you wrote about Dorinda and me?" Tiffany answers, smirking. "Bet you didn't know I knew about that one, huh, *mamacita*?"

That really gets us laughing—but not for the reason Tiffany thinks. She sounds so funny when she tries to talk like Dorinda and Chanel! Tiffany opens her pink knapsack and pulls out a pack of Twinkies—the third pack she's eaten since we've been at the concert! Since we're all pretty hungry, we stare at the Twinkies like they're lamb chops dripping with mint jelly!

"You want one?" Tiffany asks Nestor, who seems like he's gonna chomp it right out of her hand.

"Yeah!" he says, grateful.

"Okay, so lemme hear you sing the song," Tiffany says, not letting us off the hook.

"Okay, here's our song—I wrote it especially for you and Miss Dorinda," Galleria says, motioning for us to get into singing formation. "Are you ready, Cheetah Girls?"

"Ready for Freddy," I reply. And we start to sing:

"Dorinda's got a secret
and it's cutting off her flow
(Is that right, girlita?*)*
According to our sources,
She thought we didn't know
(Kats and Kittys, you'd better take notes)
Today for the first time (the very first time)
Do' Re Mi found out that she's not alone
(What are you saying?)
She found out she's got a sister
And it's making her moan and groan!

Do' Re Mi on the Q.T.
Do' Re Mi on the D.D.L.
(That ain't swell)
Do' Re Mi on the Q.T.
Do' Re Mi on the D.D.L.
(Why won't you tell?)"

Dorinda's foster brothers and sisters are clapping along, and they seem to enjoy it as much as the other people waiting outside Mariah's dressing room. Tiffany is beaming from ear to ear, too.

See, Galleria whipped up the lyrics to this particular song after Dorinda met Tiffany for the first time. Tiffany had found out she was adopted, and had a half sister in foster care, so she went and tracked Dorinda down. I can't imagine what it must have felt like to have a sister suddenly pop up out of nowhere—and a white sister at that!

It must be real confusing for Dorinda sometimes, to keep up with all that goes on in her family life. Anyway, Dorinda didn't tell us about meeting Tiffany—not until Tiffany showed up at the Battle of the Divettes competition at the Apollo Theatre and waited for us outside. (There is always some drama going on with the Cheetah Girls, that's for sure.)

"Wow, you are such a dope songwriter!" Tiffany exclaims to Galleria.

"Well, thank you, *mamacita*!" Galleria riffs back, imitating Tiffany.

"You girls are good!" says this lady wearing a caftan—kinda like the ones Daddy's girlfriend, High Priestess Abala Shaballa, wears.

"Yes, we have a singing group called the Cheetah Girls," I tell the lady proudly. Usually Galleria is the one who speaks for us, but it feels good speaking out myself for a change.

"Are you waiting for Mariah?" the lady continues. "Is she gonna help you?"

Now I feel embarrassed, and the words get stuck in my throat.

"No, we're just here on a social tip," Galleria says, piping up.

Suddenly I feel stupid. Galleria is always the one who knows just what to say to people. Just like her mother.

"I design the dancers' costumes, so let me know if you need any work done," the lady goes on to explain.

"Our manager makes our costumes," Galleria says proudly, pointing to Ms. Dorothea.

"Oh, is that right?" the lady says, like she's embarrassed. Then she heaves a deep sigh. "I wish they would hurry up so I can get Mariah to sign her album for my grandson—he just loves her to death."

"We do too!" Tiffany blurts out. "Maybe you can help us meet her."

Dorinda seems uncomfortable about what Tiffany's said. "Well, maybe we'll just go home after all—it is getting late."

Just then, the door to Mariah's dressing room opens again, and the lady with the clipboard motions for Ms. Dorothea. She whispers something in her ear, and the next thing we know, it's like Moses parted the Red Sea—because we're being ushered inside!

I grab Angie's hand real tight. "We can stay for five minutes," Ms. Dorothea whispers to us. On that cue, Galleria pulls her camera out of her bag, and we move our caravan forward. Mrs. Bosco motions to Nestor and Shawn to keep everybody quiet. We are so excited we can hardly stand it. My heart is thumping in my chest!

When we get inside Mariah's dressing room

(which feels like it's half the size of the arena), the first thing we see is millions of flowers. At first we don't see Mariah, because a crowd of people are fussing around her. "She has to go to the Angel Ball as soon as she leaves here," the clipboard lady tells Ms. Dorothea.

Now I catch a glimpse of Mariah—she is wearing a beautiful pink taffeta gown covered in silk butterflies!

"I bet you that's a Dolce & Gabbana gown," Galleria says, eyeing it carefully. Galleria knows a whole lot of stuff about fashion that Angie and I don't—but we sure can tell from here that the gown looks like "diva material."

We wait quietly until the lady motions for us to be introduced to Mariah. Mrs. Bosco is introduced first, and Mariah's face beams brightly as she shakes Mrs. Bosco's hand and looks at Gaye. She bends over to talk to Gaye, but Gaye tries to hide behind Mrs. Bosco's dress. Mariah stands there like a statue, and finally Gaye looks at her. "Hi, Gaye," Mariah says softly.

Gaye stretches out her arms for Mariah to hug her. I feel the tears forming in my eyes. After they finish hugging, the lady introduces us to Mariah. I am so nervous, I can't even hear the sound of my voice.

"Thank you so much for coming," Mariah says to us. She is so pretty, we can't stop staring at her. I can't believe we are standing here with *Mariah Carey*!

"Um, girls, let me take a picture of you with Mariah—if that's all right with you, Miss Carey?" Ms. Dorothea asks. Thank goodness she knows how to be professional while we stand there gawking!

"Of course." The five of us stand with Mariah, and Ms. Dorothea takes a picture. Galleria motions for her to take another.

"Hold your horses, darling—I've been at this rodeo before," Ms. Dorothea chuckles as she snaps the second picture. That causes Mariah to giggle.

"Can we take one, too?" Nestor asks.

The lady with the clipboard motions for Mrs. Bosco and Dorinda's foster brothers and sisters to stand with Mariah, so that Ms. Dorothea can take a picture. After that, the lady tells us, "Ms. Carey has to get to the ball now. Thank you for coming."

"Thank you for singing!" Chantelle blurts out.

"You're welcome." Mariah beams at her.

"Um, excuse me—can my, um, sister take a picture with you, too?" Dorinda squeaks and looks at Tiffany.

The lady with the clipboard is trying to be nice, so she lets Tiffany and Dorinda take a picture with Mariah. Tiffany is grinning more than the Easter Bunny does when he's delivering his eggs. I mean, she is grinning so much, her cheeks are red!

When we get back outside Mariah's dressing room, we look at the people standing there waiting, and we feel like we've won the lottery! The lady with the clipboard tells the security guard that no one else will be allowed into the room, because Mariah has another engagement to attend.

"What is the Angel Ball?" Galleria asks her mom as we walk away. "Sounds like we should be there."

"If you had a thousand dollars to buy a ticket, you could attend, darling," Ms. Dorothea quips.

"A thousand dollars?! What kind of ball is it?" Chanel asks.

"It's a charity benefit, thrown by songwriter Denise Rich, and all the monies raised are donated to cancer research," Ms. Dorothea explains. "Ms. Rich's daughter died of cancer at a young age."

"I can't wait till we can go to balls," Chanel says wistfully.

"As long as you don't pirouette down the red carpet, Chuchie," Galleria riffs, reminding Chanel how she injured herself. "I can't wait to see the pictures we took with Mariah."

"Can you get the film developed tomorrow?" Dorinda asks Galleria.

"I'm on it, doggone it," Galleria heckles. "I know *you* can't wait to get your grubby little paws on the photo ops!" When we went to Houston, Dorinda bought a cheetah photo album, and she is now officially the keeper of the Cheetah Girls scrapbook.

"Can I have a copy too?" Tiffany asks nervously. "I want to show it to my mom. She's not gonna believe I got a picture with Mariah Carey!"

"A picture is worth a thousand memories," Ms. Dorothea says, beaming at us.

"This one's gonna be worth more like a *trazillion*!" Galleria heckles.

"And a whole lot more!" Angie says, joining in the afterglow.

Once we get to the street, we kiss each other

good night. "See you in the morning," I yell after Galleria, Chanel, and Dorinda.

"See you later, *mamacitas*!" Tiffany shouts after me and Angie. Mr. Garibaldi is dropping Tiffany off at home, and she sure seems happier than a pig in a poke.

"Daddy, I think we should plaster our bedroom with copies of the photos, don't you?" I kid him as we climb into a cab.

"Let's just start with the poster, and we'll see," he says calmly.

It sure is hard getting a rise out of him. I guess he's older, so he doesn't know what it means to us, to meet someone as important as Mariah Carey.

Almost as if reading my mind, he pipes up, "I'll never forget the time I saw Miles Davis playing at Smokey Johnson's Cafe. Man, now *that* was something to see."

"When was that?" Angie asks.

"Oh, a long time ago, when I had another life—before y'all were born," Daddy says, like he's unsure of himself.

"What do you mean, 'another life'?" I ask.

"Just what I said—another life," Daddy says, and doesn't continue.

Angie and I look at each other, then shrug our shoulders. I guess he means when he was younger. He sure is acting strange tonight, though—not at all like himself. Maybe it's because he isn't feeling well.

"Did you like the concert?" Angie asks, yawning.

"Yes, I did—she sure is something special."

"She sure is. . . ." I say, closing my eyes and letting myself fall asleep.

When we reach our house, I wake up out of my stupor, and realize I was dreaming about the scary Bogo Mogo Warrior Mask that High Priestess Abala Shaballa gave Daddy as a present. It's this big ugly mask that looks like the head of a space alien, with bright-red marks across the cheeks. Daddy hung it up right at the foot of the stairs, so every time we go up or come down, it scares me to death.

High Priestess Abala says when the markings change colors, it means it's time for Hexagone to reign once again, and the world will become a more magical place. In the meantime, it's supposed to watch over us and keep away evil spirits. Well, I know *that's* not true, because High Priestess Abala is still here, hanging off Daddy like he's a prize she won at the county fair!

Up in our bedroom, Angie and I say our prayers, then tape our prized Mariah Carey poster up over the bureau. We stare at it from across the room in our twin beds, then turn off the night lamp.

"Can you help me with my math homework tomorrow?" Angie asks in the dark. I like math and chemistry more than she does, which is why I would make a good forensic pyschologist—because I like to analyze things to *death*.

"Yeah, I will," I sigh, then lay my head down on my pillow, thinking about what Daddy said to me at the Garden. "Daddy told me we can invite Dorinda and her family over for dinner—after he redecorates the living room with High Priestess Abala. Can you believe that?"

"Believe what—that he's gonna let eleven kids eat in our dining room?"

"No, that he's going to redecorate the living room!"

"No, I *can't* believe it!" Angie moans. "And I must say, I'm getting awfully worried about that woman coming around here too much. I don't like it one bit."

"Neither do I—and I don't see why she has to be all up in our business—after all the work Daddy did, and all the money he spent decorating this apartment the first time." I can feel myself getting more upset by the minute. "Daddy just doesn't seem like himself anymore."

"He sure doesn't," Angie says, concerned.

"Maybe that's why he's letting Abala talk him into bringing more ugly things into this house."

"We'd better mention it in our prayers," Angie says. And so we climb down from our beds and kneel on the floor to say our prayers—*again*.

"God, please don't let Daddy bring home any more Bogo Mogo Warrior Masks, or kooky decorations," I say.

Angie finishes the prayer for me. "Because we like everything just fine the way it is."

And then we both say, "Amen!"

Chapter 4

Of course, we can't wait to gloat to everyone at Drinka Champagne's Conservatory about our fabulous evening with Mariah Carey. We start in bragging as soon as we come through the door—with the receptionist, Miss Winnie. She has the same name as our deceased paternal grandmother, so you know we just love her to death—ha, ha, that's just a joke!

"You girls keep it up, and soon we won't be seeing any more of you," Miss Winnie says, peering over her silver-rimmed glasses. "You'll be sending us postcards from the road, complete with little red kisses in the corners!"

"Yeah, right—we haven't even heard a quack attack from Def Duck Records," Galleria says, waving her hand. "Now that Chanel is on crutches, it's just as well."

Poor Chanel looks sheepish when Galleria says this, but Miss Winnie doesn't say another bo-peep.

"Don't you worry, Miss Winnie, we won't be getting any bigheaded ideas like that any time soon—not as long as I still need work on my upper register," huffs Dorinda.

"I know what you're saying," I say. Then I notice the hurt look on Dorinda's face.

"I'm not *that* bad," she huffs back at me.

"No, I didn't mean you—I meant *all* of us need practice!" I say, embarrassed that Dorinda took it the wrong way. I just hate to hurt anybody's feelings, least of all Dorinda's. From the beginning, she has been nothing but kind to me and Angie—even when Galleria and Chanel were making fun of us. (We've never said anything, but we know they used to call us "the Huggy Bear twins" behind our backs!)

Miss Winnie smooths over the situation quickly. "Honey, after hearing Mariah Carey sing, we all should practice for ninety-nine years before we even step up to a microphone and call ourselves cute."

I almost open my mouth to say, "I know what you're saying" again—but Angie pokes me in the side. Thank goodness my better half knows how to shut my mouth sometimes.

Luckily, Dorinda is chuckling right along with Miss Winnie. "Were you a singer, too?" she asks, curious.

"Was?" Miss Winnie says, primping her hair. "I *still* give them fever—in church, anyway."

"Hi, Miss Winnie," announces Danitra, one of the other students who takes vocal class with us. She has hot-pink hair, and is in a group called Think Pink.

"Hi, Danitra, how are you doin'?" I ask.

"I could puke," Danitra blurts out. "We just found out there's another group called Pink, and the lead singer has pink hair!"

"So go yellow, mellow," Galleria tells the poor girl.

Danitra waves her hand, and runs her fingers through her hair. "How are you doing, Chanel?" Danitra asks when she sees the crutches. It's the first Saturday since she had the accident that Chanel has been back to vocal practice.

"Fine!" Chanel says excitedly, then practically

attacks Danitra with her crutches as she tells her every last detail about the Mariah Carey concert.

"You did *not* get to meet her!" Danitra squeals with disbelief.

"Sí, mamacita!" Chanel counters. "You shoulda seen all the flowers in her dressing room, and the butterflies fluttering on her gown—not the one she performed in, but afterward." Chanel makes it sound like we went to the party with Mariah!

"How did you get free tickets?" Danitra asks, still trying to figure out if we are telling a fib-ulous tale. If you ask me, I think Miss Pink-haired Danitra has been bitten by the green-eyed monster.

I just hope Chanel doesn't blurt out the truth. Dorinda is already mad enough at us for telling everybody at Kats and Kittys about her foster home situation. See, at our last meeting, the Kats members voted for Dorinda's foster mother, Mrs. Bosco, to receive a charitable donation from our volunteer fund, to be used for Gaye's welfare. Dorinda almost blew a gasket afterward. We felt terrible.

Luckily, we are saved by the bell—or rather, by the director of the conservatory herself—the former disco diva, Miss Drinka Champagne. "I see you girls are getting into the mix with your usual tricks," Miss Drinka says, chuckling, when she sees us cackling with Danitra.

We immediately straighten up our act, because Miss Drinka is very particular about professional behavior from her students—inside and outside the studio.

"Tell Drinka, darlings—mother wants to sip *every* detail, right down to Mariah's manicure!" Drinka flings her hand at us, and flashes her foot-long red claws. Whenever we think her outfits can't get any more, well, creative, Drinka outdoes herself again. Today, she's wearing red cigarette-leg pants with a matching bustier, and a cape with pom-poms and jingle bells hanging off it.

"That girl has octaves to spare," Drinka says, stomping down the hallway with us.

"We had twenty-five people in our posse!" Galleria boasts, listing everyone who came with us to the concert.

"Even our father came," I tell Drinka. She met our father once, when he came to pick us up. He just wanted to see what the conservatory was like, since he pays for our training.

"How is that handsome father of yours?" Drinka asks, her dark, dramatic eyes sparkling up a storm.

"He's fine," I say.

Don't tell me that the legendary disco queen, Drinka Champagne, likes *our father*! All of a sudden, I'm feeling disappointed inside. Why couldn't Daddy pick someone dope for a girlfriend, like Drinka Champagne? They still love her in places like Japan, and in Holland, where people tend to be more liberal-minded than we are in the States. At least if Drinka were his girlfriend, we would have some fun! She would be like a "fairy stepmother" or something. But no, Daddy has to go and meet the kookiest bird in the flock, and she has to fly her broomstick right to our house!

"Excuse me for a second, dolls," Drinka says, hurrying toward her office. "Get inside the studio—I'll see you in a New York minute."

We continue our bragging in the studio, and everyone wants the juicy details—everyone, that is, except for this tall, skinny guy in snakeskin pants (skinnier at the bottom than Drinka's) and matching jacket. We've never seen him before, and he just eyes us kinda coolly, then turns away. Another group of guys is huddled in the corner as Wolfman Lupe, the pianist, sits down on the piano bench and waits for the rest of the class to file in.

"Knucklehead alert, dead ahead," Galleria mumbles under her breath, nodding at the group of guys in the corner.

"I don't know . . . they look kinda cute," Chanel grins back. "So does the guy in the snakeskin pants."

"Oh, you *would* think so," Galleria whispers. "Let's just hope he doesn't hiss and bite."

Chanel grins right at the guy in the snakeskin pants, and he walks over to her. I guess it must help, using crutches—people think you're helpless or something. Boys never walk over to me and Angie when we smile. It always seems that guys like Galleria and Chanel anyway, because they're real pretty. Angie and I try not to let it bother us. Not that boys don't look at us—they do, sometimes—but we're not supposed to look at boys until we're sixteen, or Daddy will bury us alive!

"Hi, I'm Eddie Lizard," the skinny boy says to Chanel, flashing a beautiful smile.

Dag on, his teeth are white! I don't even realize

I'm staring at him, until he introduces himself to me, too. "Oh, hi—I'm Aquanette," I say, trying to snap myself out of it.

"Eddie Lizard," he says.

"We've never seen *you* before—we would have noticed," Chanel says, grinning.

I think Galleria must have poked Chanel in the back or something, because she seems like she's losing her balance on her crutches for a second. "That's okay, I don't need any help," she says, as Eddie Lizard extends his hand.

"I just moved here from Los Angeles," he says, folding his arms across his chest, which makes him seem very mysterious and mature. I guess he must be a little older than us—maybe in tenth or eleventh grade.

"*We've* been to Los Angeles!" I exclaim excitedly, but Eddie keeps looking at Galleria and Chanel.

"Oh, yeah?"

Galleria tells him all about our trip to Hollywood—performing in the Def Duck Records Showcase at the Tinkerbell Lounge, and staying at the Royal Rooster Hotel. If I didn't know any better, I'd think she was trying to make him like her—even though Galleria doesn't have to try very hard. *All* the boys like her.

Now I realize that Eddie *does* look familiar—and maybe that's why I've been staring at him (well, I'm sure not gonna admit that I think he's very cute. No, ma'am—especially since he doesn't seem the least bit interested in me!). *Where have I seen his face before?*

"Are you a singer?" Dorinda asks him, curious.

"No . . . well, yes—well, not exactly," Eddie Lizard says, like he's confused. He nervously toys with a silver talisman, shaped like a heart, dangling on a chain around his neck. I wonder if it's some kind of lucky charm or something. He does seem kinda mysterious. "I'm an actor, but I want to get vocal coaching, and my Dad used to know Drinka Champagne back in the day—so I came here, because everyone says she's the best."

"That she is," I reply, wondering if his dad is a singer or an actor too.

"Is that your real name—Eddie Lizard?" Galleria asks, smirking.

"Yes, it is. My father's name is Doktor Lizard," Eddie explains.

"Oh, he's a *doctor*—like a forensic pyschologist?" I ask, getting excited. Angie and I want to be doctors when our singing careers are over. I want to be a Chief Medical Examiner, and examine corpses for autopsy clues, and Angie wants to be a neurosurgeon, and operate on people's brains.

"Well, he's not *that* kind of doctor—um, it's spelled D-o-k-t-o-r Lizard. He's a hoodoo practitioner. He was the consultant on the movie *Vampire Voodoo Voyage*—maybe you saw it?"

"Are you kidding? We *love* horror movies!" Angie says excitedly.

"I played one of the corpses who falls in love with the voodoo queen Marie Fangella," Eddie says, chuckling.

"*That's* where I saw you!" I say excitedly. "I didn't recognize you with your eyeballs still in your sockets!"

"Oh, right, that was a good makeup job," Eddie chuckles in his soft way. "Now my dad is here in New York, curating the hoodoo exhibit at the African-American Museum. I, um, live with my dad, so we'll be here for a few months."

I wonder where his mother is. . . . It sure seems like we have a whole lot in common. All of a sudden, I feel something for a boy I've never felt before—except maybe for Major

"Beethead" Knowles, who tried to get my attention when I was ten years old by throwing a rock at me. He made me fall off the swing instead, and I ended up with a big gash in my left knee. Our grandmother, Big Momma, made Beethead swear he would never talk to us again, and he didn't—until we saw him in Houston on Thanksgiving this last trip.

"Is hoodoo like voodoo?" Dorinda asks, curious.

"Um, yes, it is from the same tradition—but it's practiced more in the United States. *Voudoun*, or voodoo, as you call it, was formed in Haiti," Eddie says nonchalantly.

Now Chanel looks at Eddie, really impressed. I wonder who he likes more—Galleria or Chanel—and I still can't help wishing it was me!

"I know all about Santeria and *brujeria*!" Chanel says proudly.

"Really?" Eddie asks her, getting more intrigued by the second.

"I'm Dominican and Cuban," Chanel explains.

All of a sudden, Drinka claps her hands loudly, waking us out of our cozy little chat with the Lizard. "Enough chatting and batting lashes ladies—it's time to get to work."

We all move to the center of the studio to begin our vocal warm-ups. All during the warm-ups, I'm wondering if I should tell Eddie Lizard about High Priestess Abala Shaballa. No, then he'll think I like him or something, I decide. I'd better just get all of this nonsense out of my head. *Too bad, because he sure is cute. Real cute.*

After vocal class, I grab my cheetah backpack and head for the door. I notice that Galleria is lingering inside the studio, and feeling around in her backpack like she's looking for something.

"You lost something?" I ask. But I already know the answer—she's just trying to get Eddie's attention! It works, too. After a few minutes, Eddie makes his way over to Galleria, and they are chatting with each other as we all walk to the elevator. Galleria is telling him all about the Cheetah Girls—but it doesn't look like she needs any help from us!

"The record company—Def Duck—you know, the same label that Kahlua Alexander is on—said they'd put us in the studio with producer Mouse Almighty. We're supposed to cut a few songs for a test demo or single, but we haven't heard a peep yet," Galleria laments like a damsel in distress.

Eddie acts like he's real interested in our music group, but I can tell he's even more interested in Galleria. Once we're outside, the two of them are stuck together like Popsicles—standing in front of the building, gabbing, while the rest of us just look on.

"You are mad funny," Eddie Lizard riffs, as Galleria tells him about our Cheetah Girls escapades in Hollywood.

I wonder if we're going to eat lunch together, like we usually do after Drinka's vocal class. I decide right then and there that I'm not going if the Lizard joins us. Why does it always seem like Galleria is the rooster with something to crow about? Well, that's not exactly true—'cuz the Cheetah Girls would've never gotten to Houston if it wasn't for me and Angie.

I throw Angie a look, like, "Let's go home." She just stands there, like she's mesmerized by this horse and pony show.

"Man, I went on so many auditions before I even got a gig as an extra in a crowd scene," Eddie laments, talking about his struggling acting career. I guess he wants Galleria to feel sorry for him, too.

"Really?" Galleria asks, like he's so cute, she can't believe he wouldn't just walk onto a movie set and become an instant star!

All of a sudden, a homeless man wearing a plastic bag wrapped around his body runs up to us and screams, "Satan lives! Satan lives!"

The rest of our crew try to act like it's no big deal, but Angie and I almost jump off the sidewalk, because he scared us half to death!

"Yes, he sure does," Eddie chuckles at Galleria, like he sees things like that every day in Los Angeles. "New York is such a trip, isn't it?"

"It sure is, but I grew up here, so I'm in it for the ride on the Coney Island Cyclone!" Galleria riffs at him. "Where do you go to school?"

"Because I have to travel so much with my dad, and for acting, I have a private tutor. That way I'll be able to finish high school next year."

"Oh, so you got it like that?" Dorinda pipes up. "Is it hard?"

"You mean, studying with a tutor?" Eddie asks. "Yeah—I've always got a lot of homework assignments. But, hey, listen, I've gotta go meet my father at the museum by three o'clock. Do y'all wanna go eat something around here? Where can we get our grub on?"

"Well, we're gonna go home, y'all, 'cuz we have to help Daddy with the remodeling," I blurt out.

"Come on, Aqua—I know the two of you aren't passing up a trip to Atomic Wings—not the dynamic wing-eating duo!" Galleria riffs at me and Angie.

Suddenly, I feel myself wincing inside. I know Galleria is just being her usual self, but why does she have to embarrass us like that in front of Eddie Lizard? I mean, she makes it sound like Angie and I are bone-chomping bugaboos, with incisor teeth like dinosaurs, or something country like that.

"Well, we're gonna cook something to eat at home," I respond. I'm trying to act normal, but I guess I'm just showing off. After all, one thing Galleria can't do is cook—not like me and Angie.

"Wish we were invited over!" Galleria says. But I know she's ready to head over to Atomic Wings and chow down on an order of Insanely Hot Chicken Wings, which is exactly the way *we* like to eat them.

Suddenly, I feel my mouth watering, but I decide I'm not going to back down. Out of the corner of my eye, I can see Angie looking at me like I'm crazy. "Come on, Angie, let's go," I mutter.

It's all right with me. Let Galleria hold court with Eddie without our interference. That's just fine and dandy with the fabulous Walker twins—a.k.a. the Hot Sauce twins, a.k.a. the Huggy Bear twins.

"Aqua, come on, let's stay," Angie whispers, holding my arm to keep me by her side.

"No, thank you, ma'am—the Huggy Bear twins are going to head uptown and help our father," I insist. I can see the surprised look on Galleria's face. Good. Now she knows that sometimes other people have feelings too!

"Don't go, Aqua!" Chanel says, her eyes pleading. Now I'm starting to feel a little silly for being jealous, but I'm not backing out. Big Momma says I'm stubborn, and this time, I don't mind living up to my reputation. Not one bit!

Chapter 5

When you're an identical twin, you kinda take for granted that your "other half" is gonna stick up for you all the time. But today, Angie is being real trifling—even after the way Galleria insulted us in front of that "scaly creature." I don't believe for one second that Eddie Lizard's father is a hoodoo practitioner, or whatever kind of bogus doctor he calls himself!

"I thought I'd seen it all, with the likes of High Priestess Abala Shaballa Hexagone and her kooky coven of misfits," I mumble to Angie, but she doesn't say one word.

I'll never forget the first time Abala brought her cronies over to our house: Bast Bojo, with the bald head and beady eyes; Hecate Sukoji, the only lady I've ever seen with no eyebrows; Rasputina Twia, the dwarf with the straggly-looking teeth. They sure are a motley-looking bunch!

Abala Shaballa brought them over one night to concoct a Vampire Spell, so that the Cheetah Girls would win the Apollo Amateur Hour contest. Well, we *lost*—even after drinking that dees-gusting brew, and performing the Bogo Mogo ritual with all of them!

The whole way back on the train to our house, I have my mouth poked out, and Angie doesn't say a word—until she decides to start some trouble.

"I can't believe the way you were staring at that boy," she mumbles as I put the key in our front door.

"I was *not* staring at him," I snap back.

"Yes, you were—and I can tell you're jealous because he likes Galleria and not you," Angie says, hurting my feelings.

All of a sudden, I realize that *Angie probably likes him too*! After all, we're twins, right?

"I don't care who he likes!" I say, calling her bluff, then decide I'm not going to help Angie with her math homework after all. It's her problem if she fails the test!

"Yes you do," Angie says, folding her arms across her chest. "No sense in lying to me, 'cuz I know better."

I'm going to get Angie *real* good for this. "So what if I do? It doesn't matter."

"It sure doesn't," Angie says.

I shoot her a look, because I wonder what she means by that. Not that I care anymore. Eddie Lizard can go eat a frog—and so can Galleria!

Knowing "Miss Show-off," right about now she's probably showing him all the songs in her Kitty Kat notebook, and licking chicken grease off her fingers. I hope she gets fried chicken skin stuck in between her braces! That'll make her look real cute in front of Eddie Lizard.

As I open the apartment door, I wonder why the lights are on. . . . Daddy is real particular about turning off every light when we're not in the room. I know he went out with High Priestess Abala Shaballa to the African Arts dealer to pick out some new decorations. At least, that's what he told us he was doing when we left this morning.

Angie marches straight into the kitchen, and I let out a big sigh. *Finally.* I just want to go eat some lunch, then listen to some music in my room and be by myself. I hope Angie finds something to do with herself instead of bothering me. I can't seem to shake the bad feeling I have in my chest.

I put my keys on the side mantel in the foyer, but I notice there isn't any mail there. Usually, Daddy leaves all the Saturday mail on the table, and goes through it over the rest of the weekend. Hmmm. Maybe he took the mail with him. I go back to the outside foyer, and I notice that our mailbox is jam-packed—Daddy didn't even open it!

I wonder why Daddy didn't get the mail. . . . Looking down on the floor, I realize that he didn't pick up his newspapers either, because *The Amsterdam News* and *The New York Times* are still lying where the delivery woman left them!

Daddy was probably so engrossed with High Priestess Abala Shaballa and her shenanigans that he didn't have time to read his morning newspaper in peace, while sipping his coffee and some dees-gusting shake whipped up in his new blender.

I'll bet Abala came over with a toolbox and a

tape measure, trying to figure out how she's gonna rearrange everything, then carted Daddy away to all these kooky home furnishing places where witches shop!

I put the newspapers and the mail on the side mantel, then head for the kitchen, and make myself a catfish sandwich from last night's leftovers. Plopping down at the dining room table, I ignore Angie completely. I open one of the newspapers to today's horoscope for my astrological sign—Virgo.

> *The unconditional love for which you yearn cannot be bought at any price, so don't be tempted to sell your soul to the devil. Watch out for sheep wearing wolves' clothing, and vice versa. It may not be Halloween, but many evildoers will cloak their wrongful actions in disguises you may not recognize. Due to unforeseen circumstances, now is the time to take action, despite naysayers.*

I wonder what "unforeseen circumstances" means? I almost forget that I'm mad at Angie, and open my mouth to ask her—then catch myself. She wouldn't know anyway. If *I* don't know something, *she* usually doesn't either.

"Can you believe Eddie Lizard is the same guy from *Voodoo Vampire Voyage*?" Angie says, biting into her catfish sandwich. She *would* make herself the same thing to eat as I did. "He looks a lot skinnier in person. His eyes are prettier than I would have thought, too."

"Of course they are, Angie—'cuz he didn't *have* any in the movie!" I respond.

Exasperated with my pesty sister, I go back to trying to figure out my horoscope. *"Watch out for sheep wearing wolves' clothing. . . ."* Suddenly I get alarmed. Maybe they're talking about Eddie Lizard! I wonder if that means I should forget about him. . . .

"What does the horoscope say—that you like him, and should just admit it?" Angie says, smirking and biting into her sandwich.

"Why don't you read it and find out?" I say, pushing the newspaper in front of her. I swear, if I had a can of Daddy's SWAT insect spray, I'd spray it right at her, and watch her squirm like a cockroach before it turns over on its back and croaks.

BAM! All of a sudden, we hear a loud crashing noise from upstairs. Angie jumps up from the table.

"What if it's a burglar?" I hiss at her, getting paranoid.

We know Daddy isn't home, so what else could that noise be? No wonder the lights were on!

"Let's go see if Mr. and Mrs. Elliot are home," Angie says, getting scared, too. Mr. and Mrs. Elliot are our neighbors. We live in a duplex apartment, and there are only a few other people who live in our brownstone building. We run to the front door, and Angie whispers, "Let's leave it open, just in case the burglar wants to run away!"

"No—that's stupid. We should lock him inside," I say.

"We can't lock the door from the inside—if we close it, he can still get out!" Angie hisses back at me in a hushed voice.

"Let's just go," I say, realizing she's right, this time. We run out the door, and head for the stairs in the hallway. Angie runs so fast, she almost trips me from behind, making me annoyed at her all over again.

I hope Mrs. Elliot is home! I don't smell that familiar odor of gingerbread cookies wafting into the hallway. Mrs. Elliot runs her own "cookie book" company, Delilah's Dish and Tell. She writes romance novels that come with a package of cookies, so you can eat and read at the same time. We usually see Mr. or Mrs. Elliot carting boxes up and down the stairs, and moving stuff into vans outside. Of course, when we need them the most, we don't see them.

I knock on the door impatiently, hoping somebody answers. "Come on, come on!" I mutter under my breath.

Finally, the door is opened by their housekeeper, Esmeralda, who hardly speaks any English. "Is Mrs. Elliot home?" I ask quickly.

"No home," Esmeralda responds, smiling. Now I wish Chanel were here, so she could speak Spanish to Esmeralda, and tell her how scared we are that there is a burglar in our apartment!

"Esmeralda, can you help us? Somebody broke into our apartment," I blurt out, knowing full well she's probably not going to understand one word of my mumbo jumbo. Sure enough, Esmeralda gives me a blank look, and opens her brown eyes wider.

"Come, please," I beg her, motioning for her to come downstairs with us. But she seems unsure of what to do.

"You want I come?" she asks, pointing downstairs.

"Sí!" Angie blurts out.

All the way downstairs, Esmeralda is blabbing at us in Spanish, and we are blabbing at her in English, and neither one of us understands the other.

My heart almost jumps out of my chest when we get to our apartment door and find it open. I fall back into Esmeralda, and I can see that I've scared *her* now.

Angie grabs my arm, almost causing me to jump out of my skin. "I left the door open, remember?" she whispers.

Now the *three* of us are scared to go inside the apartment. All of a sudden, my skin feels itchy and crawly, like I have lice, so I start scratching all over.

Angie opens the door all the way, and the two of us tiptoe into the foyer, standing still to see if we hear any more noise. Esmeralda is still standing on the welcome mat outside the door. I grab her hand and pull her inside. I'll bet *now* she understands exactly what we want her to do!

As I begin to climb the narrow, winding stairs to the upper floor of our duplex, something tells me to turn around and look at the Bogo Mogo Hexagone Warrior Mask. "Angie!"

I hiss, pointing to the ugly creation that has made my life miserable. "The markings have turned redder! Haven't they?"

"I guess," Angie says, sticking her face right next to the mask. "Yeah, they have!"

We begin our climb, and I try for the life of me to remember what High Priestess Abala Shaballa said. . . . *When the markings on the mask turn brighter, it will be time for Hexagone to rule the world again.* . . . I *think* that's what she said, but I'm still not sure what that means.

The three of us climb the narrow, winding stairs to the upper floor. Maybe Abala's idea of redecorating meant getting Daddy out of the apartment and taking our furniture! Everybody tells us people get robbed in New York a lot.

I peer back down the stairway and look over the living room. Well, everything downstairs seems to still be there—unless she's got some kooks coming back later to get the living room furniture.

I can feel my heart pounding as we walk into my room and look around. Then we walk into the bathroom—and lastly, into Daddy's room.

"It's Daddy!" Angie shrieks when she sees

him lying in the bed. She goes running up the bed to shake him—and steps on something that makes a cracking sound. The lamp from his nightstand is shattered on the floor! Daddy must've knocked it over, reaching for something.

"The phone is off the hook," I add, picking up the receiver and putting it back into its cradle.

Esmeralda lets out a shriek and points to the floor, babbling in Spanish. I can't see what she's pointing at, but I'm concerned about Daddy. I sit on the bed and call his name, but he doesn't answer. "Daddy, can you hear me?"

I get so scared that I shake him, until he lets out a moan.

"What's wrong, Daddy?" I ask, getting hysterical.

"Is that you, Mattie?" Daddy asks, rubbing his eyes and waking out of his unconsciousness. "I never meant to hurt you."

Mattie? "Who's Mattie?" I repeat out loud.

Daddy doesn't answer, because he isn't really conscious. I've never heard him mention that name before. And what does he mean by "I never meant to hurt you"?

"Daddy, what's wrong?" Angie asks, getting hysterical too.

"Lord, my stomach hurts, my head hurts," Daddy moans, holding his head.

"We should get him to a hospital," Angie shrieks.

Esmeralda grabs my arm, still babbling in Spanish. She is trying to show me something on the mantel. I notice there are all sorts of strange things there. . . .

"Someone has burned the black and red candles and left them sitting there," I call out to Angie. Daddy doesn't burn candles, so I know it couldn't be him—especially not without putting them on a plate or something first, so the melted wax doesn't mess up the wood.

Esmeralda picks something up from the mantel and presses it into my hand. "What is this thing?" I ask, looking at it puzzled. "It looks like a gingerbread man made out of muslin or something."

Esmeralda presses another one into my hand, and gets real excited, babbling away.

"We should call Chanel and see what Esmeralda is trying to tell us!" Angie says, taking the gingerbread people out of my hands and dropping them back on the mantel.

I figure Chanel is still eating lunch at Atomic

Wings with Dorinda and the lovebirds—Galleria and Eddie Lizard—so I try her cell phone. Dialing the number, which I know by heart, I can hear my own heart pounding.

"Hola!" Chanel says, answering the phone chirpily.

"Hello, Chanel. Are you with Galleria?"

"Sí, mamacita. Eddie is going to take us to see his father's hoodoo altar!" she says excitedly.

"Chanel, something is wrong with Daddy—and Esmeralda, the housekeeper next door, is here with us, and she doesn't speak English. She's trying to tell us something. Could you translate for us?" The words tumble out of my mouth like an avalanche.

"Well, you could at least say, 'Hello, *mamacita,*'" Chanel responds.

"This is no time for joking, Chuchie! Could you please talk to Esmeralda?"

"Okay, put her on."

I hand the receiver to Esmeralda, and wait with bated breath while the two of them talk in Spanish. Esmeralda hands the phone back to me, and Chanel isn't so chirpy anymore.

"You've got to get your father out of there—he's been hexed!" Chanel says, worried.

"Esmeralda says the place is jinxed by a *bruja*—a witch, and not a good one either. Someone has placed your father under some kind of spell, and those are voodoo dolls on the mantel!"

I hear someone mumbling in the background to Chanel, and she says, "Wait a minute, Aqua!"

I hold on while Chanel talks with someone—probably loverboy Lizard. My hands are freezing, because I'm so scared for Daddy. I knew that High Priestess Abala Shaballa was up to no good! *We have to get Daddy to a hospital!*

"Please, Chanel, hurry up." I peer up at Esmeralda and give her a look, like, "I understand." Her eyes are pleading with me.

"Eddie says don't take your father to a hospital!" Chanel says. "He needs to be looked at by a hoodoo practitioner!" I hear Eddie in the background, still talking to her.

"We are calling 911 as soon we hang up, so an ambulance can take Daddy to a hospital, Chanel," I say firmly. Eddie Lizard may have Galleria and Chanel under a spell with all his hoodoo talk, but he doesn't fool me. "We can't just leave Daddy lying here like this."

"No, no—the doctors can't help!" Chanel says excitedly.

"And I guess Eddie Lizard can?" I shoot back, annoyed.

"No, he'll call his father to come over and look at him," Chanel says.

"Daddy's going to the hospital, and that's that," I huff back.

Suddenly, Eddie Lizard gets on the phone. "Listen, um, Aqua—"

"Aquanette," I repeat, annoyed that he can't even remember my name properly.

"Yes, Aquanette—even if you do take your father to the hospital, don't touch anything in your house. Let my father come over and see what's going on."

"Well, okay—we'll call you as soon as we get back. Bye," I say, anxious to get off the phone.

"Excuse me, Aquanette—but how are you going to call without my father's phone number?"

"Oh. Right—give it to me," I say, embarrassed. I scribble it down on a pad. Then I hang up the phone, and pick it up again to dial 911.

"I don't care what Eddie Lizard says," I hiss to Angie. "Daddy is going to the hospital."

"No hospital!" Esmeralda says, placing my

palm in hers. I wonder why she's hopping on the same hoodoo bandwagon. . . .

"No, no—he's going, and that's final!" I say, determined. Nobody is gonna tell me what to do with my daddy. "And if that 'pecan nut' Abala Shaballa Cuckoo comes around here again, I'm going to hit her over her head with her own broomstick!"

Chapter 6

It seems like we've been waiting for a thousand years in the emergency room at St. Luke's Hospital for someone to come and tell us what's wrong with Daddy. The ambulance workers put him on a stretcher, and he seemed delirious the whole way over, sweating and mumbling.

We'd never ridden in the back of an ambulance before—and if we never do again, it will be too soon. I couldn't help crying, and neither could Angie. We weren't worried about scaring Daddy, because he didn't even seem to know we were there with him. He just kept mumbling strange things, and calling out to that strange woman—"Mattie, is that you? I won't leave you."

"We'd better call Ma later," Angie says, as if she's thinking out loud.

"Suit yourself," I mumble back. "I wonder if she knows who Mattie is. . . ."

"Probably," Angie says, shrugging her shoulders.

By now, I have a pretty good idea of who Mattie must be—some woman Daddy knows from his past. Angie is clutching my hand as we wait in the emergency room, which is scary in itself. As a matter of fact, we feel like we're in a bad version of *Fright of the Living Dead.*

I mean, you have to see these people in the emergency room to believe it! The man in the chair next to us, for example, is wearing a bloody ace bandage around his head, like it's an accessory or something. He keeps jumping up out of his chair and prancing back and forth, as if he's giving a fashion show.

The lady sitting across from us has eyebrows so thick, they look like a unibrow across her forehead. But that's not the worst part—she keeps belching so loud that no one will sit next to her—not even her husband! Yes, ma'am, he is sitting a few seats away with a newspaper covering his face—I guess because he's embarrassed, or else he's very interested in the articles he's reading.

He can't be more embarrassed than we are, because Angie and I won't even look up—just in case we accidentally meet the glances of the Unibrow Belcher or Mr. Bloody Ace Bandage.

See, it's hard to be inconspicuous when you're twins—everyone thinks they can just talk to you out of the blue. People always ask the same question, too—as if their eyes are on vacation. "Are you two identical twins?" Usually we don't mind, but right now, I guess I'm not too happy about being a twin—or sitting here in this awful emergency room.

As if hearing me thinking to myself, the Unibrow lady lets out a loud belch. I act like I don't hear a thing. Just another day sitting in a crazy emergency room. Yes, ma'am. I just keep staring at my sneakers, like I'm gonna discover gold any second now.

"Some people should stop makin' so much noise," says an older woman in a blue housedress with a purple sweater over it, with a big ol' cast on her left arm.

"I think we should call Galleria and Chanel, and tell them what's going on," Angie suggests calmly.

"You call them," I respond.

"Gimme a quarter," Angie mumbles under her breath. I pretend like I don't hear her.

"Come on, Aqua, gimme a quarter!"

I hand my pesty sister a quarter, and watch as she heads to the phone booth to call Galleria and Chanel. I don't know why Angie is bothering. What's Galleria gonna do about about this mess with Daddy—write a song? It's not like she can help or anything.

I get so tired of sitting there waiting that I pull out the newspaper and read my horoscope again: *The unconditional love for which you yearn cannot be bought at any price. . . . Watch out for sheep wearing wolves' clothing. . . .*

I still can't figure out what the first part means, but now I think I understand the second part. All along, I've known that High Priestess Abala Shaballa wasn't exactly Glinda the Good Witch, popping into our lives out of nowhere in her magical bubble. (Actually, Daddy met her at the annual African American Expo at the Jacob Javits Convention Center downtown.) Angie and I have always felt that Abala Shaballa is not what she appears to be!

Please, God, let Daddy be okay! I pray silently. Suddenly, I get scared that Daddy won't wake up—in more ways than one. What if he thinks we're making up this stuff about Abala? What if he thinks his illness doesn't have anything to do with her and all those hocus-pocus brews she's been making him drink?

Suddenly, I get a chill down my spine. What if his illness *doesn't* have anything to do with High Priestess Abala? After all, Esmeralda is Mrs. Elliot's housekeeper—not the Wizard of Oz. How would she know about all that stuff in Daddy's bedroom?

Just then, Angie comes back and plops back into the chair beside me. "Galleria, Chanel, and Eddie want to come over to our house and look at the stuff in Daddy's bedroom," she whispers. "They want to bring Eddie's father, too—Doktor Lizard."

"Well, I don't know if we should be inviting company over to our apartment without Daddy's permission," I shoot back.

Angie gives me a look, like, "You've got to be kidding."

"I don't believe in all this mess anyway," I continue.

Now my sister throws me that look again, and rolls her neck at the same time, which really gets on my nerves.

"Well, never mind what *I* believe in—let's just hear what the doctor has to say," I say, holding my ground. Right now, I don't feel like a Cheetah Girl at all—just a stubborn mule digging its heels in for the long haul.

"Well, I told them we're gonna call them back. I knew you would get mad if they met us at the hospital," Angie says, sucking her teeth.

"Why would you want them coming to the hospital?" I ask her. My sister just doesn't use her head sometimes. I could swear *she's* the one with a crush on Eddie Lizard. "I don't know why you're in such a hurry to have some snake doctor nosing around our house!"

"He's not a snake doctor, he's a hoodoo practitioner!" Angie says, like Miss Smarty Britches.

Luckily, just then a nurse attendant comes out of one of the examining rooms and motions to us. We jump up, following the nurse into a little waiting room.

"Your father is resting. The doctor will be in to see you shortly," she says, smiling. I try to read whatever I can into the nurse's smile, but she just leaves us sitting there. It seems like a thousand more hours before a tall doctor wearing glasses comes in to talk to us. "Is there a Mrs. Walker?"

"No—um, yes, sir, but our mother lives in Houston," I say, suddenly feeling embarrassed that Daddy is lying in some room and Ma isn't here with us.

"Okay, well, your father is going to be fine," the doctor continues. "He's quite dehydrated, and his blood pressure is low, but after a series of tests, we can't find any medical reason to detain him further. We'll release him in the morning, after we run a few more tests."

"There isn't anything wrong with him?" I ask, surprised. How can that be? I just *knew* the doctor was going to tell us something horrible. I feel the sweat breaking out on my forehead.

"Like I said—he's severely dehydrated, but we can't detect any other underlying medical conditions. His vitals are all relatively stable," the doctor says, poker-faced.

I don't care what he says—I *know* there is something wrong with our Daddy.

"Can you arrange for someone—an adult—

to come tomorrow, so we release your father in the morning?" the doctor asks.

"Yes, sir, we'll come with an adult in the morning," I say, snapping out of my daze.

As we leave the hospital, Angie looks at me and doesn't say a word. I don't want to admit it, but for once, I think she is right. I turn to her, tears welling in my eyes, and mumble, "We'd better have Doktor Snake make a house call."

Angie just holds me, and doesn't say a word, which is a blessing. Even though I always gloat about being three minutes older, for once I feel like *I'm* the younger twin.

Chapter 7

When we get back home, we both feel scared about going upstairs by ourselves.

"Let's go get Esmeralda!" Angie says.

"We've scared that poor woman enough for one day," I mutter. "We'd better be glad Esmeralda doesn't speak English so she can't tell Mrs. Elliot about the afternoon 'fright' we gave her—and all the strange things she saw in Daddy's bedroom."

"Yes, ma'am!" Angie replies knowingly.

That's all we would need, is for all our neighbors in the building to think they have a bunch of "pecan nuts" from Houston living next door to them!

Taking a deep breath, we climb the spiral

staircase. Scaredy-cat or not, I think it's high time we figure out what on earth all those strange things are in Daddy's bedroom.

"We left the light on," I say out loud, as if Daddy is still home. Even now, I can hear his voice fussing with us about that. He is real particular about us turning off all the lights, so we don't "give his money away to Con Edison."

"I didn't leave it on," Angie says, defending herself as usual.

"It doesn't matter who left it on," I shoot back, "'cuz Daddy's in the hospital." I can't even remember who left the room last after the EMS (Emergency Medical Service) workers got Daddy in the ambulance. The first thing I do is go straight for the mess on the nightstand.

"Somebody musta put all this stuff in Daddy's room after we went to Drinka Champagne's," Angie says, like she's honing her divette detective skills. I think she'd better stick to her neurosurgeon ambitions, because I am definitely better at clues than she is.

"What do you mean, *somebody*?" I huff back. "It's *obvious* who."

"Well, why would Abala do this?" Angie

says, peering at Daddy's nightstand and reaching for something.

"Now that's a dim-witted remark, Angie," I say, shaking my head at her.

She ignores me. Picking up one of the voodoo dolls, she starts shaking it.

"Don't touch anything until Doktor Lizard gets here!" I yell at her like I'm the chief investigating officer on this crime scene.

"I thought you didn't believe in any of this stuff," Angie challenges me, smirking like the Cheshire Cat.

"I don't," I say, realizing that I'm acting stubborn again. Well, I can't help it! Like Big Momma says, *A scorpion can't change its ways, so why should people?*

"I've never seen black candles before," Angie says, leaning over and looking at the burned votive candles. "I wonder what those are for?"

I stare at all the other stuff on the nightstand. Aside from the black and red candles and the funny-looking brown-cloth dolls, there are stones, powders, herbs, an old-fashioned scale, some nails, and a little sack.

"It looks like she burned something else besides the candles," I say, surprised by the pile of ashes on the nightstand. "It kinda looks like photos—people's pictures, maybe?"

Angie examines the pile of ashes. "Those are definitely the edges of photos, and magazine pages."

"Yeah, you're right—magazine pages. I didn't think of that," I say.

The doorbell rings, and we both jump.

"That must be Galleria and the snake people!" Angie says, like a smart-aleck. I know she's making fun of me.

When we open the door and see Galleria's face, I forget how I upset I got at her earlier. That is, until Eddie Lizard appears in the doorway, flashing his devilishly charming smile. That familiar voice I heard in my head all morning pays me another visit. *Why does he have to like Galleria? Why can't he like me?*

"Where's Chanel and Dorinda?" Angie asks Galleria.

"Auntie Juanita would have a fit if Chanel stayed out any longer. We put her in a cab. She's not supposed to be hopping around all day on those crutches. Miss Cuchifrita Ballerina is still a crippled Cheetah, you know." Galleria looks at me like she wants to make peace. "And you know, Dorinda has to help out Mrs. Bosco on Saturdays with cleaning."

"I know that's right," I say, catching my manners and trying not to act jealous again. Now I just feel disappointed. We've gotten used to Chanel and Dorinda being involved in everything we do, so it only seems right that they should be here with us now.

"Hi, um, Aquanette," Eddie says, trying to be polite. I look at him, and feel my heart fluttering. Then he steps aside and an older man comes into the apartment after him. Eddie's father looks just like him—except that he's older, taller, and has white hair. I know I should tell Eddie he looks just like his father, but I don't want to.

Judging from Doktor Lizard's white gauze outfit and moccasins, I can tell he's not from New York, and that he's used to living in a warmer climate. I look down at his moccasins again—the toes are pointy like Aladdin's slippers. Jack Frost must be nipping at his heels quite a bit. "I'm sorry, sir, but I'm Aquanette Walker, and this is my sister Anginette," I say, catching my manners and holding out my hand to shake his.

The peaceful-looking man covers my hand with both of his, and stands still for a second—so I don't move either. Slowly, he removes his hands, then says, "I'm Doktor Lizard—Eddie's father."

Doktor Lizard does the same exact thing to Angie. As we all walk into the living room, Galleria whispers in my ear, "He's just trying to feel your vibrations." Then she pinches my butt, which causes me to giggle.

Doktor Lizard turns in front of the couch and smiles. "Let's go see the handiwork."

"Excuse me?" I ask, feeling stupid because I don't know what he's talking about.

"Upstairs," Galleria whispers, nudging my back.

"Oh, yes. Can we get you any lemonade or something to drink first?" Angie asks.

"No, thanks—I've imbibed quite a bit already," Doktor Lizard says, smiling.

Imbibe? Lord, that's just what we need—someone else talking funny. It sure seems like we can't understand what anybody is trying to tell us today!

"This is definitely the work of a spooky kook," Galleria says, sniffing the burnt air in Daddy's bedroom.

"No. This is the work of someone who has made a pact with the devil," Doktor Lizard says, "to try and win the love of a man forever, so she can control him." He moves closer, to see the stuff on the nightstand.

I can tell by how slowly and carefully Doktor Lizard is talking that he's trying not to frighten us. Well, it isn't working—I look over at Angie, and I can tell he is scaring both of us to death!

"She burned photos—probably of women—desirable women . . . women he used to love," Doktor Lizard explains.

"Why?"

"To eliminate the competition, and to insure that he will love no other, nor harbor any lingering flames." Doktor Lizard nods knowingly. "This sort of ritual is only performed by Hexagone witches."

"Our Daddy's girlfriend's name is Abala Shaballa Hexagone!" I blurt out.

"Oh, well, then there is no mystery about what is going on here," Doktor Lizard says, picking up the pouch on the nightstand and emptying the stuff inside.

I try to peer over his shoulder and see without being rude, but I don't know what those things are he's holding in his hands.

"My, my, my—I haven't seen the likes of these in centuries," Doktor Lizard says, looking at us and smiling.

Centuries? I hope he's joking, because he can't be that old!

"A piece of elephant tusk, an alligator tooth, and the bill of a mockingbird in a bogo mojo bag." Doktor Lizard toys with the items in his hand, like he's marveling at Abala's "handiwork."

"It's all here," he says. "She's created an altar for the spell—black candles to signify the negative forces inherent within the multiverse. Red candles to incite passion. Voodoo dolls stuffed with straw, his bodily fluids, nail clippings, and clothing."

I grab Angie's hand and clutch it tight. I never believed that anything could scare us more than the horror movies we love to watch—but Doktor Lizard has succeeded!

"Stones to set the time of their romance to infinity. Nails to write the spell on the candles," Doktor Lizard continues, like he's doing his grocery list. "Scales to weigh out his love, and the exact quantities of the herbs, roots, and powders for her potions."

"She's been making him drink brews for weeks now!" I blurt out. "She tried to get *us* to drink them too."

"Yes, well, she wouldn't have gone to this extreme unless something was going wrong," Doktor Lizard says, resting his finger on his lips. "She must have discovered that his heart belonged to someone else."

Suddenly, my heart stops—maybe Daddy really *does* still love Ma! "Well, it would have to be our mother—she lives in Houston," I explain quickly.

"I see," Doktor Lizard says, while taking out a bag from his leather satchel.

"I must uncross the spell here first."

"How do you do that?" Galleria asks.

"Uncrossing oil, jinx removal, and hocus-pocus powder," Doktor Lizard says nonchalantly. He opens a bottle and sprinkles drops everywhere, while chanting: "Break the hex, blast the root, free this man from the Hexagone hoot!"

Galleria takes her Kitty Kat notebook from her backpack. *I can't believe she's gonna write this stuff down!* It figures Galleria would try to make a song out of anything—even Daddy's misery! I cut my eyes at Angie, who just shrugs.

"Now we must go examine the crossroads," Doktor Lizard mumbles, like he's talking to himself.

"What crossroads?"

"When you walk to the corner, there's a pole, and when you look up, you see the sign for the street and the avenue, pointing in two different directions," Eddie explains for his father.

"The intersection of two roads, two street signs, is a place of great magical power. It's also the best place to dispose of the remnants of a spell—leftover candle wax, incense and photo ashes, footprint dirt, ground bone fragments," Doktor Lizard says, gathering the stuff off the nightstand and putting it carefully in his bag.

"Do you want us to help you?" I ask.

"We're losing light, so we have to hurry," Eddie Lizard says quickly. "Later, you and your sister should clean the room as well as you can—before your father comes home from the hospital."

"Oh, okay," I say, trying not to look at him while he talks. I know this is silly, but Eddie Lizard just makes me feel so self-conscious. I cut a quick glance at Galleria. I can tell she is truly smitten with him.

"We have to go remove the remnants, then visit the hospital and attend to your father," Doktor Lizard calmly explains. "With all their medical expertise, doctors are never able to detect the work of a spell, hex, curse, or devil's pact."

"Can we help Daddy?" I ask hopefully.

"Well, the sun hasn't gone down yet, so we still have some time. I will do my best," Doktor Lizard says, kissing the talisman charm around his neck.

When we get to the corner of Eighty-ninth Street and Riverside Drive, Doktor Lizard instructs us to go through every piece of garbage. I feel so funny, because people are staring at us. They probably think we are homeless people—or even worse, that we're up to no good.

"That's mine!" screams a homeless woman who has appeared out of nowhere. She has bright red lipstick smeared across her mouth. "Don't touch my stuff!" she yells, lunging at me so quickly that I drop the empty milk carton I'm holding.

"This is hoodoo business, woman—scat!" Doktor Lizard says without moving a muscle. The lady gets a scared look on her face and walks off, babbling.

How did he do that? I wonder.

"The power of hoodoo is known by many," Doktor Lizard says, as if reading my mind.

Well, we sure didn't know anything about hoodoo. Not that I'm convinced that all this poking around in public garbage cans is gonna make Daddy better!

"Well, our work is done here," Doktor Lizard announces, after he quietly puts more stuff into his satchel.

"I'm real glad you came," I whisper to Galleria as we get into Doktor Lizard's blue Cadillac and head over to the hospital. When we arrive and announce that we want to see Mr. Walker, the nurse attendant looks at us rather skeptically, but she lets us go up to Daddy's room.

"What are you gonna tell your mother?" Galleria asks me as we walk down the long corridor. Galleria knows, because she stayed at our mother's house in Houston with us, that Angie and I haven't told our mother bo-peep about High Priestess Abala Shaballa. How are we supposed to tell Ma the truth *now*, after we've been fibbing all this time? *The Lord doesn't like liars*, I can hear Ma's voice ringing in my ear.

"She's gonna be so hurt that we lied to her about what was going on with Daddy and that pecan nut!" I whisper to Galleria. "We're gonna have to tell her the truth—eventually."

"She may try to take you back from your father," Galleria says nervously. "What if she wants you and Angie to move back to Houston?"

I know what Galleria is getting at. We *can't* move back to Houston and leave the Cheetah Girls behind!

"Daddy looks so peaceful," Angie sighs as we gather around his bed.

The nurse from the desk comes inside and tells us, "He's resting now, so we're gonna have to ask you to leave."

"Oh, please, ma'am—I just need to look at my father for comfort. We won't disturb a thing," I plead with her.

The nurse looks at Doktor Lizard like she's unsure what to do. "All right," she finally says.

When she leaves, I crack a smile.

"That was quite a performance—you drama queen!" Galleria whispers, complimenting me on my theatrics. I guess I have learned a thing or two, going to LaGuardia Performing Arts

Annex with a whole bunch of real-life drama queens.

Doktor Lizard reaches over the hospital bed and tries to open Daddy's eyelids. Then he touches his palms, heart, and head. "I'm gonna need your help," he says, motioning for us to help prop Daddy up in his bed.

"Anginette, go guard the door to make sure the nurse doesn't come in," Doktor Lizard commands my sister.

When we've propped Daddy up, Eddie Lizard holds him still while his father prepares something in a bowl. "This is a 'decoction'—the opposite of a concoction—it should help undo the Love Spell."

Daddy doesn't even open his eyes as we open his mouth and hold the cup to it so he can gulp down the decoction.

"She almost had him, that's for sure," Doktor Lizard comments, as he pulls out a piece of paper and a fancy-looking pen. "I'm writing your father's name on parchment paper with dragon's blood ink, to help him heal," Doktor Lizard says, looking at me until I realize he's waiting for me to tell him Daddy's name.

"Oh, I'm sorry—his name is John Walker."

After Doktor Lizard finishes writing Daddy's name, he puts the paper on the nightstand, takes out two white candles from a case, and lights them on the table. Then he places some oil on one of the voodoo dolls, and puts it on Daddy's chest. "I'm going to recite an incantation to gain the help of the healing spirits," Doktor Lizard explains. "You won't be able to understand my chant as I drift into the unknown tongue, but do not be frightened."

Galleria nods her head, and I grab her hand as we listen to Doktor Lizard making funny noises and words. *"Abba—hum, dweebie dum, raccaacaacaa, dummmmmmm."*

It just sounds like Doktor Lizard is calling somebody dumb, but I have no idea what he's really saying. Angie turns around, startled, but I motion for her to keep guarding the door. After Doktor Lizard finishes his chant, he wraps the voodoo doll and parchment paper in a piece of white cloth and places it between the two white candles.

All of a sudden, the patient in the bed next to Daddy's turns over and yells out, "Hey, if it isn't the Bobbsey Twins!"

My heart almost jumps out of my chest, until

I realize that it's Mr. Bloody Ace Bandage from the emergency room. "That's right, it's us," I whisper to him. "Shhh, we don't want to wake our Daddy!"

"Oh, okay," the man says, then turns back over.

"Don't worry, we're finished here," Doktor Lizard assures me as he packs up everything.

"Who was that wack attack?" Galleria asks, puzzled, as we flee Daddy's hospital room. "The Bobbsey Twins—funny we never thought of calling you that."

"Well, you thought of everything else to call us," I reply sarcastically, then wrap my arm under Galleria's. I'm not mad at her—I'm just anxious to find out if Doktor Lizard's ritual worked.

As if reading my mind, Doktor Lizard calmly tells us, "Now all we have to do is wait and see. You'll have to watch your father's behavior closely when he's released."

"Don't worry, we'll watch him like Houston hawks!"

"What do we do about Abala?" Angie asks, like a scaredy-cat.

"Nothing," Doktor Lizard says. "She'll know that she's failed—that he doesn't love her—and she'll find another victim."

I feel a pang in my chest, as if Doktor Lizard is talking about *me*. He probably knows a lot more about people's secrets than he's telling. He probably already knows that I like his son, and that Eddie doesn't like me.

I sit quietly in the back of the car with Galleria and Angie, while Eddie Lizard sits up front with his father. My nosy sister whispers something in Galleria's ear. Galleria whispers back, loud enough for me to hear: "No, silly willy—I'm just mackin'."

Now I know what Angie asked her—if she liked Eddie.

Suddenly, I realize what the first part of my horoscope meant—you can't make someone like you. They either like you or they don't. Well, I don't care anymore if Galleria does like Eddie, or if he likes her. They deserve each other!

Chapter 8

The next morning, Angie and I come straight home after church to call the hospital, and see if Daddy can be released.

"Yes, Mr. Walker is being discharged today," an attendant tells us over the phone.

"Really?" I ask, like I can't believe it.

"Yes, the residing doctor has ordered his discharge. Everything seems to be fine. He'll need an adult to sign him out."

"Yes, we know," I reply.

"We can pick up Daddy!" I shout to Angie, who throws her arms around my neck and hugs me, stepping on my nicely shined pumps in the process.

"Ouch, Angie—you're gonna put *me* in the hospital now!" I say.

But she just slaps me on the shoulder and smiles. "'Member how Uncle Skeeter told us that when he was younger, Big Momma used to pay him five dollars to walk around in her shoes to stretch them out?"

"Yeah—no wonder he can't keep his head on straight!" I chuckle back. "Dag on, I wish Uncle Skeeter was here right now. I could use some cheerin' up."

"Me, too," Angie mumbles.

We'd never realized until this morning—when we tried to think of an adult to bring along to check Daddy out of the hospital—how *sad* we felt about not having any relatives in New York. You have to understand, we have so many relatives spread all over down South, that when we have our annual family reunion picnic in Bayou Wildlife Park, we take up the whole eighty-six acres! Okay, maybe I'm exaggerating just a bit, but we have more relatives than most people.

"It's just plain pitiful that we had to ask Ms. Dorothea and Mr. Garibaldi to take us to St. Luke's and sign Daddy out," I say, shaking my head. We didn't know who else to ask—and believe me, it kills us to have to ask Galleria for anything, after yesterday's drama.

I know we could have asked somebody at our church—Hallelujah Tabernacle—but we don't know the people in our congregation that well. Besides, Reverend Butter, and the pastors and aides, are real busy getting everything ready for our big Christmas celebration—that's all everybody over there is talking about.

"I hope Daddy doesn't act strange in front of Ms. Dorothea," Angie mutters while we change the sheets on his bed—just like Docktor Lizard and his son Eddie suggested we do. (Of course, Angie and I were too tired to finish cleaning last night, because Galleria kept the Cheetah Girls in the chat room, swooning about Eddie Lizard, till I was bitten to death by the green-eyed monster!)

I drill Angie on how we're gonna play it with Mr. and Mrs. Garibaldi. "As far as Bubbles's parents are concerned, Daddy fell faint from dehydration and stress, and had to go the hospital for some tests. After all, they know how hard Daddy's been working at his new job at SWAT Bug Spray, whipping up marketing campaigns for the new flea spray they're launching in the spring."

We've already asked the Lord to forgive us for "withholding information"—that's what Big Momma calls it when you don't tell people the whole truth about something until the right moment.

"Should we call Ma now and tell her?" Angie asks.

"And tell her what?" I counter. "If you ask me, I'd rather wait until the sun goes down on this mess."

"But we always call her or Big Momma after church on Sundays!" Angie protests.

"Well, we're busy living our lives in the Big Apple, so I'm sure they'll understand if we call later," I snap back at her. Shoot, I may be stubborn as a mule, but Angie just plain kicks stuff around like a mindless donkey!

The doorbell rings, and I run to the door with my coat in my hand, because I know it's Mr. Garibaldi and Ms. Dorothea. Now Angie will have to move her slowpoke butt away from the telephone, and stop thinking about calling Ma or Big Momma and broadcasting Daddy's problems all over the country!

"Hi, Aquanetta!" Mr. Garibaldi exclaims, kissing me on both cheeks. I just love when he does that! (It's a European salutation, I guess.)

"Hello, Miz Aqua," Galleria says, squinting at me to keep the sun out of her eyes. If I didn't know better, I would swear Galleria is acting insecure.

"Where's Angie? Let's get this rodeo on the road," Ms. Dorothea says, clutching the collar on her fake cheetah-fur coat.

"Angie! Let's go," I yell loudly.

She finally comes downstairs, and we run outside to Mr. Garibaldi's van. "What station do you girls want to hear?" he asks once we get comfy inside.

"Hot 99, Daddy—we've gotta hear the new jammies!" Galleria blurts out, speaking for all of us as usual.

"So, what new songs are you girls working on?" Mr. Garibaldi asks excitedly. I wonder why he asks *us* that. He should be asking his daughter, since she's the one who writes all our songs.

"Um . . ." I start in, but Galleria cuts me off.

"Daddy, you know we aren't working on anything until Chanel gets better, or until we hear from the Def Duck peeps about a showcase, or getting in the studio with Mouse Almighty!"

"That's quite an earful, darling. I hope you spurt out sound bytes for interviews as quick as you spurt out your *whines*," Ms. Dorothea comments, like she's a reporter doing commentary.

"I wasn't whining, I was just saying," Galleria replies with a smirk.

The new song "Hot Diggity Dog," by Kenny Knuckles, comes on the radio, and the three of us sing along, because we know all the words:

"You can pay your rent
So you think you're heaven sent
Don't wreck my life and cause me strife
'Cuz I'm going for mine all the time
Hot Diggity Dog
Don't mean I'm the alley cat with a wack attack
Hot Diggity Dog
Don't mean I can't be down with the mack
Hot Diggity to my Dogs
Then we can all get along in this song!"

"You think they play this song enough? That's the thirtieth time this morning, and we haven't even had our breakfast yet!" Ms. Dorothea moans.

"You know how it is when a new jammy comes out, they give it major-domo airtime," Galleria says, bopping along.

"Who's the artist?" Ms. Dorothea asks. She's real interested in the new acts coming up, now that she is officially our manager.

"Kenny Knuckles," I reply.

"Kenny 'Pig' Knuckles is more like it—'cuz he's packing an extra fifty in the music video for the single," Galleria snorts.

Suddenly I feel uncomfortable. Angie and I aren't exactly fluttering doves in the weight department. Maybe, when the Cheetah Girls start getting famous, people will say the same thing about us!

"You know, you always look heavier on television than in person," I retort, crouching a little farther back into my seat so I don't take up so much room. "It's not fair that male artists can be as big as the post office, but nobody says anything. I don't like the fact that people expect female artists to be skinny, like Mariah, Kahlua, or Whitney—it just isn't right." I fall silent, hoping Ms. Dorothea will come to our defense.

"In my opinion, as long as you don't eat all the

profits from the record trough, you're entitled to a few good meals," Ms. Dorothea quips, coming through for me. But then, she asks the question I was hoping wouldn't come up this morning. "Aqua, what exactly happened yesterday?"

I get a queasy feeling in my stomach. I wonder if Galleria told her mother about Eddie Lizard. She probably even told her that I liked him!

"W-what do you mean?" I respond, stuttering.

"When you came home from vocal practice?" Ms. Dorothea asks suspiciously.

"Oh, we, um, Daddy was lying in bed, and said he didn't feel too good," I say, cutting my eyes at Angie, who throws me a glance faster than greased lightning.

"That's all?" Ms. Dorothea asks, like she doesn't believe us.

"Yes, ma'am."

"Don't you think it's odd that a grown man wouldn't have called the hospital himself?" Dorothea continues interrogating me.

"Um, yes, but I think he was waiting for us," Angie mumbles, so low that Ms. Dorothea asks her to repeat herself.

Ms. Dorothea doesn't ask us any more questions, though. I'm so glad when we finally get to the hospital, I almost jump out of the car before Mr. Garibaldi puts his foot on the brakes!

I know Ms. Dorothea doesn't believe us, but right now the only thing I care about is getting Daddy out of this place, and seeing if the spell has really been broken.

"Daddy!" Angie says excitedly when she sees our father sitting quietly in the outpatient room. Daddy stares back at us sternly, which causes my heart to flutter. I think Daddy really has recovered, and is back to his old self. Well, praise the Lord and shame that headwrap-wearing "She-devil!"

"Mr. Walker," Mr. Garibaldi starts in, putting his arm around Daddy's shoulder.

"Call me John," Daddy says politely.

"*Sí, sí*—forgive me, *Giovanni*!" Mr. Garibaldi says, grinning from ear to ear.

"I like the way your name sounds in Italian, Daddy," I say, smiling.

Daddy doesn't say a word, but Mr. Garibaldi just keeps chattering away. "Can we expect you at our dinner table at eight o'clock? The lobster fra diavolo is simmering *perfetto* right now, and waiting for you later!"

"Of course, I don't see why not—eight

o'clock, as planned," Daddy chuckles. Mr. Garibaldi could make dead people smile in their coffins if he wanted to.

"Mr. Garibaldi, what does lobster fra . . . um, you know, mean?" I ask, grinning because I cannot pronounce the word. (I'm sorry—I'm just terrible at trying to say things in other languages.)

"Lobster fra diavolo?" Mr. Garibaldi repeats, humoring me.

"Yes, sir," I shoot back.

"It means, lobster à la Friar Devil," Mr. Garibaldi explains.

My heart stops right in its tracks. *No, please, not the devil again!* Mr. Garibaldi sees the shocked look on my face, and quickly goes on to explain. "No, *cara*, it does not mean that exactly—um, how do you say—?"

"It's not a literal translation," Galleria says, throwing a smirk in my direction.

Since she knows the truth about Daddy, I guess she's entitled to get a good laugh from that one. "It's just a fancy way of saying spicy spaghetti with some seafood thrown in the mix—definitely the flavor that you two savor."

I feel a sting in my chest when Galleria says

that—and she catches it too, by the look on my face. Suddenly, I feel stupid, because I realize Galleria doesn't mean anything bad by those things she says. I'm just being overly sensitive. Shoot, before that cute boy in a snakeskin rattled his way into Drinka Champagne's, I would have paid Galleria's remarks no mind—as a matter of fact, Angie and I laugh at her jokes all the time.

"Aquanetta, you havva not lost faith in my cooking, no?" Mr. Garibaldi says, teasing me.

"Oh, no, Mr. Garibaldi, we will be at your table at eight o'clock sharp!" I reply quickly. "Dorinda and Chanel are coming too, right?"

"Yes, ma'am," Galleria says, imitating me, then putting her arm around my shoulder. "Don't forget to tell me my horror-scope later!"

I feel myself cringing *again* at Galleria's remark, but this time I stop myself. Galleria always asks me to read her "horror-scope," because she gets a kick out of it. Being the capricious Gemini she is, she's always full of tricks and surprises!

"See you later, Ms. Dorothea."

"Bye, darlings—be on time, and don't wear

white!" she quips, making a joke about the hospital uniforms, I guess.

The first thing we do when we get back inside our house is walk over to the ugly Bogo Mogo Hexagone Warrior Mask, turn to Daddy, and ask, "Is it okay if we take this thing down now?"

"Throw it out—I don't want to ever see that thing again!" Looking defeated, Daddy walks upstairs to his bedroom.

"Good-bye, Bogo," Angie mutters, as we stuff it into the trash can outside the building.

"I don't trust this thing—why don't we throw it in the garbage down the block?" I say, pulling it back out. We know we're not supposed to do that, because people are real fussy about their garbage cans in New York. One day, I saw Mrs. Elliot yelling at the people in the building next door, because they left a stack of magazines for recycling in front of our building.

"Yeah, let's put Mr. Bogo in a garbage bin far away from us!" Angie quips.

After we say good-bye to Mr. Bogo for the last time (we hope), we go straight back up to Daddy's bedroom to see if he's okay.

"How are you feelin', Daddy?" I ask. But he just sits on the edge of his bed like a robot. We sit next to him quietly, until the spirit moves me to tell him exactly what my horoscope said yesterday.

"The unconditional love for which you yearn cannot be bought at any price."

All of a sudden, Daddy puts his head down in his hands, and starts bawling like a baby! I have never seen Daddy cry like this, except for the day our parents' divorce papers came through. He sat at the dining room table that day, looked at the papers for the longest time, then cried.

"It's been so lonely up here without your mother," Daddy blurts out all of a sudden.

"We know, Daddy," Angie pipes up. "We didn't tell you, but you should have seen how lonely Ma is down there without you."

Daddy gets real quiet for a long time, then whispers, "There wasn't anything wrong with me a doctor could fix, was there?"

"No, Daddy, there wasn't," I reply calmly. "Do you remember us coming to the hospital yesterday with, um, Doktor Lizard, and his son?"

"No," Daddy says. "The last thing I remember is Abala coming over after you girls left for your vocal lessons."

"Daddy, who is Mattie?" I blurt out.

From the look on Daddy's face, I know I have stepped on a land mine. Angie gets real still.

"Why do you ask?" he asks, looking guilty.

"Because you mumbled her name when you were sleeping." I hold my breath, waiting for Daddy to answer.

"I was with her . . . before your mother," Daddy says solemnly.

Now I wish Daddy hadn't told me who Mattie was. Then I wouldn't know that he still loves her. I can tell he does by the look in his eyes.

"I told Abala that I still carried a torch for Mattie," Daddy confesses. "I mean, she was my first real love. I think that's normal, but I don't think Abala took it the right way."

"Maybe that's why she sped up the spell!" Angie says, playing divette detective again.

"Did you tell her anything about Ma?" I ask hopefully.

"Yes, I did—I told her that I still love your mother . . . very much," Daddy says, putting his hands to his face.

"Well, it sounds like Abala might have panicked, and tried to erase all the memories from your heart," I say, thinking out loud.

"Anything else?" Daddy asks sternly, looking at me and Angie, like, "The True Confessions Show is over, and stay tuned for the next episode!"

"Um, no, Daddy—we just wanted to make sure you're okay," I say, heaving a deep sigh. Daddy has had enough drama this weekend to last until—well, until Ma calls, anyway.

"I feel fine," he says, still threatening us with his eyes. "And don't you girls have homework to do?"

"Yes, we do!" Angie and I say in unison, smiling with relief. We turn to go, but Daddy stops us.

"Tell me one thing—" he says.

"Yes, Daddy?" I hold my breath. *Please, God, don't let him know that I had a crush on Eddie Lizard. I hope he hasn't figured that out!*

"You didn't tell your mother I was in the hospital, did you?"

"No, Daddy, we didn't," I say softly.

"Good. Please don't say anything—yet," he says firmly.

"Okay," I say, relieved that Daddy doesn't know anything about Eddie Lizard. Daddy doesn't take kindly to us liking boys, I don't care *what* spell he is under! Like I said, he doesn't want us dating until we're sixteen, and that's that.

"Um, Daddy—you just have to promise us one thing," I tell him.

"I can't promise till I know what it is!" Daddy barks, just like he used to before all this happened. "Come on, out with it!"

"Please don't bring any more of those nasty shakes in this house!" (I'm talking about all those herbs he drank, instead of good meals like we're used to cooking—and Daddy is used to *eating*!)

"That's a promise," Daddy says, breaking out into a small smile, which on him looks bigger than the one on the Cheshire Cat.

We both kiss Daddy on his forehead and run off to our room. "You're gonna help me with my math homework, right?" Angie starts in.

"All right, Miss Smarty-Britches—but you owe me one!" I am determined to make my sister pay for all those snide comments she made yesterday. "And I do not like Eddie Lizard one bit!" I hiss, as she lies on her bed and opens her math notebook.

"I *know* you do!" Angie shoots back, smirking at me.

"It's a long time till sundown, sister, so you'd better pray you don't end up tied to some voodoo doll that looks like a crawling Lizard," I warn her.

"That's right," she says, "'cuz you'll just untie me and tie yourself to it!"

Angie screams as I wrestle her to the floor.

"I thought you girls were doing your homework," Daddy yells from his bedroom.

For the first time, we're dee-lirious that Daddy is yelling at us about something, 'cuz we know he's back to his good old gruffy self again!

Chapter 9

Just as we're all leaving our apartment to go to Ms. Dorothea's for dinner, the phone rings. It's probably Ma, I think to myself. She must be crawling with crickets because we didn't call her today!

Angie rushes to answer the phone, but I wrestle it from her. I'm sorry, but I still don't trust Angie to talk to Ma yet. She might tell her about what happened, even though Daddy said not to.

"Hello?" The blood drains from my face like a vampire when I hear the voice of High Priestess Abala Shaballa, the woman who hurt our Daddy in the name of love.

"Daddy doesn't want to speak to you anymore, so please don't call our house," I mutter into the phone. I know Daddy can't hear me, because he went to get his Cadillac out of the garage, but I still feel nervous about messing in grown-ups' business.

The High Priestess starts talking, in that breathy voice of hers that makes her sound supernatural. "Well, I do declare, um—"

"It's Aquanette," I say politely.

"Well, Aquanette, perhaps you'd better let me speak to your father. I can see you don't understand—"

"Oh, yes, ma'am, we understand all right. As a matter of fact, we *over*stand, because we don't take too kindly to you putting a stupid love spell on our father. He's *through* with you and your brews," I shout. "So go park your broomstick somewhere else! Good-bye!"

"I see," Abala says, like she's embarrassed. "You're quite mistaken, but perhaps I'll call—"

"No, *you* don't understand," I huff, "if you call here again, we're reporting you to the FBI, the CIA, and UFO headquarters!"

"UFO?" Abala repeats, balking.

"Yes, ma'am—because you're definitely from

another planet! Personally, we suggest that you go back to Hexagonia for a brushup course, 'cuz your witchcraft skills *stink*!"

High Priestess Abala Shaballa hangs up in my ear.

"You think she'll call back here?" Angie asks as we walk to Daddy's car.

"I don't think so," I answer firmly. "She has definitely flown the coop!"

By the time we get to Galleria's apartment on the Upper East Side, we have forgotten all about High Priestess Abala—and I *hope* she has forgotten about *us*! We're excited, because this is the first time we're having dinner at the Garibaldis'. I plan on having a good time, and maybe even being nice to Miss Galleria after yesterday's drama.

"You're not still mad at Galleria, are you?" pesty Angie asks me as Daddy's parking the car near Galleria's apartment building on Sixty-seventh Street.

"She can have Eddie Lizard if she wants," I say, acting nonchalant. "He's too skinny for me anyway."

Angie chuckles her silly little laugh, and

leaves me alone. I swear, she has a mind like a meat cleaver!

"Wazzup, buttercup?" Galleria says, when she opens the door and sees me and Angie. I feel myself cringe inside. Is this another one of Galleria's Southern slanders? She probably thinks we make butter out of buttercup flowers in our backyard!

"Hi, Galleria," Angie says, giving her a kiss on both cheeks the way Mr. Garibaldi does it. Galleria giggles, and does it to me. I kiss her back—on both cheeks—because I know I'm being ree-diculous.

Mr. Garibaldi's face lights up like a Christmas tree when he sees us. "I'm so happy to see my *caras* again—especially sitting at my dinner table," Mr. Garibaldi says, kissing us both twice on each cheek, which causes us to giggle again. "And how are you feeling, Mr. Walker?"

Daddy clears his throat and nods his head, saying, "Fine, fine." I think Daddy must be embarrassed that Mr. Garibaldi picked him up from the hospital—even though we've assured him that we didn't tell Ms. Dorothea or Mr. Garibaldi one bo-peep about his love spell, or uncrossing the hex.

It's funny, but in the four months we've known her, we've never been in Galleria's apartment before—we always hang out down at Ms. Dorothea's store, Toto in New York—or at Chanel's mom's loft, which has its own dance studio. The Garibaldis' place is just like I imagined it—the most beautiful animal kingdom in the world. "Oh, this is real nice," I tell her quietly as I look around.

"Ooo, look, even the candles are cheetah!" Angie exclaims, pointing at the huge cheetah wax candles in their cheetah candlestick holders.

Galleria's face lights up, like she just got an idea. "*Wazzup, buttercup*—that could be a line in the new song I'm writing!" She picks up her Kitty Kat notebook and plops down on the couch, scribbling away. Dorinda and Chanel are sitting on the couch, too—playing Scrabble.

"Don't get up!" I shout at Chanel. She breaks into a big grin. "It sure doesn't take much for you to start hopping around—and we don't want that!" Then I turn to Dorinda.

"Dorinda, where is your, um, family?" I ask, surprised when I see that she is by herself.

"Mrs. Bosco called and said she'll bring the kids another time. She wanted me to spend time alone with my crew," Dorinda says, breaking into a grin. I can sure tell that she's relieved she isn't "baby-sitting" tonight. "We got the Mariah photos," she adds proudly, pulling out the Cheetah Girls scrapbook that she has started for us.

"Oooh, she looks beautiful even in the photo," I gasp, as I look at the picture of us with Mariah Carey in her dressing room.

"Lemme see!" Mr. Garibaldi says excitedly. He stares at the photos, exclaiming, *"Ah, ché bella!"*

"We do look dope together, right?" Dorinda says proudly.

"Ay, *Madonna*! I forgot the clams oreganato!" Mr. Garibaldi cries, then runs back to the kitchen to get his Italian creation out of the oven.

"Daddy should have his own cooking show," Galleria says, looking up from her notebook for a second.

"I saw you yesterday with Eddie Lizard," Chanel whispers in my ear. "Aqua has her first crush!"

"I do not," I whisper back. I cannot believe she is saying this with Galleria sitting right over there on the sofa! "*You* have a crush on him."

"I do not!" Chanel says, her brown eyes getting bigger than Ring Dings. "Well, maybe for a second—but then I remembered, I'm saving myself for Krusher!"

Angie snickers, and I cut my eyes at her. Krusher is Chanel's favorite singer—but not ours.

Meanwhile, Ms. Dorothea drops a pan, and it makes a loud noise, almost scaring us to death. We're all still jumpy after the weekend's events. Ms. Dorothea sticks her head out of the kitchen and snaps, "Galleria, please put the good glasses on the table like I asked you to. And get your nose out of that notebook!"

Galleria reluctantly obeys.

"It would be one thing if you were doing your homework, but I know you're writing a song," Ms. Dorothea continues, shooing their dog Toto into the kitchen to eat his dinner from his bowl. "My goodness, you probably have enough songs to give to the Goodwill by now!"

Oooh, I know *that* hurt! I never heard Ms. Dorothea fussing at Galleria before about writing songs. I guess Galleria must have done *something* to upset her mom, and I'm sure we're gonna hear about it later tonight, when we go into the chat room on the Internet for our Cheetah Girls Council meeting.

"Done, diddly, done, Mom," Galleria says, jumping up and plopping her Kitty Kat notebook on the chair. "Someone find me the key to the doghouse, pleez!"

"Well, one more phone call from that amphibian boy, and you'll be living in a snake pit!" Ms. Dorothea hisses. "Back in my day, a boy called the house once a day to keep the doctor away—not every hour, like he's on the admitting team in ER!"

We gather from the tone in Ms. Dorothea's voice that Eddie Lizard must be wearing out his welcome with Ma Bell—at least at the Garibaldi residence! Galleria clams up, and keeps rubbing one of the glasses with a napkin, like she's removing an invisible spot.

"That's enough, Galleria!" Ms. Dorothea snaps. "You'd think you were rubbing Aladdin's lamp to make three wishes!"

"The glasses are beautiful," Dorinda pipes up.

"Thank you—we got them at the Galleria," Ms. Dorothea says, then lets out a little smile.

"Oh? When did you go to the Galleria?" I ask, surprised. I know Ms. Dorothea wanted to come down to Houston for Thanksgiving, but had to stay and work on her winter collection for her store.

"Darling, I mean the Galleria in Milan."

"Oh," I say, surprised. "I didn't know they had a Galleria in Milan—um, Italy?" I know Bubbles was named after the Galleria Mall in Houston. Ms. Dorothea told us that the first time we met her.

"Oh, you didn't know, Aquanetta?" Mr. Garibaldi says, his eyes lighting up. "The *original* Galleria is in Milano—it's been there for centuries. The one in Houston is copied after that—the gigantic, glasslike roof, the marvelous cafes, *everything*. But they are both beautiful, of course!"

"We didn't even know that, and we're from Houston," Angie exclaims, impressed.

"Are you ready for a feast?" Mr. Garibaldi says, "because this is one you'll never forget."

"Yes, we are!"

Finally, Ms. Dorothea plops herself down at the head of the dining room table, and massages her temples like she has a headache. "What a day I had. Queen Latifah's stylist came in, and worked my store over like a rattlesnake in sand! I mean, she left not one grain unturned. I have nothing left to sell but a few boas!"

"Word?" Dorinda responds, amused. She majors in fashion design at school, so she's very into it, and laps up everything Ms. Dorothea says like a cat with a bowl of condensed milk.

Mr. Garibaldi sets all the food on the table, and we start salivating. Whatever he calls the dish he's made, it looks dee-licious.

"Lobster fra diavolo, just like my mother used to make for us on Sundays," Mr. Garibaldi says proudly. "Believe me, this recipe has been in the Garibaldi family long before that other Garibaldi freed Rome!"

"What other Garibaldi?" Angie asks, curious.

"In Italy, he's like our Martin Luther King. You know, a hero who fought for the people and led a revolution," Galleria explains proudly.

"Is that right?" Daddy asks, sucking up his pasta dish. I can't believe how much Daddy is eating—like a horse after winning the Kentucky Derby!

The phone rings, and Galleria jumps up to get it. "No, *I'll* get it," Ms. Dorothea says firmly, standing up—and almost touching the ceiling because she is so *tall*. "I'm warning you now, Galleria, if that Lizard boy is calling you again, then I'm calling Batman and having him thrown out of Gotham!"

"What's he calling for?" Dorinda asks, raising her eyebrows innocently. Bless her heart, I don't think Dorinda even knows exactly what's going on!

"Oh, he just wants to talk about a little something, something," Galleria says, without looking up from her plate.

"Yeah, well, it sounds like a whole lot of nothing, nothing, if you ask me!" Ms. Dorothea huffs as she picks up the phone.

Angie and I look at each other, and I know we're thinking the same thing: *Can you believe the telephone is cheetah, too?*

"Hello?" Ms. Dorothea says, in her sweet phone voice.

I look at Galleria, but she's trying to act like she doesn't care who's on the phone.

"Oh, hello, Mr. Mouse Almighty! Pardon me for saying this, but fancy hearing from you at dinnertime on a Sunday night!"

I almost choke on the strand of linguini I'm sucking into my mouth. Now all five of us look at each other, like, "She did not say Mouse

Almighty, the producer from Def Duck Records, did she!?!"

"Oh, we're just having some lobster fra diavolo, clams oreganato, and homemade gelato with chocolate cannolis for dessert—but nothing special, just another Sunday dinner."

Ms. Dorothea walks back to the dinner table with the phone. "Oh, heavens, no. I couldn't cook an egg with a timer. No, my husband gets all the credit. Perhaps we can tempt you. . . . No? Okay, but I insist you come another time. Yes, yes, I understand. It must be difficult. Yes, the girls will be delighted. I'll check with their schedule and get back to you. Hmm. Hmm. Good-bye."

We stare at Ms. Dorothea like she has swallowed the fortune cookie with the fortune still inside.

"Was that *the* Mouse?" Galleria asks, like she's holding her breath.

"Yes, Mouse is definitely in the house," Ms. Dorothea says slowly, picking up her fork to resume eating her dinner.

"Where is he?" Galleria asks, like she's bursting.

"He's in the park, feeding pigeons," Ms. Dorothea says, smirking. "Where do you think he is—in the studio, where we have to go see him!"

"Omigod!" I say, letting out a big sigh.

"I must say, these music biz people are strange birds," Ms. Dorothea says, shaking her head. "He says he's been up all night finishing Kahlua's album, but in the next breath he says he's ready to get the Cheetah Girls into the studio. I don't think he knew what day of the week it was, or what time."

"Well, *we* know what time it is!" Galleria shrieks, beside herself—and believe me, she's not alone! Angie and I can barely sit still in our chairs! If our daddy wasn't here, we would get up and start "whoopin' and hollerin'." 'Cuz believe me, this news is something to get excited about. *Hee-haw!*

"So, when are you girls available to go into the studio?" Ms. Dorothea asks, but she already knows the answer.

"Tomorrow at sunrise!" Galleria shouts out.

"Well, we have a little matter that I didn't want to discuss with Mouse," Ms. Dorothea says, looking right at Chanel. "There is no need for Mouse Almighty to know about Chanel's little ballet escapade."

Chanel turns five shades of red, and begins to protest. "But, *Madrina*—"

"No buts, Chanel—especially after you landed on yours during that audition!" Ms. Dorothea continues, like a locomotive couldn't stop her if it tried. "We're going to wait until Chanel can walk without crutches, which shouldn't be more than another week."

"I can walk without them *now*! *Te juro*—I swear! I only use them because *Mamí* makes me!" Chanel's big brown eyes are pleading like a puppy dog's.

"Well, I'm going to call Mouse back tomorrow, and make an appointment for next week. That will give you all time to practice together, and for Chanel to get her balance back. Is that a deal?"

"A wheela-deala!" Galleria says.

"*Ma che fortuna!* Look at the luck that Sunday dinner together brought you," exclaims Mr. Garibaldi. He's waving his fork and knife in both hands, like a kid who just got a big, shiny, red Mack truck for his birthday!

"You are right, Mr. Garibaldi—this is a feast we'll *never* forget!" I say. I'm so grateful for everything—for being in the Cheetah Girls, for helping Daddy come back to his senses, and for living in New York City—even though we miss Ma terribly.

"At long last, we're in the house with Mouse!" Galleria says, reaching over to hug her mother. "And that definitely means mo' betta chedda for the Cheetah Girls!"

Do' Re Mi on the Q.T.

This is Galleria and this is Chanel
We are coming to you live
From Cheetah Girls Central
Where we process the data that matters
And even mad chatter
But today we're here to tell you
About our friend, Do' Re Mi
(That's Miss Dorinda to you)
Kats and Kittys, the drama
Has gotten so radikkio
Just when we thought we knew our crew
Bam! The scandal was told!

There's a new girl in town
That's Miss Dorinda to you,
She bounced into our lives
But now she's part of our crew

Do' Re Mi on the Q.T.
Do' Re Mi on the D.D.L.

(That ain't swell)
Do' Re Mi on the Q.T.
Do' Re Mi on the D.D.L.
(Why won't you tell?)

Dorinda's got a secret
And it's cutting off her flow
(Is that right, girlita*?)*
According to our sources,
She thought we didn't know
(Kats and Kittys, you'd better take notes)
Today for the first time (the very first time)
Do' Re Mi found out she's not alone
(What are you saying?)
She found out she got a sister
And it's making her moan and groan!

There's a new girl in town
That's Miss Dorinda to you,
She bounced into our lives
But now she's part of our crew

Do' Re Mi on the Q.T.
Do' Re Mi on the D.D.L.
(That ain't swell)
Do' Re Mi on the Q.T.

Do' Re Mi on the D.D.L.
(Why won't you tell?)
But we peeped you!
And now we beeped you!
So what you know about that, huh?

Let's tell Miss Dorinda
That she's got all the flavor
And when she keeps things to herself
It's Do' Re Mi that we savor
Don't turn quiet on us
Like you got nothing to say
We found out you got a sister
So why can't she come out and play?

Do' Re Mi on the Q.T.
Do' Re Mi on the D.D.L.
(That ain't swell)
Do' Re Mi on the Q.T.
Do' Re Mi on the D.D.L.
(Why won't you tell, tell, tell!)
We said Do' Re Mi's on the Q.T.
(That's the sneak tip)
Do' Re Mi on the D.D.L.
(That's the down, down low)
Do' Re Mi on the Q.T.

Do' Re Mi on the D.D.L.

Do' Re Mi on the Q.T.
Who you trying to be?
Do' Re Mi on the D.D.L.
That's right, you know that's fowl
like a nearsighted owl
Do' Re Mi on the Q.T.
Why you got secrets
that make us growl?
Do' Re Mi on the D.D.L.
(Is that really true her sister is—Ahhhh!
Yes, mamacita *. . .)*

(Fade with growl sounds)

The Cheetah Girls Glossary

Bugaboo: Country hick. Pain in the neck. A boy who is kinda annoying.

Cigarette-leg pants: Fitted pants that taper down the bottom to a skinny leg. Very popular in the 1950s with poodle-carrying divas.

Crawling with crickets: Upset. Jumpy.

D.D.L.: On the down, down low. For example: You told Rerun that you couldn't go to the movies with him because you had homework to do, but then you go to the mall with your posse, and see him hanging with his. You run into the girls' room, and stay on the D.D.L. until the coast is clear.

Disco diva: Someone who reigned during the disco music period in the 1970s. Famous disco divas include Grace Jones, Donna Summer, and Gloria Gaynor, who defined the disco period with her anthem, "I Will Survive."

Fib-ulous tale: Something that only happened in your imagination.

Green-eyed monster: Jealousy. Envy. Example: "Dalissa was mackin' my new outfit so hard, I could tell she got bitten by the green-eyed monster."

Horse and pony show: Showing off. Drawing attention. Example: "At Brittany's birthday party, this rhythmless boy and girl were in the middle of the dance floor, putting on a horse and pony show!"

Imbibe: Fancy way of saying drinking, or sipping liquid refreshments.

Inconspicuous: Out of sight. Hard to notice. For example, "Why don't you sit in the corner and try to be inconspicuous for a change and some coins."

Intervene: To get in the mix; cut in. Example: "Daddy is not feeling my report card, so maybe I'd better intervene on my behalf, and tell him I'll try harder next term."

Mackin': Checking something—or someone—over to the max.

Mo' betta chedda: More juice. More "ops." More caviar for the crackers!

Overstand: When you can see things like they really are—without a crystal ball.

Pecan nut: Someone who is fruitier than Froot

Loops, and definitely doesn't have an elevator that goes all the way to the penthouse! In other words, a little cuckoo!

Q.T.: On the hush-hush, sneak-sneaky, or the quick tip.

Salutation: Greeting. Example: "Hey, Dim Sum, where's the yum-yum?"

Shabby: Terrible. Tacky. Shameless. Example: "Her outfit is so shabby."

Sound bytes: Tasty, quick riffs you do when you're giving radio or television interviews, and wanna sound like you're at the top of your game.

Talisman charm: A symbolic item used in spells or for good luck. Can be worn around the neck, carried in a pouch, or placed on a worship altar.

Withholding information: Not exactly a fiberoni or white lie; more like keeping a secret.